MW00830776

DUTY BOUND

BLACKTHORN SECURITY
BOOK ONE

GEMMA FORD

Duty Bound

Copyright © 2024 by Gemma Ford

All rights reserved.

No part of this book may be reproduced in any form or by any electronic or mechanical means, including information storage and retrieval systems, without written permission from the author, except for the use of brief quotations in a book review.

Mortlake Press

ISBN: 978-1-7385403-2-7

First Edition

Cover design by Deranged Doctor

Disclaimer: This is a work of fiction. Names, characters, places, and incidents are the products of the author's imagination or used in a fictitious manner. Any resemblance to actual persons, living or dead, or actual events is purely coincidental.

CHAPTER 1

*L*ily stood outside Hamid Karzai International Airport, feeling like she was in some alternate universe.

The whole place was mayhem—screaming kids, people throwing elbows, and every once in a while, bang! A shot cracked off, then everybody dived to the dirt like it was the world's worst game of dodgeball.

She bobbed in a sea of chaos, staring at the little pop-up tent cities that had sprouted up everywhere, and extended into the distance as far as the eye could see. People waved passports like they were some kind of magic tickets out of there, but the guys with guns just shrugged.

And the heat. . . it was like standing in a pizza oven, and not in a good, cheesy way.

Every so often, a roar sounded overhead—some big military bird clawing at the sky. Lily could almost see everybody's heart sink as they stared at it thinking, *Why not me?*

The choppers buzzed above like annoying bees, a stark reminder that the whole place had gone sideways.

In the last twenty-four hours, U.S. and NATO forces had

pulled out of Afghanistan, causing all hell to break loose. The Taliban had taken control, ousting the existing Afghan government, leading to widespread panic and a mass exodus.

Hence the absolute mayhem at the international airport.

Lily stood alone in the crowd, gripping her suitcase in a sweaty palm, the last ten months of her life crammed into something that weighed less than fifty pounds. She'd never felt so out of place, or more vulnerable.

She glimpsed a little kid looking up at her, eyes wide, like he'd just lost his best friend. Lily smiled at him, but he burst into tears.

Understandable. She felt like doing the same thing herself. Was she ever going to get out of here?

An old man leaned against the fence. He looked like he'd walked straight out of a history book—no case, no belongings. Nothing. He slumped to the ground, defeat etched on his face.

Lily couldn't believe the taxi had dropped her off smack in the middle of this madness. This morning, she'd been sipping a latte at her desk. Now she was sprinting for her life, trying to get the last flight out of Dodge.

The line, inching incrementally forward, suddenly surged. Someone elbowed her in the ribs. A woman holding a baby raced by, screaming incoherently. The guards fired in the air to maintain some crowd control.

The gunshot reverberated through her, making her ears ring.

It felt like a mosh pit at a rock concert, only the music was just chopper blades and distant gunfire.

Damn, the Afghan sun was hot. Sweat poured down her cleavage and under her arms. She put down her suitcase, removed her jacket, then draped it over her arm. It wasn't just the heat—it was the pressure-cooker tension of the crowd. All these scared, desperate faces looking for a way out while knowing so few would find one.

Out of the blue, a convoy of banged-up vans rolled up. Lily's heart skipped a beat as a bunch of robed, heavily armed men hopped out. These guys were not asking for tickets or handing out refreshments. They had that "we mean business" look in their eyes, the kind that sent people running in the opposite direction.

Despite the overcrowding, the throng of people somehow dissipated. Lily tried to back away and blend in with the retreating masses, but she was too slow, too awkward with her heavy suitcase and cabin bag slung over her shoulder.

One of the men grabbed her arm, his calloused hand rough on her skin, his grip biting painfully into her flesh. He yanked, hard, and dragged her forward. She lost her jacket.

"No!" She tugged and thrashed but could not break free. The bag slung over her shoulder slipped off and was lost underfoot.

What the *hell* was happening?

She clung to her suitcase, but he ripped it from her hand then flung it on the ground. It popped open, her whole life reduced to a yard sale on the tarmac.

"What are you doing?"

Her cry fell on deaf ears.

Despite her wild struggles, he hauled her into the van. She squished in with four other weathered, grim-faced strangers, all wearing lanyards that said CNN. Film crew.

The doors slammed shut, cutting them off from the mayhem and enclosing them in darkness. The roar of the crowd became a muted backdrop. Lily's heart thumped a mile a minute, her mind racing faster than the van's battered engine.

Were they being kidnapped? Was that what this was? An abduction?

They sped off, the echoes of chaos fading away. Lily couldn't believe she'd been forced to leave behind everything she owned, her last shred of normalcy, on the hot concrete.

She stared through the darkness, barely able to make out the fear-numbed faces of her fellow victims. None of them had seen this coming, and none knew what to expect.

One thing she knew for sure. It wasn't good.

CHAPTER 2

*I*t was past midnight when Blade cruised back into the void that was Fayetteville, North Carolina. He could still taste the open road on his tongue and feel the wind in his hair.

He'd pushed his motorcycle to the limit, trying to outrun the hell hounds in his head. The sleek Suzuki was more than a ride—it was his escape, his therapy on two wheels, cutting a path through the darkness like a knife through silence. But not even the throaty growl of the GSX-R could silence the screams.

His buddy Spade's last moments... the anguished yell as the bullet found its mark... blood on the dusty ground.

He heard himself yelling—no, begging—Spade not to die. To hang on, help was coming. Even though he knew it wasn't.

His friend had bled out in his arms, on the mountain path, whispering the words, "*Tell Lily I love her.*"

Blade had ridden hard, leaned into the curves with a reckless abandon, pushing for a velocity high enough to set him free from the haunting memories. Spade wasn't the only one who'd died that day. Blaster and Ricky had fallen too. Shot down by a sniper's bullet.

Blade had tried to outrun the guilt, the what-ifs, the could-have-beens, but the ambush that took their lives was his cross to bear. His and his alone. No one else was left to share the burden.

Blade killed the engine, silence hanging heavy in the air. The stillness revealed a black SUV squatting curbside. His eyes narrowed as he removed his helmet, then he swung his leg over his bike. That wasn't usually there.

"Evenin', Blade." The voice cut through the hush.

Blade's heart kicked up a notch at the tough, gravelly timbre. "Pat?"

Pat was one tough son of a gun, a former Navy SEAL who'd weathered life's storms, including the loss of his wife and his early retirement. Blade hadn't seen the man shed a tear until his boy, Spade, was laid to rest ten months ago.

He had gotten to know Pat fairly well over the last few years, thanks to his friendship with Spade, but since he'd gotten his walking papers from the doc, they hadn't spoken much.

"Yeah. How are you doin', Blade?"

He smirked. Was Pat really asking if he was okay? "I'm standing, aren't I?" He squared up to the wise ex-officer. Facing Pat was like staring down the barrel of the past, and the first time he'd done it, he'd nearly fallen apart.

The memory of the ambush was still a fresh wound... the chopper ride, the blur of debriefs, and the tremor in his hands that wouldn't quit for two straight days. He'd lost three brothers that day, four counting Stitch, who had gone AWOL right after. Blade hadn't left Helmand until he'd brought their bodies home.

"You sure you're good?" Pat prodded, his gaze sharp.

Blade swallowed over the lump in his throat. "As good as I can be." Pat just nodded—he knew the score.

"So, what's with the surprise visit?" Blade eyed the SUV again.

The corners of Pat's mouth turned up. "I was in the neighborhood."

"At this ungodly hour?"

"Just swinging by." His easy smile reminded Blade so much of Spade it hurt.

"You may as well come inside then." Blade led him indoors as the moon slipped behind a cloud. Once in the living room, he reached for the whiskey. "Drink?"

"Why the hell not?"

Blade poured two, handed one to Pat, then picked up his glass and sat down. Pat had already settled on an armchair in the living area. Seemed he was planning to stay a while.

"Still having nightmares?" Pat's gaze flicked to the pile of old newspapers, books, and DVDs on the coffee table—a stack of distractions for the sleepless.

He gave a dry laugh. "That obvious?"

Pat snorted and raised his glass. "To Joe." Spade's real name. Blade used it so rarely, he'd almost forgotten what it was.

"To Spade."

They sipped in silence until Blade murmured, "I can't shake it, Pat. It's like a shadow glued to my heels."

"What went down in Helmand... it's not on you. It was a snake pit. They all knew it." His voice was strong, his tone firm.

Blade's gaze was fixed on the amber liquid, his jaw clenched. "Should've seen it coming."

"You're not clairvoyant, son."

He just grunted.

"You keeping busy?" Pat changed tack.

"Riding, fishing…" Trying to stave off the boredom.

Pat leaned in, eyes glinting. "Good. Glad you're not otherwise engaged. I've got a job for you."

Blade perked up. This was it—the reason Pat was here, in the dead of night.

"You remember Joe's girlfriend, Lily?"

Blade frowned. "Lily? The computer geek?" The image of a waifish girl with a pixie cut and thick eyeglasses came to mind. She always seemed like a bit of an oddball to him, more at home among servers than soldiers.

Pat gave a nod, confirming. "She's a smart girl. Employed by the Agency now."

His eyes widened. "The CIA? For real?" He couldn't imagine her running around in the field playing spy games.

Another nod from Pat. "She's cyber. Was out in Afghanistan."

Blade's brows shot to his hairline. "Afghanistan? Spade never mentioned that."

"She went afterward. Guess it was her way of dealing with what happened."

That hit home. He was still clinging to the fringes of the base where he trained, where he lived the life before... Before everything went to hell and took Spade and the others with it.

"Why are you telling me this?"

Pat's gaze was hard as stone. "She's MIA, Blade. Snatched on her way out of Kabul, when everything went to shit."

Blade's gut twisted. "Kidnapped? You're kidding me?"

"Wish I was. We recently discovered she got caught in the mayhem at the airport. Thousands trying to get out and she got grabbed, along with a couple of reporters."

The news had been a constant drone in the background.

Kabul falling. The world watching, helpless. And now Lily, a face in the crowd, taken.

"We?" Blade's voice was sharp. "I thought you'd hung up your boots?"

Pat's smile was thin. "Let's just say I'm consulting for Uncle Sam—unofficially, of course."

Blade arched his brows.

Pat shrugged. "It keeps me busy."

He wasn't judging, just surprised. "You could've told me."

Pat's face was unreadable. "I'm telling you now."

Blade understood that all too well. The pull of duty didn't just let go. It sunk in its claws then hung on tight.

"So, what's Lily got to do with all this?"

"She was working with the Afghans, setting up a system, codename *Hawkeye*, to keep an eye on the Taliban." His quiet words hit hard.

"So, they nabbed her to shut it down?"

Pat let out a dry laugh. "It's live. Lily did her part. According to my DOD sources, she is one of a small number of individuals who have the top-secret codes they need to dismantle the system. I don't know who the others are, but apparently she was the easier target."

Blade's mind raced. With those codes, the Taliban could shut them out. They'd have even less intel than before.

"If they get those codes, everything she did is for nothing." Pat's words were heavy with emotion. Lines of worry etched deep in his face. This was personal to him.

Blade frowned. "Why are you telling me this?"

Pat's eyes were like flint. "I'm going in after her, Blade."

"Are you crazy? That's a job for Delta Force. Hostage rescue is their specialty. You know as well as I do, nobody does it better."

"The brass won't touch it. Not officially. It's no-man's land out there."

Blade knew the score. The troops were gone, the region was a void, and now Lily was somewhere in the middle of it.

"Have you talked to them? Made any deals?"

Pat scoffed. "They're not going to go for it. We've got witnesses. She was forced into a van, left her stuff scattered outside the airport."

Blade was on autopilot, the operator in him kicking into gear. "Tracked her phone? Got any eyes in the sky on this?" He sucked in a breath.

Stop.

Those days were over. This was not his problem.

"We've got drones looking."

"But no rescue team?"

Pat's look was all the answer he needed.

"Unofficial doesn't mean not happening."

A mission in the shadows. He raised a hand. "No. Don't even start." But Pat leaned closer, laying out the details.

"We need a squad of at least four operators, including me. I've organized a ride on a civilian aircraft to Kabul tomorrow at oh six hundred. We're going in as aid workers, it's the only way. A contact in the city will kit us out."

Blade exhaled slowly, trying to keep his shit together.

No fucking way was he going back there.

Hell, he'd barely made it out alive the first time.

Now Pat was asking him to go back? Lily was the only link the man had left to his son, and he wanted to do something to help her. Blade got that. Understood it on a cellular level. Still…

He swallowed over the rising panic, struggling to keep the fear out of his voice. "I know this means a lot to you, but you've got the wrong guy." This was not the answer. *He* was not the answer.

"I'm not the man for the job. After what happened…" He couldn't think the words, let alone speak them.

"I'm asking you to put Helmand aside, Blade," Pat said, tersely. "I need to do this. For Lily. She's like family to me. I can't just leave her in that hellhole. You know the score. You know I can't do this alone. I need your help."

Blade's gut clenched. He'd re-up in a heartbeat if things were different. Dive back into the fray, earn his stripes again. He'd been at his best when he was operating and missed that version of himself. But the truth was stark in his mind—he was a shadow of who he had been. He had a panic attack when a firecracker went off, for fuck's sake.

He met Pat's gaze, unflinching. "I'd be a liability, man. I'll help you find a team, but I can't go out there."

Pat stood, towering over the table like some avenging angel. "You led one of the fiercest teams the military ever put together. You've still got that fire."

"That was then, Pat. Not now. Besides, I'm not combat ready. I wouldn't be able to ruck 20Ks without stopping."

Pat's eyebrow quirked, a silent call-out on Blade's bullshit. The guy was still an iron fortress, running and lifting like his life depended on it. His spare room was a damn home gym. Old soldiers never really died. They just bench pressed their sorrows away.

"Blade, she needs us. We're the only chance she's got."

Blade chewed his lip, the old wounds throbbing. Going back to that sandbox would rip open every scar. But Lily... she didn't deserve to be a pawn in that messed-up game.

"What about gear? You can't take it on a commercial jet." He was looking for a reason not to go. Any reason.

"Got it sorted. My guy's got gear and a chopper to take us into the mountains."

Blade raked a hand through his hair. "Christ, Pat. I don't know if I can."

Pat stood solid as an oak. "Joe believed in you. Don't you forget that. And he'd want you to help her."

Damn it to hell and back

Tell Lily I love her.

Blade hadn't done that yet. To be fair, she hadn't been around to tell, but maybe it was time he did.

"Okay, Commander. You win. I'm in."

CHAPTER 3

*L*ily opened her eyes. For a heart-stopping second, she didn't know where she was. Then reality crashed down—voices raised in anger, the staccato of gunfire, clawing panic.

She bolted upright then winced. Every part of her body ached. They'd walked for a grueling eight hours yesterday over rocky and uneven terrain, and her feet were riddled with blisters.

It was late last night when they'd finally arrived at this sorry excuse for a shelter. Exhausted, she hadn't been able to do much more than collapse before crying herself to sleep.

Now, in the harsh light of day, her skin crawled as she eyed the dirty room—small and stifling, with no furniture other than a bucket in the corner, a filthy mattress on the floor, and a wooden chair with a missing leg that wouldn't support anybody's weight. She vaguely remembered trying it last night, only to end up on the hard, unforgiving ground.

Outside, children wailed and dogs barked incessantly… faint sounds of life indicative of a small town or village. The aroma of cooking food wafted on a stale current of air, making her stomach rumble.

Damn, she was hungry. No one had offered her as much as a morsel or a sip since she'd been taken.

It sucked that she'd been separated from the other hostages and locked in here for the night. Talking with the reporters had made the nightmare more bearable and staved off the creeping dread.

One of them had even spoken Pashto and translated for the rest of the group so they'd known what was going on.

This way!

Keep going!

Don't fall behind!

Basic commands, punctuated by the prod of a gun barrel or poke of a stick, but it was much better knowing what their kidnappers were shouting at them than being left to wonder.

Now she had no way of communicating with her captors unless they spoke English.

Lily knew the score. Four months in Kabul had given her a front-row seat to the workings of the place. The Taliban factions were a mixed bag—some dragged into the fray, others true believers trying to stitch their country back together after the West pulled out.

She also knew why she'd been taken.

Hawkeye.

The official codename for the military software system she'd helped to develop. They wanted it, needed it, and she was the key, with the access codes locked up tight in her head.

No one else knew the codes apart from the two Afghan software developers on her team who she'd personally trained. She'd made sure each held the job title "Office Administrator" so no one hacking into the facility's employment records would suspect them.

A copy of the codes was also stored in the Commander of the Afghan Army's safe in an undisclosed location, but she'd heard he'd destroyed them when Kabul had fallen to the Taliban.

She was the weakest link.

Panic threatened to choke her.

The small window above her head let in a hard shaft of light, the beams of which picked up the dust hovering around the room. That grimy pane of glass was her only connection to the outside world.

Lily crossed the floor to stand under the sunbeam then turned her face up to the light. What a pain her eyeglasses had been in her lost luggage.

Shivering, she thought back to the chaos at the airport. Desperation and fear in the air, the crush of bodies, the helpless cries. Then the world had erupted—gunfire, screams, hands yanking her into the unknown.

She wrapped her arms around herself and waited until the tremors subsided. It had been a nightmare—and it was only just beginning.

Lily blinked at the sun. Judging by the temperature and the position, it was late morning. She'd been in this stinking room for over twelve hours. Someone must come for her soon.

She tried not to think about what lay ahead. Torture, for sure, as they tried to extricate the codes from her. Death… eventually. A sob caught in her throat.

If she played dumb, pretended she didn't know anything about the codes, she might be able to buy herself some time. But time for what? Besides, she didn't think that charade would last for long.

Lily swallowed thickly, trying to generate some saliva. Her mouth was drier than a sand dune. What little water she'd had on her had been left in the van. As well as her jacket with her passport.

Crap.

Without that, she wasn't going anywhere even if she did somehow escape.

Weariness—or maybe it was despair—crashed over her, and she collapsed back onto the mattress. Who cared about a few pesky bedbugs? She'd be dead in a couple of days. Unless they left her here to dehydrate and starve to death before they tortured her, hoping to make her more compliant?

Maybe their main focus was the reporters, and she'd just been in the wrong place at the wrong time. Under the circumstances, that would be the preferable option. She gave a dismal snort.

A scratch at the door made her jolt upright. She scoured the room for a weapon but found nothing but that wobbly chair.

The door creaked open. A woman, face veiled, stepped in bearing a tray which she placed at the foot of the mattress.

Relief washed over her.

After a little bow, the woman retraced her steps toward the door. "Wait," Lily called out, her voice hoarse. The woman paused, eyes downcast. "Thank you."

Lily mirrored the woman's bow, but she left without a word, the clicking lock echoing through the empty room. So much for trying to establish contact.

Lily was alone again. She wanted to run and scream and kick at the door, but she knew it wouldn't do any good.

Sighing, she eyed the tray. On the bright side, she now had something to eat and drink. It wasn't much, just a flatbread and water, but to her it was a feast.

She'd barely finished eating when the door flew open again. Lily scrambled to her feet, heart thundering. A man filled the doorway, his gesture clear.

Follow me.

Was this it? The moment her torment would begin?

Lily steadied herself then stepped forward, muscles aching and blisters screaming with each step. Still, the pain was nothing compared to what she knew was coming.

Gritting her teeth, she followed the man into the unknown.

THE DRIVE NORTH took another whole day but as long as they were on the move, she wasn't being tortured. They would leave that task to some big-shot Taliban honcho, someone with the authority to squeeze the information out of her and the know-how with which to do it.

Most of the ride, she had a grimy sack over her head, which didn't help with motion sickness, but she kept listening in the hopes of identifying where she was going.

It didn't do a stitch of good. Apart from the spluttering and ticking over of the old clunker's engine, she couldn't determine anything distinctive. The men spoke Pashto, which meant she couldn't understand a word they said, and apart from fastening her seat belt for her, they ignored her completely.

She couldn't help wondering about the reporters who'd been snatched with her. What had become of them? Were they to be transported separately? Ransomed off? She'd heard kidnapping had turned into a booming market in these parts. Governments, wealthy families, even high-profile companies would pay big bucks to have their citizens, employees, and loved ones returned. And, of course, that cash would be used to purchase weapons and put more people in danger.

Hot tears rolled down her cheeks, but she didn't care. Under the stinking sack, nobody could see them.

The reality was, she was in some serious shit. There was no one back home to pay her ransom. She'd never known her father, and her mother had died in a car wreck when she was sixteen. Since then, she'd only ever had Joe.

Her heart twisted painfully. It still felt so raw, it was hard to believe he'd been gone almost a year already.

Darling Joe, her rock… The person she'd clung to, who had always been there for her through thick and thin.

Why did you have to die?

Living with a Special Forces soldier, she'd prepped for the worst, but even so, she'd been unprepared to face the reality.

They'd been together for nearly ten years, since high school. Since her mother's death had left her homeless and his family had taken her in. He was the only man she'd ever loved, the only home she'd ever had.

She sobbed underneath the foul-smelling bag. Joe would have come to rescue her, she knew that without a doubt, but now there was no one. She was on her own.

The car stopped.

Lily sniffed and blinked to clear her eyes of tears. Was this it? Was this the place where she would be tortured? Where she would die?

The car door groaned open, and a blast of cold air slapped her in the face. It was way colder than back in the town. She tensed, ready for the grab-and-drag.

There was no chance of rescue. She wasn't important enough. Not like a high-powered politician or powerbroker upon whose shoulders rested a fragile peace agreement. She was just a tech geek who'd done some work for the Afghan government. Expendable.

And now, impossible to find. They'd moved her from the village to the mountains, judging by the drop in temperature and the fact that the car had been traveling steadily uphill since they'd set off.

But she had one card left to play. The military software codes. She was the human key to that lock, so she was more useful to them breathing than not. It was a small comfort, but she'd take it.

Showtime. An arm reached across her to unbuckle her seatbelt. She was dragged from the vehicle, then the sack was ripped from her head.

The blinding sun made her eyes water. At least it would mask the crying.

"Where am I?" Nobody answered.

The scenery was dramatic. Mountain peaks towered above, while a river snaked through the valley below, twisting like liquid silver.

Two men gripped her arms then pulled her toward the ridge.

Where the hell were they taking her? There was nothing here but solid rock.

They rounded an outcrop, and a dark slit materialized. Her eyes widened. It was a freakin' cave, but the entrance was disguised to look like part of the mountain. The perfect hideaway.

Her heart sank. No one would ever find her here. There were no signs of life anywhere, nobody to call on for help. Just a rocky mountain and below that, acres of green valley stretching down to the river. It was beautiful, though, in a stark, hopeless way.

The men forced her into the cave. On the way, a sharp edge snagged her arm.

"Hey!" she cried out, but no one took any notice.

One of the men made her sit with her back against the cold stone wall, while the other, much younger, chained her ankles to two iron rings bolted into the solid ground. Crude, but effective. With the shackles on, she wasn't going anywhere.

The older man left the cave.

"Can I have some water?" The younger guy shrugged, like he couldn't understand.

"Water." She made a drinking motion with her right hand. He gave a nod then disappeared, leaving her alone.

She looked around, surveying her new home. Nothing but rock. She couldn't even see the entrance from where she sat.

Shifting her position, she tried to get more comfortable. Sharp edges dug into her back, and the ground was hard and unrelenting.

Lily didn't have to wait long before an old man with a long beard and flowing robes came in with a flask of water. Judging by the way he carried himself, she guessed he was the one in charge.

He sat opposite her on the floor, crossed-legged, and set the water down on the ground just out of arm's reach.

"Salaam," he said politely, although his face remained impassive. "I hope you are not too uncomfortable."

Was he freakin' kidding? She was terrified, cold, desperate to pee, parched, starving, and smelled like a camel after three days of not showering. Otherwise, she was just peachy.

At least she'd had a bucket in the filthy room. This cave didn't even have that courtesy. And damned if she'd ask this guy for one. Or anything else.

"I'm fine." She kept her gaze down like she'd seen the women at work do when talking to their male superiors. It wasn't out of respect, she was too damn terrified to look at him.

He nodded in approval. "Do you know why you are here?" His English was heavily accented but grammatically correct, and she got the impression he was well educated. Definitely the one calling the shots.

She shook her head. "For ransom?" It was, she hoped, a convincing lie. No way was she going to let on she knew about the military software system and the codes. That was a last-option bargaining chip, and she still had one other option. If she could convince them that they had the wrong person, she might have a fighting chance of getting out of here alive.

"What is your name?" His eyes were dark and piercing. Did the question mean he wasn't sure?

Hope flared within her. If only she could convince him she wasn't who he thought she was.

"Jo Burke," she blurted out, using the first name that sprang to her mind—Joe's. In a strange way, it gave her strength. He wouldn't have backed down in this situation. Joe was a fighter.

She swallowed hard, the memories of him swelling in her throat, masquerading as a tremble of fear.

The man sucked in air over his teeth, his eyes tightening. "You're lying. Your name is Lilian Devereux, and you work for the Afghan government."

Shit.

They knew.

The realization left her cold, and she had to suck in air to prevent being sick. Still, she stuck to her guns.

"I am Jo Burke, and I am a reporter with The Wall Street Journal." The other hostages had worked for CNN. Hopefully, the correlation would give her story credibility.

"Liar! You are Lilian Devereux. Here is your picture." He threw a laminated ID card at her feet.

Looking down, she stifled a sob. It was her work keycard. She'd used it every day for the last four months to get inside the secure government building.

How the hell had he gotten hold of it? They must have bribed someone or had a man on the inside.

Tears rolled down her cheeks, she couldn't stop them. Faced with the damning evidence, she couldn't very well keep on lying. Her little charade was over.

"Now, I ask again. Do you know why you are here?"

Taking a shuddering breath, she shook her head. She might be Lilian Devereux, but she wasn't going to give him the luxury of answering his questions. If he wanted her to speak, he'd have to force the words out of her mouth.

He smirked, knowing he'd won this round. "I will tell you why. You are here because you have something we want. Something that is very valuable to the new regime. I think you know what that is?"

Go to hell.

She kept her mouth shut and her eyes cast down. God, that jug of water looked inviting. She fantasized about gulping down the cool, thirst-quenching liquid and began to salivate.

"You can have it. I brought it for you." His voice was back to being calm and conversational. "Once you tell me what I need to know."

Want to know, she thought savagely. *You don't need to know anything. You want to know so you can prevent the former Afghani officials from monitoring your activities here in Helmand Province.*

The opium-rich region had been terrorized by the Taliban for decades. Local farming communities were divided—half slaving in the fields to line the tribal leaders' pockets while the other half tried to make an honest living without being killed for it.

Since the coup, she'd heard rumors that girls would no longer attend school and women would not be allowed to work. The Taliban were going to renege on everything they'd promised before assuming power.

Lily clamped her mouth shut even harder.

After a long moment, the chief got up and sighed. "I'm

sorry you feel that way. You are making things very hard on yourself." He picked up the water flask and left the cave.

She spent a miserable day—alone, frightened, cold, parched, and starving. He returned later that night, this time with a plate of food in addition to the flask of water, as well as some blankets and a lantern. It was freezing in the cave now that the sun had set.

To make things worse, an icy wind buffeted her from the side, colder than any AC she'd ever felt, but when she peered in that direction, all she saw was shadows.

Gazing longingly at the blanket, she imagined wrapping it around herself, protecting herself from the draft.

As she'd done earlier in the afternoon, she kept her eyes lowered and refused to speak. The man left again, taking everything with him but the lantern.

She still hadn't gone to the toilet or eaten or drunk anything. Her last bite had been earlier that morning in the village, when the robed woman had brought her the tray.

Food and drink she could last without for a while longer, but the same couldn't be said for a bathroom. She desperately needed to pee.

Their plan was as clear as day. They expected her modesty to make her beg them to take her to a toilet, then they'd refuse unless she gave them the codes. The same went for the food and water—she'd get nothing until she cooperated.

What they didn't realize was she didn't give a damn about modesty. Not in a situation like this. Lily Devereaux was made of sterner stuff. And deprivation was way better than being tortured. She'd heard Joe and his father talk about waterboarding and other ways of extracting information from prisoners. They'd been trained to resist interrogation, to survive in situations such as this, but she hadn't.

Still, she didn't want to think about that right now.

Shuffling in a semicircle, she positioned herself as far from her previous spot as she could get. Her ankles twisted painfully in their metal bindings, but she didn't want to have to sleep in a wet spot, so she stretched as far as she could, pulled down her trousers, tugged her underwear to the side, then relaxed.

Luckily, the cave had a gentle slant, so the liquid ran away from her.

Take that.

They couldn't use that against her anymore.

She resumed her position, hugging herself to generate some heat, grateful for the lantern that offered a glimmer of light in the darkness. Without it she might have succumbed to the fear. She'd never been fond of the dark, not since her mother's accident. Joe always left a light on in the hallway for her.

The cold was her biggest worry. If they didn't give her a blanket or light a fire, there was a very real possibility she might succumb to hypothermia during the night. Then again, if she froze to death, she couldn't give them the codes. That would stump them. Her snigger was tinged with hysteria.

The man didn't come back again, obviously deciding to let her stew overnight. In the morning, when the cold, hunger and thirst had taken its toll, he'd try again.

Lily shut her eyes, giving in to the exhaustion. It would help if she could sleep through the worst of the cold. She was just dozing off when she heard a loud ruckus outside.

What was that?

Heart pounding, she squinted into the gloom. The lantern flickered in the draft, creating shadows around the cave. What the hell was going on out there?

There were a series of loud bangs.

She gasped. Was that *gunfire*?

Fully awake now, she huddled against the wall, trembling.

Was this part of their plan? Had they come to frighten her, or worse, to harm her in some way in an attempt to get her to cooperate?

She yelped as she heard another burst of gunfire. It wasn't continuous, but rather several short bursts followed by shouting and sporadic blasts of return fire.

Were they being attacked? Had the Afghan forces found her?

She held her breath, hardly daring to hope.

Holy crap, that was loud!

The shooting was right outside the entrance to the cave now. It reverberated off the stone interior, making her ears ring. The Taliban youth ran in, waving his weapon above his head, yelling at her in Pashto. She couldn't understand him, but she did know it wasn't good, so she curled up in a ball and tried to make herself as small a target as possible.

More yelling and shooting, then a beast of a man burst into the cave. He looked like something out of a futuristic horror movie, with a flashlight strapped around his head, a night vision scope covering half his face, and an enormous rifle aimed at the terrified Taliban fighter.

Before she had a chance to shout out, the beast pulled the trigger and cut the young man down in two short bursts from his gun.

Then he turned it on her.

CHAPTER 4

"*L*ilian Devereux?" the beast asked.

Stunned, she stared at the bloodied mess that had been the Taliban fighter, and then up at the shooter's gun. He'd been so young.

"Lilian! Is that you?"

American. He was American. It filtered through her addled mind that he must be here for her.

"Yes," she whispered, but he couldn't hear her over the incessant shouting outside.

"What?"

"Yes!" She forced strength into her voice and bobbed her head.

"Good. I'm going to get you out of here." Pushing the weapon over his shoulder, he bent down to inspect her shackles, then pulled out a lethal-looking combat knife. Her eyes widened as she recognized it. Joe had an identical one.

She gasped. "You're Special Forces."

The man pried the lock loose. He was pure Spec Ops, every move screamed it. He had that same chiseled-soldier look—all business, all mission.

With a grunt, he hauled her to her feet. Her ankles whined and blisters screamed, but with his arm wrapped around her—his grip like iron but not unkind—she was able to walk. "Let's move out."

They edged toward the mouth of the cave, the air turning colder. They almost made it, too, then all hell broke loose. Bullets flew from all directions.

He shoved her away and shouted, "Back!"

She crashed to the ground then covered her head.

The cave became a storm of sound and shrapnel. He was on comms, his voice a low growl of command. "Team, get the hostages clear. I've got Lilian."

Something about the way he said her name sounded familiar, but she couldn't quite pinpoint it. Was this one of Joe's Green Beret's buddies? Had their paths crossed before? She strained to get a clearer view of him, but it was dark in the cave and the blinding head light created a blurry halo around him, on top of which, the night-vision scope obscured part of his face.

He barked into his comms, the tension in his voice like a tightrope. "That's a negative. I don't want history repeating itself. Get those hostages to safety. That's an order."

This was not good.

"Other hostages?" She stared at him. "They're here too?"

"Yeah, we tracked them via satellite. That's how we knew where you were." Grabbing her wrist, he pulled her to the back of the cave. "Any other exits?"

All she could think about was their near escape, and now they were trapped. A sob gurgled up in her throat.

"Lilian, look at me."

She strained her neck. A beast of a man, but haloed by the bright head light, he was all shadow.

"Is there another way out?"

She tried to think, then pointed to a draft she'd felt earlier. "Maybe there?"

He was quick to check it out. "You're right. There is a narrow tunnel here. It's pretty tight, but it could be something."

"Can we fit?" It was very narrow, only about four feet wide by three feet tall.

"There won't be much wriggle room, and I'll have to leave my pack behind, but it's our best option. We can't get out the front without support."

Which you sent away, she added silently.

He began rooting through his bag, tucking what he could into pockets and through belt loops. "I'm going to set a trap." He was all business again. "Stand back."

"What?" She blinked at him. Was he insane? "You're going to blow up the entrance?"

"It'll buy us some time."

"But—what if we can't get through the tunnel? We'll be stuck. We won't be able to get out."

She saw a flash of white teeth below the head light. "Yeah, but the enemy won't be able to get in, either."

Fantastic. He was going to turn their escape route into a rock pile and take his chances in the narrow tunnel. The *dark*, narrow tunnel.

Sporadic bursts of gunfire—far too close for comfort—sounded outside as he prepped C4 like it was Play-Doh. Once the cave mouth was wired to blow, he stood back to admire his handiwork.

Lily yelped as a stray bullet ricocheted off the rock not far from where she stood, spraying sediment into her face.

"Stand back!" He lunged for her, pushed her behind him, gave her a quick once-over for injuries. Whatever he saw—or didn't see—satisfied him, because he continued with his plan. "Get ready. It's going to get dusty in here."

"Are you sure—?"

He depressed the lever, then the world shook.

She screamed, flattening herself against the back wall of the cave, tensing for a barrage of shrapnel and falling rock.

But the blast was angled outward. Apart from a storm cloud of dust, nothing happened in the cave. Then a deep rumble sounded.

"Here we go," he said.

Hundreds of tons of mountainside tumbled over the exit.

She stared at the wall of rock and started to hyperventilate. Now they were well and truly stuck.

"Lilian, come on."

Still, she didn't move. Her breath came in short, rapid gasps. The cave was hazy with dust, and the lantern glowed red behind them.

"Lily," he said more quietly.

She turned, as if in a daze. Joe had called her Lily, and his father, Pat, but no one else.

His head light danced in front of her eyes. That combined with her breathlessness made her vision swim.

Dear God, don't let me pass out.

"Come on, Lily. We've gotta get out of here."

She followed him in the direction of the tunnel. Even without his backpack he was a giant of a man, like Hercules slaying the monster, except she had no idea how he was going to get them out of this one.

He secured the weapon over his back and crouched down. The gap was so small, how on earth would he fit? It didn't look big enough for *her*.

Shit, he was going to go for it. Not that they had a better option. Or even a worse one.

It was so *black* in there…

"I'll go first. Keep behind me."

She gulped as he eased himself into the tunnel. The light

from his head-mounted flashlight danced off the narrow, rocky walls, and she heaved a sigh of relief. At least they weren't going to be swallowed by the darkness.

His massive shoulders took some maneuvering, but then he was in. He actually did it. She watched as he leopard-crawled along for a few yards, her eyes dropping to his tight, khaki-clad butt.

Catching herself, she blinked. What the hell? This was hardly the time. Still, she had to admit, it was a great butt. Hard, taut, muscular.

"You coming?" he called, but it was too narrow for him to turn around.

"Does it lead anywhere?" She really, really didn't want to go in there, but what choice did she have? He'd demolished their only other way out.

"Looks safe enough. The breeze is strong. I think we'll be okay." A few seconds later, he started moving again.

Oh, God. She was actually doing this.

If he can fit, so can I.

Lily got down on all fours.

Here goes...

Taking a shuddering breath, she crawled in after him. The ground under her hands was cold and crumbly with a metallic smell that would have been sharp and pungent had it not been diluted by the breeze.

They progressed slowly, inch by inch, for about twenty yards, him in front of her and her focusing solely on his wiggling butt. As silly as it sounded, that perfect backside helped keep the panic at bay.

Eventually, the passage widened into a small, rounded alcove where they could sit side by side. The soldier pushed his night vision scope aside and wiped sweat from his face. "We can rest for five minutes."

"Thank goodness." Lily sat next to him, back against the

wall. The stiff breeze made the confined space more bearable, and she wanted to believe the hilltop and freedom were only a short distance away.

"You okay?" he asked. The head light was still on, so his features were a dark haze. That was okay with her. It would be pitch black in the tunnel without it, which would probably send her over the edge. This way was better.

His voice was familiar. She tried to place it but couldn't. "Yes, I… I think so."

"Good." He pulled a compass out of his pocket then studied it. "We've been going steadily west and at an upwards trajectory, so it shouldn't be long until we reach the outside. I'm guessing another twenty, thirty minutes. Do you think you can handle that?"

Like she had a choice. "Yeah."

He turned his head, and the alcove was plunged into darkness. Nearly there, she told herself. Just keep going. It was dark and claustrophobic, and she couldn't stop thinking about what would happen if the tunnel narrowed to a point where they couldn't get through. What then?

A muffled blast made her jump and sent a puff of dust down the narrow tunnel.

"What was that?"

"They're trying to blast their way into the cave." His voice was controlled, measured. Meantime, she was about to have a full-blown panic attack. There was no going back.

He must have sensed her terror, because he turned around and laid a firm, calloused hand on her arm. "Stay calm, Lily, and keep breathing normally. We're almost out."

"Okay," she whispered. "I'll try."

"Good."

"Um, I have to ask. Do we know each other?" It was the familiarity with which he said her name. She couldn't see his eyes but sensed he was looking right at her. Her face, on the other hand, would be illuminated by his head light.

"Yeah, we've met, I'm Blade Wilson, Spade—sorry—*Joe's* friend. I haven't been able to get in touch before now because you left so soon after he... passed away. I was with him when... anyway, he gave me a message for you. He said to tell you he loves you."

CHAPTER 5

Okay, so he wouldn't win any prizes for his delivery, but at least he'd said it. He'd told her. One mission complete. One to go.

The look on her face was complete astonishment. She opened her mouth to speak, but he held up a hand cutting her off. Now was not the time. "Come on, let's move on. We can talk when we're safe."

She shut her mouth and gave a dazed nod.

Turning his back on her, he adjusted the head lamp, lowered his scope, then crawled farther along the tunnel. The angle was noticeably steeper now, and the breeze was stronger than before. It felt cool on his face, and just for a moment, he closed his eyes and savored the fresh air. They were on the right track. Escape, evasion, survival. That's what he'd been trained for, and during his operational days, he'd crawled through way worse than this to stay alive.

They all had.

He thought about Phoenix, Boomer, Viper, and Pat—the makeshift unit guiding the other hostages through the thick, impenetrable forest that covered the valley to the rendezvous point where a chopper waited to transport them to freedom. They were a good bunch of guys. He'd served with all of them at one time or another during his Special Forces career. All except Pat, who was the driving force behind this mission. They were effective, able, and deadly. Even though the Taliban fighters would be close on their tail, he was confident they'd get the hostages out in time.

Blade peered through the night vision scope ahead into the tunnel. He guessed they had at least twenty to thirty yards to go before they broke ground. It was doable, as long as the enemy weren't waiting for them at the other side.

Things hardly ever went according to plan, this mission a classic case in point. Prepare down to the finest detail but inevitably something would happen to fuck things up. The enemy was an unknown force, impossible to control. Hence the constant question—what if?

What if there were more fighters than they'd expected? What if the hostages weren't there? What if one of them was injured? What if the helicopter couldn't make it to the emergency rendezvous point?

Good thing Blade had plenty of contingency plans.

At the covert air base in the desert, before the Black Hawk had brought them to the mountains, he'd studied drone footage of the area and knew tunnels crisscrossed for miles from cave to cave. He was betting the enemy below hadn't yet realized they'd found another exit. That would give him several hours to get Lily as far away as humanly possible.

It was pitch-black in the tunnel, and he used both the NVG and the head light to show them the way. They must be close to the end now, but it just seemed to go on and on. Nothing to tell them how far they had to go. The only clue he had was the cooler air making his eyes water. They must be close.

The tunnel curved, so he crawled around it—and hit a dead end.

What the—?

He reached out with his hand but all he could feel was cold, hard stone. His heart sank. No, this couldn't be. He heard Lily scampering up behind him. "Why have we stopped?"

He hesitated. How could he tell her there was nowhere to go?

Another blast of icy air hit him. It was coming from above. He glanced up.

Hell, yeah! He hadn't noticed it before, but the tunnel made a ninety degree turn upwards. A hole loomed above them through which he could see the stars and a scant canopy of leaves.

Brilliant. They'd made it.

There was a crescent moon tonight, which was perfect. It would give them enough light to see by but wouldn't leave them too exposed, and the trees and crags would provide plenty of shadows in which to hide.

The only problem was getting up there. He judged the distance to be about ten feet. Too high for him to reach by himself, but together they might have a shot.

"We're at the end," he called to Lily who'd stopped behind him. "There's a hole vertically above us, but it's high. We're both going to have to squeeze in here for me to lift you up there."

"There is? Oh, thank God." He heard the relief in her voice.

"I'm going to stand, then you crawl until you reach my legs. Use my body like a ladder to climb until you're standing next to me. From there, I'll boost you up. Okay?"

"Got it."

He got to his knees, scraping his back against the stone

roof of the tunnel. Sometimes, being this tall had its drawbacks. Gritting his teeth, he maneuvered himself into the vertical shaft and held onto the walls as he straightened up. It was tight, but there was just enough room for the two of them. The problem would be getting her into a standing position.

His shoulders raked the sides. Pressing his back to the rock, he tried to leave enough space for her to stand. Jagged edges dug into his back, but he ignored them. "Your turn."

He heard her scramble forward until he felt a hand on his shin.

"That's it. Come as far forward as you can before angling up. Try to stand too soon and your back won't be clear."

Lily put one hand on his knee. Another on his thigh. She gasped and let go of him.

"You okay? Did you scrape your back?"

"I'm fine." Her voice carried a small tremble.

"Alright, then. Time to work your way up the shaft. It's a tight fit, but it's doable."

"I don't know if I can." Her voice was tight and high pitched. She was seconds away from panicking. "There isn't enough room."

"Listen, Lily. The only way we're going to get you out of here is if you climb up my body. I can help you, but you've got to get to your feet first. Don't worry about hurting me. Push against me as hard as you have to, but stand up."

Whether it was the urgency in his voice or her own fear, he couldn't tell, but she shuffled forward. He pressed tighter against the wall to create as much space as possible.

Her head banged into his knees, then his thighs, and then into his groin. He tensed, willing his body not to react to her closeness in case he put her off. It was almost pitch dark. He'd switched off his headlamp when he'd stood so as not to attract any unwanted attention from above. The milky glimmer from the unseen crescent moon was their only light source.

Grunting, she turned her face sideways, so it wouldn't be plastered against his stomach, but his T-shirt was rising along with her head. He felt her hair on his skin. Slowly, she got to her knees then finally to her feet. She'd filled out since he'd last seen her, which admittedly was almost a decade ago. Her curvy hips dug into his and her plump breasts pressed against his torso. With every breath, he felt the softness of her chest expand into his.

"Are you sure about this?" she whispered, her face less than an inch from his. Damn if he couldn't feel her breath on his lips.

"I'm sure." He kept his voice calm and steady, even if inside he was anything but. Her hair cascaded around her face and tickled his neck, like it would if he woke with her in his arms.

He swallowed. Where the hell had *that* thought come from?

Lily tilted her head to glance up at the hole, but her nose bumped his. She whispered, "Sorry."

He sensed infinite discomfort in those two small syllables.

"Let's get you out of here." Enough was enough. He couldn't handle the close proximity. His body was seconds away from getting the wrong idea—and that would not be good. "I'm going to lift you from the waist as far as I can. Use your knees and feet to climb me, your hands to pull you up the walls. When you're high enough, stand on my shoulders, from there, you should be able to reach the top and haul yourself out of the shaft."

She nodded, her nose rubbing against his again almost like an Eskimo kiss. Their breath mingled in the darkness, and he felt so close to her that for a fleeting minute he considered leaning in to let their mouths meet. It wouldn't take much, less than an inch. What would she feel like? Taste like? Would she respond?

What the hell?

Get a grip, soldier!

This was Spade's nerdy girlfriend, except she wasn't so geeky anymore. Her lush body played havoc with his senses, and for some reason, he couldn't stop thinking about it.

"I'm ready," she whispered.

He placed his hands around her waist then lifted her, her body flush against his. Her breasts bounced into his face, and he nearly came undone. Sucking in a harsh breath, he twisted his head to the side. It wasn't to avoid embarrassing her nearly as much as to avoid embarrassing himself. Fuck, they were incredible breasts. He inhaled deeply. It took all his willpower not to bend his head and nuzzle them.

What the hell was wrong with him? Sure, it had been a while since he'd been laid, but this was totally unprofessional behavior. She was a hostage and his best buddy's girl. He needed to stay focused—not react like an adolescent teenager on prom night.

Her petite frame weighed next to nothing, so he was able to lift her high enough so that her hips were level with his ears. He grimaced as his back scraped against the hard rock. "Can you grab onto anything?"

She bent her knees and hesitantly placed one on each of his shoulders, stabilizing herself. Her groin was right in his face, but she was too busy looking up to notice. She was wearing lightweight cotton trousers, and damn if he couldn't feel the lace from her panties right through them.

Lace, for fuck's sake.

That conjured a bunch of inappropriate images, which was crazy since he'd never found her attractive before. He exhaled. The sooner he got her out of here the better.

"I can feel a plant or a root or something." She stretched higher, tilting her pelvis so her crotch was right in his nose.

Fucking hell.

"Grab it." Quickly.

She managed to get enough leverage to pull herself up until she trod lightly on his shoulders. Thank God for that.

He put his hands under her feet and pressed up. Combined with her efforts to pull and claw her way to the surface, she managed to scramble out.

"Keep low," he called quietly, looking up.

Her face filled the opening, hair tumbling down. She whispered back into the darkness, "I am. How are you going to get out?"

"Take this." He undid a length of rope that he'd tied around his belt then tossed it up. "Tie it to that tree but stay alert for anyone who might be creeping around." The last thing he wanted was for a Taliban sniper to spot her, although they'd be under strict orders to shoot but not kill. She was useless to them dead. They needed her alive for the codes. He, on the other hand, would be toast.

Before long, there would be fighters crawling all over the hillside searching for them. When the five of them formulated the rescue plan, they hadn't counted on a fighting force descending from over the ridge. He still didn't know exactly where they'd come from. They must have emerged from the cave network that riddled the mountains. It was obviously larger than anyone anticipated.

An army colonel once told him to make sure his unit's Plan B could function as a Plan A because in many cases it was the one ultimately put into action.

At least Pat, Phoenix, Viper, and Boomer had secured the four other hostages and had escaped into the forests in the valley below. It had taken him longer to find Lily. Her captors had kept her separate, probably to interrogate her in private. She was first prize. The others were collateral—an added bonus to use for ransom.

From what he'd seen, Lily didn't appear to be injured or harmed in any way, which was one reason why they'd inserted as soon as possible, perhaps to the detriment of more thorough reconnaissance. It was vitally important she didn't sabotage all her hard work by giving the Taliban the access codes. Pat had outlined how important her military system was to the Afghans, even more so now that the Taliban had assumed control. Unfortunately, that meant they'd stop at nothing to extract those codes from her.

The end of the rope dropped down into the tunnel. She'd done it! He gave it a firm tug. Satisfied her knot would hold, he climbed to the surface.

CHAPTER 6

With the cold night air on their faces, they crouched low and raced across the rocky terrain toward the green zone—an area of dense vegetation alongside a river in a valley such as this one—roughly five hundred yards below.

Despite it being spring, the temperature had dropped close to zero overnight, and their breaths misted in front of them. Particularly Lily's, which was how Blade noticed she was breathing harder than normal.

"When did you last eat or drink anything?" he asked.

"Not for a while." They reached the trees. She stopped, doubling over to catch her breath.

Another complication he hadn't accounted for. She was fading fast, her blood sugar dangerously low due to dehydration and lack of food. "Let's rest here. We should be okay for a moment."

Lily wobbled, possibly due to lightheadedness.

He looped his arm around her. "You alright?"

"I just need to close my eyes for one second." She leaned backwards against a tree.

"No, don't close your eyes. Lily. Lily!"

Her legs buckled, then she sank to the ground.

Blade crouched beside her, studied her face. She was barely conscious.

Damn it. He didn't want to stop for long, but she needed sustenance. A quick glance around told him they were alone, and he hadn't spotted anyone on the trail down the mountain. The cave collapse would take most of the night to clear, and until then, the kidnappers would assume they were trapped inside.

But once they were in, it wouldn't take long to realize they'd escaped. By then it would be morning. Daylight. A dangerous time to be on the move, but beneficial for their pursuers. They'd follow the tunnel, then start scouring the hilltops, eventually tracking them into the valley, which was the only logical escape route.

He detached his water flask from his utility belt and pulled a squishy energy bar from his pocket. "Here. Drink."

She was so weak, it seemed an effort to open her eyes. He held the flask to her lips and watched while she drank—first a tentative sip, then thirsty gulps.

"Easy," he cautioned. "Don't choke."

After she'd drunk half the bottle, he handed her the energy bar. "Eat this."

She tore it open, took a greedy bite, then moaned and closed her eyes as she savored the pleasure.

He couldn't tear his attention from her mouth. His hunger was far different from hers, and completely inappropriate given her relationship with Spade and their current predicament. Finally, he managed to banish the impure thoughts from his mind. Thank goodness it was too dark for her to notice his intense gaze. "Better?"

"Much."

She sounded stronger. That was a good sign. Maybe they could make some progress now. They'd need to put as much distance as possible between them and the Taliban, and she'd need all the energy she could muster.

Lily crinkled the wrapper and looked around, unsure of where to put it.

He held out a hand. "Any trash we leave behind will let them know we were here and which way we went."

She handed him the trash, her soft fingers lingering a second too long for his comfort. "I remember you now. You're the team leader of Joe's unit. I saw you together a couple of times in the early days." Before she'd wrapped Joe around her little finger, and he'd stopped hanging out with the guys in his unit.

Blade wondered if they were thinking the same thing—they hadn't taken to each other when they'd first met. He'd thought Lily, or Lilian as she was known back then, too stuck up for her own good. Definitely too smart to mix with the likes of them. She used to dismiss him with a flat glance on the rare occasions that they'd crossed paths.

"*Was* the leader. I left the army after..." He shrugged.

"After Joe died?" Her clear, brown-eyed gaze lingered on his face, almost as if she was trying to figure him out.

Good thing she couldn't read minds. She'd be horrified to know what he'd been thinking—about her then and now. Lord knew he wasn't proud of either thought, but his body seemed to have developed a mind of its own where she was concerned.

He nodded. "Yeah."

She glanced down at the damp ground. "I heard he wasn't the only one who lost his life that day."

Blade swallowed over the massive lump in his throat. "I was the only one who made it home."

After a few weeks had passed, he'd heard Stitch had taken refuge in a small Afghan village where he'd converted to Islam and integrated into the community. He hadn't tried to make contact. If that's what the former medical officer wanted, then who was Blade to tell him any different? They each had their own demons to live with.

"Will you tell me what happened? I know the official version from Pat, but I want to know what really happened."

Oh, boy.

Her whisper made his heart race, though he wasn't sure if it was the woman or the question she asked. Blade stared at the ground, wishing it would swallow him up, but he knew this wasn't a conversation he could avoid. Coming here, facing *her*. It was inevitable it would come up. "The official version isn't incorrect," he began, willing his heart rate to return to normal. "Pat would have given it to you straight."

She chuckled, the outburst softening her features. "That's where you're wrong. Pat tried to protect me, just like everybody else, but I don't want the watered-down version. I want to know the cold, hard truth about how Joe died."

Blade studied her as best he could in the dim light. Wide, brown eyes tilted up at the ends. Cute, button nose. Kissable, heart-shaped lips. Since he'd last seen her, she'd grown her ash blonde hair and lost the glasses—thick, black-rimmed things that did nothing for her looks. Without them, she was a knockout. Her huge eyes now held dozens of questions, and her lips pursed as she waited for answers.

How could he tell her what had happened? The details still kept him awake at night. She'd loved Spade. They'd been together forever. He didn't want to ruin the image she had of him.

"Please. I need to know. No matter what."

God, she was going to regret that. But he couldn't tell her

no. He took a deep breath. "We were on a goodwill mission. It wasn't supposed to be dangerous, although every mission has the potential to blow up over here. One minute we were hiking over a mountain pass, the next we were walking straight into an ambush."

Her eyes grew wide. "What happened?"

"Insurgents on both sides, as far as the eye could see. They opened fire. There was very little cover." He glared up into the hills, the feeling of helplessness close to overwhelming. Anxiety made his chest pound, his body cold and clammy.

Lily watched him closely through the dark. The whites of her eyes and hardness of her gaze forced him to continue, even though guilt threatened to crush him.

"Our guide was a Taliban sympathizer and, unknown to us, had given away our location. I should have seen it coming but didn't. He led us straight into that ambush."

"Oh, God." The words came through a whimper. She was probably picturing the situation, but not even the most vivid imagination could be as bad as the real thing.

Dust mixed with cordite... His men screaming... Blood on the barren path...

Blade shook his head to get rid of the visuals, but they kept coming. All he could do was narrate through the pain. "The mountain pass was surrounded by hills on either side. It was a perfect natural trap. We were completely exposed."

"What did you do?"

"Nothing. It happened too fast. Spade took a bullet in the thigh and went down. I was ahead and turned around when he screamed. Blaster and Ricky had both been hit, too." His voice broke. "There was nothing I could do to help them."

Lily's face was blank. He had no idea what she was thinking.

"Stitch provided cover fire while I went to help Spade, but he took another round in the chest. I couldn't save him." His voice turned into a groan, and he exhaled slowly through pursed lips. It still hurt so goddamn much.

His shrink said he should talk about it, but he wasn't sure that helped. All that did was make him relive the nightmare again… and again. He preferred to keep the memory buried, like some bittersweet home movie stuffed into the bottom of a drawer, to be viewed and cried over only when extremely drunk.

"What about Stitch?"

He raised an eyebrow. She knew the names of Spade's fallen colleagues, but not his? Maybe she would have remembered if he'd also died on the mountain pass like he should have.

"Stitch couldn't cope with what happened. He went AWOL later that day. As far as I know, he's still in the wind."

"You were the only one who came home." She made it sound like an accusation.

He didn't blame her. For months he'd thought the same thing. How had he made it out in one piece? Had it been blind luck? Or was God tormenting him by making him live with the guilt for evermore? Was that his punishment?

"Yeah, I made it to a later rendezvous point and got on a chopper out of there."

"What about their bodies?" Her voice cracked. Her eyes glimmered with tears.

The urge to put his arms around her and weep with her was strong, but he got the feeling she wouldn't appreciate that. "They were retrieved later that day, when it was safe to return to the region." When the Afghan army, assisted by an airstrike by 101st Airborne Division, had taken out as many of the Taliban fighters as they could. The rest had disappeared back into their tunnels to fight another day.

Lily cleared her throat. "You brought him home?"

Them. He'd brought *them* home.

Blade nodded, not trusting himself to speak.

Then he'd buried them.

A thought struck him. "I don't remember seeing you at the funeral."

"I couldn't do it." Her voice was heavy with emotion. "I couldn't go. I paid my respects privately."

He packed the water back in his belt holder. "It's none of my business. You don't need to explain."

They started walking again. Despite her exhaustion, she fell into step beside him. "A few days before… before he died, the Agency offered me a position in Kabul. I took it because I thought it was a way to be closer to Joe, and it was a chance to do something to help end the opium wars in Helmand Province." A bitter laugh escaped her. "I was so naive."

Blade didn't reply. They all were, to a certain degree. Naive to think they could have made a difference.

"I know it's not the same as being out there fighting, but it was better than sitting at home worrying."

He could only imagine what that felt like. He'd much rather be in the warzone than at home worrying whether a loved one would come back alive. It was one of the reasons he'd stayed single. No accountability. No one to leave without a boyfriend or a husband. No kids to leave without a daddy.

"Besides," Lily continued, "if the Afghan government could use it to restore peace in that region, I would have accomplished something."

"Can't argue with you there."

She trudged along beside him, her words heavy as her footfalls. "After it happened, I decided to take the job anyway. It was… easier than being alone. I needed to get away from the memories. Everything at home reminded me of him."

Blade could understand that. "I'm sorry," he murmured, keeping an eye on the hillside. "It was my fault we got ambushed. I didn't vet the guide thoroughly enough. It was my job as team leader to double-check all third parties, and I let them down."

He felt her gaze on his face but kept walking. If he'd been more careful and had scrutinized Sayed more closely then maybe, just maybe, his friends would still be alive.

They walked some way in silence. Blade forced himself to focus on their immediate surroundings, not back in the past where his mind really wanted to go. It wasn't good to wallow, his shrink had told him. Best to stay in the present.

"I don't blame you for what happened," she said, eventually. "You couldn't have foreseen that ambush. Pat told me you'd relied on faulty intelligence. That's not on you."

He scowled into the darkness. Pat had divulged a lot more than was necessary, but then Lily was the type to demand details. The former SEAL probably hadn't told her anything she didn't already know.

"Thank you." It was nice of her to say, not that he believed it.

"But I do blame you for making him sign up for the Green Berets to begin with."

He thought he'd misheard. "Excuse me?"

"It was *you* who convinced him it was a good idea to sign up. I know it was." She took an angry breath. "He was happy in the Ordnance Corps. He didn't want to be a killer."

Blade couldn't deny it. That was exactly what they were. Glorified killers, trained to take out the enemy with extreme prejudice and capable of excessive force when necessary. And he was proud of it. But he hadn't coerced his friend. That wasn't true.

"Spade wanted to try out for the Green Berets," he said

slowly. "There was a selection process. We went through it together."

"He joined the army to train as an engineer. *You* put the stupid idea of the Green Berets into his head."

Every syllable pierced his heart.

"If it wasn't for you, Joe would still be alive."

CHAPTER 7

*I*t was hard to believe this was the same guy she
remembered. Blade Wilson. The girls who
flocked around the base couldn't even say his name without
swooning. He'd been something of a god at Fort Bragg.
From his broad, muscular shoulders and washboard abs to
his sexy, carefree smile and witty banter, he was every
woman's wet dream. Tough too, outperforming most of the
others in the training exercises and, according to Pat, a
natural leader.

Personally, she'd always wondered what the fuss had been
about. She didn't deny he'd been good looking, if you liked
the whole blue-eyed, bad-boy thing, but he'd lacked
substance. There'd been something shallow and dismissive
about him that had turned her off.

No one ever stayed with Blade for very long. He'd love
you and leave you, but then, his women knew what they
were getting. She masked a snort as she struggled to keep
pace with him. His commitment phobia didn't change those
women's minds. They looked at it like a challenge, each
wanting to be the one to tame him. But no one ever did.

Blade's only loyalty, as far as she could see, was to his country and to his friends.

Then, there was the brooding hulk of a man he'd become. He was still good looking—she'd be a fool not to see that—but in a haunted, brutal kind of way. The easy smile had vanished, and the blue eyes no longer laughed. Instead, they gleamed with an intensity that made her nervous.

Joe had looked up to him, almost hero-worshiped him, a trait that had irritated her. Joe had been a smart guy, but he'd lacked confidence, particularly in the beginning. She supposed the unit had cured him of that. He'd always been able to figure out how anything worked, take it apart and put it back together again. He would have made a brilliant engineer, but that wasn't what he wanted. He'd wanted to follow his cocky, self-assured friend into what she secretly called the death squad.

Deep down, she'd always known it would end this way.

Joe wasn't like Blade and Ricky and the others. He was strong, had been well-trained, but he was a softie at heart and killing bothered him. He'd struggled to process what he'd done. He'd had nightmares. Once, a few weeks before he'd deployed that last time, she'd woken up to find his hands around her neck. Luckily, he'd come to his senses and realized what he was doing before he'd done her any harm.

When she suggested he get some help, he'd flatly refused, saying they'd kick him out of the army if he was diagnosed with PTSD. Unfortunately, he was right, that would have ended his career as an operator. Not that it would have been such a bad thing, in her opinion. But he'd made her promise not to tell anyone about the incident, not even his father. The unit was his life. His teammates were his family. And Blade? Joe looked up to him as an older brother.

On they marched, Blade with a look of intense concentration on his face, his shooting hand gripping the pistol, ready to go should there be a problem, the muzzle in front of his nose, the weapon angled at forty-five degrees. There was another sidearm in a holster strapped to his leg. She tried not to notice how thick his thigh was, how it filled out his cargo pants.

The growly beast had clammed up since her little outburst and hadn't uttered a single word for at least two miles now. Did she feel bad about what she'd said? Hell, no. She did blame him, but she also blamed Joe. Maybe she should have added that.

Basically, she was just pissed he was dead and needed a target for her anger. Blade made a big target.

Hot tears stung her eyes, but she blinked them away. Now wasn't the time to have a moment, now was the time to stay focused and get out of there, far away from the men who wanted the codes.

"When do you think they'll realize we've gone?" she asked, to break the silence.

"Not long."

Great. Now he was giving her the silent treatment.

It would take her captives some time to clear the debris caused by Blade's explosive device, but it had already been a couple of hours. Exactly how long, she had no idea. The miles seemed to blend into each other, and she was walking on autopilot.

Blade stalked rather than walked, always a step or two ahead of her, his head moving like a homing beacon. Wary, cautious, alert.

To raise her spirits, she thought about what might have been. She and Joe would be married by now, maybe even have a baby on the way. He'd be working at Fort Bragg as an engineer, building airplanes, tanks, or something else he was passionate about, while she went to work at her computer job, comfortable knowing her husband would be home safe and sound when she got back.

Sadly, that's all it was. A dream. Her fantasy.

Not Joe's.

His had been to join the Special Forces.

Glaring daggers at Blade's back, she followed him farther into the forest. Dense trees blocked out the moonlight, and dark shadows loomed in front of them.

"You do know where you're going, right?"

He shot her a look hinging on disbelief.

"Okay, fine. Sorry I asked."

But she had noticed that every few yards he'd turn to check on her, to make sure she was still stumbling along behind him. He was a good soldier, she'd give him that much.

On they went. Her feet were aching, her back breaking. Weren't they ever going to stop? There was no more talking, the only noise—other than her footsteps—came from small animals scurrying into their burrows as they approached.

Blade seemed to glide through the undergrowth, barely making a sound, which was bizarre given his immense frame and those enormous boots he was wearing. Easily six foot four or five, with muscles bursting out from under his shirt and shoulders that could carry two men.

He was strong too. When he'd lifted her up in the vertical tunnel, he'd done so effortlessly, as if she weighed nothing more than that blasted rifle he carried with him. Heat stole into her cheeks as she thought of how she'd had to rub against him to get out.

No way was she going to dwell on how hard his body had been, how firm. How he'd smelled so masculine that it had awakened a longing in her that she hadn't experienced since Joe.

Lily stumbled, only just catching her footing.

"You okay?" he growled, barely turning his head.

"I'm fine." God, how she missed Joe's body. Missed having his arms around her at night. Most of all, she missed his smile of delight when he woke up next to her in the morning, like she was this wonderful surprise he hadn't been expecting. Even after ten years together, he still did it.

Had done it.

Joe was gone. Why couldn't she get her thick head around that?

They walked on for another hour, until the sun started to poke its sleepy head over the distant purple mountains. Her breath had grown ragged, her body beyond fatigued. "How much longer?"

He stopped so suddenly, she bumped into his back. An oomph escaped her.

Solid. Wall.

Yet she was too exhausted to apologize.

His dark eyes roamed over her. Was that concern she saw in them? Couldn't be. She must have imagined it. He didn't give a damn about her. He just wanted to get her out of here so he could go home. It was written all over his body. She was just another job, a mission he had to fulfill.

"There's a cabin not far from here. I was hoping to reach it before daylight."

She gave a weary nod.

He handed her the water bottle. "Drink."

Hey, she wasn't about to argue. Lily downed what she could, dribbling down her chin. Who would have thought water tasted so good?

"Easy," he said softly.

She wiped her mouth and handed it back. "Thanks."

"You think you can manage another mile or so?"

Another mile. Shoot. At this point she didn't know if she could manage another step. "I can try."

He gave a curt nod, then re-attached the water bottle. It

was nearly empty now. Hopefully there were supplies at this cabin, wherever that was.

They set off again, but it was too much. Her mind was willing, but her body rebelled. When was the last time she slept? Twenty-four hours ago? Forty-eight? She was too tired to work it out.

In the east, the horizon shimmered with an electric blue glow. They were almost out of time. "I can't—"

Her legs gave way.

He moved quickly, so quickly she didn't realize what was happening. Strong arms caught her before she hit the ground.

"I'm sorry."

"It's not a problem. I can carry you." His dark eyes softened with concern, like the sky.

God.

It was easier hating him.

He scooped her into his arms.

With every step toward the cabin, she felt his heart beating, firm and steady. He smelled good too, like a man. Like Joe smelled when he got back from a day at the base. It had been so long since she'd smelled that manly scent that she inhaled deeply, savoring it. As they gained more ground, her mind grew groggy. Before she knew it, she'd lapsed into an exhausted sleep.

CHAPTER 8

*B*lade knew the instant Lily fell asleep.

Her body went limp, and her head relaxed against his arm. He glanced down and for the first time, took a long, hard look at the woman he'd rescued. The anger on her face softened in the warm hues of the rosy dawn. The cresting sun illuminated her features, highlighting the gentle curve of her cheeks and the fullness of her lips, slightly parted as if…

Well, he wasn't going to go there.

Her eyelashes, long and delicate, rested against her skin, just above the faint purple shadows underneath that spoke of the ordeal she'd undergone.

Docile, vulnerable, exhausted. Lily was an enigma. Full of fear when he'd first rescued her, then simmering with fiery indignation. She was tough, though. He'd pushed her hard, mostly because he'd wanted to get under cover before daylight hit, but also because he was mad at what she'd said about him. That he'd convinced Spade to join the unit.

He ground his jaw. No way. She'd been wrong about that. Spade had signed up on his own accord. No persuading necessary. As had Ricky and Blaster and all the other guys he knew.

He cast his mind back. It was so damn long ago he could hardly remember. He'd met Spade, or Joe as he was called back then, at a training camp. Spade was an infantryman in the Ordnance Corps, and Blade had recently returned from a tour in Iraq with the 82nd Airborne Division. Blade was older than Spade by about five years, but when you served together, age didn't mean a thing. They became fast friends. Spade had always been bright, and he was—had been—an asset to their unit. The guy had been a genius with machinery. Anything from their patrol vehicle to a jammed anti-tank weapon, he could take apart and fix.

Blade remembered the moment he'd decided to try out for the Special Forces. His Commanding Officer had pulled him aside and told him he was a good fit. Blade had needed a change. The constant partying and mayhem while off-duty was taking its toll. He didn't like the person he'd become. To win the respect of his buddies, he had to drink more, stay up later, and get up to more shit, and after four years, he was over it.

The decider had been when he'd met one of the Green Berets on a training operation. He'd been in the canteen when the atmosphere had changed. It suddenly buzzed with energy like an electric current had been fed through the room, and in walked a massive, tattooed man wearing a green beret with a silver emblem on it—an arrowhead and dagger.

He'd stared at the man with respect and admiration. The entire canteen had gone quiet, as if the sheer power of this one man had rendered them all speechless. This was a member of the U.S. Army Special Forces, one of the army's most elite fighting forces.

As soon as he could, he'd gone straight to his CO and

applied for the Q Course, the grueling year-long recruitment process for the Special Forces.

Perhaps his determination had rubbed off on Spade, but he was certain of one thing—his buddy wouldn't have signed up if he hadn't wanted to. Spade had been as driven as he was. During training, which was one of the toughest courses in the world, they'd both managed to keep it together and neither had broken.

If Spade hadn't wanted to be there, he wouldn't have made it through the physical endurance, jungle, escape and evasion, or interrogation trainings. He wouldn't have coped with the hunger and thirst, intimidation tactics, or sheer exhaustion they'd experienced for days with no apparent end in sight. No one without a hundred percent commitment would have.

Blade had the utmost respect for anyone willing to put themselves through that grueling process. There was no shame in bugging out. Many good men had. Not everyone was cut out to be part of the Special Forces, but Spade wasn't one of them.

He grimaced. Whatever Lily might think about him, she was wrong about that. Sure, he might have talked about it, but Spade had made up his own mind about joining and had been all-in from the get-go.

Finally, he reached the cabin. It was hidden away in the densest part of the forest, barely visible unless you knew it was there. Abandoned for many years, it would once have been a half-way house for bandits and rebels. Now, given its dilapidated state, it had been left to rot.

His buddy Phoenix, with whom Blade had done basic training before Phoenix had switched sides and joined the U.S. Navy, had rebuilt the front door yesterday morning after the chopper dropped them off. He'd attached new hinges and repaired the lock so it could be bolted from the inside. The windows had been boarded up, apart from a tiny slit at the very top, so not only was it pretty dark inside, but no one could enter that way unless they had a rocket propelled grenade.

Supporting Lily with one arm, he used his free hand to unlock the door then kicked it open. He knew immediately the other members of Pat's team had been back. There were two fully stacked backpacks in the corner.

Thank you, guys.

These were definitely going to come in handy since he'd left his own pack behind in the cave.

He glanced at his watch, badly scratched by the tunnel— oh five twenty. By now, the rest of his team would have been extracted from the RV point, and the hostages would be enjoying a cold soda on their flight back home.

Mission accomplished.

All except his part.

He laid Lily gently on the floor, folded up a blanket, then placed it under her head. She stirred but didn't wake.

He smiled when he saw a note in Pat's barely legible scrawl on the table.

Glad you made it out. Left you some supplies. Good luck—and thank you.

It was unsigned. No clue for the enemy in case they'd found the cabin before Blade had made it back here.

The supplies were in the backpacks. Blade began to unpack them, taking an inventory. Rations and water, a first-aid kit, five pounds of Semtex including detonators, stun grenades, hand grenades, blankets, a sleeping bag, and a small gas cooker—everything an SF operative would need behind enemy lines. Unfortunately, but for obvious reasons, they'd taken the radio equipment with them. It wouldn't do to have that falling into the wrong hands.

Blade secured the premises as best he could. He set an

early warning system outside using a tiny amount of explo-sive, so if anyone approached the cabin, he'd hear them. Next, he bolted the door from the inside. Once satisfied with his security measures, he finally sat to eat and drink something.

The last forty-eight hours had been intense. Pat had been right to ask for his help. Blade had mobilized the guys almost immediately. No one had needed much convincing.

He'd called Phoenix first. The former Navy SEAL had left the unit earlier this year after an operation in Iran went south. Blade didn't know all the details, but it sounded like Phoenix had gone against his instinct and followed orders, and people had died. Soldiers had died. He couldn't carry on after that.

Boomer was also itching for action. Six months ago, in a twist of fate, he'd taken two bullets to the chest in an op that went south. In addition to spending a month in hospital coughing up blood, and another two rebuilding his strength, he'd been ordered to compulsory therapy sessions. His military career was over. To say he was pissed was an understatement. Boomer lived for the action, and as an explosives expert, was calm and steadfast, a real benefit to any team.

Then there was Viper, a former sniper, deadly, insanely accurate. He'd been out for a year already. When Blade had called about the unofficial op, he'd jumped at the chance.

Damn shame he hadn't gotten Lily out of that cave in time to make the RV. Still, after what had happened on his last mission, he wasn't about to risk his team getting blown to bits. Better this way.

He couldn't add any more dead men to the ones he already carried around in his head. He would just have to get Lily out of Afghanistan alone.

Blade yawned. Christ, he was tired. He'd been awake since the flight to Afghanistan the previous night, and while he'd been through worse, that faint sense of disassociation that came with severe fatigue was setting in.

He looked at Lily curled up on the blanket. As he watched her sleep, her curvaceous form began to swim before his eyes. He needed some shut eye. Sighing, he lay down next to her then pulled the extra blanket over them both. Within seconds, he was out.

"Joe…" It was little more than a soft moan in his ear.

Must be dreaming.

Then an arm snaked over his chest, and there was no mistaking Lily's whisper. "Joe."

Eyes wide open, he lay stock still, heart thumping. Should he wake her? She'd been so exhausted she'd passed out a mile from the cabin. Clearly she needed the rest. They couldn't go anywhere until it got dark anyway.

"Mmm…" She snuggled into him, her hair soft against his cheek, her hand stroking his chest. Her touch was light, tantalizing, erotic. What the hell was she doing?

His dick didn't know either but decided to rise to the occasion, just in case.

Fuck.

Okay. Time to wake up.

He lay a hand on her shoulder and gave a gentle shake. "Lily, wake up."

"Uh-uh," she murmured and nuzzled some more.

Goddamn if he didn't want to pull her into his arms. Hold her, nurture her, devour her. But he wasn't Joe.

"Lily," he said louder. In response, her hand moved lower, caressing his stomach. He groaned. She was killing him. "Lily, wake up."

"I don't want to," she muttered, draping a leg over his.

What the hell?

Was she awake? He lifted his head and glanced down at her face. Her eyes were closed, her lips curved upwards in the beginnings of a smile. How come he'd never noticed how gorgeous she was before? He suddenly saw what Spade had seen in her, and what he'd been blinded to by her superior attitude and fast put-downs. The geeky glasses hadn't helped either.

Her leg moved up and down, massaging his thigh.

It felt good.

She felt good.

He brushed a stray hair off her face, resisting the urge to kiss her. Her body was languid and warm, curving into him. A part of him didn't want her to move. A big, rock-solid part. As much as he was enjoying this, he couldn't let her continue. She'd be so embarrassed when she woke up. As would he.

Blade turned toward her and shook her shoulder. "Lily, come on. It's time to wake up."

"Kiss me…" she whispered, her hand snaking into his hair.

Whoa!

She angled her face upwards and found his lips with her own. His heartbeat escalated like the rapid exchange of gunfire. He had to put a stop to this before—

Hell.

She was kissing him. Soft, butterfly kisses that made his gut clench and his breath catch in his throat. He mustn't respond, yet it was so hard not to. Her lips nudged his open, then she slipped her hot tongue into his mouth.

All rational thought vanished.

He growled, a low sound in the back of his throat, and kissed her back. Long, velvety kisses. Delving into her mouth more than he meant to, holding her tighter than he wanted to, inhaling her scent more than he needed to.

He was losing himself in that kiss.

Losing it. Period.

But damn, it felt so good. *She* felt so good. Before he realized it, he'd hooked an arm around her waist and was crushing her against him.

Then she stopped moving. Stopped moaning. Stopped kissing.

Stopped *everything*.

Blade also froze. He'd pushed it too far.

Fuck.

He released her.

Slowly, she opened her eyes and stared at him with horror. "You are not Joe."

CHAPTER 9

*S*hit. *Shit.*
Double shit.
What had she done?

Why the hell was she draped around Blade Wilson? And why had she been kissing him like he was the last man on earth? Worse, she'd been enjoying it.

Heart slamming against her ribs, she recoiled like he was a poisonous snake.

"Sorry," he said, immediately. "I don't know what happened. I was asleep and then—"

She held up her hand. "Don't. Just don't."

His dark blue eyes turned smokey. "You kissed me, and I—"

"I know." She remembered that part, thank you very much. Heat flamed her cheeks. God, how could she have been so stupid. "I thought you were Joe."

"I'm not."

No shit.

She scooted away from him, shaking her head. Thank God it was dark in the cabin, and he couldn't see her scorching cheeks.

"I shouldn't have responded. It was a mistake."

"Damn right it was a mistake. What were you thinking? Didn't you know I was dreaming?"

"You were pretty insistent."

Unfortunately, she remembered every vivid detail of her erotic "dream." His hard body next to hers... His manly scent... His stubble...

Her muddled, traitorous brain had thought it was Joe. She'd wanted to believe it, wanted it to be him so badly that she'd practically sexually assaulted the guy. Only when he'd started kissing her back did she realize it wasn't Joe.

Joe's kisses had been soft and gentle, filled with tenderness. He'd kissed her like he was afraid she'd break if he was too rough.

Blade had no such qualms.

That's when she knew.

"Okay, stop. I'm sorry. There, I said it." She huffed and folded her arms across her chest.

"It's okay. Really. Don't sweat it. I'm sorry too." His eyes flickered, and she could have sworn his lips threatened to turn up at the sides.

"Are you finding this funny?"

He sat up and pulled the blanket over his lap. It was then she realized he had a honking big hard-on, not that he seemed fazed by it. There was amusement in his dark blue eyes. This was more like the Blade Wilson she remembered.

"You have to admit, it's a unique situation. Before I fell asleep, I didn't think I'd be woken in hostile territory in such a friendly fashion."

She gave him a blistering look. "It's not funny."

It was mortifying, that's what it was.

And disturbing.

"I know. How about we put this behind us and move on?"

Except his molten lava gaze said he wanted to do the complete opposite.

"Okay, fine." She gave a stiff nod.

It would help if she couldn't still smell him on her skin and taste him on her tongue. Her body tingled where he'd touched her. "Is there somewhere I can freshen up?"

"There's a bucket of water in the corner." He nodded towards the back of the cabin.

She got up, relieved to turn her back on him.

"I left some food out for you, so once you've washed up, you can have something to eat." He hesitated. "Then we need to talk."

"Talk?" She spun around. What was there to talk about?

He got to his feet and began folding up the blankets. "Yeah, about our next steps. The evacuation helicopter has gone, but we have a few other options."

"Okay."

She let out a shaky breath. For a moment, she thought he meant talking about what happened between them, but that was ridiculous. This was Blade, Special Forces operative and all-round tough guy. He didn't talk about anything as sensitive as emotions.

Besides, nothing had happened between them.

Only a mistake.

It was too bad they'd missed the evacuation but good to know they still had options. She didn't have a clue what they were, but she'd soon find out. After all, that was what *he* did.

Survive. Evade. Resist. Extract.

She'd heard Joe say it many times, particularly at the beginning of his Special Forces career.

Lily walked over to the bucket of water. It wasn't so bad. This time yesterday her prospects had been bleaker. She never would have expected to be rescued, particularly by

Blade Wilson, of all people. Now they were on the run from the Taliban, hiding out in an abandoned cabin.

Things were looking up.

If anyone could get them out alive, it was Blade. According to Joe and Pat, operators weren't made much better than him.

Lily gasped as she stuck her hand into the bucket. It was icy cold.

"No heating," was all he said.

No privacy, either. She glanced over her shoulder to check whether he was watching her.

He was.

"I'll go outside until you're done," he said, and left the cabin without another word.

At least he had some intuition.

Left alone, Lily got to work. She needed this wash. It had been three days since her last shower, and she'd done a lot of miles in that time. God, she must stink. How could he have come near her, let alone kissed her.

Like that.

Stripping down to her underwear, she used the rag and a bar of soap that had been left on the shelf next to the bucket and got to work. She washed every inch of herself, including her hair, removing all traces of the last few days.

The traumatic hike at gunpoint to the village, the fetid mattress, the dirty cave, the escape through the tunnel, and the long walk here.

Added to that was Blade's touch, his smell, and the way he made her feel.

At least the icy water had cooled her cheeks.

When she was done, she used one of the army blankets to dry herself. The fibers were harsh and scratched her skin, but she didn't care. It felt glorious to be dirt-free.

Next, she shook her clothes vigorously, wincing at the

dust that puffed out. They were dirty and stained, but she didn't have anything else. She eyed out the backpacks. Pulling the blanket around her, she went to the door.

"Er, Blade?"

He spun around, his gaze locking on the blanket. "Yeah?" She saw his jaw muscles working.

"Is there a clean shirt or something I can put on? My clothes are disgusting." She bit her lip, waiting for his response. He looked furious for some reason, his neck and shoulders so tense the veins were sticking out.

He cleared his throat. "Yeah, in the packs."

She stood back as he entered the cabin. He skirted around her, back to the door frame, keeping his distance like she had the plague. Maybe he thought she was going to kiss him again.

Well, no worries there. She wouldn't make that mistake again.

"I would have washed them," she said, "but there's nowhere to hang them up, and I wasn't sure how long we were going to be here."

"Not that long."

She'd figured that much.

He opened one of the packs and rifled around. With a grunt, he pulled out a plain, khaki green T-shirt. "Knew there was one in here somewhere."

It was a man's size, but she didn't care. It was clean.

"Thanks."

His gaze locked on her, heat radiating off him. She turned her back and a few seconds later, heard him go outside and close the door.

The fresh T-shirt felt amazing, but there was no getting around the dirty jeans, which she pulled back on, cringing at the dirt stains on the knees. Finally, she put on her tennis shoes, which used to be white but were now an interesting brown-gray. Her blisters were beginning to turn into calluses, so at least her shoes didn't hurt her feet. She'd lost her jacket in Kabul and would probably never again see it or anything from her suitcase.

Lily opened the door to find Blade, rifle in hand, staring out into the forest. He appeared to be deep in thought. The sun beat down on his head, highlighting the natural blond streaks in his brown hair. His profile was strong and noble, his jaw glistening with golden stubble. She blew a damp strand off her face. God definitely knew what He was doing when He made this one. "Everything okay?"

He gave a tight nod. "So far, so good."

She stepped outside and glanced up at the sun, still hot, but beginning to sag over the top of the hills on the other side of the valley. "What time is it?"

"Nearly two o'clock." He didn't check his wristwatch.

That meant she'd been asleep most of the morning. Strange, it had felt like no time at all. Her captors would definitely have cleared the rubble from the explosion by now and realized she wasn't in the cave. They'd know the only way out was via the tunnel. Were they already scouring the hills, searching for her? Could they be making their way through the lush valley towards the cabin?

"Isn't staying here giving them a chance to catch us up?"

"Yeah, but the alternative could get us killed. We're too exposed during the day."

"When does the sun go down?"

"Here in the woods, might be dark enough in another three or four hours."

Three or four hours. That long. Knowing her enemies were on her trail made her on edge. Her instinct was to keep moving, keep running, but she had to trust him. He was the expert, after all.

"Okay." She tried to keep her voice upbeat. "What did you want to talk about?"

CHAPTER 10

What was she trying to do? Torture him?

He couldn't get rid of the image of Lily standing there in nothing but a blanket, her pearly white shoulders in full view, her cleavage taunting him.

Soaking freaking *wet*.

Damp tendrils of hair falling over her shoulders, like some sexy river nymph.

It was all he could do to concentrate on what she was saying. For a moment, his brain had frozen.

The effect this woman had on him…

Not *this* woman. *Spade's* woman.

As if he could forget that. He was beginning to understand why his buddy hadn't brought her out with the guys like some of the others did. The wider Special Forces units were fairly incestuous. Maybe Spade had wanted to keep her all to himself, and not run the risk of anyone hitting on her.

Not that she would have cheated on him. She was loyal, he could see that. She'd loved Spade.

Her words came back to haunt him.

I needed to get away from the memories. Everything at home reminded me of him.

His heart twisted painfully.

Everything still did.

Blade pushed thoughts of Spade aside and spread the topographical map out over the worn, wooden table. It had a wonky leg and kept listing over, but it was good enough for their purposes.

"What if they find us here?" she whispered.

He saw real fear in her eyes and his heart twisted again. Now he wanted to protect her. Tell her everything was going to be alright. Wipe that fear from her eyes.

Except she wasn't safe. Not yet.

They had a long way to go still before they were in the clear.

"They won't have expected us to have gotten this far."

She gave an uncertain nod, her gaze turning to the map. "Where are we?"

"Here." He pointed to a vast green space—a nameless area in the valley region.

"I had no idea we were so close to the river." She traced the blue, squiggly line with her finger. It was a cute, child-like gesture, but then he realized she was working out how long it was. "Pity we don't have a boat."

"The river is in full flow right now thanks to the spring thaw. We don't want to cross it unless we have to."

"How wide is it?"

"As wide as a basketball court. Wider in parts."

"Where are we headed?" She scanned the topography with experienced eyes. As a military software designer, she'd be used to reading maps.

"Here."

She glanced up at him. "Kabul?"

"Yeah, it's our best chance of getting you out of

Afghanistan now that Bagram is controlled by Taliban forces." The U.S. air base north of Kabul in Parwan Province would have been his preferred option, but since U.S. and NATO troops had withdrawn from the country, that was now a no-go zone.

She frowned. "But it's over a hundred miles away. Impossible by foot."

For her, maybe. He'd rucked farther than that before. Still, he was blown away by how quickly she'd worked out the distance. "I know, but hear me out."

She rested her gaze on him.

"Plan A. Find some sort of transport to get to the city undetected. Don't forget we're deep in Taliban territory here, so the villagers will be sympathizers. Two westerners like us will stick out like burning flares."

"Especially with you dressed like you're going into battle." She cast a pointed look at his camo trousers, khaki long-sleeved shirt, and rifle.

He grunted. "We'll stick to the off-road areas and skirt the villages."

She was still studying his gun. "Don't you ever take that thing off?"

"No."

He'd have thought she'd known that, after living with a soldier for ten years. One of the first things you were taught in the armed forces was to never let go of your weapon. Even when he slept, he kept one hand on the comforting cold barrel. It was his version of a safety blanket.

She sighed. "What's Plan B?"

"We head to the nearest village and call for an emergency extraction. There are people in neighboring countries I can contact to fly us out."

"I thought you said the villagers would be Taliban sympathizers?"

"Most are, and those who aren't may be too scared to help us."

Her lip trembled. "They could betray us, and we'd be captured again."

He gave a small nod. "It will be risky. We might find someone brave enough to let us use their telephone, but I wouldn't count on it. If they're seen cooperating with us, it could be dangerous for them."

"You mean they'd be killed for helping us?" Her shoulders slumped. She'd been in the country long enough to know how these things worked.

"Yeah."

"Pity we don't have access to *Hawkeye*."

"Your software system?

"Yeah, my predictive threat software."

"How would that help us?" Pat hadn't told him exactly what it did.

"It's an AI-based system that utilizes machine learning and big data to analyze vast quantities of intelligence to predict enemy movements and tactics. It helps in preempting attacks, identifies vulnerabilities in defenses, and optimizes resource allocation on the battlefield."

She'd lost him at AI.

He hadn't gotten on board with all of that yet, although it was working its way into military operations, logistics and training exercises, particularly drone management and cybercrime. If it was half as impressive as it sounded, he could see why the Taliban were so keen to destroy it. "How long have they had this?"

"Before the coup, the Afghan government was using it to locate Taliban strongholds and assess threat levels. They saw this coming, but without international support, were powerless to defend themselves."

"Why is it such a threat?"

"Because we can use it too. The United States has access and can see the same data."

"But they need you to do that?"

"They need me *and* the codes to do that." She shuddered and wrapped her arms around her body like she was giving herself a hug. The fear was back, flickering in the depths of those deep, brown eyes.

"I won't let anything happen to you," he said quietly.

"You can't make that promise."

"Trust me, Lily. I'll get you out of here, one way or another."

"I hope you're right." Her voice was a whisper.

Blade turned back to the map. "I think we should go for Plan A, and if that doesn't work, we switch to Plan B."

"Isn't there a Plan C?"

"There is." He hesitated. "But that involves trekking over four hundred miles through the mountains to Pakistan."

"You mean the Khyber Pass?"

He nodded.

She blinked at him. "Let's go with Plan A."

CHAPTER 11

*L*ily watched the sun sink over the mountains, dragging the light with it. A short while later, the valley was plunged into a deep, unforgiving darkness.

"It's time," Blade said.

For the last few hours, he'd stared at the map, planning their route. Then he'd planned their backup route, and finally their backup-backup route, God forbid they had to use it. She couldn't imagine hiking over the Khyber Pass.

He'd also studied the towns and villages in the region. When she asked him why, as they didn't intend to visit any of them, he'd muttered something about a possible contact in one of them.

Blade heaved on his backpack, obviously expecting her to do the same. And she'd have complied already if she could have figured out how. She stared at the complicated array of straps, different partitions, and assortment of survival para-phernalia that went inside.

Seriously?

Not to mention the darn thing was bigger than she was.

He guessed her predicament, as the corners of his mouth turned up. "Here, let me help."

She scowled at his amusement.

Blade picked up the pack as if it weighed nothing more than a child's rucksack. She turned her back to him, then he slid it up over her shoulders. "Turn around."

Lily faced him, irritated she had to ask for help.

He adjusted the padded straps over her shoulders so it was more comfortable then fastened the stabilizing strap across her breasts. She tried not to flinch when his hand grazed her nipple.

"How's that?" His rough, growling voice softened.

She cleared her throat. "Fine, I think."

They set off, Blade taking the lead. Unnerved by the dark and the cacophony of unfamiliar sounds, Lily stayed close to his heels. She didn't want to think about the men out there, hunting them.

He moved like a big cat, silently prowling over the entangled terrain, while she stomped and stumbled and crunched her way along the invisible trail he was taking. Unlike her, he was dressed in full combat gear, thanks to the supplies his team had left for them, including lightweight body armor and belt-kit over his camouflage fatigues, his rifle in the ready position like he was expecting an attack.

He'd given her a vest too, which she wore over her khaki T-shirt. It added a level of warmth, although in the valley, it wasn't too cold. Not like it had been in the mountains.

Although he'd turned off his head light, presumably so they didn't attract unwanted attention, the night-vision scope he'd worn in the cave was still positioned over one eye, so he could safely lead them through the undergrowth. As before, he turned every few minutes to make sure she was still behind him.

"You okay?" he asked after they'd walked about a mile.

"Yeah." Complaining wouldn't get her anywhere, and she didn't want to slow them down. According to the map, the road leading out of the valley toward Kabul was over ten miles away, which meant they still had a long way to go.

She'd have to conserve her energy.

One step at a time. She fixed her gaze on Blade's sculpted shoulders, which supported his heavy pack with ease. After a while, she focused on his sturdy, resilient waist, then that oh-so-firm butt. She couldn't help but stare as the fabric of his pants hugged his glutes with enviable precision.

He turned to check on her.

Lily glanced up, heat flooding her cheeks. Had he just caught her ogling his butt? "Not much of a moon tonight," she murmured, raising her flaming face skyward. A scattering of clouds blotted the dark canvas with gray.

"The cloud cover is good for us," he replied. "This is the most dangerous part of our journey. The enemy will be in the valley now, looking for us. They'll guess which way we're heading."

"Maybe we should've taken another route." She peered into the bushes. "Confused them."

He shrugged as if they were discussing nothing more than which diner to go to for coffee. "We still could, but it would mean crossing the river, and then crossing it again to get back to the road. But if the shit hits the fan, we will."

She didn't like the sound of that.

Please, God, don't let the shit hit the fan.

Lily glanced around. In the darkness, the trees looked like soldiers, their branches like rifles pointing at them. Low bushes evoked images of crouching Taliban fighters.

"Relax, it'll be okay."

Relax? Was he crazy?

They were trekking through an Afghan valley pursued by angry men with guns. How could she relax?

Shooting daggers at his back, she trudged on.

After another half a mile had passed, Lily asked, "Do you remember the first time we met?"

He shot her a blank look.

Clearly she hadn't made the same kind of impression on him as he'd made on her.

"It was family day at the base. I was there with Joe and his father. Joe introduced us." She had this image of him casually leaning against the wall, a lazy, knowing smirk playing on his lips. He'd pushed away, shook Pat's hand, then nodded to her and said hello.

Actually, it's wasn't as polite as that.

He'd glanced at her—so self-assured, so confident—smiled that cocky smile, then dismissed her almost immediately by turning back to the others. She'd been intimidated by his blatant, physical masculinity. It had radiated off him like heat from a blazing fire, undeniable and potent. It was easy to see why the girls living around the base had fawned over him.

Not her though.

Raised, for the most part, by a single mother, her upbringing had been fairly sheltered. No brothers to jostle with, no father to show her what men ought to be like. Joe had been her first and only love.

When her mother died, Joe's family took her in. She'd been sixteen at the time, and Joe had been her lifesaver. She'd been lost and he'd rescued her. Then she'd met his army buddies—in particular Blade, with his sexy grin and cocksure attitude—and she'd recoiled. Determined not to like him, and terrified his cavalier attitude would rub off on Joe, she'd made up her mind about him before she'd even had a chance to get to know him.

Cocky, arrogant womanizer. That's how she'd pegged him. And for ten years, she'd believed it to be true.

Looking at him now, however, focused and vigilant, still turning to check on her every few minutes, she realized she might have got it wrong.

Sure, he was all those things, or had been, but he was also considerate, thoughtful, and passionate. Traits she had never attributed to him before.

Boy, was he passionate.

Not going there.

She forced her attention back to the terrain but couldn't help a little shiver passing through her.

Tearing her thoughts back to the present, she shook her head and muttered, "Never mind. You probably don't remember."

On they walked, mile after mile, not speaking. The silence unnerved her, especially in the dark. But she didn't want to put her foot in her mouth again.

Finally, Blade called a stop. "Do you need a break?" The eye without the night vision scope settled on her.

"Yeah, please." Her legs felt like lead, and her neck and shoulders ached from the unfamiliar weight of the backpack. "I just need a few moments to recover."

Annoyingly, Blade wasn't sweating. Wasn't winded. Wasn't tired. This was like a Sunday stroll to him, and he seemed totally relaxed. She, on the other hand, was a hot, sweaty mess—and not in a good way.

"If you pop open those buckles, I'll help you take it off," he offered. "Give your shoulders a break."

Lily popped, then the straps burst apart over her chest. Standing behind her, he lowered the backpack to the ground. She sank down after it with a groan, resting against the lumpy bulk.

"Don't get too comfortable." He didn't remove his pack. "We're not stopping for long."

"How far until we reach the road?" She'd lost track of how far they'd walked.

"We're about halfway there."

God. How was she ever going to manage this? She took a woeful sip from her water flask then leaned her head back and closed her eyes.

Blade patrolled the area around her, weaving in and out of the trees, pausing only once to consult the map. The moments ticked by.

Now that she knew how exposed they were, she couldn't relax. Feeling slightly better, she struggled to her feet.

Wordlessly, Blade lifted her backpack then slid it onto her shoulders. This time she fastened the buckles herself, but in memory of his touch, her traitorous nipples puckered. She avoided eye contact. The whole situation was ridiculous.

"Shh..." He held up a hand.

Lily froze, listening. Her senses had become fine-tuned to their surroundings, but she couldn't hear anything other than the rustle of leaves and the occasional scamper of a small animal. Then a twig cracked somewhere behind her in the shadows.

She gasped, and her hand flew to her mouth.

It was them!

He put a finger over his lips, crouched down, then gestured for her to follow him, and to bring her backpack with her. Seconds later, he'd melted into the shadows.

Crap! Her heart almost leaped out of her chest.

Where'd he go?

One blink and he'd vanished. She ducked after him, panic setting in, but then saw his shadowy figure behind a tree.

Thank God.

He took her pack, then led her silently through the bush toward a small ditch. She looked at him questioningly, and he gestured for her to climb down into it.

There was no talking now. Heart pounding, she followed his instructions and lay flat on her belly, not caring about the damp mud seeping through her pants or the acrid smell of decaying leaves.

He quickly gathered some foliage, ripping off a branch or two with a sudden display of strength and then climbed in next to her. He pulled a hessian net out of his backpack's top fold and threw it over them, then he positioned the branches on top of that. They were effectively camouflaged.

"Don't move," he whispered. He maneuvered into a sitting position behind his rifle, the muzzle poking ominously through the netting.

Lily hardly dared to breathe. She had an awful feeling the shit he'd mentioned was about to hit the fan in a big way. Sure enough, five minutes later she heard heavy, crunching footsteps. Shortly after that, three Taliban fighters, armed with rifles similar to Blade's, appeared. They were searching the woods. For her.

Lily's heart thumped so loudly, she was convinced Blade could hear it.

Please don't find us.

Was this it? Would they be gunned down and left to die in this muddy ditch? Biting her lip, she tried not to think the worst, but the terror rose to choke her. She glanced over at Blade, seeking reassurance, but he was staring straight ahead. She couldn't even hear him breathing. He was frozen, his finger on the trigger, ready to open fire on the three soldiers.

Even though she'd lived with Joe for ten years, she'd never seen him in action. She'd refused to go to any of the military events, not even the pub after a successful mission. Other wives and girlfriends did, but Lily bucked that long-standing tradition. Joe used to go, of course, and on those nights she knew not to wait up. Sometimes he'd stay over at Blade's and not come home until the next day, which never sat well with her. As a result of her non-participation, she'd never seen him fire his weapon, not even during a training exercise. And he never talked about his work. She was given to understand none of them did. So, of course, this level of intensity boggled her mind. She'd never witnessed anything like it.

How could Blade stay so calm? The soldiers were only yards away, moving in their direction.

Closer… Closer…

Soon they'd reach the ditch.

Still Blade didn't move. No muscle twitched, no limb flexed. No finger or toe quivered with pent-up anticipation. He was just a relaxed, controlled body beside her, motionless but lethal, waiting for his opportunity.

One of the men murmured something in a low voice, then all three halted. The man closest to them gestured toward the ditch, but the original speaker shook his head and pointed back the way they'd come.

Go away.

No such luck.

The men continued to approach. They got to the edge of the ditch and looked around. The closest one spoke again. It felt like he was standing directly above them. Lily peered through the hessian coverage. He stood less than a yard away. If she stuck out her hand, she could touch his foot.

She waited, desperately hoping they'd retreat.

Then it happened. The man closest to them stepped into the ditch, his boot clipping Lily's shoulder. She winced, causing him to glance down. With a yell of surprise, he lifted his rifle and pointed it at her.

CHAPTER 12

*B*lade didn't hesitate. He opened fire and let off a short, sharp volley of shots. One in the head, one in the chest. The soldier fell to the ground, the expression of surprise still on his face. Lily screamed and put her hands over her ears.

The other two men spun around, but Blade was faster. He gunned one down with another lethal double-tap before the fighter managed to get off a shot. The remaining soldier fired, but his enthusiasm compromised his aim. The bullets flew harmlessly over their heads. Before he could bring his weapon under control, Blade shot it out of his hands. It fell to the ground, leaving his hands damaged and bloody. The man didn't have time to register the pain before Blade gunned him down with another controlled burst.

Lily stared at the three dead men, slack-jawed and gasping.

There was no time to comfort her or help her process this. No time to do anything other than move.

"Come on! We've got to go. The gunfire will have given our position away."

He grabbed the netting and stuffed it back into his backpack in one practiced motion.

She didn't move, her attention still fixed on the dead men.

"Lily! We have to go."

"You shot them." Her voice was a hoarse whisper.

"I had to. They were going to kill us. Now, let's get out of here before their buddies find us." He pulled her out of the ditch. It was like leading a zombie, but at least she let him guide her through the undergrowth and around the trees. He was desperate and determined to put some space between them and their compromised position.

"We'll head to the river." If they could find a way across, at least they'd have a chance. He was pretty sure the Taliban fighters wouldn't cross the raging river, as many of them couldn't swim. Not right now, anyhow. They'd wait until they could find a boat.

Additionally, the enemy also wouldn't expect them to go that way. It was dangerous, and in the opposite direction to where they needed to go. Kabul. The fighters would know that was their final destination, their only hope of getting Lily out of the country.

Blade was running now, pulling Lily behind him. Her breathing was erratic, but she kept up. For a moment there, he'd thought she was going to fall apart, but somehow she'd held herself together.

He recalled the disbelief on her face after he'd dispatched the young Taliban guard in the cave. That had probably been her first. Now she'd witnessed three men gunned down in front of her in the forest. It was a lot to take in when not used to it. Plus, a weapon discharging that close to your ear was deafening. Both the traumatic visuals and the loud noise would contribute to her shock.

Her face was a mask of concentration, her eyes gleamed

with determination. Blade didn't know her, what drove her. Not really. But she was stronger than she looked.

He wanted to get to know her, to learn the answers to his questions. The thought hit him like a damp branch to the face. For the first time in God only knew how long, he actually wanted to get to know someone. And for longer than just one night.

Problem was, she was out of bounds. A no-go area.

Blade pushed on, keeping a tight hold on Lily's hand, until the trees began to thin out. Before long, they were in the open air. Fresh, cold air tinged with mud and silt. He muttered, "Nearly there."

The earth was softer there, their shoes sinking into the fertile soil. It made walking difficult, so he slowed for her and released her hand. A patchwork quilt of agricultural fields lay between them and the river, each demarcated by a low, stone wall.

"Come on." He nodded to one of the barriers. They clambered over it then slunk across the dark field to the next one. The soft roar of rushing water told him they neared the river.

Lily stumbled, and he turned to help her, but she'd collapsed on the other side of the wall with a sob. The horror of what she'd seen had set in, and her body had shut down. To be honest, he was surprised they'd gotten as far as they had before shock set in.

He sat beside her and put an arm around her. "Shh… it's okay. We're safe."

For a little while, at least.

She was probably trying to get a grip, but he recognized the signs of horror overriding control. Chest heaving, eyes wild and unfocused… her brain was failing to work through what she'd seen.

He didn't blame her. How could she process such an

extreme level of violence? It was difficult enough for soldiers, who were trained to do it on a regular basis. But for civilians?

Her breath came in shallow gasps, like she couldn't get enough air.

"Lily, look at me."

Panicked eyes swung toward him but didn't settle. She was hyperventilating, in the throes of an anxiety attack.

He had to get her breathing under control.

A distraction, that's what he needed, but there was nothing out here but fields.

So he did the next thing that popped into his head, trying not to think about the ramifications.

He kissed her.

When he captured her mouth with his, she gave a little moan of protest and tried to push him away, but he held her head securely in place, curving his fingers around the back of her neck. After a few rapid heartbeats, he felt her relax against him. The wetness on his cheeks told him she was crying silent tears of fear and horror.

It sucked that she was out here, fleeing for her life.

She didn't deserve this.

Didn't deserve to see the level of death and destruction that he'd wrought on their enemy and would again if the need arose.

He couldn't erase the images in her brain. She'd have to live with it for the rest of her life. All he could do was take her mind off it, get her anxiety under control.

He kept his lips pressed against hers, gentler now that she wasn't so tense. She yielded, her mouth opening under the pressure of his lips. His tongue slid against hers, and he was relieved to feel her reciprocate. He kept the kiss light, not delving too deeply, not wanting to startle her any more than she already was.

It was hard because damn, she tasted good.

She felt good too. Her body was soft, with desirable curves in all the right places.

With a muffled sob, she flung her hands around his neck. He released her mouth and gave her space to cry. She clung to him, her tears wet against his face, and they sat like that for a moment. Before he expected, she gave a deep, shuddering breath and got herself under control.

Slowly, he pulled away. Her curious eyes glistened with tears, but they weren't glazed over with shock anymore, and her breathing appeared to be normal.

His approach might have been unorthodox, but it worked.

Lily let go of him and scooted over.

He removed his arm from around her shoulders, giving her space, and was surprised to find himself wishing it was still there.

"Sorry, I didn't mean to fall apart. It's just… I've never seen anyone shot before yesterday, and now—"

"I know." He gave a stiff nod. "I'm sorry you had to see that. I wouldn't have done it if it hadn't been necessary."

A reluctant nod. "I knew it would happen at some point, but I didn't think it would affect me so much."

"It always does, the first time."

"Even for you?" She stared up at him, looking for reassurance.

"Even for me." He'd stopped thinking about his first kill years ago, but at the time, it had affected him. How could it not?

"Joe used to have nightmares," she said, after a beat.

Blade frowned. "He did?"

She gave a sad nod. "He'd wake up screaming, drenched in sweat. Once, he even tried to strangle me in my sleep. He thought I was the enemy." Her shoulders heaved in a desolate shrug. "But then he woke up and realized what he was doing."

"Christ." Blade was appalled. "Why didn't he say anything?"

Spade hadn't mentioned he was suffering from nightmares or flashbacks. His performance in the unit had been stellar. If he'd been struggling with PTSD, he'd managed to keep it under wraps.

"He didn't want to be kicked out of the squad."

Blade sighed. If they'd known, they would have had to suspend him pending a psych evaluation. "I'm sorry, Lily. I didn't know."

She shook her head sadly, "It's not your fault. He didn't tell anyone. Not even his father."

"Pat would have insisted he get help."

She sniffed.

"Exactly."

* * *

"You ready to get going?" Blade asked.

Lily gave a weary nod, then her gaze flicked to his lips.

She was remembering their kiss, and she wasn't the only one. It had been soft and tender, completely different to the first time, back in the cabin when she'd thought he was Joe.

"Blade?"

Now wasn't the time.

Besides, he didn't know what to say. He didn't know what this thing was between them. This weird magnetic pull drawing him to her like a moth to a flame. A cliché, but it was true. But the attraction didn't matter. She wasn't available. Never would be. For him, anyway.

He had to stop thinking like that.

The thought made him wince, almost like a physical pain.

What the hell was that all about? He never got this hung up on anyone. And certainly not while on mission.

"Once we're across the river, we can rest for a while. Maybe get some sleep."

She gave a tight nod.

Damn, he'd sounded harsher than he'd meant to. Holding out a hand, he said, "Not far to go now."

After a second's hesitation, she took it. Once he pulled her to her feet, she immediately let go.

Blade led her across another couple of fields and over a few more low, stone walls. Finally, they reached the river—a broad, dark oil slick curving through the pre-dawn landscape.

It ran thick and fast. White specks on the surface rolled over onto each other, spitting up spray. It hissed angrily as it rushed past.

Lily halted, her eyes widening. "We're going to cross *that?*"

"You can swim, can't you?" He hadn't thought to ask. Shit, if she couldn't, they'd have a problem.

"Yeah, of course."

He exhaled. "Good. We're going to wade across. It's deep in the middle, so we'll have to swim that part, but I'll make sure we're tied together, so you won't get washed downstream."

Lily stared at the frothy channel in the middle.

"It'll be okay," he muttered, praying he was right. The danger with water was often not the current or the temperature. It was the panic. When people freaked out, they were done for. Flailing around would only make things worse.

But they didn't have much of a choice. It was cross the river or be caught.

Blade glanced back the way they'd come. After their mad dash across the fields, he half expected the enemy to come charging toward them, tipped off by a surprised farmer. The darkness worked in their favor, and if anyone had seen them, the message would take a while to filter back to the Taliban camp.

They had some time. Not a lot, but a small window in which to vanish across the river.

"I'll tie us together using the rope." With her rucksack weighing her down and the powerful current, she'd battle to cross on her own. Anyone would.

"Okay." Her gaze was fixed on the raging river.

Reaching around her waist, he wrapped the rope and tied it in a bowline knot. Perfect for a rescue situation, it held up best when there was constant pressure pulling against the knot, like in a moving current. Then he repeated the process, securing the rope around himself, but leaving a decent amount of slack between them. Enough to give them swimming space, but short enough to haul her in should she run into trouble.

Next, he shrugged off his backpack, took out a thick, black plastic bag.

"What's that for?" she asked, finally dragging her eyes from the water.

"To keep some of our stuff dry," he said.

"Our backpacks?" He noticed she was shivering, but whether it was from the cold or the shock, he couldn't be sure. Probably both.

"No, we're going to wear those. They'll help keep us afloat. This is so we can get warm on the other side."

He took out the sleeping bag, wishing he had dry clothing to add to it, but he'd had to leave his original backpack in the damn cave. The team hadn't given them any extra jackets or sweaters, only a down sleeping bag in one of the emergency packs. After this, keeping warm was going to be one of their biggest problems, but he didn't mention that now.

One dilemma at a time.

Right now, getting across this river was their priority.

After tying the black bag firmly, he placed it at the top of his pack, then refastened the straps. "Okay, we're good to go."

Lily wrapped her arms around her, a gesture he'd come to know—she felt scared and vulnerable.

"You got this." He forced a smile.

She bit her lip. "Is it cold?"

"Yeah." It was going to be freezing, no way to sugarcoat that. "But we'll be across in under ten minutes."

She gave a little nod. "Do we get undressed?"

"Remove the body armor, and stuff it into your pack. You can keep the rest on. Wade in as far as possible. The longer you keep your feet under you, the less ground we lose. When you can't stand anymore and have to swim, try to keep your feet up as high as you can." That was enough of a warning without mentioning an undertow. "Don't be alarmed when you start moving rapidly downstream. At that point, we have to let the current take us. As soon as we can stand again, we'll be able to go straight to the other side. Got it?"

Her lip quivered, but she gave a brave nod.

"Don't worry. I've got you. I'll pull you across if you get into trouble."

A shaky breath. "Let's get this over with."

"That's the spirit."

Blade went first, his weapon on his back, secured to his body along with the backpack. He needed both arms free to swim. After a few steps, he felt the rope tighten around his waist, then slacken again as she followed him in.

This was it.

They had to make it across undetected.

* * *

HOLY CRAP!

The water was freezing.

Lily gasped as a million little icicles pierced her legs, then her stomach, then her chest, threatening to squeeze all the breath out of her.

Already, her toes had gone numb.

She exhaled, long and slow, trying to keep calm.

"You okay?" Blade cast a worried glance in her direction.

I can do this.

Frigid water lapped at her shoulders. She'd caused enough bother over the last hour, so she wouldn't bail out now no matter how much she wanted to. And boy, did she want to. Icy tentacles clawed at her, drawing her in. Teeth pressed together to stop them from chattering, she muttered, "I'm okay."

The riverbed was slippery, and her feet felt weird under the water—heavy, but at the same time unable to grip the sandy bottom.

"Keep going. You're doing great."

How'd he keep so goddamn calm all the time? She tried not to freak out as they moved farther into the middle of the fast-moving channel in the center. The current tugged at her legs, and she fought to keep her feet down.

"I think I'm losing my grip." She panted through the exertion. The undertow strengthened and threatened to pull her downstream by her clothing, her backpack, her legs.

"Go with it."

Fine for him to say. He was a head taller than her and wasn't having the same problem.

Lily felt like she was walking on the moon—long, loping hops instead of normal steps, the buoyancy of the water lifting her up.

She yelped as the ground disappeared and her legs were sucked out from under her. The current washed her quickly downstream. It was much faster than she realized, and for a moment, she fought a flicker of sheer panic. Forcing her feet down, she tried to stand. Couldn't reach the bottom. The undertow caught her, dragged her under. Flailing her arms, kicking her legs, she surfaced, spluttering.

Blade shouted, "Relax. I've got you. Don't fight it."

The rope went taut. Her pace slowed.

Oh, thank God.

Desperately trying to keep her head above water, she put her faith in Blade. How the hell did he do it? No longer walking, he swam, taking big, powerful strokes toward the opposite bank. It felt like they were getting nowhere because of how quickly they moved downstream. The landscape flashed by in a blur.

Panic hovered, but then she began to calm down. They were, in fact, making progress. The bank looked like it was getting closer. Blade was doing most of the work, even though she was swimming as hard as she could, which wasn't easy with a rope around her waist and a huge backpack on her back. He was right, though, it did help to keep her afloat. So did her frantic flutter kicks.

Breathe. Stroke left, stroke right. Breathe. Stroke left, stroke right. Breathe...

She talked herself through the motions, trying to build up some sort of rhythm, like in the communal swimming pool back in her hometown. The current, however, had other ideas. It tossed her around, buffeted her, and slapped her in the face. Once, she almost rolled over onto her back.

After what felt like an eternity, they rounded a bend in the river and the current slowed down. They'd reached the point bar of the meander. Blade stood. A second later, the rope tightened, jolting her and halting her downstream momentum.

He pulled her toward him. "You should be able to put your feet down."

Tentatively, she reached out and managed to touch the bottom.

Yes!

She could stand.

After a few more tugs, she found much firmer footing. It wasn't long before Lily trudged out of the water behind Blade. Her clothes and pack weighed her down like they'd absorbed half the river. Her legs wobbled from the exertion.

"We made it." Lily turned and stared back across the river for their point of entry, but it was around the bend. They'd traveled roughly half a mile downstream thanks to the current.

Blade undid the rope from around his waist, then took it off hers. He looped it around his arm then clipped it back onto his belt. "We're out of sight here. Let's have a rest while we dry off."

"Okay."

His intense gaze unnerved her. It conveyed thousands of messages while keeping countless secrets.

That look mingled with a sense of pride swelling inside her. The combination elicited a strange sensation in her core that made her stomach tighten.

"You did great."

She grinned. "Thanks."

For the first time since her capture, she didn't feel in immediate danger.

"We should get warm."

Strangely enough, she was so numb from the frigid water that the cold night air felt burning hot against her skin.

"How are we going to do that?" Everything in her backpack was wet.

"We've got one dry sleeping bag. You can use that."

"What about you?"

"I'll be okay. I'm used to it."

"You're sure?"

He grunted and stalked off up the bank.

A dry, warm sleeping bag sounded great. Finding her footing, Lily scrambled after him.

CHAPTER 13

*B*lade didn't get it.

Blue lips, chattering teeth, soaking wet—yet she still looked sexy as hell. Maybe it had something to do with the way her trousers sucked against her shapely legs, dripping river water on the bank. Or the way her oversized khaki T-shirt was glued to her breasts, outlining their generous shape, and showing him just how cold she was.

"We need to get you warm," he said, gruffly.

"C—Can we light a fire?" she asked, trembling.

"No, too dangerous." Both sides of the river consisted of populated farmland. They may as well send up a flare saying, *We're here! Come and get us.*

Ideally, he'd have liked to have avoided the lush valley plains. Water meant agriculture which meant people. But, getting her warm was more important than moving farther inland. She was shaking violently. It wouldn't take long before hypothermia set in.

He'd seen soldiers climb into their sleeping bags and be rendered unconscious from hypothermia during the night because their bodies hadn't been able to generate heat themselves.

"We need to get out of these clothes," he said, once they'd reached the outskirts of the farming area. "They're only going to make us colder."

Several fields separated them from the river, and like on the opposite side, they were all demarcated by handmade stone walls. Traditional mud dwellings dotted the landscape seemingly at random, but each farmer had erected his house strategically to watch over his crops.

Blade looked around. They'd be safe here. No smoke from the chimneys, no lights on inside the huts. It was still several hours until daybreak.

"Let's rest up."

He chose a spot where two walls intersected and formed a natural shelter. The corner faced away from the wind and looked out at the tree-covered hillside roughly a mile away.

"These are p-poppy fields, aren't they?" Teeth chattering and body shivering, Lily gazed at the vivid splashes of color.

He tore his attention from her to the flowers. Petals ranged from the deepest reds to the softest whites and boasted every shade of pink between. Each bloom gyrated in the stiff breeze, strong and beautiful.

Kind of like her.

They weren't open, however, their heads bowed in the darkness. In the light of day, they'd be quite spectacular.

Blade studied her again. He was concerned. Her body was losing heat faster than she could replace it. That's why she was shivering so violently. It was the body's way of creating energy to warm her up.

"Yeah. Poppies bring in more money than any other agricultural crop. The farmers guard their plots obsessively, particularly during the harvest. It's not unusual to see armed guards on patrol around here."

She peered through the darkness, her brow furrowed with concern.

"Don't worry. It's too early in the season." Plus, he hadn't seen anyone through the night vision scope. "Here, let me help you with your backpack."

"I-I don't think I've ever been this c-cold." After he took it off her shoulders, she slunk down against the wall and hugged herself. "I can't feel any of my t-toes."

Even her words were stilted and slurred. That was a dangerous sign. Her body was slowing down, affecting her reflexes and coordination. She would continue to cool down unless she got heat from an external source.

One of the most effective ways to warm someone up in that situation was to put them in a sleeping bag with another person with a normal body temperature—and that's exactly what he was going to do.

He just wasn't sure how she'd feel about it.

Sitting next to her, he shimmied out of his backpack. He retrieved the sleeping bag—still dry, thanks to the black bag.

"Lily, you need to get out of those wet clothes and climb in here with me."

"What?" Her eyes widened. Her jaw dropped. She curled into a tighter ball.

He'd expected that reaction. Maybe his delivery was inelegant, but they were running out of time.

"It's the only way I can warm you up. You're becoming hypothermic, which means your body can't heat itself. If you want to survive, you're going to have to do as I say."

"Can't I do jumping jacks or something?"

He snorted but shook his head. "Won't work. Your internal thermostat has shut down. You need my body heat."

She swallowed. "You want me to get naked?"

"Leave your underwear on, if you like." It would have

been better if she'd removed it, but he didn't think *he'd* be able to handle that, let alone her.

Keep it real, he told himself sternly. This was a life-or-death situation. He couldn't rescue the hostage only to lose her to hypo-fucking-thermia in a freezing valley. Pat would string him up when he got back.

He was more scared of Pat than an almost naked Lily.

Turning her back to him, she peeled off her dripping trousers and was about to hang them over the wall, when he shook his head. "Too noticeable. Here, give them to me."

He hung them over a couple of rocks. That way if any of the farmers looked out of their hut windows, they wouldn't see the trousers flapping in the wind.

While she stripped off the soaked T-shirt, he undressed, and arranged his clothes where they had the most chance of drying. Out of modesty, he'd left his boxers on, but that didn't stop him from feeling strangely vulnerable when he caught her staring at him.

"You okay?" Normally he didn't give a shit about getting naked. It was part of life in the military. You showered, shaved, and went to the toilet alongside your fellow soldiers. Any modesty evaporated during the first few months of training.

This wasn't a "normal" situation.

Her eyes raked over his chest, but she nodded. "Yeah."

"Good."

He climbed into the sleeping bag, which wasn't really big enough for two. It would be a tight squeeze, but that was the point.

Lily eyed it like it was an unexploded bomb.

She was shivering so violently now, he worried she'd break something. He growled, "Get in."

She took a tentative step toward him, her hands over her breasts. That was all the farther she got.

"Lily, I'm serious. I've lost men to hypothermia before. It's no joke."

A blush crept into her cheeks, and he thought how wild and untamed she looked in that moment—naked, wild hair cascading around her face, bare shoulders, breasts catching the moonlight.

Fuck, she was exquisite.

He was doing this for Joe. For Pat. If he didn't, she was going to die. That much he knew for sure.

All he had to do was stay focused—on the situation, not on the rise of her breasts or the curve of her butt.

He exhaled, low and hard.

Not an easy thing to do.

Wordlessly, she climbed in beside him. Fucking hell, she was freezing.

All inappropriate thoughts flew from his mind as his training took over.

"Come here."

Back to him, she snuggled closer, and he wrapped his arms around her. Might as well have been hugging an ice sculpture but for the waves of intense tremors assaulting her body, draining her of energy.

He drew her closer, spooning her tightly. She fit perfectly into the outline of his body. "You're okay now. I've got you."

Because his body was cold too, it took a while for him to start generating heat, but he was nowhere near as frozen as her. He absorbed her tremors, willing his metabolism to kick in. When it did, his body temperature rose and finally, through transference, she began to thaw out.

He could tell because she began to relax. Her muscles untensed, the shivering slowed, and the frantic shudders grew less frequent.

"How's that?" he whispered in her ear.

"It's working." He was glad she was recovering, but

damned if he didn't want her to stay exactly where she was. She fit so snuggly against him, her buttock curved into his groin, her back arched against his chest.

Fuck. Far too snug.

Holding Lily, her soft curves nestled against his body, was driving him crazy. Needing a distraction, he calculated how long they could safely stay here before they had to move on.

If the enemy deduced they'd crossed the river, which was a distinct possibility, they were very exposed, lying here naked less than five hundred yards from the riverbank.

"Once you've warmed up, we should head out." His voice was huskier than he'd have liked.

"Oh, okay."

Was that disappointment?

"It's too dangerous to stay here for long. We need to put some distance between us and the enemy."

He felt a lingering tremor and stroked his hand up and down her arm. He didn't mean to, it was a natural response, but as soon as he'd done it, he knew it was a mistake.

She gave a soft moan that reverberated through him like a 20,000-ton freight train. He felt his cock surge to life and froze, praying she hadn't noticed.

"Blade?" she whispered.

"Yeah." He tried to ignore the throbbing in his boxers.

Here it comes.

"Do you really think we're going to get out of here?"

Now *that* he hadn't been expecting.

You're a dick, maybe. *Get a hold of yourself*, definitely. But *that*… no.

He breathed deeply. "Yeah, I told you we would."

"I know, but I wasn't sure if you were trying to pacify me or if you really meant it."

He frowned. "I don't say things I don't mean."

"Yeah, that's what Joe said."

He froze. "What?"

"He said you're one of the most honest men he's ever met." She hesitated, and he felt her adjust her position, wriggling her behind into his crotch.

Don't do that.

Please, don't do that.

"Even with women."

That made him pause. "What did he mean, *with women*?"

It was news to him that Joe had spoken to Lily about him. It wasn't like they knew each other. Then again, he and Joe were best buddies, so of course Joe would talk about him and the unit when he was at home. With her.

Suddenly, Blade envied Joe for what he'd had.

Lily. To himself. Every night.

Then he remembered the nightmares. What she'd said about Joe trying to strangle her. He grew angry. Joe should have said something, dammit. If he was suffering from PTSD, he should never have been on that mission with them. If he hadn't, he might still be alive.

Tension radiated through his body, and he had to force himself to calm down. He focused on Lily's newfound warmth, her softness, the swell of her breast that he could just feel underneath his arm.

Now he was hot in a different way.

Maybe it was time to move. Get the hell out of this sleeping bag. Get away from her.

"He said you might have a different woman every time you're on leave, but you never lied to them."

"I didn't." And he hadn't had a different woman every time he was on leave. There were a handful he'd had fun with who understood how he operated. No complications. No strings.

"I couldn't afford to be distracted." He tried to explain, hoping she'd understand. Hoping she wouldn't think he was a womanizing prick. "A serious relationship would have been a distraction."

"Joe had me." Her voice was a whisper.

"And you were the last thing he thought about when he died."

"Is that such a bad thing?"

Blade ground his jaw. "No, but I didn't want to worry about leaving someone I loved behind, or wondering what they were doing when I wasn't around. I didn't want to think about them when I went into battle."

He wasn't doing a very good job of explaining this.

"Clarity of thought is everything on a mission, like when you're operating behind enemy lines. You can't afford any lapses in judgment. One mistake and that's it. You're dead, and so is your team." He ground his teeth, feeling on edge.

Ironic how that's exactly what had happened.

One mistake.

His.

Not a girl, though.

"I get it," she said softly.

He didn't respond, letting the waves of regret wash over him. Joe, Blaster. Stitch.

Lily's voice cut through his lamenting. "Didn't you get lonely?"

"No." Not then.

"What about now?"

He hesitated. "I think you're good to go."

He shifted position, and cool air thrust between them. The closeness had gone, and along with it, the right to ask personal questions.

Lily sat up, her eyes lingering on him thoughtfully.

"Get dressed." He tugged on his wet clothes. "We'll warm up once we start moving. You won't have a problem now your metabolism has kicked in again."

Lily got up and pulled on her clothes. She turned her back but thrust her perfectly rounded butt at him when she bent over to pull on her pants.

God help him.

What had he just been saying?

He let out a long, slow breath. The last thing he wanted was to be a hypocrite, but this woman was one hell of a distraction.

CHAPTER 14

*L*ily was glad to be out of that sleeping bag.

Away from him.

Sure, he'd saved her life by giving her the warmth from his body so she hadn't succumbed to hypothermia, but *holy crap*, that had been intense.

His smoldering, bare-chested body wrapped protectively around her, his legs touching hers, his heart beating through her, making her feel things she hadn't felt in a really long time.

Not since Joe.

Closing her eyes, Lily took a steadying breath. She wasn't even sure she wanted to feel those things again. Somehow, with this guy, it seemed impossible not to. He just had that strong, protective way about him. Capable. Safe. With mind-numbingly well-developed biceps.

To be fair, it hadn't been her idea to climb into the sleeping bag with him. Once she had… What girl wouldn't melt with *those* arms around her?

But, she'd had an effect on him too.

He'd tried to hide it, but something like that… Uh-uh.

That made her feel marginally better. Still, they were victims of circumstance, stuck out here in the middle of nowhere together. It was like one of those reality TV programs where extreme conditions and near isolation drove unlikely people to partner up. In *every* way.

She shuddered at the thought.

It wasn't real. It was a moment in time, that's all. Once this was over, they'd go back to their separate lives. She mustn't read more into it than there was.

He had a job to do, a mission to complete. They couldn't afford to let anything interfere with that.

Like he'd said… *no distractions.*

"When are we crossing back over?" Lily focused on their current predicament. Her wet clothes were uncomfortable, but she was nowhere near as frozen as before. Blade had been right. Now her body had kicked into gear, and she was fine.

"Not for a while. We'll put some miles between us first. Hopefully they'll have given up looking by the time we cross back."

She watched as he repacked his backpack, folding up the sleeping bag and stuffing it inside. He was carrying a much heavier load. Blade reattached his utility belt, with the rope clipped to it, then the holster around his thigh carrying that lethal-looking knife.

"Here." He picked up her pack then held it out so she could slip her arms into it.

Why did he have to be so goddamn attentive?

Lips pressed together, she wriggled into it. His hands were warm on her shoulders as he adjusted the straps so they didn't hurt her.

"I got it." She took a step forward. She wasn't ungrateful, but every time he touched her, her brain went into meltdown.

He grunted and turned to survey the hillside.

Lily fastened the chest strap. It suddenly became clear what had happened when she'd first met Blade ten years ago. She'd felt it then, the power of his attraction. And it had frightened her.

That first meeting at the base. Off duty, he'd been wearing jeans and a T-shirt. He'd grinned at her, his blue eyes sparkling with vitality and mirth, and shaken her hand, holding it that little bit longer than was necessary.

Then a blonde woman in a tank-top and skinny jeans had sauntered up behind him and put an arm possessively around his waist. He'd kissed her, full on the lips, right in front of them, causing her to blush and look away. She'd been very naive back then, only eighteen and barely out of secondary school. His blatant sexuality had disturbed her, and she'd made up her mind to disapprove of him, right then and there.

Not only that, but she'd also feared his influence over her boyfriend. Joe admired Blade, looked up to him. What if Blade's cavalier attitude and arrogance rubbed off on her Joe, leading him astray?

She'd lose the only definite thing in her life, the only man she could depend on.

Consequently, she'd done all she could to keep Joe away from him. It was impossible, given they were in the same unit, but when Joe was on leave, she'd kept him to herself, integrating him into her group of friends and refusing to socialize with his teammates.

It wasn't right, but she'd been scared.

Lily exhaled.

The revelation that Blade had this strange power over her, even back then, made her decidedly uneasy. Especially since it hadn't been reciprocated.

Not then.

That day at the barracks, he'd said how good it was to meet her then disappeared with his blonde without so much as a backward glance. She'd stared after him, filled with a sense of foreboding.

Now, she watched Blade sweep the ground with his foot, eradicating any sign that they'd been there. He swung his much heavier pack onto his back then fastened the straps, his weapon sandwiched between his legs. That rifle was never far from his body, never out of reach. Always connected to him like an extension of himself.

The only time he'd put it down had been when he'd been holding her.

Lily followed Blade as best she could while he navigated the tree line in the darkness. The ground was rugged and uneven, with lots of clumps of vegetation and long grass growing between the trunks, which made walking difficult. On top of that, they were constantly hiking at an angle, which made her feel lopsided.

Blade moved like a leopard, sure footed and silent, while she stomped along behind him, trying not to fall on her face. They were averaging about two and a half miles an hour thanks to the terrain.

Every now and then he'd guide them deeper into the vegetation to avoid a dwelling or group of dwellings. The simple, rectangular houses clung precariously to the steep hillside, like a stack of matchboxes positioned on top of one another. If something happened to the bottom one, she was convinced they'd all fall down.

Blade glanced at the sky. "It'll be light soon."

That meant they weren't covering enough ground. If only her glasses hadn't been broken, she might be able to see the clumps of vegetation better. "How long have we got?"

"Another hour. At most."

Shit. After that, it would be too dangerous to continue.

She picked up her speed, ignoring the ache in her shoulders and the rumble in her stomach. It had been a long time since they'd eaten, but getting out of the danger zone took priority. The hillside and indeed the lush valley plains were filled with shepherds, farmers, fishermen, and any number of people during the day. They had to hide until it was dark again.

Grimacing, she trudged on. Traveling only at night made their progress very slow.

"As soon as daylight breaks, we'll hole up and eat something."

Lily gave a weary nod.

Her clothes were still damp but drying from the warmth of her body. The vigorous marching had warmed her up, despite the coolness of the early morning. She'd actually worked up a sweat. Still, it beat freezing. Seemed in this place there was no in-between.

Finally, Blade called a halt.

Thank God. She leaned against a tree, weak with exhaustion and hunger.

"This looks like a good place. It's out of sight from anyone who might happen to walk by."

Lily raised her head. He'd found a clump of trees growing so close together that they provided all-round coverage like a green, circular hedge. Their roots intertwined in the middle, creating natural armchairs for them to sink into.

"Looks perfect," she murmured, shrugging off her pack. It slid down her arms to the ground. "How do we get in?"

He pulled a couple of branches back. It wasn't easy, and if he let them go, they'd snap back into place. Lily slipped through, dragging her pack with her.

"I'll get it," he said, taking it out of her hand.

"Thanks."

He nodded, setting it down beside her. "You okay?"

"I'll be fine after some food and a nap." She didn't want to complain, but she could hardly keep her eyes open.

Blade began setting up camp and unpacking his pack. Outside their little hideaway, the sun had come up, and everything seemed a little bit brighter. Warmth percolated into the forest, dissolving the last of the chill.

Lily leaned back against her pack and closed her eyes. She didn't even remember falling asleep.

CHAPTER 15

*B*lade kept vigil while Lily slept.

She'd gone out like a light. To be fair, they'd battled a mighty river, frozen half to death, then walked close to five miles before stopping, so it was no wonder she was exhausted.

Once again, he'd been impressed by her stamina. She was tough. He knew her eyesight wasn't a hundred percent without glasses, which made her stumble occasionally, yet she never complained.

He couldn't understand why he'd never noticed Lily before. Apart from that first meeting a decade ago, he hadn't seen her much. Maybe not at all. She'd kept to herself. Plenty of times he'd invited Spade to hang with the guys at the bar or to go away for a weekend, but he always declined. If he was on leave, he was with Lily. Spade kept the two parts of his life separate, and Blade respected that.

He assumed it was because he didn't want to drag his work into his relationship. What they did hardly made for good dinner conversation. A man's home life was private, his family sacred. Blade, on the other hand, preferred not to have a family—for all the reasons he'd given Lily when they were lying together.

Joe had figured out how to juggle a homelife and the Special Forces, but Blade never had. Now he wouldn't need to. There was no more Special Forces. No unit. He scoffed and turned his face up to the sun. It was blasting through the trees, turning the lush valley into a steaming sauna.

Soon, it would be sweltering, and they'd have to hydrate frequently to avoid dehydration. He shook his head. Talk about extremes.

A random thought popped into his head. Would he be willing to juggle a relationship and the unit if it had been Lily?

It was an interesting question. Lately, he was thinking maybe it wasn't that he couldn't manage it but that he hadn't found the right girl. If he'd had someone like Lily, with her sharp mind, lush curves, soft lips… Hell, he wouldn't have wanted to say goodbye in the morning either. Then again, she wasn't the type of girl to pick up a soldier in a bar.

He sighed and checked the perimeter of their little hide-out. Nobody would even know it was there. It was unlikely that their enemy would come up into the hills to search for them. Unlikely, but not impossible.

Once the Taliban realized they weren't on the west side of the river, they'd cross it and come east, looking for signs they'd been there. Hunting them down. They'd rely on local intel too, the villagers and farmers whose land they'd been crossing. A soldier and a woman wouldn't be hard to spot.

Don't you get lonely?

That question had been spinning around in his mind as they'd marched here. These last ten months had been the loneliest of his life. Not only was he grappling with the grief of losing his best friend, but guilt from the failed mission was eating him up inside.

He'd filled the hours with working out like a maniac, fishing, going for long motorcycle rides, even getting drunk. Anything to numb the pain.

Now, for the first time in a long while, he'd found a semblance of peace. Being out here, rescuing Lily, had given him a purpose again. Even if she did drive him crazy with her sensual looks, quirky attitude, and curvy butt.

He thought about the sleeping bag and shook his head. Never, and he meant *never*, had he wanted anyone so much. Just thinking about the way she fit into him made his stomach knot with a tight heat.

But it was more than just a physical sensation. He wanted to protect her from the scumbags who wanted her dead. He wanted to drown in her arms and shut out the world. Pretend none of this had ever happened. That it was just the two of them.

He exhaled. What the hell had come over him?

He was never like this.

Was that how Joe had felt when he'd returned home from a mission, knowing she was waiting for him?

A vision of Lily standing in her underwear in the silver moonlight made him catch his breath. Damned if he didn't want to make her moan again, like she had before. But this time he'd see to it she didn't stop.

A loud crack made him swing around, but there was nothing there. He listened, careful not to move a muscle. The slightest sound, a twig breaking, a leaf rustling, would give him away. In this part of the forest, shadows were scarce and visibility was good. A sudden movement would draw the eye.

There it was again.

Footsteps.

The trees and foliage had a way of distorting sound, so it

was hard to pinpoint their exact location, but he thought there were two of them. Two distinct voices talking in Pashto. Careless and unaware, a sound out of place amongst the natural melody of the forest.

In these mountains, there were many rural communities and tribes. Of course, the most likely scenario was they were Taliban fighters, or sympathizers, but they could also be local farmers who felt it was in their best interests to assist in the search for two westerners on the run.

Slowly, Blade got to his feet, his weapon ready. He held it with practiced ease, the barrel pointed safely toward the ground but ready to be brought to bear in an instant. His finger rested alongside the trigger guard, but the safety was off.

He was ready.

He inched forward, his movements deliberate, keeping to the denser foliage. It offered heavier camouflage but also obscured his view.

Another rustle, louder now. The adversary was moving closer.

There!

He was right.

Two turbaned men in flowing robes having a smoke. He crouched down and watched for a while, thinking if they moved on, away from their hiding place, it might be okay.

Unfortunately—for them—they didn't.

As they turned, Blade noticed an AK-47 hanging off the one man's shoulder. It had been hidden amongst his robes, escaping immediate notice.

His mind cleared with only one thought present.

Neutralize.

Blade slunk through the undergrowth, not making a sound, until he was directly behind the two men. He could gun them down right here, right now, but the noise would be deafening. It would alert anyone else nearby that something had gone down.

One of the men flicked his cigarette butt on the ground, said something to his friend, and disappeared around a tree to take a leak. Blade watched as he leaned his weapon against a tree.

Big mistake.

In a fluid motion, he drew his knife. He'd always preferred it as a weapon. Silent, efficient, deadly. It was his proficiency with the weapon that had earned him his nickname in the unit.

With a swift motion, he was upon his enemy, one hand clamping down on the mouth to silence any potential outcry, the other drawing the blade across the throat in a swift, merciful action.

The man made a soft gurgling sound then crumpled to the ground. Blade supported his weight to prevent any noise, then he melted back into the forest.

The second guy was easy to locate. He paced back and forth, clearly agitated, weapon over his shoulder, no thought to the noise he was making.

He called for his friend but got no reply, so after making an annoyed sound in the back of his throat, he went looking for him.

Blade followed.

Before the man reached the lifeless body of his friend, Blade pounced. There was no warning, no prelude. His knife found its mark with a precision that was almost surgical, slicing through flesh and sinew with ease.

This time, no sound. Not even a gurgle.

Blade laid the second man to rest beside his comrade, then pulled some foliage over them to prevent anyone finding them soon. He buried the two rifles inside a dense, prickly bush, where it was unlikely they'd be found.

The forest was silent again.

Still, their position had been compromised. These two might be missed, and he didn't want a search party of fighters combing the woods near his and Lily's hiding spot. It was time to move on.

He went back to the camp to wake her.

CHAPTER 16

"**W**hy are we leaving?"

Lily scampered to keep up with Blade. "What's going on?"

"I told you. I heard voices and thought we'd better head out. Our position there was no longer safe."

She shook her head to clear the fog. Ten minutes ago she'd been in dreamland, and now they were trampling through the forest again, zigzagging around various flora and tripping over hidden roots.

Well, she was tripping. He was doing his usual Rambo thing.

"Did you see anyone?"

"Here, eat this." Blade handed her an energy bar. "It should keep you going until I can find us somewhere else to camp, then you can have some of the rations."

She grabbed the bar. Rations would be good too, as she was ravenous. Her last meal was a distant memory.

Blade had warned her against dehydration, so she'd been sipping her water regularly. They carried enough between the two of them to last three days if they were careful. But she was conscious that she was drinking far more than Blade.

She studied him as he turned to make sure she was keeping up. Disheveled hair, grim expression, haunted eyes underlined with shadows. The beard was an interesting addition. It made him look older, harder. More devastating. "You didn't sleep, did you?"

"I kept watch."

"That's when you saw them?" She hadn't known him for long, but she could tell when he was hiding something.

He gave a curt nod.

"Taliban?"

"I don't know. Didn't wait around long enough to find out."

"So, it could have been nothing? A harmless farmer or goat herder?"

"It wasn't nothing." His jaw jutted out stubbornly. "And no one here is harmless."

"Then you did see who they were."

"They had guns, okay? Goat herders don't sneak around armed with AK-47s."

That was pretty definitive. Lily ate her energy bar in silence, wondering how close they'd really come. By the tension in those powerful shoulders and his constant alertness, pretty damn close.

When she was done, she scrunched up the wrapper, earning herself another annoyed look.

"Sorry," she whispered.

"Give it to me."

She handed it over and he stuffed it into his pocket to dispose of later. No evidence. No clues to leave their enemy.

They marched in silence, Lily barely keeping up. Blade made it clear that talking was not allowed, not now while they were potentially surrounded by the enemy.

Fine with her.

He was in a gruff mood anyway, all snarly and sullen. The men with the guns had really pissed him off.

A back-breaking hour later, they came to a dilapidated pile of stones that looked like it might once have been a dwelling of some sort. The rear wall was half-standing, but the top had toppled forward onto the rest of the rubble.

"Wait here." Blade did a lap of the ruins. "It looks safe enough. The vegetation will give us some extra cover." It was surrounded by foliage, providing a natural camouflage, although, if someone looked closely, they'd see the rocks through the trees.

Lily followed him behind the building and sat, or rather fell, down with a long sigh. Her backpack had caught her off-balance and pulled her down. Sometimes, gravity sucked.

"You okay?" A raised eyebrow.

"Yep." She kept her voice light, even though she'd landed on a pebble and would have a nice little bruise later. That was the least of her worries.

They were still on the far side of the river, which meant at some point they'd have to cross back over, right into enemy territory. She wasn't looking forward to that. It seemed everywhere they turned, the enemy waited.

Blade prowled around like a predator, the veins in his neck bulging. He seemed wired, on edge.

"Why don't you take a nap?"

He glanced at her and shook his head. "I'm okay."

"You don't look okay."

He spun around. "What do you mean?"

"You're jumpy and tense, and you haven't slept since yesterday. I don't want a zombie protecting me if we come under attack."

At his sardonic look, she added, "Don't worry, I'll wake you at the first sign of danger."

He did another lap of the broken-down building, just to be sure, then came back and shrugged off his backpack. Placing it next to him, he sat, his rifle's sling still around his body, hands on the weapon.

"You're going to sleep holding your rifle?"

"Yeah." Obviously, his look said. "The threat level is still high."

She shrugged. The place seemed pretty deserted to her, but what did she know?

"Give me an hour." He leaned back against his rucksack and shut his eyes.

A few seconds later, his rhythmic breathing told her he was asleep.

Left to her own devices, Lily took the opportunity to relieve herself, then assumed a position where she could see in all directions but was out of the line of sight in case anyone should come wandering through the clearing.

The sun was deliciously warm, and she tilted her face up to it. How different the day temperatures were from the night. Her clothes were completely dry now, and the freezing hypothermic episode of the early hours was fading into the background.

While Blade slept, she watched the tiny creatures scurrying around amidst the stones, oblivious to the plight of the westerners using their home as a makeshift camp. A squirrel, or something similar with a bushy tail, carried a nut in its mouth as it whipped across the clearing then into a crevice.

With detached curiosity, she listened to the rustling leaves and the scampering animals in the wood around them. The sounds of Blade's steady breathing reminded her how fragile their little bubble of security was and how, without him, she was incredibly vulnerable.

He took care of everything, including her. Blade might be her late boyfriend's best friend, but she hadn't known him at all. Hadn't wanted to get to know him. Maybe if she had, this would have been easier.

Maybe there wouldn't be this crazy sexual tension between them, or whatever it was. Too late to do anything about it now. Joe was dead, and it seemed she couldn't get close to Blade without making a fool of herself. The awkwardness would be her constant companion until this ordeal ended.

The day wore on, and after an hour—at least she thought it was an hour—she got up to wake Blade. As she reached back to the wall, a tinkling sound wafted across the dry air. She crouched beside him and listened.

There it was again. Definitely a bell.

Crap.

She poked Blade on the shoulder.

His eyes flew open. "What's up?"

"I heard something. A bell, I think."

He jumped to his feet, rifle positioned against his shoulder, then moved stealthily to the corner of the stone wall. Lily, stunned by how fast he'd gotten up, froze as the bell sounded again.

She met his gaze, and what she saw frightened her.

"Wait here," Blade said for the second time that afternoon, then he disappeared around the corner.

Lily didn't move a muscle. Didn't breathe. Didn't blink.

Who was it? Soldiers didn't wear bells.

A shepherd? The hair on her back stood up.

Then, Blade was back, a deep frown on his face. "Goat herder."

Lily breathed out, relieved. How dangerous could a goat herder be?

Footsteps sounded, nearing the pile of stones.

"Get down," he whispered.

They both slouched behind the wall.

Blade, rifle over his shoulder, peered through a crack while Lily prayed the herder would go away.

He didn't.

Whistling, the man sat on the wall and lit a roll-up cigarette he pulled from behind his ear. Without a sound, Blade unsheathed his knife.

Lily did a double take. Was that *blood*?

Holy crap. Was it *recent*?

Blade's face was a grim mask of determination. He'd had the same look when he'd shot those two gunmen in the forest.

He was going to kill the guy. And for what? Herding goats? The goat herder had no idea Blade was less than a meter behind him.

Lily stared at the knife in alarm.

She shook her head violently, but Blade ignored her. He was totally focused on the man sitting on the wall. A loud *baa* accompanied ringing bells. A handful of scrawny goats gathered around the herder, pulling tufts of grass from between cracks in the stones.

Lily could smell the cigarette smoke as she squatted against the wall, gaze riveted on Blade.

He was stock-still, crouching behind the wall, knife glinting in his right hand.

The goat herder leaned back.

Lily knew Blade was going to react. Heart pounding, she grabbed his arm and shook her head violently. She mouthed, "No."

He glared at her and shook off her hand but did pause. The herder jumped down off the wall then went to tend to his goats. A few minutes later, he walked away, still whistling to himself.

Lily only relaxed when the sound of the bells faded into the distance.

CHAPTER 17

"*D*on't ever grab my arm like that again!"

Blade was furious. He paced up and down, adrenalin pounding in his ears. He'd been about to neutralize the threat, and she'd stopped him, potentially putting them both at risk.

Her eyes flashed like flaming opals. "You were going to kill him? A harmless goat herder?"

"Yeah, I was."

"Why? He wasn't a threat to us."

He turned to face her, blood boiling. "Until he gets home and mentions to his buddies that he saw two foreigners up in the hills. Word gets back to the fighters, and before you know it we have an army hunting us down on this side of the river too."

Lily paused, thinking. "He didn't see us."

"Let's hope you're right." Blade took a ragged breath, trying to calm down. Right now, he was acting like a dick. She didn't deserve that. Lily was a civilian, not a killer like him. She didn't understand the need for fast, aggressive action.

"You think he was pretending?"

"Anything's possible. That's why we can't take chances. We're not just evading an army. Everyone in this region is hostile toward us. There are eyes and ears everywhere."

"Violence isn't always the answer, you know." She glared at him. "There are other ways to resolve conflict."

"Not out here, there aren't." He sheathed his knife. Even now, that goat herder could be racing back to tell his friends how close he came to getting his throat slit by an enemy soldier. It would make a good drinking story. "Do you think if we'd asked that guy nicely not to tell anyone we were here, he would have listened?"

"Maybe." Her defensive expression belied her words.

"Don't be naive. It would be in his best interests to tell what he saw. That way he'd ingratiate himself with the men in control of the area."

She stood her ground. "I'm telling you, he didn't see us."

Blade clenched his jaw, hoping she was right. "It's still not worth the risk. Every action has consequences here. A footprint, a discarded wrapper, a word spoken too loudly. Anything can give us away."

"Okay, I get it. Geez."

She pulled on her backpack, wrestling with the weight of it. Blade wanted to help but didn't think it would be particularly welcome right now. Besides, he was still simmering with pent-up aggression. The sooner they got out of there, the better.

They marched in silence, him storming ahead trying to work out his tension, Lily several paces behind. He wanted to put as much distance between them and their last rest stop as possible. The niggling feeling the goat herder wasn't as harmless as he'd seemed wouldn't go away. And over the course of several ops, he'd learned to trust his gut.

That plus being out in the open in broad daylight made

Blade set a grueling pace. As they ate up the miles, the forest thinned in favor of low-lying shrubs and bushes, which meant less coverage. In the valley, the lush floodplains expanded and contracted with the meanders in the river.

Blade couldn't stop thinking about the goat herder. Something about the whole situation bothered him, but he couldn't put his finger on it. Maybe it was his whistle—too contrived, too deliberate.

On the other hand, maybe he was just being paranoid, and like Lily had said, the guy was harmless.

The sun was dipping over the hills when his temper cooled. Though he still couldn't shake his suspicions, he felt better about the distance they'd covered. He also felt bad about pushing Lily so hard. Though she hadn't said a word, she'd been panting behind him for some time. "Let's stop here."

Silently, she dropped down onto a tree stump and bent over.

"You okay?"

She gave a sullen nod, either still mad at him or totally spent. Or both.

He couldn't blame her for being angry. He hadn't handled the situation very well. Actually, that was an understatement. He'd fucked up. Royally.

"I'm sorry I lost my temper." He handed her a water bottle. "I shouldn't have spoken to you like that."

"You were just doing your job." She took it but didn't look up. Instead, she unscrewed the cap and took a long pull.

Her hair had gone all wispy and curled around her face, softening her features. When she finished drinking, a few droplets remained on her lips.

He fought the urge to lick them off.

"I was, but that wasn't the way to handle it."

She bobbed her head, the movement short and terse.

"Apology accepted. I'm sorry I grabbed your hand. Actually, no, I'm not. I didn't want to see you kill that man."

"I know." He wasn't going to go there again. She was entitled to her opinion, and it was probably best she didn't live by his rules, anyway.

His world wasn't a particularly pretty one.

She shook out her hair, then tilted her head back and closed her eyes, exposing her elegant neck.

Was it bad to want to run his tongue all the way down it to her breasts?

The heat must be getting to him.

But damn, she was beautiful when she was angry. All flushed and desirable, amber eyes shooting fire at him. Their exchange had left him edgy and frustrated. Needing something to do, he took out the map and focused on that. "If we move to higher ground, we might be able to find a small cave or crevice to shelter in until the sun sets. We shouldn't be out here in the open."

"Sounds like a plan."

"You ready?"

She answered by climbing to her feet.

* * *

THE NEXT MILE WAS UPHILL. It was tough going, and Blade slowed his pace so Lily could keep up. The ground beneath their feet changed again from spongy grass and clumps of foliage to dry dirt and pebbles.

As they got to the rugged peaks, he took Lily's hand to stop her slipping and sliding on the gravel. He was also conscious that they were visible from the valley below by anyone with a pair of binoculars. He had to get them undercover as soon as possible.

"Here." He stopped beside a horizontal rock crevice just wide enough for both of them to lie in.

"You sure?" She looked out over the valley.

"Yeah, the shadow will protect us from prying eyes below, and we can shelter from what's left of the sun."

Lily removed her backpack and shimmied into the crevice. He handed her the flask again. "Thanks."

"We should be safe here for a spell." He climbed in beside her. There was just enough height for them to sit, in a reclining position. The view was spectacular, but neither of them could enjoy it.

Lily seemed lost in her own world, while he plotted their next steps. So far so good, but their pursuers wouldn't quit. She was too damn valuable for them to stop chasing.

Well, she was also too damn valuable for him to give up on. One way or another, he'd get her out of here.

"Are you always so suspicious of people?" she asked, startling him.

He answered carefully. "In enemy territory, yes. Are you always so trusting?"

She chuckled, easing the tension. "Actually, no. Usually I'm the one with trust issues, although there are two people I trust implicitly."

"Spade?" he guessed.

She nodded. "And Pat."

"Pat's a good guy."

'Yeah. Joe was there for me when I needed him most. When my mother died, I had nobody. Joe asked me to move in with him, and his folks sort of adopted me. They were wonderful. I owe them so much."

"I'm sorry, I didn't know." Spade hadn't told him Lily had lost her parents. Spade hadn't talked about her at all, come to think of it.

"It was a long time ago now, but I don't know what I would have done without them."

He turned toward her. "How'd they die?"

"My father disappeared when I was little, so I never knew him. My mother died in a car wreck when I was sixteen."

He could see why she had trust issues. Everyone she'd ever loved had left her.

Even Joe.

He ground his teeth together. Sometimes life could be a bitch.

"It was Pat who asked me to come and get you. He was worried about you."

Her gaze softened. "He's like a father to me. A real sweetie."

Blade thought of the barrel-chested bear of a former Navy SEAL and laughed. "I haven't heard Pat described like that before."

"He's got a softer side."

If he had, Blade hadn't seen it.

"I trust you," she said, out of nowhere.

He glanced at her, surprised. "You hardly know me."

"I know you'll do everything in your power to get me home safely."

He didn't reply. Hell, he'd move mountains to get her home.

Not for Pat.

Not even for Joe.

For himself.

He might never be able to have her, but there was no damn way he was gonna leave her out there at the mercy of killers.

The way she was looking at him. *God* help him.

"I want you to know I'm grateful, even if I don't show it.

You didn't have to come here. After what happened to Joe, I'm surprised you did."

"I owed it to Spade."

She threaded her fingers through his. "You're a good friend, Blade."

He stared at her, his big hand enveloping her small one. Suddenly, all the tension of the last few hours rose up to strangle him. "Lily, I—"

"Shh." She leaned in. "Just kiss me."

CHAPTER 18

*I*t was madness, she knew this.

Yet she did it anyway.

She *needed* this. Needed him. To kiss away the fear and the weariness and make her feel safe again.

"God, Lily," he growled, raking a hand through his hair. "We can't."

"Why not?" she whispered, her lips trailing along his jawbone.

He groaned and closed his eyes. "Spade loved you."

"I know he did, and I loved him back, but this isn't about Joe. This is about you and me." She began nuzzling his neck.

Blade stiffened, hot tension radiating off him. "Pat would kill me if he found out."

"He doesn't need to know."

"Fuck." He reached behind her head and pulled her toward him, crushing her lips against his. She gasped, the sound swallowed by his mouth opening under hers. His sudden agreement had her heart slamming against her ribs. Gone were the excuses. He was all fiery passion, rock hard body, and scorching tongue.

She surrendered to his embrace, the animal inside him devouring her. She'd expected a gentle kiss, like Joe's, but should have known better. Blade was nothing like Joe. He was all physical passion and wild sexuality. Hadn't that first kiss in the cabin when she'd been half asleep proved it?

Freakin' hell.

He slid his hands under her bottom then hauled her onto his lap. The space between them vanished. Senses in overdrive, Lily recognized she was a hot, wet, writhing mess. Any hotter and she'd spontaneously combust.

She'd wanted to forget this frightening place with its violent people and ever-increasing peril. Hoped for a soft, pleasant distraction in Blade's arms. She'd expected he'd be a welcome diversion. But she hadn't expected *this*. She was on fire, the heat he stoked inside her threatening to consume her.

He growled and crushed her against him. There was nowhere to go, not that she wanted to leave. She wanted to stay. Wanted this kiss. Wanted *him*.

Time distorted as she succumbed to her desires. Heart racing, she tangled her fingers in his hair, pulling him somehow even closer, as if trying to meld into one being.

Blade's kiss deepened, an intoxicating mix of urgency and yearning that threatened to overwhelm her completely. She was lost in the storm of *him*, a tempest of emotion and raw need she'd never experienced before.

It drove out the ugliness of the goat herder incident. Banished her fear of the men chasing them. Lily forgot when it was and where she was in favor of focusing on *who* she was with. She was done fighting her attraction to this man. He'd affected her from the day they'd met, and right now she wanted to embrace that.

If this experience had taught her anything, it was that life was too short to hold back. Anything could happen. They might not make it to the main road. They might die tonight crossing the river. There were a hundred ways her life could end in this country. She didn't want to go with any regrets. And she'd regret not knowing how this would feel. She'd regret not knowing *him*.

Trembling, she clung to his thick, powerful shoulders. Thrilled as they rippled underneath her fingers as he moved. He hoisted her higher, and there was no denying how rigid he was beneath her. He wanted her too, as much as she wanted him. The realization spurred her on. She closed her eyes and gave in to the surge of emotions coursing through her.

It was too much, this blood-boiling chaos. Shaking, out of control, tears trailed down her cheeks, and a sob caught in her throat.

Blade stiffened and broke away, his eyes immediately filling with regret. "God, Lily. I'm sorry."

"No." She shook her head.

He shifted, putting some space between them. She slid off his lap, her lips still throbbing with the taste of him.

"Please, don't apologize. It was just…" She couldn't find the words. Never in her life had she experienced that level of desire. Her heart raced, her skin tingled. Every atom in her body vibrated at a frequency she couldn't control.

How could she tell him she wanted this. Wanted *him*.

It was all just so overwhelming.

He glanced away, his jaw clenched, wrestling with his own turmoil. "I didn't mean to be so rough. I'd never intentionally scare you." Guilt knotted his brow.

Lily reached out, her hand trembling as she touched his cheek, guiding his gaze back to hers. "You didn't scare me. I was overwhelmed, but not by fear. By the intensity of… of everything. Of us." She held his gaze, begging him to understand.

For a moment, they were suspended in time, the world around them receding into the background. The potential dangers of their situation, the risk of death that loomed like a specter over their every move, seemed momentarily insignificant against the raw honesty of their connection.

Blade's expression softened, the harsh lines of tension easing as understanding dawned. He reached for her, his movements hesitant.

She threw her arms around his neck and held him tight.

"Lily," he murmured against her hair. He held her for a long moment before slowly releasing her. "I'm sorry, I—"

She waited for him to say something, but no more words came. Pulling back, she saw the anguish in his expression. It was like a bucket of ice-cold water splashing her in the face.

There was no *us*. Not now, not ever.

Blade wouldn't do that to Joe.

Her heart plunged down the hillside and smashed on the rocks below. "I know."

CHAPTER 19

*H*e'd fucked up.

Blade stared stormily out over the valley while Lily slept next to him.

That kiss.

Holy shit.

He couldn't help himself. It had been boiling for so long, this unbridled passion between them. Finally, unleashed by her gentle pleading, he'd let himself go.

And made her cry.

Shit. What a jerk.

Then, he'd had the audacity to tell her he couldn't go through with it. That he couldn't do that to Spade. Couldn't betray his friend's memory.

Hell, they'd crossed *that* line days ago.

Deep down, he questioned whether that was the real reason he'd pulled back. Maybe he was just scared. Seeing her tears, knowing how much it had affected her… it had shocked him.

No, it had fucking terrified him.

That came with a whole new level of responsibility. A

level far beyond his capacity. It always had been. That's why he always kept it light. Fun. No strings.

This crazy, helter-skelter, all-consuming longing he felt whenever he kissed her was so completely foreign, he couldn't get his head around it.

A shout somewhere far below brought him out of his daze. He'd been thinking about Lily when he should have been figuring out their next move. More proof why whatever was happening between them was a bad idea. He had to stay alert, keep a clear head if he was going to get her out of there.

After she was back home, things would revert to normal. She'd forget about him and this nightmare. People did that with trauma, pushed it to the back of their minds and pretended it hadn't happened.

Most of the time.

Blade took another look at the map. The river was at its narrowest two klicks south. That would be the best place to cross. There might be a raft or a boat he could steal so Lily wouldn't have to get soaked again.

He didn't want a repeat of that episode. He tightened his jaw, willing away the memory of her soft skin against his.

The problem with crossing there, however, was that they were more vulnerable to an ambush. The valley narrowed at that point, becoming more rugged with less vegetation and fewer places to hide. The rocky outcrops on the steep valley sides also provided excellent cover for snipers.

He scanned the map, following the river. Ideally, he'd head south for another ten klicks before crossing, but that would result in a more difficult swim, and it was much farther to go. Spending yet another day out here would be suicide. He wanted them on the road to Kabul by nightfall.

Using his high magnification spotting scope, he scanned the length of the river, or as much of it as he could see from up here, but couldn't spot anything out of the ordinary.

Workers in the poppy fields, a couple of boats moored alongside a jetty—nothing that aroused his suspicion.

When the sun had sunk below the hills and the sky was turning a dark indigo, he woke Lily up.

Her eyes fluttered open. "Blade. Hmm…" She scrambled up. "Is everything okay?"

"Everything's fine," he reassured her, his tone crisp. His heart lurched as he saw the disappointment in her eyes. Damn, he hated himself for this. For hurting her.

But he was a pro. She was the hostage, and this was a rescue op, not a romantic getaway. He had to stay focused.

"Are we going?"

He gave a stiff nod. "Yeah, we should move out. Last push until we hit the road."

"Okay."

He gave her a moment to get herself together then helped her on with her backpack. "Why didn't you and Spade ever come out with us?" The question surprised him. He hadn't intended to ask, but it been on his mind for some time.

She hesitated. "It's complicated."

"Complicated how?"

She stretched, ironing out her curves. "Looking back now, it seems ridiculous, but I was scared that I'd lose him."

"Who? Spade? No way. He was nuts about you."

"I know." She paused, her wide, brown eyes settling on him. "It wasn't him I was worried about. It was you."

He scowled. "Me?"

"I thought you might rub off on him."

He didn't say anything for a long moment, and when he did, his voice was husky. "You thought I was a bad influence on Spade?"

Lily looked out over the darkened valley. "Do you blame me? You were with a different girl every time you were back in town. Joe told me so."

"I explained that," he snapped.

She held up her hands in a gesture of defeat. "I know you did. I was wrong, okay. I admit it. I didn't know you back then. All I saw was this hot, broad-shouldered guy with perfect teeth and a blonde hanging off his arm."

"You didn't take the time to get to know me." He blinked. "Wait a minute. You thought I was hot?"

She flushed. "That's not the point. I made an assumption, and it was wrong. I'm sorry."

His chest tightened. "All that time, I thought you were just a stuck up bi—" He cleared his throat. "That you thought you were too good for us. Too smart to be seen with the likes of us."

She gasped. "It was nothing like that."

He fixed his gaze on her. "We were both wrong."

She didn't smile, but there was warmth in her eyes. "Yes, we were."

* * *

THEY SET OFF, treading carefully over the loose gravel. Blade led the way, more used to the terrain that she was. Lily followed close behind, mimicking his steps, squinting at the loose ground in front of her.

The path, if it could be called that, wound its way down the mountain, following the contours. After Lily slipped a couple of times, Blade took her hand. He'd promised himself no contact, but he couldn't let her fall to her death. A purely professional connection.

That was his story, and he was sticking to it.

They walked on, him helping her over the more difficult parts of the descent, until they stopped for a water break.

"You know you said you thought I was a bad influence on Joe?" He couldn't keep that question to himself, either.

She glanced up, surprised. "Yeah?"

"Well, you might find this strange, but it was actually the other way round."

"I don't get it. You're saying Joe was a bad influence on you?"

"Yeah." He worked his jaw, unsure how to proceed, but she should know the truth about the man she'd been living with. "Spade was always the one who got a little out of hand when we went out. It was like he had all this pent-up aggression and didn't know what to do with it. More than a few times I had to pull him out of a fight or take him back to my place to sleep it off."

Lily was staring at him like he'd grown horns or something. "Joe? My Joe?"

Blade nodded. "He said it was because he wanted to let his hair down, have some fun, you know? I suppose he was always so well behaved at home. His father expected a lot of him, and then there was you—" He bit down on his lip.

Shit, he'd said too much.

It was all true though. Spade had been a firebrand when they went out drinking. He'd once how said how perfect Lily was, and trying to match that standard kept him from relaxing. Said he couldn't be his usual carefree, foul-mouthed self around her. At the time, Blade had thought she'd been the one with unreasonable expectations of him, but what did he know? He'd never been in a long-term relationship. Now he was starting to think Spade had put those expectations on himself.

"What about me?" Her voice was a tight whisper.

"Spade thought the world of you. I think he wanted to be the kind of man you deserved. And I think he tried hard to be that guy."

"In other words, not himself."

Blade winced. "I'm sorry. I shouldn't have said anything."

Tears swum in her eyes. "I had no idea he felt like that. I wish he would have told me."

"Maybe he didn't want to lose you."

Her lip quivered. "He wouldn't have lost me. We'd have worked it out."

Blade didn't reply.

There was nothing wrong with wanting to be a better man.

His chest tightened at the sight of her blinking back tears, her face pale and drawn, yet determined.

No, nothing wrong with that at all.

The incline gradually lessened, the loose gravel becoming interspersed with patches of hard-packed dirt and sparse vegetation. He let go of her hand.

"We were very young when we got together. Joe was my first boyfriend. The only man I'd ever been with."

He inhaled sharply as memories came flooding back—her lips on his neck, their bodies crushing together, his tongue in her mouth.

"It's hard to believe he kept his true self from me."

"I saw a different side to him, that's all." Blade wished to hell he hadn't said anything. "Out in the field, Spade was decisive, brave, and loyal. He had your back, you know."

She nodded.

"Back home, he was just Spade. Rowdy, free-spirited, always pushing the boundaries."

Lily shook her head. "That sounds like a completely different Joe than the one I knew."

"I guess he had many sides to his personality, just like we all do."

Her eyes were sad. He wanted to hold her, to kiss away the pain, but he couldn't. It wasn't his to take on.

"I guess so. I just wish we'd had more time."

"Spade was a good guy, an excellent soldier, and my best

friend. That's all that counts." The guilt cut through him, making him clench his hands around his rifle.

Spade was a better man than him.

Not only had he moved in on Spade's girl, but he'd also bad-mouthed his dead buddy in front of her. God, he was a prick.

He just didn't want Lily thinking he was the one to blame. That he was the bad influence. Her opinion of him mattered. A lot.

Way more than he thought it would.

"You were with him when he died?"

He gave a stiff nod. "Yeah. He passed away in my arms, right there on that mountain pass."

Tears flowed freely down her face. "I didn't know he died in your arms. Why didn't you tell me?"

The energy leaked out of him like he'd been hit by a bullet. The memory was still so vivid, probably because he'd replayed it so many times in his head. There was no bandage for this injury. The raw, gaping wound would never heal.

"I don't know. Does it make a difference?"

Her chest rose. "Yes, it makes a difference. It helps knowing he wasn't alone. That you were with him."

At least that brought her comfort.

"That's when he said to tell you he loved you," Blade croaked.

She swiped at her eyes. "I loved him too."

His heart shattered into a million pieces.

That's why they could never be together.

CHAPTER 20

*S*he'd been wrong about everything.

The more she thought about it, the more she realized Blade was right. Joe had always been well-behaved at home, always polite and attentive like he was playing a part.

He never let his hair down—not with her, anyway.

When they went out, it was usually with her friends, which meant he had to maintain his perfect boyfriend facade. It was only with his Special Forces buddies, his true friends, that he'd allowed himself to let loose.

How the hell had she missed that? Ten years, and she felt like she hadn't known him at all.

Yet that wasn't the only mistake she'd made.

Her stupid notion that Blade had forced him to sign up. That Blade had led him astray. It was all bogus.

The real Joe probably wanted to break free from his preordained, orderly life. He'd have been itching for a thrill like the Green Berets offered, for the brotherhood of a tight-knit unit, for the chance to truly be himself.

She shook her head as she traipsed along behind Blade.

How had she been so blind?

It was too late now, that's what sucked about it. She couldn't tell Joe how sorry she was.

They'd been little more than kids when they'd gotten together, and since they'd lived under the same roof since she was just sixteen, he'd never had a chance to go wild and have fun. He'd stepped up and done the right thing, taking her on and looking after her.

A pang caused her to catch her breath.

Had he been happy?

The change in the terrain was more noticeable now. The path they were on wound through a field of wildflowers, their dark heads bobbing in the breeze. Blade had become tenser, more vigilant. He stalked ahead, his gun in the ready position, his finger flat against the trigger guard.

"Let's aim for those trees." His voice was a low growl.

They were moving into the danger zone. Any security she'd felt up in the mountains vanished, and the tight knot of anxiety in her stomach was back. She pushed all thoughts of Joe out of her head and concentrated on what was happening around her.

Lily followed Blade into the wooded area. This was where the narrow band of forest started and would give them some cover. She was hoping they'd be able to stay camouflaged all the way to the river.

Suddenly, Blade stopped walking and raised his hand, signaling to her to stop.

She froze.

"What is it?" she whispered.

"Something doesn't feel right."

A chill crawled up her spine. She trusted Blade's instincts. "What should we do?"

"Get back into those trees and stay put. I'm going to take a look." There was an urgency to his tone that scared her.

"But—"

"Don't move, Lily. Hide in the leaves and wait for me." Then he slunk off into the night.

Panic threatened to overwhelm her, so she mentally went through the commands on her computer program to keep her mind busy. It helped. The fear subsided.

Minutes ticked by.

How long had it been?

Her fear reared up.

She peered into the darkness but couldn't see anything. Where the hell was Blade? Was he alright? Had something happened?

What if he never came back?

After what felt like an eternity, he reappeared like a specter. She hadn't heard a sound. He raised a finger to his lips. "Keep your voice down."

She nodded to show she understood.

"We can't go this way. They're planning an ambush up ahead. Twenty, thirty men. All armed."

Her heart sank.

"An ambush?" What the hell? "How did they know we were here?"

Then she got it.

"The goat herder."

He nodded. "Yeah, he must have seen us."

Shit. That was her fault.

How many times could she be wrong in one day? She bit her lip. "I'm sorry. I should have let you—"

He cut her off. "No time to worry about that now. We've gotta get out of here."

She looked around. "Where to?"

The only way was down to the river.

"Plan B."

She gasped. "We're going into one of the villages to ask for help. Around here?"

"Not around here. About twenty klicks over that hill, into the next province."

She glanced up at the hill they'd just climbed down. "Twenty kilometers? You're kidding?"

"Wish I was."

"Why there?" Lily didn't know if she could walk that far. Wasn't there a closer village?

"They're not as sympathetic to the Taliban, and I might have a contact who can help us."

Lily stared at him in amazement. "And you only thought to mention this now?"

"It's a long shot." He shrugged. "I'm not even sure he's still there."

She gritted her teeth. "So we might walk twenty kilometers for nothing?"

He took a glug from the water bottle, readjusted his rifle, then looked at her. "Not for nothing. Someone there might be able to help us."

At least it was away from the soldiers waiting to ambush them.

Lily took a deep breath. This seemed to be their only option.

"You ready?" he asked.

She gave a firm nod. "Let's go."

* * *

LILY WAS BEYOND EXHAUSTED. They walked most of the night with very few breaks. The sky was lightning in the east, and soon they'd lose the protective cover of darkness. They had to get out of sight soon. Even now, lights flickered in some of the windows in the sleepy hollow. She collapsed on the ground behind a copse of trees on the outskirts of a small village.

It was more of a hamlet than a village, with about a dozen brick houses scattered about in no apparent pattern. There was a dry, picked-over field for livestock and, on the far side, a dirt road leading away from the village.

She had no idea where they were, other than miles from their intended path, far from both the river and the road that led to Kabul.

Part of her felt like crying, she was so tired. But another trusted Blade. He'd get her out. Somehow. She had to stay strong.

"Who's your contact?"

Blade slid off his pack then sat next to her. The lines clawing at his eyes and the tension in his jaw showed his exhaustion too. They both needed rest and sustenance to continue.

"Stitch. The guy that went AWOL after our last op."

She knew that name. "The medic?"

"That's him."

Lily frowned. "What makes you think he lives out here?"

"I tracked him down after he went AWOL. I was his Commanding Officer, after all."

She tilted her head to look at him. "Yet you didn't tell anyone where he was?"

He shrugged. "I figured he needed time, just like the rest of us."

Joe had told her what happened to people who went AWOL. They were considered deserters. She supposed they *were* deserters. If Blade had given up Stitch's location, he would have faced court martial and if found guilty may have been dishonorably discharged, fined, or even imprisoned. After what had happened to the unit, any of those options felt like undue punishment.

"Why did Stitch come here?" she whispered. "Why not go home and get help?"

"He met a local girl on a fact-finding mission a few months before our last op. I was with him, actually. So were Spade and Blaster. We went in as a four-man team. I knew he was soft on her, so I guessed he might come back here."

Lily leaned her head back against the tree. "Great. That's all you've got to go on. A girl he was soft on?"

"It's not like we have a lot of options."

She closed her eyes, trying not to give in to the urge to cry.

"Lily, look at me."

With a superhuman effort, she opened her eyes and turned to face him.

"I've been to this village. The elder will remember me. Even if Stitch isn't here, there's a strong possibility they'll help us."

She perked up. That was promising. "So what do we do now? We can't go around knocking on doors."

"I'll take a look around."

"Okay. Yeah, I know. Wait here."

He threw her a rare grin then, leaving his pack on the ground beside her, melted into the shadows.

CHAPTER 21

*B*lade headed toward the dark dwellings. He had no idea which, if any, was Stitch's house but if his former teammate was there, he'd recognize their unit's call-sign and come to him.

He slipped behind the first house, a single-story stone rectangle with a small patio out front and whistled. The sound was designed to sound like a bird indigenous to the region, although the sun was already coming up, so there was a possibility Stitch might think it really was a tweeting bird.

At the seventh house, he heard someone moving inside, then a door creaked. Blade stood behind the dwelling, upright and in full sight. He didn't want Stitch to be in any doubt as to who he was.

The next moment, a hand clamped over his mouth, and cold steel touched the base of his neck.

What the fuck?

Blade spun out of the person's grasp, gun raised.

Stitch stood there, grinning.

He sighed and lowered his hands. "You nearly gave me a freakin' heart attack."

149

"I thought I was dreaming." Stitch sheathed his knife.

It took a moment for Blade's pulse to return to normal. Trust Stitch to pull that one on him. "Great to see you, buddy."

The two men hugged.

"I see you haven't lost your skills," Blade said wryly.

Stitch chuckled, his teeth white against the darkness. "What the hell are you doing here? More importantly, how did you find me?"

"I remembered that girl you were soft on in the village," said Blade. "It didn't take a genius to figure you'd come back here."

"I only hope the rest of 'em don't figure that out, else my days here are numbered."

"No chance. I didn't tell anyone."

He nodded his thanks.

Blade grinned. It was great seeing Stitch again. He was thinner—lost most of his bulk since he wasn't pumping weights anymore. But he was the same old Stitch. "You look well."

"Life here suits me."

"Glad to hear it." He put a hand on Stitch's arm. "Listen, I wish I could say this was a social call, but it's not. I need your help. I've got a hostage with me, and the Taliban are up our asses. I need to get her to Kabul. Can you help?"

"Christ, you don't ask much, do you?"

Blade looked him in the eye. "This is a personal mission."

Stitch frowned.

"For Spade. It's his girlfriend who got kidnapped. I don't know if you ever met Lily. She's a hot-shot software designer working for the CIA."

"The CIA. Wow." He gave a thoughtful nod. "I think I remember her. Blonde hair, glasses, pretty smile."

"That's the one." How come he'd never noticed her pretty smile?

Stitch peered behind Blade into the darkness. "Where is she now? Back there?"

It wasn't a guess. He knew how Blade operated. He'd have her hide in the hills while he came down to scout out the landscape.

"Yeah, we need a place to lie low during the day and then safe passage out of here. Do you have a phone we can use?"

"Nah, buddy. No cell reception out here and not a sat phone in sight. I do have a car we can use, though. Why don't you get Spade's old lady and come inside? We can talk there."

Spade's old lady.

He tensed at the phrase but gave a grateful nod.

"Thanks, man. Appreciate it."

* * *

Twenty minutes later, Blade and Lily sat on an intricately woven Afghan rug adorning the floor of Stitch's living area. The house was traditionally decorated, which meant no western furniture, but it didn't matter. The edges of the room were piled with big comfy cushions that were so inviting, he had to resist the urge to lie down on them and go to sleep.

Despite the chill outside, it was warm and cozy here. Elaborate tapestries hung over the windows to ward off the cold, and two gas lamps burned in the interior since there was no electricity. Heat lingered from the fireplace, though the flames had burned down during the night.

Simple living, but for a guy like Stitch who was used to roughing it outdoors, it was more than adequate.

"So, you're married?" Blade smiled as Stitch walked in carrying a plate of sandwiches and tea. The question was merely to break the silence. No westerner would be allowed to live here with a local woman if he wasn't.

"Yeah, Soraya's asleep."

Again, Blade suspected Soraya knew they had guests but wouldn't make an appearance until she was dressed and ready to receive them properly.

Stitch handed Lily a cup of hot tea. "So, you're Spade's girlfriend? I think we met once or twice over the years."

"I remember you." She smiled and accepted the tea.

Blade noticed how her gaze flickered over Stitch. He was a handsome man, even with the beard, and was a hell of a lot more charming and sociable than he was. He was a good guy, too. Had fixed him up more damn times than he could count.

"Sorry for your loss. Spade was a good man and a great friend."

"Thank you."

A flash of sadness crossed her face, but her eyes were still glittering. A stupid, territorial part of him caused him to tense. He needed a change of subject.

"How's married life treating you?"

Stitch chuckled. "It's good. We live simply, but I'm happy here. The people are warm and accepting, and they like having someone with my skills around."

Lily frowned. "A soldier?"

"A doctor. I joined the army straight out of med school."

"Oh, yeah. I forgot." Genuine interest laced her tone. "What made you do that?"

"My father was in the military, and after he was shot and killed while overseas, I decided I wanted to use my skills to help people like him."

"I'm sorry." She flushed. "It's a noble goal, though."

Stitch shrugged. "Don't be. It's our past experiences that make us who we are."

Good old Stitch, still philosophizing about life. No

surprise he'd settled here so comfortably. "I'm glad it's worked out for you," Blade said, and he meant it. "I was worried when you took off."

"Adapt and overcome, isn't that what they taught us?" But there was an edge to his voice.

After the tea and sandwiches, Stitch got up. "Why don't you get some shut eye, you both look shattered. We'll pick this up in a couple of hours and figure out how to get you home." He smiled at Lily.

She nodded gratefully, her eyelids heavy.

"Alright if we sleep here?" Blade nodded at the cushions.

"Sure, man. Make yourself at home. *Mi casa, su casa.*"

For the first time since he'd arrived back in Afghanistan, Blade felt like he didn't have to sleep with one eye open. After making sure Lily was comfortable, he sighed, leaned back onto the soft cushions, then drifted into blissful oblivion.

* * *

BLADE WOKE to the sound of a kettle whistling over a gas stove. A woman dressed in a flowing robe and wearing a teal scarf on her head was working in the kitchen. From her profile, and the small bump of her belly, it was obvious she was newly pregnant.

Now *that* was something Stitch hadn't mentioned.

He sat then smoothing down his wayward hair. After three days of hiking, there wasn't much hope. "Hello, you must be Soraya."

He heard Lily stir.

The woman turned and smiled. She was very beautiful, with smooth, olive skin and eyes the color of her headscarf. He could see why Stitch was smitten.

"Yes, you're Blade?"

He nodded and got to his foot. "Can I help you with that?"

Stitch came in and immediately went to her side. "Soraya, love, I told you not to come down."

"I know." She looped an arm around her husband. "But it's not often we have guests, particularly friends of yours. I wanted to meet them."

With a roll of his eyes, Stitch introduced them.

Lily rose and rubbed her eyes. "It's wonderful to meet you, Soraya."

"I'll take that." Blade grinned at his buddy as he took the tray with the teapot and cups from her.

Soraya had just the right amount of curiosity and feistiness to keep her American husband on his toes. She was exactly what Stitch needed in his life.

"Thank you."

"I'm sorry for the intrusion," Lily said as Blade put down the tray. "It's my fault we're here."

Blade wasn't sure if she meant because she'd been abducted or because she'd prevented him from killing the goat herder.

"I'm sure that's not true." Soraya knelt and began pouring the tea. "I've always been curious about Stitch's past, and of course he's told me all about his friends in the unit."

"Has he now?" Blade raised an eyebrow.

Stitch laughed. "Soraya knows everything about me, including my time in the Green Berets, but it goes no further. The rest of the village think I'm an army doctor."

"Which you are." Soraya smiled up at her husband. It was clear she adored him.

He winked at her. "Amongst other things."

They were very much in love.

Blade stole a glance at Lily. She had a sad, wistful expression on her face that made his gut tighten. Was she thinking about Joe? What they might have had?

"Why the long face?" Stitch asked, glancing at him.

Damn. Was he that obvious?

"Thinking about how we're going to get Lily out of Afghanistan."

"You mentioned the Taliban were on your tail," said Stitch. "Could you be more specific? How long have we got?"

Blade smiled at the use of "we." Old habits died hard.

Lily flashed him a nervous look then glanced at Soraya.

"None of the people here like the Taliban." Stitch, as intuitive as ever, guessed what she was thinking. "We try not to get involved in politics."

"We have no poppies, you see," Soraya explained mostly for Lily's benefit. "So there is little to bring them to our village."

"We narrowly avoided walking into an ambush about twenty klicks over the mountain." Blade nodded in the general direction of the hills. "They'll be looking for us, for certain. They know we were there. It won't take long for them to figure out which way we came."

Lily gnawed on her lower lip. Blade knew she was thinking about the goat herder.

He reached over and squeezed her hand. "It's not your fault."

She gave him a watery smile.

Stitch shot Blade an inquisitive look, which he pointedly ignored.

Soraya just smiled at Lily. "Why don't I show you where the bathroom is, and you can get cleaned up while we let the men talk. I'm sure they've got some planning to do."

Blade smiled his thanks as Stitch's wife guided Lily out of the room.

"She's great," Blade said, nodding after them.

"What's going on, Blade?" Stitch came right out with it.

"Nothing."

Damn. He hated that defensive tone of his.

"You sure?" There was a pause, where Stitch studied him. "Tell me you're not sleeping with Spade's girl."

"Fucking hell. Of course not," blurted out Blade. That much was true, at least. During their time in the unit, they'd never lied to each other because trust was everything.

"You like her, though."

"Yeah, she's a nice person." Smart, spirited, motivated, sexy as hell. He coiled his hand into a fist.

"If you really dig her, that's one thing, but don't mess her around." His army buddy knew only too well his 'no strings' policy.

"Stitch, there's nothing going on." He'd made sure of that. He knew not to disrespect the bond they had. He'd never "mess her around" as Stitch put it.

Stitch didn't push it, but Blade could tell he wasn't convinced.

"Why does she think it's her fault?" he asked, changing the topic.

Blade told him what had happened at the ruins.

Stitch shook his head. "That's a tough call. I'd have done the same thing. Better not to take a chance. Remember those Iraqi kids back in 2011? We let them go—almost cost us our lives."

Blade nodded. That had been a close shave. The kids had run straight to the Iraqi soldiers. Minutes later, the team had a full-on firefight on their hands. Ricky had taken a bullet in the shoulder, and they only just managed to get the upper hand and get to the emergency rendezvous point on time.

Kids were different, though. He couldn't kill a kid. None of them could, even if it meant getting shot up.

"Did you know Spade was suffering from PTSD?"

Stitch looked shifty. "I suspected something was up, but I figured if it was bad enough, he'd get help."

Blade shook his head. "He didn't. Lily said he was having nightmares—bad ones." He left out the strangling incident. Spade wouldn't want anyone knowing about that.

"I had no idea it was so bad. He kept that under wraps, didn't he?"

They talked about Lily, and how she'd come to be captured. Stitch was interested in her work on *Hawkeye*.

"Excellent." Respect tinged his voice. "It at least gives the Afghans a fighting chance. The Taliban wreak havoc on these rural communities. I've seen it happen. I've helped pick up the pieces."

They discussed the situation in Afghanistan for a while longer, then Stitch downed the last of his tea. "Okay, buddy. Time to work. Let's talk about logistics."

"You mentioned a vehicle?"

"Yeah, I've got an old Land Rover—ex-US army, as luck would have it—bought at a sale in Kabul last month. I can drive you to Kabul, if you want."

"You sure?" Stitch had gone AWOL to get away from the violence. The last thing he wanted to do was drag him back into it.

The sides of his eyes crinkled. "I'm sure. Not much excitement around here."

He had a pregnant wife. Blade could never live with himself if anything happened to Stitch. "I don't want to put you in the shit. We can manage. You don't have to get involved."

"I want to. For Spade."

Blade nodded.

It was how he'd felt too.

CHAPTER 22

*W*hile Blade and Stitch plotted their escape, Lily helped Soraya warm up two enormous buckets of water in the stone washroom adjoining the house.

"You can wash here. I've laid out some clothes for you to wear afterward. You won't want to get back into those." She wrinkled her nose as what Lily was wearing.

Lily laughed. She was so refreshingly genuine. "Thank you. Are you sure you don't mind?" The simple skirt and blouse were pretty enough, but not bright or stylish enough to attracted undue attention.

"Of course not."

"You know I can't return them."

Soraya waved away the words with a flick of her hand then left Lily to bathe.

God, it felt so good to be clean.

She took her time, luxuriating in the hot water and the scented homemade soap. She washed her hair then poured water over it, the stress of the last few days rinsing away with the suds.

When she'd finished, she went back to the house, where

Soraya worked in the kitchen. The air carried the scent of cumin and coriander. Whatever bubbled in the pot smelled delicious.

The men were still hunched together in the living area, talking in hushed tones.

"Can I give you a hand?"

Soraya smiled, her hands skillfully patting dough into rounds for flatbreads. She gestured toward a bowl of fresh vegetables. "You could prepare the salad."

Lily began chopping cucumbers and tomatoes. "I can't tell you what a relief it is to be clean again."

Soraya laughed, her unusually green eyes lighting up. With her smooth skin, raised cheekbones, and slanted cat eyes, she was gorgeous—exotic by Western standards. Even covered with an apron and several weeks pregnant, her beauty was striking.

Lily felt quite bland beside her.

"How long have you been traveling?" Soraya began cooking the flatbreads. She moved with a natural rhythm around the kitchen.

Lily stopped chopping. "I was captured four days ago on my way to the airport." A shiver shot through her. She'd never forget the rough hands, snarling voices, confusion. "Blade rescued me from a cave, high in the mountains, and we've been on the run ever since."

"Did they hurt you?" Soraya's eyes clouded with concern.

"No, I was lucky. They didn't have a chance before I was rescued."

"By your hero soldier." She gave a sly smile.

Lily felt the heat steal into her cheeks.

"He looks after you well."

Lily wasn't sure what she meant. "Er… Yes, he's been very attentive."

"Handsome, too," she added with a mischievous smile.

"I suppose he is." Lily stared diligently at the cutting board.

"I think he cares for you. I see it when he looks at you."

Lily's heart did a strange flip-flop. She glanced up at Soraya. "Do you think so?"

She nodded while flipping the flatbreads. "How do you feel about him?"

Okay, now her face was on fire.

"I'm sorry," Soraya said, "My English is not so good, so I am quite direct. I hope I haven't offended you?"

Lily got the impression her English was *much* better than she made out.

"Not at all, and your English is outstanding. It's definitely better than my Pashto or Dari." She chuckled ruefully at her shortcomings. Ten months in Kabul, and she couldn't utter more than a few basic sentences. Languages were not her thing.

Soraya smiled modestly at the compliment. "I was fortunate to attend the International School in Kabul. My father, being an elder in our village, placed great value on education." Her smile faded slightly, her gaze lowering. "But that was before the Taliban's resurgence. Now, females are barred from continuing their education past a certain grade."

"That's incredibly sad." Lily had read about the potential rollback of women's rights, including the proposed closure of schools for girls and restrictions on women's public participation. "It will be a huge loss, not just for the women and girls but for the entire country."

"Yes, it will be a setback." She slid the breads out of the pan onto a rack to cool. "But we will find ways to keep learning. Our thirst for knowledge hasn't diminished."

Lily turned her attention to the tomato. "I'm relieved to hear it. Education is a right, not a privilege to be taken away."

"Let's talk about happier things," Soraya said, now

simmering lamb with onions and a melody of spices. It smelled glorious. "Are you in love with your American soldier?"

Holy shit.

The woman sure as hell didn't mince her words, language barrier or not.

"Of course not. I've only known him for three days."

"But you know Stitch?" Her eyes filled with confusion. "How come you don't know his friend?"

Lily sighed. "It's complicated. I knew about Blade but didn't *know* him."

"Ah," she smiled and nodded. "He was your boyfriend's friend, yes?"

"Best friend, yeah."

"But you didn't know him?" She furrowed her brow.

Lily stared at her. What the hell. Why not tell Soraya the story? It wasn't like she was going to see her again, anyway, and it felt good to talk to someone about the mash-up of emotions she'd been experiencing.

"I met him once, a long time ago."

Soraya stirred the stew, nodding encouragingly.

"I didn't much like him. I thought he was cocky, self-assured, and one of the most arrogant men I'd ever met."

Soraya laughed. "But you were mistaken?"

"Very. He's not like that at all."

"I understand. He has made a strong impression on you, yes?"

Lily nodded miserably. Strong was an understatement. Heart-racing, heat-provoking, leg-weakening. Any—or all—of those would be more appropriate. Not to mention the effect he had on other areas of her anatomy.

Soraya shrugged. "The past is the past, we cannot change it. It's the present that's important. You still have control over that. You can decide what happens next with you and this handsome, arrogant man."

Lily's heart twisted painfully. "There can be no future for us. Spade was his best friend. Blade won't betray his memory."

"That's a shame." Soraya pursed her lips. "You two look good together."

She shrugged. It was what it was. "I feel so safe around him. Maybe I'm mistaking that for attraction."

"Having a man capable of protecting you is very attractive." Soraya nodded knowingly. "That's what attracted me to Stitch when he first came to my village. He was here asking questions about the Taliban and seemed so powerful. So... how do you say? Macho?"

Lily nodded.

Yeah. Macho was a good way to describe him.

Them.

Blade.

She felt a surge of longing so strong it almost made her wince, but Soraya hadn't noticed. "Yet he wasn't aggressive like the other soldiers I'd met. He was kind. I could see it in his eyes."

"Blade said that's how you two met." An odd match, but at the same time, they were so perfect for each other.

"My father was ill, and Stitch treated him with an antibiotic. I thanked him by cooking a meal for him and his friends. After that, I knew he was the man for me."

"But he went away again?" Lily had thought they'd only gotten together when Stitch had gone AWOL.

Soraya looked up. "He was in a bad way when he came back. The Taliban killed his friends. He'd witnessed it and had been unable to help them. You can imagine how a doctor might feel after that. Badly in need of a break, he left his unit. He needed time to emotionally heal and didn't want anyone to know where he was. My father, who is a very important man in the village, took him in. We hid him for weeks, until he recovered."

"That was very brave of your father."

"He is a brave man."

"What happened then?"

"Stitch became part of the family. It helped that he spoke Pashto. He helped my father, treated people in the village—everybody fell in love with him."

Lily could see that happening. Stitch, with his good looks, wide smile, and easy charm would easily have integrated himself into the community.

"Including you?" It was a romantic story.

"My father was against the union, at first." Soraya checked the stew. "But eventually he came around."

"I'm glad it worked out for you," Lily said wistfully. She dumped the chopped tomatoes into the bowl.

"Maybe it will work out for you and your soldier man too."

"I don't think that's going to happen."

Soraya gave one of her enigmatic smiles. "Don't lose hope. Perhaps he just needs to get used to the idea."

* * *

Lily didn't know when last she'd had such a nice time. It seemed surreal, considering their situation, but Blade and Stitch's joking comradery made her forget, just for a moment, her life was in danger.

"I first met Blade when I joined the army," Stitch told them at lunch. "I'd come straight from med school and didn't know the first thing about soldiering."

"You weren't so bad." Blade smiled.

"I was a complete rookie." He rolled his eyes.

Blade chuckled. "Luckily for you, you were a fast learner."

"Still, I always preferred patching guys up to killing them." Soraya put her hand over her husband's.

Not only was Stitch as gorgeous as Blade, but he was a decent guy too. Moralistic and kind. It was hard to imagine him killing people.

"When we lost Spade," his voice dropped. "I was messed up. He bled out on that mountain pass, and I was powerless to save him."

"That makes two of us," Blade murmured.

"I knew I had to get out of there," he said. "Away from the stench of death. So I came here. To the village. To Soraya."

She flushed, but her eyes were shining. "You were lost, and we took you in."

He nodded, his gaze dropping to her baby bump. "And now we're starting a family. Strange how life works out. If it hadn't been for the ambush—"

"I'm glad something good came out of it." Lily glanced at Blade. The look of utter devastation in his eyes made her heart skip a beat. An urge to make him see it wasn't his fault swept over her. He wasn't responsible for what happened. Wasn't to blame for the guide selling them out.

She wanted to eradicate his guilt and unhappiness. Replace it with something else. Something good and wholesome and pure.

He met her gaze. The pain in his eyes vanished, exchanged for a brief flash of longing. But then it was gone, so quickly she'd wondered if she'd imagined it. He looked down at his plate and went back to eating his meal.

CHAPTER 23

*A*fter helping Soraya clean up, Lily returned to the living area. "Where's Stitch?"

Blade looked up from the map and fixed his deep blue eyes on her. "He had patients to check up on. He'll be gone for a couple of hours."

"Oh." She hovered, unsure what to do. There were some books in the corner, so she went to take a closer look, but they were all in Pashto.

"Lily, I think we should talk."

"What about?" She sank to her knees and perched on the cushion next to him. "How we're going to get out of here?"

"Among other things."

A surge of something she couldn't quite explain erupted from inside her.

"Tomorrow is going to be extremely dangerous," he said.

"I know." The river crossing was fraught with danger. It was a natural checkpoint, so they'd decided to drive across, even though they'd be fully exposed, at risk of being recognized. "Soraya's given me a full-length robe, so they won't see my face."

"That's good." He fell silent, his gaze penetrating.

She swallowed. "Is something wrong?"

He inhaled, and she watched his broad chest expand. "While Stitch drives you across, I'll hide in the back."

"Is that wise?" She had no idea what they'd been planning, but the Land Rover she'd seen outside didn't look like it had enough hiding places for a man Blade's size. "What if they search our vehicle?"

"It's risky. I'm hard to miss."

He had that right. It wasn't as if he was a small man who could fit into a footwell, or under the spare tire. He was all brawn and bulk and bulging muscles. Six feet four or five of raw power.

"Maybe you should drive."

He tilted his head, acknowledging her idea. "I think Stitch passes for a better local, don't you? Plus, he speaks the lingo."

Lily suddenly found it hard to breathe. "What if they spot you?"

"We have a game plan."

She nodded, knowing deep down she wasn't going to like this.

"If I get noticed, Stitch is going to say I flagged you down a mile back and threatened you at gunpoint to give me a ride. You had no choice. That should get you off the hook."

Lily swallow, her mouth suddenly dry. "What about you?"

He didn't meet her gaze. "I'll run for it. There's plenty of foliage either side of the river. I'll dive in if I have to. It'll be fine."

She wasn't so sure.

"That's only if they find you, right? I mean it's more likely they won't, that we'll get through."

"That's right." His offhanded manner made her very uneasy.

A shock ran though her.

166

This could be her last chance to tell him how grateful she was.

"Blade," she whispered. "I just want you to know—in case anything happens, which it won't—I'm so thankful for what you've done. Bringing me here. Rescuing me from that cave. Looking after me. I won't ever forget it."

Won't forget *him*.

Lily didn't know whether he saw it in her eyes or was responding to her words, but he edged closer, so close she could see the different color flecks of blue in his eyes.

Suddenly, she was drowning, floundering in the desire that she saw there. Blue flames calling to her, drawing her in.

"Blade, if we don't make it—"

He didn't wait for her to finish. With a low moan, he looped a big hand around her neck and pulled her toward him. The whole cushion moved, shifting her closer until she was practically sitting on his lap.

"Fuck, Lily. *Fuck*."

She knew what he meant. She felt it too, this magnetic pull neither of them could control. It seemed to drive them together no matter how hard they fought it.

Not even Joe's memory could prevent it from happening.

Or maybe it was because of it.

When they left here tomorrow, they might not make it home. Might not get another chance.

Lily leaned in, telling him it was okay, that she also felt it. Also wanted it.

She touched her lips to his, feeling him resist for half a second before exhaling. His hand tightened behind her neck, tilting her head and pulling her closer. Blade's lips crashed against her, and he growled like an injured bear, leaving her no doubt who was in control.

Lily's heart surged, pulse racing erratically. She gave up trying to fight her feelings. This was it—what she'd wanted since that first kiss in the cabin when she'd thought he was Joe.

A sob burst from her as they locked together. Heat flowed between them. Scorching, flaming, bursting sparks that only grew stronger the more they kissed.

Holy shit, she was burning alive.

Molten lava surged through her blood, making her pulse at her very core. She pushed aside thoughts of the men hunting her, the fear plaguing her, the anxiety weighing on her about tomorrow's escape. All she felt was delicious, gut-wrenching desire, proof of what it meant to be alive, to be here with Blade.

Lily had no idea how she ended up kneeling over him, reveling in the feel of his thick thighs beneath hers and basking in the sensation of his hands reaching under her blouse, spreading over her back, crushing her against his rock-hard torso.

He groaned again, a low guttural sound at the back of his throat that sent delicious shivers through her.

His shoulders tensed under her hands. Desperate to get closer, she hung on to him, writhed against him. Wished their clothing would just disappear and he would take her right then, right there. With a ragged gasp, she hiked her skirt up and over his legs, so she could feel him properly.

Holy smoke, he was hard, straining against the material of his cargo pants. Against her.

"Christ, Lily," he groaned. "I want you so bad. Is this okay?" Sapphire flames blasted into her, begging her to say yes.

Seriously, she had no problem with that.

"Yes," she whispered, punctuating the word with a nod.

"Are you… I mean, can we…?"

His voice was ragged, his hands melting over her back, snaking under her bra strap. She could hardly think.

She gave a nod. "Once a month shot. We're good."

It was like he'd been unleashed. Any thought of holding back had vanished, and it was just him and her.

Feverish now, he reclaimed her lips and ravished her so hard, so passionately, her head spun when they broke for air.

He gripped her ass and positioned her on top of his straining cock. Even though it was buried beneath his clothing, she could tell he was huge. For a panicked second, she wondered if it would fit. Joe hadn't been as big.

Then again, she was so ready to find out.

He massaged her ass, making her writhe on top of him.

God, she wanted him so bad she could scarcely contain herself. Never had she felt so utterly abandoned, so out of control, as she did with this man.

Blade yanked her blouse over her head then cupped her breasts over the lace, the friction exquisite. He ran his thumbs over her nipples until she panted under his ministrations.

Momentarily unable to speak, she moaned.

He gazed into her eyes, and the deep swirling pools of blue darkened. "God, Lily, you're so beautiful."

His words made her sing.

"More." The plea came as a sigh.

He unclasped her bra, pulled the straps down her arms, then tossed it aside.

Cool air and hot breath mingled on her naked flesh, her pleasure building by the second. He caressed her breasts with his callused hands, driving her wild.

It felt *so* good.

He traced circles around her nipples, his featherlight touch at once frustrating and exhilarating. A few flicks made them somehow more sensitive, more demanding. She gasped as he squeezed them into hard buds, first gently, then with more urgency.

169

She yelped as heat flooded her pussy, like invisible wires sending electrical impulses south. It was a miracle she didn't come right then.

Bending his head, he drew one nipple into his mouth and sucked on it. She arched her back and moaned, the sound throaty and deep, tinged with longing.

His biceps flexed under her hands as he repositioned her. When he turned his hot mouth to her other breast, Lily thought she was going to die.

What a wonderful way to go.

When she was about to combust, he looked up, his heated gaze boring a hole right thought her. There was no chance of stopping now. They both wanted this, both needed it.

She stared into his soul and in turn opened hers to him, trusting him with her vulnerabilities, allowing him to read all the emotions running through her mind, all the desires surging through her body. Though unwilling and unable to stop such an intimate exchange, it terrified her to open herself up like this again, when tomorrow—

She didn't want to think about tomorrow.

His eyes burned, blazing with a depth of emotion that made her shiver. She clawed at his chest, gripping handfuls of T-shirt, desperate to get rid of all barriers between them.

In one move, he peeled it off and tossed it aside. They collided again, and she exulted in the contact, his skin soft velvet covering solid steel.

His lips slanted against hers, softer now. At the same time his fingers slid under her panties then he pulled them aside. Straddling him left her wide open to his touch, and she was so wet, so ready. There was no resistance at all. His finger slid straight inside her, filling a space that was crying out for his touch.

He growled against her mouth, swallowing her moan. She

rocked her hips, grinding against his hand, every atom of her body on fire.

She didn't know it could feel like this. So frantic.

So desperate.

She clung to him as his thumb began to stroke her clit, driving her to the edge. She gyrated and bore down, needing more. Craving release. Unwilling to slow down until his cock could fill her.

Then he slid his finger back out.

"No!" It was a half-gasp, half-moan.

"Wait for me, sweetheart." Blade shifted her to unfasten and lower his pants. He tugged them and his boxers down to his knees, grabbed her ass, then positioned her over him.

The anticipation was killing her. She heard herself whimpering, begging... Then he entered her.

Lily squealed as his cock took the place of his finger. Hard and thick and swollen with need, filling her so completely she thought she'd split open.

He snarled and thrust upward, driving her into another level of ecstasy. How was such pleasure possible? She was lost, heading toward a place she'd never been before. Her hands tangled in his hair, her only tether to reality as the rest of her body was somewhere unimaginable.

Every stroke made her tremble from temples to toes. Every thrust sent sparks flying from her core to her extremities. She clung to him, whimpering with each surge, flying higher and faster into the unknown.

"Oh, God," Lily cried out when she didn't think I could take it anymore. "Oh, *God*. Blade."

"Come with me, baby," he murmured, hauling her down as he jerked upwards, sending spasms through her, unleashing the explosion that had been building since their first kiss.

She came hard, screaming with the release. Rapid convulsluts consumed her. She jerked spasmodically, crying out his name and digging her fingers into his back.

He held her tight against him, gripping her waist, pistoning his hips. His body went rigid, his head tipped back, and he roared as he went over the edge. She kissed him hard as he exploded inside her, thinking it was the perfect way to end this perfect union.

But it wasn't over.

The spasms lingered, extended by his primitive thrusts, building again by his renewed attention to her breasts. He sucked a nipple into his mouth and teased it with his teeth while reaching between her legs. Still pumping, still driving, he stroked her clit. The surge built with dizzying speed and delirious desperation until she shattered, her body at once thrumming with electricity and numbed into immobility.

She collapsed on top of him, a swirling pool of roiling emotion.

He held her for a long while. She couldn't move, couldn't speak. She lay in his arms, savoring the moment, cataloging every feeling, every sensation, as the memory might have to last a lifetime. What they'd just shared was incredible, and knowing it may never happen again… It was too intense. She began to sob, her tears a mixture of emotion and desire and overwhelming release.

"Shh." He kissed the wet trails on her cheeks then the drops on her eyelashes. Finally, his mouth found her lips.

It was different now. Gentle, tender. It felt like they'd both given everything and now were broken. There was nothing to hide, no walls between them. Just brutal honesty and raw emotion.

He knew. Just like she knew.

Whatever happened tomorrow, they'd always have this.

CHAPTER 24

*B*lade checked his backpack, stopping every now and then to kiss Lily full on the lips before carrying on. It felt like the most natural thing in the world.

Even though it wasn't.

As far as mistakes went, this was probably the biggest fucking one he'd ever made. But it was worth it. *She* was worth it.

Hell, he'd do it again in a heartbeat if he got the opportunity.

Lily laughed and swatted him away. "You have to stay focused."

She wasn't wrong.

Still, it was fun to pretend, even if for a short time.

Blade went back to sorting his pack. He was traveling light, as the damn thing needed to fit in the spare tire well of Stitch's Land Rover—along with the tire. He hoped to hell they didn't search the vehicle at the checkpoint.

The odds of them getting through were about fifty-fifty. Not great, but he and Stitch had ruled out all the other options. The river was wild and flowing fast, the land around

It built up and populated. They couldn't cross without a boat, which would be seen, making them sitting ducks. And they couldn't walk. Without a vehicle, they wouldn't have a hope in hell of getting Lily to Kabul.

They'd both freshened up after their frantic love making, and he'd dressed back in his army fatigues, ready for the arduous journey ahead. They were leaving at first light to catch the guards before they changed shift, when they were dopey with fatigue, not inclined to work hard, and unlikely to react fast if the shit hit the fan.

Lily was curled up on a cushion, watching him. Blade couldn't believe how easy it was with her. Like he'd been doing this all his life.

He loved her lingering kisses, her soft hugs, and the way her eyes shone as she looked at him. Nobody had looked at him like that in a *long* time.

Nobody he'd cared about, *ever*.

It was a heady feeling.

He was still reeling from her encasing him. She was so tight, so warm. Shit, he was getting a hard on just thinking about it. He crouched, kissed her again, then muttered, "Can't help it."

She pulled him close. Each moment felt loaded, like it could be their last. They were both trying to make the most of it, clinging to what little time they had.

The sound of the front door opening shook them apart. Blade stood and turned away to tighten the straps on his pack. Lily straightened her skirt and looked up as Stitch walked in.

"Hey, you two. Feeling better?"

Blade turned. "Yeah, rested up. Ready to go."

"I think so." Lily smiled nervously at Stitch.

"Great. Soraya's on her way. We'll have supper then turn in early, that way we can head off at first light."

Blade gave a steady nod. "Sounds like a plan."

Dinner was more subdued than lunch, the air thick with a sense of expectancy. Soraya took Lily upstairs, leaving the guys to talk. Blade watched her go, his stomach in knots.

He wanted to protect her so goddamn badly, yet he didn't know if he could. She'd been through so much. First she's lost her parents and home. Then she'd lost Joe. After that, she'd been kidnapped and imprisoned. Her rescue resulted in hiking endlessly, nearly freezing to death, and watching him kill people—not to mention suffering the constant swell of fear. She'd endured a week of hell getting to this point.

What if it all went to shit now?

"Don't do that," Stitch said, quietly.

"Huh?"

"Don't think about the what ifs. Stay focused on the plan."

He nodded. Stitch was right. Letting his mind wander wouldn't do any good.

Except he suddenly had so much more to hang on to.

He had Lily.

"I'm focused," he muttered, scowling at Stitch. "Listen, if it all goes to hell and I get shot, you have to make sure she gets away."

Stitch knew better than to argue. They'd made their peace with death a long time ago, all of them. Doing what they had done for a living, you couldn't not.

Still, none of them wanted to go.

"I'll do my best," he promised.

Blade gave a satisfied nod. "Thanks, Stitch."

"No problem."

* * *

"Nobody will recognize me in that," Lily said as Soraya held up a traditional Afghani burqa. It was a two-piece ensemble made from a high quality synthetic black material and included a meshed veil that covered her face.

"That's the plan." Soraya smiled and placed it on the bed, which was little more than a double mattress on the floor. There was a thick rug beneath it to keep out the cold, and colorful scatter cushions over the top.

Lily tried it on. "It's perfect." She thanked her and took the burqa downstairs.

Soraya gave them some blankets, and Stitch left the coals to burn down in the fireplace, so the room was toasty warm.

"See you at oh-five-hundred," he said before heading to bed with his wife.

The house grew quiet. Without electricity, they could see the stars shining brightly through the windows. Once they were certain their hosts had gone to bed, Lily scampered over to Blade and curled up against him. There was no urgency now, no rush. They were both spent from earlier in the day, and they didn't want to make noise and disturb their hosts, not after they'd been so kind and hospitable.

Lily lay in Blade's arms, savoring his strength, feeling safe for what might be the last time. He stroked her hair, his arm wrapped around her.

"I'm scared," she whispered.

He kissed her and held her tight. "I won't let anything happen to you."

"Promise?"

"I promise."

But it was the words he didn't say that had her worried.

* * *

BLADE WOKE her up before dawn, whispering in her ear.

"It's time to get ready."

She yawned, stretched, then kissed him lazily on the

mouth. He lingered, closing his eyes briefly as if trying to commit the moment to memory, then got up.

A few moments later, Stitch walked into the room, followed by Soraya. She made coffee, rich and black, and they sipped it while they got ready.

Lily put on the burqa, and with Soraya's help, attached the veil over her face. Now she was invisible.

Blade said very little as they loaded the Land Rover. His expression was grim, his shoulders tense, and he walked around with his hands coiled in fists.

This was a high-risk strategy, she knew that.

They might even get killed.

Except what was the alternative? An ambush? Dying on a dusty mountain path, like Joe. Lily swallowed and held back her fear as she said goodbye to Soraya.

"Thank you for helping us," she whispered. "I'll never forget it."

"It's important. We have to get you out of Afghanistan and make sure your system is safe."

Lily hugged her hard. "We'll send Stitch home to you in one piece, I promise."

"*Inshallah*," Soraya whispered.

God willing.

CHAPTER 25

*G*oddamn it.

This was *bad*.

His stomach was knotted so tight, it felt like a fuse wired to an unexploded bomb, each second ticking toward an inevitable detonation.

"Checkpoint is ten klicks south," Stitch called as they took the bumpy dirt road out of the village. The Land Rover bounced along, kicking up a cloud of dust behind them.

The only thing that mattered was getting Lily across undetected. He had to admit, she didn't look like a western woman. Soraya had done a fantastic job hiding her blonde hair. Add the veil, and she'd be unrecognizable.

He met her gaze in the rearview mirror. The eyeliner made her brown eyes seem enormous and brought out the gold flecks in her irises. He knew she was scared, saw it in the way she looked at him—a silent plea, like she wanted to fly straight into his arms.

If only.

Shit. She was tearing him apart.

Normally, he kept a professional distance from hostages.

They did what he said, and he helped as best he could. But with her... He heaved a silent sigh.

Lily was different.

Breaking eye contact, he tried to focus on the operation ahead. If anything, he was the more vulnerable party. Stitch, in his traditional clothes, blended right in, while he, with his army fatigues, gear and rifle, looked exactly like what he was.

The enemy.

Still, he wasn't prepared to abandon his gear for the sake of a disguise that probably wouldn't work anyway. He didn't have the dark, bearded looks of the Afghan men, and his physique practically screamed military. If they were stopped and searched, he'd much rather be ready for it than not.

The Land Rover featured a spacious backseat, and a glass partition separated it from the front, where Stitch and Lily sat side by side. Initially, they kept the divider open for easy conversation, but as they neared the checkpoint, Stitch slid it shut, concealing their hidden passenger in the back to avoid raising the guards' suspicions.

Lily pulled up her face veil and glanced once more in the mirror. He shook his head. No one must know he was there.

She turned her gaze forward, took a deep breath, and stiffened her shoulders.

How fucking brave was she? After all she'd been through.

A real trooper.

Having evaded the Taliban for so long, they were now heading straight for them. It seemed counter-intuitive, but it was the quickest way to get Lily to Kabul, where they'd be able to fly her out.

Blade hunkered down and pulled a dark blanket over himself. His backpack was stored in the spare tire well in the trunk area, and his rifle was on his lap, ready to fire. It was virtually invisible without a thorough search.

Plan A was for them to get through the checkpoint unnoticed. If not and Blade was discovered, Plan B was for them to claim he'd hijacked them and they were transporting him under duress.

He'd be arrested, but they might make it through.

They hadn't told Lily that part. If it came to it, he prayed she'd go along with it.

Traffic backed up as they approached the bridge. Stitch, with his flawless Pashto, would quite easily be accepted as a local villager. The Land Rover posed a small problem since it was an ex-army vehicle, but since the Americans had cleared out of the country, there were a lot of similar vehicles about. It wasn't a stretch that a respectable Afghan doctor had purchased one on the cheap.

Just in case, Stitch had an AK hidden beside the handbrake and a combat knife concealed under his robes.

"One klick out," Stitch said for his benefit.

He had to rely on his buddy's updates because he couldn't see shit with his head under the blanket. Adrenaline surged, elevating his heart rate, but he controlled it by concentrating on his breathing.

"Eight guards spread out along the checkpoint. Two more in the hut." Stitch's voice was steady, years of training kicking in.

Fuck.

Ten armed men were too many to take out if there was a problem. They could all be killed in the ensuing gunfight, along with Lily and a bunch of innocent civilians.

"I've got your back, buddy." Stitch had come to the same conclusion.

Blade didn't doubt it. He'd do the same if the roles were reversed.

He prayed it wouldn't come to that.

"Contact," Stitch murmured. "Guard approaching driver's window."

The locational references were so Blade had the best chance of escape if shit hit the fan.

He hunkered down, hands on his weapon, forcing his body to relax. No movement. Nothing to arouse their suspicion.

A tap on the window. He heard Stitch slide it down. There was an exchange of words, but it was all in Pashto. Blade couldn't follow what they were saying.

The guard said something about the woman. He caught that, and went cold.

Stitch replied, and there was a rustling of papers. He was showing the guards his documents. Forged, on his part, and Soraya's for Lily.

Blade tensed. Were they going to have a problem?

Footsteps around the vehicle, a tap on the passenger window.

"Don't move," Stitch whispered to her. "Keep your eyes down."

The guard tapped again, harder this time, then barked an order. He wanted Lily to get out of the Land Rover.

"What do I do?" she whispered.

"Stay put." Stitch knew as well as he did, that once they got out of the car, they were as good as done for. It was a lot easier to get away if you were still in your vehicle.

Stitch leaned across Lily, putting his hand on his weapon as he did so, and shouted at the guard. It was something along the lines of: What are you doing? My wife and I want to go shopping in Kabul.

That was their cover story.

The guard kept trying the door, but Stitch wouldn't unlock it.

Then he banged on it with the butt of his rifle. There was no mistaking his meaning. He wanted Lily to get out.

Well, that was never going to happen.

The guard moved to the rear door and tried to open that one. Blade was seconds away from being discovered.

"Now," murmured Stitch.

Without removing the blanket, Blade pulled the trigger and the glass window exploded. Lily screamed, and the checkpoint guard reeled backward, his face a bloody mess.

"Stitch, make sure you both get out of here!" Blade opened the door.

Lily spun round. "No!"

Stitch pulled her roughly back. "Stay still. Put up your hands."

"Hands up? Why?"

"Lily, listen to Stitch."

She raised her hands, her face ashen. Stitch did the same, leaving his gun where it was.

Nine armed guards sprinted toward them, weapons raised. It was a miracle they hadn't opened fire.

"You sure?" Stitch asked, over his shoulder.

"Stick to the story." Blade wasn't going to create a bloodbath.

Lily was crying now.

"Take care of her."

Stitch nodded.

Blade walked away from the car, his hands in the air.

CHAPTER 26

"They're going to kill him," Lily sobbed, through her tears.

Blade walked onto the bridge, unarmed, his hands in the air. Within seconds, he was surrounded by security personnel, nine lethal assault rifles pointed at his head.

"Not yet," Stitch said, grimly. "They'll want to know what he's up to first."

Blade was pushed face-down into the dirt. One of the guards put his foot on his head. They yanked his hands behind his back to handcuff him.

"Oh, God." Lily couldn't breathe.

This couldn't be happening.

Two men grabbed Blade roughly by the arms, hauled him to his feet, then dragged him off.

"I should have known he'd do this." Stitch bashed his hand against the steering wheel.

"You mean he *planned* this?" Lily turned on him. "But why? Why would he give himself up like that?"

"To save your life." Stitch's voice was strained and raw. "And mine. That guard knew who you were. If Blade had made a run for it, he would have been shot down in seconds, and so would I because I'd have covered him. There'd be no one to get you to safety. The bastard knew this was the only option."

Lily gasped. Their Land Rover was surrounded by angry-faced guards, rifles drawn. Her head was still spinning after what had happened.

"Oh, Lord."

Stitch kept his hands in the air. "Let me handle this."

One of the guards pulled open the door.

Lily kept her eyes down, hoping they wouldn't notice the tears on her face.

It had all gone terribly, terribly wrong. Blade had sacrificed himself for her and Stitch.

Headstrong, stubborn man.

The scheming bastard had planned for this. *That's* why he'd been so distracted on the drive here.

The guard gestured for Stitch to get out of the vehicle. He did so, hands in the air. She remained in the Land Rover, a guard at her window.

Lily looked up beneath her lashes. She couldn't even see Blade anymore. They'd taken him into the hut.

Stitch had said they wouldn't kill him, not without interrogating him first. But he'd killed one of their soldiers, so they wouldn't go easy on him. Spade had told her what could happen if a Special Forces soldier got caught.

She squeezed her eyes shut, blocking out the million terrifying thoughts flying through her head.

Stitch's voice broke through her thoughts. Glancing sideways, she saw him gesticulating back up the road in the direction they'd come. He was acting out their cover story.

The American soldier had forced them to stop, held them at gunpoint, and made them drive across the checkpoint. His gun was still in the back, see.

The soldier ripped open the back door and retrieved Blade's weapon.

Thankfully, they didn't search the rest of the car.

Another guard peered in the passenger window at her, but she kept her head down like Stitch had told her.

Please don't let him recognize her.

He didn't.

A few minutes later, the guard gestured for Stitch to get back into the car and waved them on their way.

Lily felt weak with relief.

They'd bought it.

Stitch drove slowly and cautiously over the bridge. Once they were clear of the checkpoint, Lily spun on him.

"What's going to happen to him?"

"They'll interrogate him. Find out why he's here."

Torture him, more like.

"Stitch, please. We can't leave him here."

"Blade's a survivor. If anyone can get out of this, it's him." She could hear by the flatness in his voice that he didn't mean it. He was just trying to give her hope.

"You know as well as I do they're going to kill him. After what he did—" She gestured back to the bridge.

Stitch was silent.

"Stop the car. I'm not leaving without Blade." She put her hand on the door handle.

Stitch glanced in the mirror then pulled over. The Land Rover screeched to a stop, dust whirling from beneath the tires. "Lily, listen to me. Blade did this for you. I'm not going to risk your life by going to get him. He wouldn't want that."

Lily stared at him. She was numb. Broken. Destroyed.

Blade was back there, being beaten to a pulp, and she was supposed to just walk away?

Emotion choked her, and she burst into tears. She couldn't help it.

Blade had sacrificed himself for her. He'd willingly given up his life for hers.

"Who does that?" She was crying so hard she could hardly speak. "Who gives up their life for a hostage they barely know."

"A Green Beret," said Stitch simply. "He's just doing his job."

She shook her head, blinded by tears. "They'll kill him."

Stitch scowled, and she noticed how white his knuckles were as he gripped the wheel. "He's trained to withstand interrogation. He'll drag this out. It will take them a while to figure out exactly who he is."

"Do you think they'll realize he rescued me?"

"If they do, they'll question him about you. That'll take some time. Once they figure out you were in the car with me and they let you go—"

He hesitated. "They'll launch a man hunt for the Land Rover."

"Won't they know it's registered to you?"

"I'm not that stupid."

She sniffed. "They can't trace anything back to you?"

"No, Lily. We made sure of that."

She covered her face with her hands. It was too much. "I know what they're going to do to him," she murmured. "Spade told me stories."

Stitch knew too. She could tell by the way he ground his jaw.

Lily imagined Blade being stripped naked and beaten until he was semi-conscious. She pictured him hunched over, his glorious body bruised and broken, eyelids swollen, blood seeping from multiple wounds.

"I think I'm going to be sick."

"Really?"

She nodded and opened the door.

Stitch waited, engine still running, as she threw up the contents of her stomach. Even when she was done, she kept retching.

"Lily, we have to go. We have to put some distance between us and the checkpoint."

He was right. She knew he was right.

Lily gave a surly nod.

Stitch put his foot down and the Land Rover growled into gear. He increased the speed until they were racing toward the road to Kabul.

The miles flashed by. Lily barely noticed. Her head was filled with Blade. How he'd held her. How he'd kissed her.

How he'd given his goddamn life for her.

Stitch said very little, focusing on the road. Twenty minutes later, they turned onto the Kabul highway. It wasn't big enough for a highway, more of a main road with lots of traffic squeezed into two lanes heading in each direction.

Stitch drove a couple of miles toward Kabul, then cursed under his breath, and pulled over into what looked like a make-shift rest area. The only thing there was a small store selling fruit.

Lily turned to him. "What are we doing?"

"Wait here."

He climbed out of the car and approached the store. A man and a woman were standing in front of the fruit display, picking out some fresh produce.

Lily watched as Stitch started talking to them. What the hell was he doing? Grief-stricken, tired, confused, she threw up her hands and leaned back.

She didn't care anymore.

Maybe he was getting supplies, although eating was the last thing on her mind right now.

When he got back to the car, she opened her eyes.

"Are we done?"

"You're getting out."

"What?" She gawked at him. "Why?"

"I'm going back."

She gasped and threw her hands around his neck. "Thank you!"

"Easy now." He disentangled her. "This couple will take you to Kabul. It's probably safer that you're not seen in the Land Rover, anyway."

Lily smiled through her tears.

She was okay with that. More than okay.

If it meant Blade had a chance.

"When you get to Kabul, call Pat. he'll know what to do."

"I will. Thank you, Stitch."

"Good luck, Lily." He paused. "And for what it's worth, I think Spade would have been happy to see you two end up together."

CHAPTER 27

*B*lade had been stripped, his wrists bound, his body thrown unceremoniously to the floor. He lay in filth in a world of pain while the enemy kicked the shit out of him.

"Who are you?" The voice yelled in his ear.

He didn't reply.

Another kick to the ribs, then another, which coincided with a muted crack. He winced.

Fuck, it hurt to breathe.

His left arm, already awkwardly positioned beneath him, felt wrong. A sharp, searing pain confirmed his suspicion—broken, likely from the way they'd twisted and slammed him down earlier.

He tried to curl into a ball but was hauled to his knees.

"What is your name?"

Blade caught a whiff of stale coffee and cigarettes.

A fist connected with his jaw, and he tasted blood. He spat it out at the man's feet. Another blow, this time to his head. He keeled over, seeing stars.

A boot connected with his face, crunching his nose in a

way that caused blood to immediately flood his mouth and dribble down his chin. Darkness encroached on his vision. Maybe he'd pass out. Then he wouldn't feel any more pain.

He welcomed it.

The only thought in his head was Lily. Stitch had gotten her through the checkpoint. She'd be on her way to Kabul right now. To freedom.

Away from the men hunting her.

Away from here.

"Who are you?" the man shouted again.

Being naked and screamed at was supposed to unsettle him, but he'd gone through worse during training. He'd been here before, and that gave him some comfort. This wasn't a new experience for him.

Blade let his head drop and tried to appear as subdued and as feeble as he could. It was what they wanted. If he'd gone all gung-ho and said fuck you, they'd only continue the violence. Better to play into their hands.

"You are U.S. Army." The other man sneered then spat on the floor.

Blade looked contrite, like he'd been found out.

Army was one thing. If they discovered he was Special Forces, they'd assume he'd been part of the hostage rescue. It didn't matter that he was no longer in the unit.

So far, his capture hadn't reached the Taliban leaders up in the mountains who were presumably still searching for them, but it would soon.

When that happened, all bets were off.

When he didn't answer, he got a rifle butt in the head. The shock sent him reeling over onto his side again.

He didn't move, tottering on the edge of consciousness. Maybe they'd think he'd been knocked out.

They kicked him in the back to make sure, so he moaned

incoherently but didn't move. Hopefully, they'd think he was too far gone to continue with the interrogation.

They weren't giving it their all, anyway. It was a half-assed attempt to discover his identity. From what he'd seen so far, these guys were not particularly organized, and there was no clear chain of command. All things that acted in his favor.

Blade curled up in the fetal position on the cold, concrete floor and let the darkness envelope him. There was nothing else he could do right now.

When his head cleared, he'd take stock of his surroundings and try to figure out how the hell to get out before Lily's captors came for him. As long as they didn't know who he really was, he had a fighting chance.

Blade drifted in and out of consciousness. He had no idea how long he lay there. Eventually, he opened his eyes— rather, his one eye that wasn't swollen shut—and looked around. He was in a concrete room, about twenty by twenty, with the door behind him and two windows in front. The blinds were broken, causing thin shards of light to shoot across the floor.

It was still daylight.

He grimaced as he tried to move.

Fuck, everything hurt.

They'd definitely busted a rib. Probably his collarbone too. He tried to move, then gasped as a deep, searing pain radiated through his left arm.

Christ.

His hands were still tied together, but he couldn't move the right one without the left exploding in agony. Eyes watering, he added that to the injury list.

The room tilted a little. The wooziness was from a concussion caused by the repeated kicks to the head. At least it was no longer pounding like a goddamn jackhammer. That was a good sign.

After several false starts, he managed to get himself into a sitting position. It took a few wheezing seconds to recover. Using the wall for support, Blade staggered to his feet.

First thing's first. Check the door and windows. He didn't think they'd be stupid enough to leave them open, but you never knew.

The door was locked, the windows didn't open.

Shit.

Outside was a yard of some sort.

"Well, I'll be…" This wasn't a secure compound. It was a house, and he was looking out onto a barren backyard. As he watched, an armed guard walked by.

Blade pulled back behind the blind. The man didn't spot him.

After a moment, he peered through the slats again, wincing at the explosion of pain in his left arm. He couldn't see anyone else. The guard lit up a cigarette and had a smoke.

Common sense told him there would be more guards, maybe in the house. Maybe on rotation. Soon enough, a chief interrogator from Kabul would arrive and take over.

He did not want to be around for that.

If he was going to get the hell out of here, now was his chance. The house was relatively insecure, there were no bars on the windows, and the door didn't appear to be reinforced.

Blade looked around for a weapon, but there was nothing in the room except a wooden chair and a small puddle of fresh blood, which belonged to him.

He stumbled back to the window. It was old style glass, thin, but not shatterproof. That gave him an idea.

The guard finished his smoke and disappeared.

Blade waited, counting the seconds until he came back again.

Three hundred Mississippis.

Five minutes.

That's how long it took to patrol the perimeter.

As soon as he disappeared the second time, Blade pulled the blind aside and clenched his hands together. He punched a small square out of the window.

There was a soft tinkle as the tiny shards landed on the dirt outside.

He waited, but no one came.

Without wasting any more time, he used the shards that remained in the pane to saw through his plastic ties. They separated with a snap, but the sudden jolt to his left arm nearly made him pass out.

Gritting his teeth, he contemplated his options. Kick down the door or go through the window. Both were risky. Breaking all that glass would draw the guard, but kicking down the door would draw the attention of whoever was still in the house.

He chose the second option.

Blade picked up the chair and using his good arm, hurled it at the window. Glass shattered, leaving dangerous shards glinting around the edges. Pulling the blind off its railing, he knocked out most of the glass and clambered out. Despite this, it still cut his hands and legs.

As expected, he heard the sound of running footsteps, but made it to the corner of the house in time to stick out his fist and send the guard flying.

He bent down to pick up the fallen AK-47.

Shit, if only he could use his left arm. He was still wrestling with it when he heard a voice shout, "Put down the weapon!"

Slowly, he turned to see two more guards standing in the doorway, pointing their semi-automatics at him.

Fuck.

He considered taking them both out, but knew the odds were against him. On the other hand, surrendering would mean getting hauled back inside and given another beating, and this time they wouldn't be so lenient.

He hesitated, feeling strangely detached, like he was in someone else's body. The two men watched him warily, waiting to see what he'd do.

Their instructions were to guard him, not kill him. He might have information that was useful, failing which, he could be ransomed.

What these guys didn't know was the Taliban leaders wouldn't be thinking along the same lines. That decided it for him.

Damn it all.

He wasn't going to give them the satisfaction.

Blade reached for the trigger.

CHAPTER 28

*B*lade was about to pull the trigger, when he heard a familiar voice yell, "Get down!"

He threw himself hard to the ground.

A volley of shots from behind drilled into the two guards, sending them flying. The next minute, an arm reached out and grabbed him.

Stitch.

"What the fuck are you doing here?" he snarled, grimacing at the pain in his side. "You're supposed to be with Lily."

"Relax. Lily's fine. She's on her way to Kabul."

He crumpled, leaning against his friend.

"Christ, they've done a number on you."

He grunted in response.

"Let's get you out of here." Stitch helped him back to the Land Rover parked around the corner, out of sight.

"You crazy bastard, you were going to go for it, weren't you?"

Blade gave a snort. "Always wanted to go out in a blaze of glory."

Stitch shook his head. "Get in, this isn't over yet." Shouts and gunfire sounded behind them. "Let's get the fuck out of here."

Stitch put his foot down, nearly flattening two Taliban fighters in the process. They dived out of the way just in time.

The Land Rover raced down the suburban street, spraying their pursuers with dust and pebbles. Blade turned and saw the two soldiers pick themselves up off the ground. Soon, they were joined by two more. All four raised their weapons and fired at the speeding Land Rover. The back window exploded, shattering glass fragments over the back of his head.

He ducked, groaning at the pain in his rib and shoulder. His left arm hung limply at his side. Stitch gave a cackle and gave them the finger.

"Thanks, pal," Blade said, once they'd put some distance between themselves and the house where he'd been held captive. "I owe you one."

"Don't mention it. You'd do the same for me."

It was true, he would. In a heartbeat.

"How's Lily getting to Kabul?"

"I've arranged for another ride." Seeing Blade's concerned look, he explained further. "I paid an Afghani couple to take her. It's safer this way. They won't draw as much attention as an American SUV barreling down the road."

Blade gave a gruff nod.

"Don't worry, I gave them more than enough so that they wouldn't turn her in."

"Thanks, I'll pay you back."

He waved a hand in the air.

"How'd you track me down?" Blade inquired.

"I figured they'd stash you somewhere close until the security services could pick you up, so I doubled back and tailed them to the safe house then waited for the perfect chance to make a move."

"I had it handled," he said through a grimace.

"Sure." Stitch glanced over at him. "Looks like it."

He coughed and held his ribcage. "I've had worse."

Stitch shook his head.

"To be honest, I was expecting more of a beating, but they didn't realize I was Special Forces."

"Not yet," Stitch said grimly, checking the rearview mirror.

Blade nodded. "Yeah."

A cacophony of sirens wailed in the distance. They were coming.

"We've gotta get this car off the road," Blade muttered.

Stitch ground his jaw. "I know that. I've got a plan." He floored it down the Kabul road, swung hard into the rest-area, then parked behind the fruit store.

Blade, unable to move, watched as Stitch jumped out, approached a man with a shitty Toyota—literally the worst car in the spot—then offered to do a swap.

The man stared at him, like he was nuts.

Stitch gestured with his hand, urgent and impassioned. The dust hadn't even settled around the Land Rover yet.

With a sly grin, the man agreed. Stitch handed him the keys, raced back to the SUV and helped Blade get out.

Once they were firmly in the Toyota, Stitch took off out of there, passing a swarm of police vehicles racing in.

Blade ducked, breathing hard from the effort, as Stitch laughed and turned onto the Kabul road. The move wouldn't stall them for long, but it would buy them some time.

"I told him not to say anything," Stitch murmured, checking the mirrors again. No cop cars were giving chase.

The road behind them was blissfully silent.

"You think he will?"

"Maybe. No one wants to mess with the Taliban-run police force. He'll know it's not in his best interests to keep quiet. But by the time they figure out we've switched cars, we'll be somewhere safe."

"Safe?" Blade glanced over. He was wheezing heavily now. "Aren't we going to Kabul? They're just going to put up another roadblock on the outskirts of the city."

"No, my friend. We are not going to Kabul. That would be suicide."

He leaned back against the headrest. "Then where are we going?"

"Somewhere I can take a look at that broken rib, and every other part of you they've kicked to shit."

"I'm fine."

"Like hell you are."

"I just need to sleep." He started drifting off.

"Wake up, Blade." Stitch tapped him on the leg.

"Huh?"

"Can't sleep yet, buddy. Not with that concussion."

"Fuck off," he growled.

"I can't believe you pulled that stunt back there. What the hell, man?"

He knew Stitch was keeping him talking so he could monitor him for signs of a cranial bleed or loss of orientation. Anything that would signal a traumatic brain injury. "Couldn't risk you and Lily getting shot."

He thought he was making sense.

Kind of.

"We might have made it. There were only ten of them."

Blade laughed, but it hurt so damn much, he coughed instead. He couldn't see shit out of one eye, either, but that would just take time. "Where are we headed?"

"I've got a contact."

"Good to see domestic life hasn't made you soft."

Stitch grinned. "Farzaad is a good man. He'll have our backs."

Blade offered a half-nod. He trusted Stitch.

The beat-up Toyota chewed through the miles. There were no more sirens. Blade closed his eyes, only to get another jab from Stitch.

"You must really care about Spade's girl to put yourself on the line like that. I know it wasn't just for me."

It was a loaded question, meant to stir him up. Meant to keep him awake when all he wanted was to crash.

It was smart too because he didn't have the energy to dispute it.

"Yeah."

Stitch glanced over at him. "She's vulnerable. You know that, right?"

"I know," he growled. "That's why nothing happened."

Not strictly true.

"I'm sorry for what I said before." Stitch kept his eyes on the road. "I was out of line. I didn't know how strongly you felt for her."

Blade closed his eyes. "It doesn't matter how I feel. She's Spade's girl, remember? I did this for him."

"She *was* Spade's girl, but from what I could see, she's now very much yours."

"What?" Blade squinted out of his good eye. "You're full of it."

"No, man. She wanted to go back for you. That was real emotion I saw there, not just heat-of-the-moment crap. She needs you."

Blade mulled it over.

She needed him.

Out here, yeah, but what about back home? Would she need him then? He was nobody. An out of work soldier with

PTSD. Didn't have a job, nor any likelihood of getting one. Weren't many jobs for former soldiers.

He didn't have engineering skills like Joe or medical training like Stitch. All he knew was how to kill, and he was damn good at it. Problem was that didn't translate into civilian life too well.

He had nothing to offer a woman like Lily.

Weariness and pain overwhelmed him, and he couldn't stay awake. He heard Stitch talking, but the words were a jumbled mess.

The Toyota turned off the main road onto a dirt track, and the jolt made him catch his breath. Waves of nausea flowed over him. Darkness pulled him down, and he couldn't keep his eyes open anymore.

"Blade!" Stitch's voice barely registered.

He was losing the battle.

Thankfully, the pain started to diminish, and then there was nothing.

CHAPTER 29

*L*ily stared up at the Airbus A320 that was going to take her to Istanbul. The situation at the airport was still chaotic, but one of Pat's local contacts, a former Afghani official still working undercover in Kabul, had managed to get her a ticket under an assumed name. She wore a full burqa, including the mesh screen over her eyes, and traveled with a man she did not know.

A local woman traveling alone would raise too many questions.

Once they landed in Turkey, she'd lose her chaperone, switch planes, and get on an American Airline flight to Charlotte Douglas International Airport.

"Do I use the same passport?" she'd asked Pat. God only knew what had happened to hers. Probably stolen by now.

"Yeah. It's not ideal but was the best we could come up with under the circumstances."

Lily was incredibly grateful to the woman whose passport she was using.

"If someone else uses your original passport, it'll confuse

the hell out of them," Pat had told her with a dry laugh. "We'll reissue you a new one when you get home."

Home.

How unfamiliar that word sounded. She'd been away almost eleven months now. The home she'd shared with Joe would be full of memories, and she didn't want to go there.

Yet, she had no choice.

Except now, she'd be missing both of them, not just Joe. He'd always have a place in her heart, but it was Blade who consumed her thoughts.

Had Stitch found him?

Was he even alive?

How would they get out of there?

So many unanswered questions. She sighed and climbed onboard, feeling like she was leaving a huge part of herself on the shimmering tarmac behind.

Blade.

Her hero.

She still couldn't believe he'd voluntarily sacrificed himself like that.

For her. For Stitch.

She found her seat and curled into it, wishing it would swallow her up. *God*, how she missed him.

Pat had moved fast. He hadn't wanted to risk the Taliban locking down the airports. "We're banking on them not having figured out who Blade is yet. Once they connect him to you, they'll launch a major manhunt. You'll be the talk of the town."

"What about Blade?"

Pat had remained stoic. "He's a big boy. He can look after himself."

"What if they kill him, Pat?" She hadn't been able to keep the fear from her voice.

He didn't answer for a long while. "He's trained for this, Lily. Stitch is going after him. Have a little faith."

She wished she could, but it was so hard.

She didn't want to believe he was dead, that she'd never see him again.

It was just… she had so much to lose.

The doors closed, then the plane began to taxi along the runway. The anxiety she'd felt up to now began to dissipate. A few more seconds then they'd be airborne.

Pat had said as soon as they left Afghanistan airspace, she'd be safe. Home free. The sparse, dry scenery flew past the window, faster and faster, until it became one long, yellow-green blur. The plane groaned and the wheels lifted. They were up.

She leaned back, eyes closed. Didn't want to open them until she was safe. How long until they flew into Iran airspace? Ten minutes, twenty?

An hour later, she was finally able to relax.

They'd done it. She was free.

Blade had done it. He'd gotten her out, just like he'd promised.

Pity he wasn't here to share the moment with her. They should be celebrating right now with a glass of bubbly. Stitch should be home with Soraya.

So many people had pulled together to make this happen, and she was the one getting out. They were stuck there, God only knew in what state.

It didn't feel right.

* * *

LILY FELT the plane start to descend and opened her eyes. She'd slept most of the way from Turkey to Charlotte. Now, about to land in her home state, she felt the weight of the past week lift.

Reality was settling in. She was safe.

They wouldn't come for her here. Too late, they'd lost their chance. She'd give the codes to the authorities, and it would no longer be her problem. Pat had said a team would be waiting at the airport to debrief her. CIA, NSA, and goodness knows who else.

All she cared about was that the nightmare was over.

A cloudless, cobalt sky welcomed her home. A bright sunny day in Charlotte, NC.

She couldn't enjoy it. Not with Blade still out there, whereabouts unknown.

Maybe Pat had heard from Stitch in the interim. It had been a long flight. Two flights, in fact. She'd left her travel partner in Turkey and gone on to board the American Airlines plane with no problems. She'd even removed the burqa after takeoff. Lily left Turkey as the borrowed-passport woman, but she arrived in America as herself.

Holy shit. Pat wasn't kidding about the debrief.

She stepped off the plane, carry-on slung over her shoulder, then walked into the terminal. A SWAT team greeted her.

Seriously?

Was scaring the daylights out of her really necessary? After everything she'd just gone through, this felt like total overkill.

But they led her to a private room where three stern-looking guys and one equally no-nonsense lady waited around a conference table.

The room was stark, illuminated by harsh fluorescent lights that put her on edge. There were no pictures on the walls, no furniture other than the table and a few chairs. It felt cold, almost clinical—a stark contrast to the warmth of sunlight she'd just left behind on the tarmac.

Lily sat then placed her carry-on beside her chair. The air was thick with anticipation, or maybe it was just the recycled air conditioning. Either way, it made her skin prickle.

One of the men introduced himself as Agent Thompson. He attempted a smile, which made him look constipated, and said, "Thanks for joining us."

Like she'd had a choice?

"I'm glad to be back."

"I'm sure." The woman spoke for the first time. "You've suffered a terrible ordeal."

No shit.

"You didn't have any problems on your way home?"

She shook her head.

"Can we have your passport?"

Lily took it from her jacket pocket then slid it across the table.

The woman nodded.

Agent Thompson spoke. "Lily, the software codes…" He let the sentence hang, an implicit invitation for her to fill in the blanks.

She glanced at them. They were practically drooling over the table. This was a chance to track not just the Taliban, but any enemy, anywhere. The software she'd helped develop would provide data they could use to strengthen America's borders, assist their allies, and understand their adversaries better. It was all about the information.

"Can I have a piece of paper?"

He had one ready.

Slowly, and with precision, she wrote down the strings of code that would get them access to *Hawkeye*.

"Just to be clear," another agent added, "this is everything?"

She gave another nod. "That's everything. Can I go now?"

The fourth man grimaced. "I'm afraid not. I'm with the Department of Defense, and we'd like you to talk us through everything that happened over there, beginning with your abduction."

She sighed. Really? They were doing this now.

Someone knocked.

"Excuse me one second." The man stood then opened the door a crack.

Pat's voice flowed into the room, terse, demanding, abrupt. The debrief could wait. She'd been through enough. He was taking her home.

"I suppose it can wait a day or two," the DOD man said reluctantly.

Lily threw herself into his arms. "Pat, thank goodness. It's so good to see you!"

He hugged her, a great big bear of a hug. Keeping a protective arm around her, he turned to the other agents, towering above them. "She's coming with me."

Lily couldn't have been more eager to leave.

As they left the airport building, Pat said, "I was thinking you should come and stay with at my place for a while. If you want to, that is."

Her eyes welled up. Damnit, she hated crying in front of him, but she was so relieved to not have to go home. "That would be great."

He gave a happy nod. "Let's go then. Let's get you home."

CHAPTER 30

"Where am I?"

Blade tried to lift his head, but it felt like a ton of bricks was pushing down on him.

"Don't worry, you're safe."

Stitch.

Slowly the events of the last few days came rushing back. The checkpoint, the capture, the beating… He took in an experimental breath and was surprised to find it hurt less.

"You've patched me up?"

"Somewhat." Stitch's voice was grim. "I've set your broken arm best I can, but you might want to get it looked at by a specialist when you get back to the States. I've put back your dislocated collarbone—probably a good thing you were out for that—and I've iced your black eye. Nothing I can do about the three broken ribs, unfortunately. That'll take some time to heal."

"Three broken ribs?" He looked down to find he was wearing a loose-fitting robe.

"Yeah, they did a number on you, pal. You're lucky you were able to walk out of there."

He grunted. "Thanks, Stitch."

"Not the first time, but I sure as hell hope it's the last."

"So do I."

Blade flexed his left hand, it felt strange, like his nerves weren't working properly. Everything would take time to heal, including his heart.

"Lily?" he muttered. "Did she get away?"

"I haven't heard anything, so I assume so. Farzaad's been scanning the local news stations, but there's been no mention of her. No disturbance on the local police channels either, other than hunting for your sorry ass. My guess is she's home free."

Yet they wouldn't know for sure until he'd talked to Pat.

"Got a cell phone?" he asked, knowing it was a long shot.

"Yeah, right."

So much for that. Out here, there was minimal cell reception, and no Wi-Fi. Even in the cities, it was sporadic. And highly censored.

"You're going to have to hang tight, buddy. Once you're feeling better, you can head back to Kabul."

"How? They're going to come after me like a buck during hunting season."

"I have a surprise for you."

Blade recognized that wide, sly grin.

"Oh, yeah?"

"Yeah, but you have to get up to see it. I can't bring it to you."

Blade huffed. This was Stitch's attempt at getting him moving. He knew the dangers of muscle atrophy and staying too long in one place.

"Okay, give me a sec." Using his good arm, he pushed himself into a sitting position. The room swam, momentarily, but after a hard blink, it stabilized.

"You good?" Stitch was frowning.

"Yeah, I think so."

He swung his legs out of bed, the concrete floor felt hard and cool under his bare feet. Unnatural, since it had been a while since he'd walked.

"How long have I been out?"

"Twenty-four hours, give or take."

"Shit."

"Yeah, you were worse than I thought. It's still gonna take a while, so don't be a hero."

"How long?"

"Couple of weeks, at least."

Fuck.

"You're safe here," Stitch repeated. "Farzaad doesn't mind if you stay."

Blade hobbled across the room, assisted by Stitch. His legs wobbled, but he gritted his teeth and aimed for the door.

"Who is this guy?"

"He's a friend. I met him shortly after I arrived. He's a good guy, you can trust him."

"How do I know?"

"Because I delivered his baby twins earlier this year, and they'd have died without me. He owes me big time."

A smiling, turbaned man walked toward them. He extended a hand. "Hello. I am Farzaad."

They shook.

"Farzaad doesn't speak much English." Stitch grinned. "But he's a great cook. He works in a restaurant in the next town. You won't go hungry."

Blade nodded. The guy looked genuine, and he trusted Stitch, but until he'd spent some time with the chef, he would reserve judgment.

They made their way to a side door. Farzaad opened it to reveal a garage.

No way.

Farzaad had a shiny Honda CRF450L, parked in the center, looking like it was just waiting to hit the road.

"Fuck, yeah." The sleek, aggressive lines of the bike screamed performance, while its sturdy build spoke of reliability.

"This is your ride out of here." Stitch patted the motorcycle.

Holding on to the wall for support, Blade inspected the 449cc liquid-cooled single-cylinder engine and six-speed transmission. It had plenty of grunt for off-road but would be a smooth ride on the highways too. Plus, it had the range to get him to Kabul.

Blade turned to Farzaad. "You don't mind?"

He shook his head and patted Stitch on the shoulder. "Anything for Ḍākṭar Sahib's friend."

Blade raised an eyebrow.

"That's what they call me here." A self-conscious smile lifted one corner of Stitch's lips.

"I'll look after it."

"Easy now," Stitch warned. "You're not going anywhere until I say so."

"What are you? My doctor?" He grinned, then winced.

"Two weeks, minimum." He helped Blade back to bed. "I've got to head back, but I'll check up on you in a few days."

"Okay, thanks, Stitch." He meant it.

"Just like old times, eh?" The medic grinned. "Stay out of trouble till I get back."

"Will do."

Blade lay back down on the bed. Stitch's voice came through the thin walls as he said goodbye to Farzaad and left instructions not to let him go anywhere. No worries there.

He couldn't right now if he wanted to.

If only he knew Lily was alright. If she got away safely.

Patience was not his strongest point, but like with his broken body, answers would have to wait.

CHAPTER 31

*L*ily was going slowly *insane*.

She'd been back a week, and they'd heard nothing.

Pat had pulled all the strings he could. He'd spoken to his contacts in Kabul—those in the new government and those still in hiding—but no one knew anything about the former Special Forces squad leader.

"It's like he's disappeared off the face of the earth."

"That's how they're trained," Pat told her. "If he's on the run, he's keeping a low profile. Staying under the radar."

"But for so long?"

"It's complicated out there, you know that."

She sure did. Escaping wouldn't be easy, even with Stitch's help.

The Department of Defense man had reappeared. They'd sat at Pat's dining table while she told him everything about what had happened, starting with Blade rescuing her from the cave network in the mountains.

"We didn't sanction any military evacuation," the man had barked.

Pat cleared his throat. "No, but your boss did. Off the record."

The DoD man didn't mention it again. "How'd you get through the checkpoint?"

Lily told him about the guard recognizing her, and Blade shooting him. Then he'd surrendered, allowing her to escape.

"Brave fella."

Pat gave a knowing grunt.

"And who drove you?"

"Someone he bribed into service." No way would she give up Stitch.

"So, a local couple gave you a lift to Kabul?"

"That's right, and when I got there I called Pat."

Pat took over then, keeping it brief and not giving away any of his contacts. Most of the people he'd dealt with were in hiding and would be executed if discovered by the Taliban.

The meeting ended, and Pat saw the DoD guy out. Lily was glad that was over, although part of her was still in Afghanistan with Blade.

* * *

ANOTHER WEEK PASSED. Lily had gnawed off all her fingernails. Even Pat walked around with a long, hang-dog face.

"There must be something we can do."

Pat worked his jaw. "The boys know what to do. They'll get themselves out of this."

But she could tell by his tone he was beginning to fear the worst.

STAYING at Pat's house reminded her of when her mother had passed away and Joe's parents had taken her into their home.

Nothing much had changed. The furnishings were still the same, albeit a little more threadbare, but the photos on the mantelpiece were exactly how she remembered.

Pat and his wife on their wedding day. Joe as a baby. A family shot on the beach. Joe in his army uniform. She stared at that for some time. He looked so handsome, so happy.

He'd died doing something he'd loved, being the person he'd wanted to be. That was something, at least.

She poured Pat a fresh cup of coffee and took it into his office. He seemed to enjoy having her there, and she didn't mind. It was better than being alone, and this place had happy memories for her.

"Thanks, Lily." He shot her a sad smile as she set the mug down on the desk.

"Anything?"

He shook his head.

They'd spent the evenings talking about the situation in the Middle East, about the role of the armed forces, about his time in the Navy SEALs. He'd been captured once and managed to escape, so he was under no illusions about what Blade might be going through.

"It took me a month to get away," he told her, his gaze knowing. "You just have to hang in there, and hope for the best."

Easier said than done.

Even after two weeks, Lily wasn't sure exactly what Pat did for a living. He was in and out, sometimes flying to D.C. for meetings, other times spending long hours in his study on secretive phone calls. Occasionally men in suits came to visit, but they never stayed long.

Pat was an enigma.

One evening, they were sitting in the garden together as had become their habit. Lily was scanning the Internet on her laptop, looking for any news of a captured American soldier, while Pat read the newspaper.

"You know, Lily—"

She glanced up.

"We might never know."

A chill swept over her. She didn't want to acknowledge that he might not be coming back. It had been three weeks with no news. Interminable to her, but not long for a Green Beret who'd escaped and was in hiding.

"Don't." She shook her head.

He put down the paper. "Sweetheart, sometimes they don't come home."

A red-hot poker stabbed her in the heart. She couldn't handle it. Couldn't let herself think along those lines.

"Don't say that," she croaked.

Pat studied her. "You care for him, don't you?"

Lily hesitated. How could she tell him?

Would he be upset that she'd moved on from his son? That she'd fallen in love with Joe's best friend?

He nodded at her laptop. "You're barely off that thing, you jump every time the phone rings, and you're the first one outside when a car pulls up. We're both desperate for information, but it strikes me this goes a little deeper for you."

A sob escaped her. "He sacrificed his life for mine." She couldn't meet his gaze. "I thought it was because he'd rescued me, that it was just infatuation and it would pass, but—" She sniffed. "I can't handle the thought of life without him."

He reached over and squeezed her hand. "I understand. It was an intense situation."

"You do?" Her eyes filled with tears.

"Of course. Blade's a great guy. I understand why you might have feelings for him."

"But I feel so guilty." She took a shaky breath. "What about Joe?"

"Joe would understand." Sadness crept into his eyes.

"Would he?" She shook her head.

"You know he would. He'd want you to be happy."

She closed her laptop. "You know I'll never forget what you and Val did for me."

"You're like a daughter to me, Lily." His voice was gruff, very unlike Pat.

She got up and hugged him. "Thank you, for everything."

"I only wish it had turned out different. I feel responsible for sending him over there."

"It's not your fault," she whispered. It was nobody's fault. God, why did she have to say that so much?

"If it's any consolation, he's a tough bastard, and with Stitch helping him, there's a good chance they'll make it out alive."

Lily knew he was saying that to make her feel better, but she prayed he was right.

CHAPTER 32

*L*ily perched on a wrought-iron chair on the front porch, thumbing through a magazine without much interest. Pat had cleared out, leaving her to stew alone in the quiet, empty house.

The sun bore down, unforgiving, slanting through the branches to splatter the grass with harsh shadows and spots of blinding light.

It matched her mood—patches of clarity cut through with stretches of dark unease, the kind that comes when you're left to think a little too long about things better left buried.

She didn't know when she'd started to give up on the idea that Blade was ever coming home. Accepting the inevitable was better than dwelling on the possibility he might still be alive. Her heart couldn't break anymore, and she was all out of tears.

A motorcycle pulled up outside the house. Strange, as she wasn't expecting anyone. It roared quietly, more like a hum, while the man on it stared at her through his helmet from across the lawn.

A surge of anxiety shot through her. Who the hell was this? Should she be worried? Should she run inside the house and lock the door?

He climbed off the bike. Something about him was familiar. His stature, his stride…

It couldn't be.

Her heart surged. She leaped up, the magazine falling from her hands.

He took off the helmet, placed it over the handlebars, then squinted into the sunlight.

She'd recognize that hair anywhere.

With a squeal, Lily sprinted down the steps, crossed the lawn, then threw herself into his arms. "Oh, my God! It's really you!"

Blade winced, then laughed and hugged her gently.

Tears streamed down her face, but she didn't care. He was here. Standing outside Pat's house. In the flesh.

She could scarcely believe it.

"I thought you were dead," she sobbed.

"Takes more than a bunch of armed guards to kill me." He held her at arm's length so he could take a good look at her. "Damn, you look amazing."

"So do you." She smiled up at him. Kissed him on the lips. Hugged him again.

He wrapped his arm around her. "God, I missed you."

"How did you get out?" She pulled away to look at him. "I've been so worried. So has Pat. We were sure something terrible had happened."

"I know. I'm sorry I couldn't call. I was staying with one of Stitch's friends, and there was no way to get in touch."

"Pat said that might be what had happened." She wished she'd believed him now. He'd said Blade was a survivor, and here he was, alive and well.

Now she didn't want to let him go.

Ever.

Blade beamed down at her. He'd shaved off his beard, giving her a good look at his face. God, he was so handsome. But at the same time, damaged. He had a faint bruise around his eye and a new scar near his hairline. Only then did she notice a sling around his neck, not that he had an arm in it.

"Broken arm." He nodded at it. "Stitch told me to wear it for a few more weeks, but I can't ride my motorcycle with it on." He grinned.

She shook her head. Typical.

He wore black jeans over his thick thighs, and under his leather biker jacket, a loosely buttoned shirt afforded her a glimpse of his glorious chest. Still a beast of a man, although she thought he'd lost some weight.

"How is Stitch?"

"Just fine. So is Soraya. They send their love."

Afghanistan seemed like an eternity ago, another life, but she'd never forget the people she'd met there.

Blade touched her cheek. "What do you say we go inside and talk?"

She nodded. Even though his eyes were sparkling, there was a serious undertone.

"Pat around?"

"He's out, but he'll be back soon."

She led him inside, and they sat next to each other on the couch. Lily was dying to touch him, to hold him, but she didn't know if she should. How did he feel about her now? Back in Afghanistan, they hadn't known if they were going to make it out, and because of that, they'd let themselves get carried away.

She didn't regret it, not for one moment. The memories had carried her through these last hellish weeks without him. It was what she'd thought about at night, alone in bed, when her heart cried out for him.

"Lily, I've been thinking a lot about us and about what happened between us."

Her heart sank. This was it. He was going to tell her he couldn't do it, not now they were both free.

"You have?"

He scoffed. "Hell, it's all I have been thinking about."

She bit her lip.

"I… I just wanted to say… Fuck." He shook his head.

Her heart smashed into a million little pieces.

"I know," she whispered, trying not to cry. "I know there can never be anything between us. You don't have to say it."

"I wasn't going to."

"You weren't?"

He shook his head. The sparkle was still there. She clung to that.

"I'm sorry about the things I said over there. I was messed up. About Spade, about what happened. About you."

Lily held her breath.

"Stitch told me the translator had been coerced. His family had been threatened, so even if I had vetted him more thoroughly, it wouldn't have made any difference."

She smiled, glad he'd forgiven himself.

"I know Spade would have wanted you to be happy." He chuckled to himself. "I'm not sure he had me in mind, but if you'll have me, I promise to take care of you."

Tears welled in her eyes. "Of course I'll have you. Joe gave us a gift when he died. If it wasn't for him, you wouldn't have felt duty bound to come and get me. You saved my life, Blade."

He kissed her, long and slow. When he broke away, she was breathless. Damn, she'd never get tired of him doing that to her.

"How can this be wrong?" he murmured.

She looked in his eyes and saw such tenderness, it made her melt. "It's not wrong. I think we both know that."

He smiled slowly.

Could a girl melt twice?

"How do you feel about going for a ride?"

"On *that*?"

He nodded.

"Er, yeah. Why not?" She'd never been on a motorcycle before.

"Hold that thought," he said, as Pat strode into the room.

"Fucking hell, Blade. About time you showed up." He pumped Blade's hand and thumped him on the shoulder.

Blade grimaced.

"You okay?"

"I am now."

Pat chuckled. "Glad to hear it. Are you going to tell us how the hell you got out?" He glanced at Lily. "Or have you already done that?"

"No, I was just going to." He met Lily's eye and winked.

She grinned. Now that she knew how he felt, she didn't mind waiting. They'd have time to catch up later.

* * *

BLADE GAVE Pat the rundown on his capture, skipping the brutal highlights—no need to spook Lily with those.

Pat laughed. "You rode that motorcycle all the way to Kabul?"

"Not Kabul. Pakistan."

Pat's eyes widened. "You're serious?"

"Taliban closed the road into Kabul, put checkpoints every which way. I couldn't risk it."

"Were they looking for me?" Lily asked, her voice a whisper.

"Yeah. They put two and two together and realized I was the one who'd rescued you from the cave. That city shut down tighter than Fort Knox. Nothing was getting in or out of there."

"That's why you took so long," muttered Pat.

"Yeah, I laid low for a couple of weeks then had the journey on top of that."

Pat shot him a knowing look—that weathered look of a man who's experienced his fair share of danger. "Glad you had a safe place to hunker down."

"Yeah, and a motorcycle sturdy enough to handle the off-road terrain. Made it a lot easier—until I ran out of fuel."

"What did you do then?" Lily asked, her eyes wide.

"Kept going on foot, over the Khyber Pass."

"Plan C?"

He flashed a grin. "You got it, Plan C."

"Hit any snags?" Pat asked.

He leveled the former SEALs gaze. "Nothing I couldn't handle."

Pat's nod was full of respect. "Damn good to have you back, son."

Lily's hand in his was a surprise, a warm affirmation. He hadn't expected her to have told Pat about how she felt, him being Spade's father and all.

Pat was all grins. Their closeness didn't appear to bother him. "I'm happy for you two."

"Really?"

Pat's blessing hit deep. Without folks of his own, Pat's opinion was the one that mattered most to him.

"I think Joe would approve." Pat nodded at the photograph of his fallen son.

Blade felt the weight and warmth in Lily's grip as much as in Pat's words. "That means everything."

They talked for a while longer, then Lily turned to Blade. "I do believe you promised me a motorcycle ride."

Pat laughed. "You kids have fun."

Blade shook Pat's hand—firm, brief, meaningful. It was a soldier's bond. "She's in safe hands."

He wasn't just talking about the ride.

Pat's grip was iron. "I don't doubt it for a second."

EPILOGUE

 *ne month later...*

BLADE GRINNED as Pat pumped his hand before turning to Lily and giving her a bear hug. "Congratulations. I couldn't be happier for you two."

After the last month, Blade knew without a doubt he wanted to make Lily his—forever. As it was, they'd spent every possible moment together since he'd returned, and the thought of her not being in his life wasn't just unbearable. It was unthinkable.

That's when he'd dropped to one knee.

A toast with champagne had barely settled, when Pat cleared his throat, a crafty glint in his eye. "Blade, I have a proposition for you."

Blade looked weary. "What sort of proposition? If it involves a whiff of desert sand, I'm not interested."

"Water, actually," said Pat, laughing. "The Gulf of Mexico. There's a security job on an oil rig..."

Both Blade and Lily stared at him like he was mad.

"We're about to get married, Pat," Lily began, her voice firm, protective even. "Blade can't go anywhere right now."

"I'm not talking about Blade," Pat said mysteriously. "I was thinking Phoenix would be perfect for this job."

"Phoenix?" Blade narrowed his eyes. "What are you taking about, Pat?"

"Well, I've been spending a lot of time at the DOD lately, and I've realized there's a gap to fill—perfect for an off-the-books team with all the skills and none of the red tape. A ghost unit that can move where the normal guys can't."

Blade narrowed his eyes. "For example?"

"Hostage rescue, close protection, security… You get the picture."

"A private security outfit?"

Pat nodded. "I pitched the idea today. They're seriously considering it. Short-term, it would help them out of a sticky spot. Long-term, it would help them out of a lot of them. There are situations when they need prompt action and there isn't time to go through the official channels."

"We'd run our own unit?" Blade's heart skipped a beat. Could this be the answer he'd been looking for?

Lately, he'd been pondering what the hell he was going to do with himself now that his military career was over. He'd have to work, that much was non negotiable. He was getting married.

Blade's respect for Pat skyrocketed. He should have known the crafty former SEAL wouldn't leave him out to dry.

Lily had already gone back to work, leaving him at loose ends. He wanted to earn a decent living, but most guys in his position ended up as glorified security guards. Or they joined the police force, which was a better option. There weren't many other opportunities for trained killers.

"A shadow unit," said Pat. "I was thinking of called it Blackthorn Security."

"Blackthorn?" Lily scratched her head. "Isn't that a tree?"

He gave a sly grin. "Yeah, known for its rugged resilience."

Blade could tell he'd thought hard about this. "I like it."

"Whoa! Hang on a minute." Lily glanced between the two of them. "Are you saying Blade would be heading out on dangerous missions again?"

Lily, all protective fire, made his heart lurch. He loved that she cared so deeply about him. It was a novel experience. In the past, when he'd gone on operations, it was only his Commanding Officer who cared whether he came back or not—and not for any warm, fuzzy reason either.

Sure, it had been his own decision, his choice not to let anyone get too close. No strings. Except it was clear to him now that it hadn't been by design. He just hadn't met the right girl.

"I want Blade to lead it."

He turned to Blade. "I'll be the link with the DOD. You can pick and choose the assignments. Operate as a unit, or individually, depending on the requirement."

Blade's nod was like the closing of the deal, the kind that didn't need paperwork. Pat knew he was in.

Lily's gaze rested on his face. "You've already decided, haven't you? You want to do this?"

Blade shot her an apologetic grin. "I have to work, love, and you heard Pat, we can pick and choose our ops. As the leader, I'll mostly be involved in strategy and planning, and I promise you now, I'll never set foot in Afghanistan again."

Lily leaned over and kissed him hard on the lips. "I'm going to hold you to that."

Pat grinned and leaned back in his chair. "Fantastic. As soon as you get the others on board, we can set up shop."

Blade looked up. "Others?"

"Yeah, I've got some guys in mind. I'm sure you have too. Ex-military, brave men. Out for one reason or another."

"I know a few, yeah." He met Pat's gaze.

"Awesome. I'll see to the paperwork, you start building our team."

"After the wedding," Lily cut in, shooting Pat a stern look.

He gave a happy nod. "Of course. After the wedding."

"Nah." Blade winked at Lily. "After the honeymoon."

HONOR CODE

BLACKTHORN SECURITY - BOOK 2

CHAPTER 1

*I*t was still pitch dark when Ellie woke up. The long-haul flight from Europe had left her tired and cranky. She groaned—jet lag could be a bitch.

Reaching over, she checked the time on her phone.

Five a.m.

Was it too early for a yoga session?

Her whole body ached. She desperately needed to stretch out the kinks. Her yoga mat stood in the corner by the door, beckoning to her.

Suzi, her roommate, was still fast asleep, her breathing deep and rhythmic. Careful not to wake her, Ellie slid out of bed, pulled on some leggings and a T-shirt, then grabbed her yoga mat. After scraping her hair back into a ponytail, she snuck out of the room.

The corridors on the oil rig were dark and eerie, bathed in that familiar ghostly green light that cast long shadows on the steel walls. The first time she'd been on an offshore platform, she'd been unnerved by the ethereal glow, but after five years of working in the field, she was used to it.

She made her way up the narrow steel stairway to the top

deck, expecting to see some signs of life, but the place was deserted. Then again, it was stupid o'clock. The first shift only begun at eight.

The tropical air caressed her skin, warm and serene—so different from the frigid conditions in the North Sea where she'd worked before. She closed her eyes and let the balmy breeze wash over her, savoring the moment.

With her mat tucked under her arm, she ventured along the gangway, navigating around the now-silent steel structure, with its cranes, multi-level platforms, and columns of drilling equipment, in search of a tranquil corner in which to exercise.

At the railing, she paused and gazed out at the dark expanse of ocean. It never failed to move her, the idea that she was a tiny dot in the middle of an enormous ocean. Maybe it was because nobody could get to her out here. She was safe. Protected by thousands of miles of water.

At least she'd thought she was. That was until Suzi had mentioned the threat from eco-terrorists. This was a very sensitive area of the Gulf, ecologically fragile—she'd read the impact assessments before she'd come out here. If she'd known about the threats, she might have thought twice before accepting the job.

After what had happened last time…

No, she wasn't going to go there. Ellie took a steadying breath. This was different. Eco-terrorists chained themselves to structures, got in the way, temporarily disrupted operations. They didn't threaten anyone's personal safety.

Even so, the threat did explain the presence of the armed patrols she'd seen yesterday when she'd arrived on the chopper from Corpus Christi. Two beefy security operatives standing watch on the deck. They put her mind at ease.

Tiredness made her neck stiff, and she stretched, then

wandered over to the helipad, the flattest, clearest space she could find. It was deserted, the chopper yet to return.

Perfect.

She rolled out her mat and was just standing upright when a sudden gust of wind made her spin around. In an instant, she was blindsided and taken down hard. Her breath whooshed out of her as she was flattened on the deck.

Panic surged through her.

No! Not again.

She thrashed and squirmed, trying to throw off her attacker, who had her pinned to the ground. A thousand terrifying thoughts stampeded through her head, scrambling her brain. Blood pumped in her ears, adding to her confusion.

"Get off me!" Her high-pitched cry shattered the quiet.

SHE WAS BACK IN BOSTON, standing in Raphael's apartment, his arm tight around her waist. The sharp edge of the blade he held pressed against her throat. Cold, uncompromising. One small slash, and she'd bleed out.

"Don't move," he hissed in her ear.

She couldn't; she was too terrified.

"Put down the knife," the police officer ordered, pointing his firearm at them. At Raphael, who used her as his shield. She was the one who'd get shot. The bullet would probably go right through her and hit Raphael too, but she didn't want to put it to the test.

Hot tears stung her eyes. "Rafe, please."

"Shut up," he growled, the blade digging deeper into her skin. A warm trickle dripped down her neck. She was bleeding.

Oh, God. I'm going to die.

That was all she could think about. She'd never see her family again and would die in Raphael's living room, either by his hand or a police bullet. Either way, death loomed, just seconds away.

. . .

A HAND, large and suffocating, clamped over her mouth. In the dim light, her attacker was just a shape, an indistinct mass overwhelming her. She kicked out, connecting with a soft body part, and heard a satisfying grunt of pain.

No way. This was not happening.

She would not be a victim—again.

The subsequent years of self-defense training kicked in, and she fought with every fiber of her being, but he was strong and countered her desperate thrusts. Finally, her knee connected with his groin, and he swore under his breath, yet his grip remained unyielding.

What did it take to unseat this monster?

Suddenly, he shifted, his weight settling on her pelvis. Massive hands forced her arms above her head, her T-shirt rode up, exposing her midriff. Trapped, she opened her mouth to scream.

"Don't," came a gruff command, chilling in its calmness. "I just want to talk."

Pinned down, the hard floor of the helipad pressing into her back, she glared angrily up at the man who'd shattered her early morning peace, along with her nerves.

Who the hell was he?

And what did he want with her?

* * *

"WHO ARE YOU?" Phoenix growled, securing the intruder with his full weight. She was light; it wasn't hard to subdue her, but she'd caught him by surprise. He hadn't expected such a frenzied attack.

Damn if his groin didn't throb where the hellcat had kicked him, and now she'd left claw marks down his forearm.

The woman had fought like her life depended on it. Trained, but not by any military—he knew that much. Not a serious threat, then. Maybe an eco-warrior? One of those passionate planet defenders who didn't realize the danger they put themselves in.

"What's your name?" he repeated. He'd been warned there had been threats.

She squirmed beneath him, but he held her steady, pressing her wrists into the hard floor. He regretted the use of force, but she wasn't going anywhere until she'd answered some questions.

"Ellie," she gasped, and he noticed—more than noticed— the way her T-shirt twisted under her breasts, exposing her smooth, flat stomach.

He forced his gaze to her face. It was then he noticed the small, straight scar on her neck, silver in the ethereal light on the deck. "Who do you work for?"

"Xonex, the energy company."

He frowned. Xonex, the same company that had hired him for his expertise in handling situations exactly like this. It didn't add up. Why was she dressed in black, prowling around the deck in the early hours?

She was staring up at him, terrified. Her eyes, a soft brown flecked with gold, were wide and frantic. She was beautiful. Fierce, yet vulnerable. He eased off a little on her wrists, but not enough that she could wriggle free. He had to be sure.

"You work here? On the Explorer?"

"That's what I've been telling you." Angry eyes glared at him, and she tossed some messy chocolate-brown strands of hair out of her face.

"Then why are you dressed like a cat burglar?"

She spluttered. "Cat burglar? This is my yoga outfit."

"Yoga? You're kidding." Now he'd heard it all.

"I'm an engineer. I told you, I work here."

Confused, he stared at her, trying to get her measure. Lean and curved in all the right places, with cascades of deep brown hair framing a pale, pretty face, she didn't look anything like an engineer—then again, she didn't look like any intruder he'd ever encountered either. A yoga guru, yes. Ironically, that was the easiest to believe.

"Where is your ID?" he asked, his face so close he could breathe in her scent. Vanilla—warm, inviting, disarming.

She grimaced. "I–I left it in my room."

He sighed.

Really?

"You have no ID, but you expect me to believe you work here?"

"I do." She gave a sexy pout.

He narrowed his eyes. "How come I haven't seen you before?"

"I flew in yesterday. Actually, I saw you and your friend up on deck last night, but you didn't see me."

He frowned. He hadn't noticed her. Could be a convenient excuse. "What are you doing prowling around the deck at five in the morning?"

She wriggled again, her hips digging into his thighs. For a small woman, she was remarkably strong. He pressed down, then wished he hadn't. A surge of heat spread to his groin, which was still pulsing from connecting with her knee.

"Isn't it obvious? I'm doing yoga." Irritation replaced the fear. That was something, at least. He hadn't liked seeing how panicked she'd been back there. He knew fear, and hers had been very real. Desperate, terrifying, irrational fear. Experience had taught him he wasn't the reason. Something else had caused that fear, something bad, and a while back. But she hadn't let it go.

"Yoga, right…" His voice petered off.

The way she was looking at him… all bristly and defiant, her tiger's eyes flashing in the predawn light. He wanted to believe her, but he had to check it out fully before he let her go.

She could just be a really good liar. The whole yoga thing might be nothing but a smokescreen. For all he knew, an activist group had sent a bombshell like her to stir up trouble over the oil drilling.

This wasn't new territory for him. After a solid twenty years in the service, with a good chunk as a Navy SEAL, he was no stranger to diehards on a mission. People got pretty intense when they truly believed in a cause.

"Look, I just got here yesterday." She snapped, clearly ticked off. "If you get off me, I'll take you to my cabin and show you my ID. Then we can clear this whole mess up."

Now that was the first sensible thing he'd heard her say.

"Sounds like a plan." Letting go, he released her hands. He'd check her out, and if she was telling the truth… well, then he'd owe her an apology. Somehow, he didn't mind that too much.

She huffed. "Can I get up now?"

"All right, but just so we're clear, you're sticking with me until I know you're legit."

She gave a quick nod and another small exhale.

He backed off, then offered a hand up.

She ignoring it, got to her feet, then brushed herself off, but not before throwing him a look that could melt steel.

"After you," he gestured, resisting a grin. She really was a hellcat.

She walked ahead of him along the narrow gangway, swishing her hips as she went. Groaning silently, he followed. Was she toying with him? Trying to provoke him? He followed that sexy ass down the corridor, trying to stay focused, but damn if she wasn't making it difficult.

They reached the door that descended into the crow's quarters, and she glanced back—big eyes, asking permission, but not without a mocking glare.

He nodded and down they went, the greenish glow of emergency lights bathing everything in an eerie tint, the rig creaking around them. He had to admit, she seemed to know where she was going.

"My roommate is still sleeping." She hesitated outside one of the cabin doors.

"I'll wait here."

So, the little vixen had been telling the truth, but he had to play by the book. Everyone onboard had to wear their ID card. No exceptions.

She slipped into her room, leaving the door cracked just enough so he could see inside. Last time he'd let his guard down, back in Helmand, it had almost cost him. He wasn't about to make the same mistake twice. Women could be full of surprises.

Then she was back, dangling her ID right in his face. "Satisfied?"

Phoenix checked it out, squinting in the dim, green light.

Eleanor Rider, Chemical Engineer, Xonex Energy Services.

Okay, so she was on the level.

He handed it back to her, meeting her triumphant gaze. "Thank you, Eleanor Rider. Sorry about the inconvenience. I had to make sure. You understand. We take security very seriously on the Explorer."

He saw a flicker of fear return, but she covered it well. "I suppose you were just doing your job."

He gave a mock salute. "Yes, ma'am."

She sniffed, not quite ready to forgive him. "You should think twice next time you jump a stranger." Her gaze roamed over his physique, and he thought he detected a reluctant flash of appreciation. "A man your size, you could hurt somebody."

"In my line of work, a delay could mean loss of life." His eyes bore into hers. "Just remember to wear your ID in future. It will save further... misunderstandings."

She tossed her ponytail over her shoulder as she spun around to go back inside the cabin. "Don't worry, I will."

HONOR CODE

Want to read more? The Blackthorn Security series is available in paperback format from www.authorgemmaford.com, and on Amazon. You can purchase the ebook from https://www.amazon.com/gp/product/B0CW18QPQN.

ABOUT THE AUTHOR

Gemma Ford is a romantic suspense novelist who enjoys writing about feisty, independent women and their brave, warm-hearted men. *Duty Bound* is the first book in Gemma's Blackthorn Security romantic suspense series.

You can browse the rest of the series or sign up to Gemma's mailing list for discounts, promos and the occasional freebie at her website: www.authorgemmaford.com.

CHRISTMAS 2013
TO DEAR TOM

WITH LOVE FROM

GRANDPA + GRANNY.

ESSENTIAL KNOTS

Published by Adlard Coles Nautical
an imprint of A & C Black Publishers Ltd
36 Soho Square, London W1D 3QY
www.adlardcoles.com

First edition published 2011

Conceived and produced by Weldon Owen Pty Ltd
59-61 Victoria Street, McMahons Point
Sydney, NSW 2060, Australia
Copyright © 2010 Weldon Owen Pty Ltd

WELDON OWEN PTY LTD

Chief Executive Officer Sheena Coupe
Creative Director Sue Burk

Senior Vice President, International Sales Stuart Laurence
Sales Manager: United States Ellen Towell
Vice President, Sales: Asia and Latin America Dawn L. Owen
Administration Manager, International Sales Kristine Ravn
Production Director Todd Rechner
Production Controller Lisa Conway
Production Coordinator Mike Crowton
Production Assistant Nathan Grice

Concept Design Arthur Brown/Cooling Brown
Senior Editor Barbara Sheppard
Editor Shan Wolody
Designers Kristin Mack Alnaes, Christina McInerney
Editorial Assistant Natalie Ryan

Photography Joe Filshie
Photographic styling Georgina Dolling
Photographic retouching Steve Crozier
Hand models Mike Crowton, Jasmine Parker
Index Jo Rudd

All rights reserved. No part of this publication may be reproduced in any form or by any means
 – graphic, electronic or mechanical, including photocopying, recording, taping or information
storage and retrieval systems – without the prior permission in writing of the publishers.

ISBN 978-1-4081-3276-0

 The right of the author to be identified as the author of this work has been asserted by him in
accordance with the Copyright, Designs and Patents Act, 1988.

A CIP catalogue record for this book is available from the British Library.

This book is produced using paper that is made from wood grown in managed, sustainable forests.
It is natural, renewable and recyclable. The logging and manufacturing processes conform to the
environmental regulations of the country of origin.

Typeset in Myriad Pro Light, 11pt
Printed and bound in China by Toppan Leefung Printing Limited

10 9 8 7 6 5 4 3 2 1

Note: while all reasonable care has been taken in the publication of this book, the publisher takes
no responsibility for the use of the methods or products described in the book.

ESSENTIAL

CAMPING · CLIMBING · FISHING · SAILING · SCOUTING

KNOTS

The step-by-step guide to tying the *perfect* knot for every situation

NEVILLE OLLIFFE
MADELEINE ROWLES-OLLIFFE

ADLARD COLES NAUTICAL
LONDON

CONTENTS

INTRODUCTION

People have been making cordage from animal skin and intestine, fibers, and plant material since the beginning of recorded history. Early uses included making shelters, weaving, fishing, and tethering animals. The methods shown, in most cases, are but one way of tying the knots; with practice you may develop other methods, or learn new ones from fellow enthusiasts. Where practical, the tying processes in this book progress from left to right, and turns and rotations are clockwise, or away from you.

HOW TO USE THIS BOOK

Divided into sections by knot type, this book is a collection of practical knots. Some you might simply want to tie for decoration. Similar knots —in a progression from simple to more complex—are presented together. To help determine which type of knot will best suit the task, each knot includes an explanation about what it can be used for, and how difficult untying might be.

Icons
Icons included with each knot indicate suggested use. Some knots have broad applications; others are quite specialized.

 General

 Fishing

 Camping

 Sailing

 Climbing

 Scouting

Star rating
Numbers indicate level of difficulty or complexity of the knot shown.

 Easy

 Intermediate

 Advanced

Directional arrows
Arrows placed on the step-by-step photographs show the path of cord movement. They are included to reinforce the text.

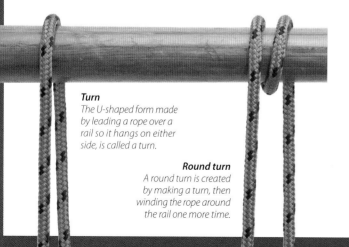

Turn
The U-shaped form made by leading a rope over a rail so it hangs on either side, is called a turn.

Round turn
A round turn is created by making a turn, then winding the rope around the rail one more time.

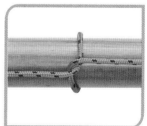

Half hitch
A half hitch is formed when rope is passed around a rail, then either under, or both under and over, itself.

Two half hitches
Two half hitches that are connected and placed directly beside each other make a clove hitch (p. 72).

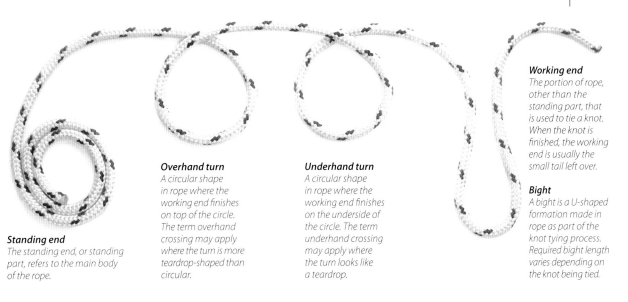

Working end
The portion of rope, other than the standing part, that is used to tie a knot. When the knot is finished, the working end is usually the small tail left over.

Bight
A bight is a U-shaped formation made in rope as part of the knot tying process. Required bight length varies depending on the knot being tied.

Overhand turn
A circular shape in rope where the working end finishes on top of the circle. The term overhand crossing may apply where the turn is more teardrop-shaped than circular.

Underhand turn
A circular shape in rope where the working end finishes on the underside of the circle. The term underhand crossing may apply where the turn looks like a teardrop.

Standing end
The standing end, or standing part, refers to the main body of the rope.

ROPE BASICS

Laid rope is the name given to cordage where the strands—usually three—wind in either a right-handed or left-handed direction. Most braided cordage contains an inner core and an outer layer. The outer component is usually composed of 16 or more woven elements, and the core, the strongest part, is made up of about eight loosely plaited strands.

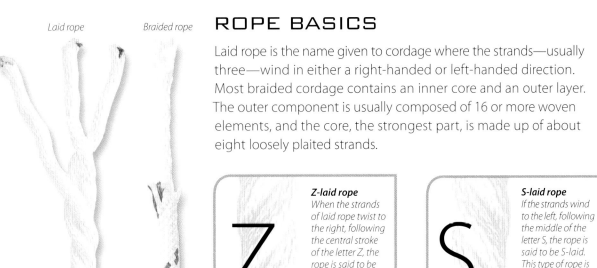

Laid rope

Braided rope

Z-laid rope
When the strands of laid rope twist to the right, following the central stroke of the letter Z, the rope is said to be Z-laid. This is the most common form of laid rope.

S-laid rope
If the strands wind to the left, following the middle of the letter S, the rope is said to be S-laid. This type of rope is less common and is usually reserved for special purposes.

TYPES OF CORDAGE

Rope has undergone major changes since the days of natural fibers. Cotton, flax, jute, sisal, coir, hemp, and manila have given way to synthetics that are strong and resistant to rot and shrinkage. Today, polyester is the most common of the plaited and braided ropes. It is often combined with other fibers to produce ropes of extremely high strength and low stretch. Other synthetic materials include polypropylene and polyethylene, which are most frequently used in the manufacture of laid rope.

Rope care

- Keep rope clean: wash to remove salt and any abrasive matter.
- Avoid abrasion: don't lead rope through sand, or over rock, unprotected corners, and edges.
- Synthetic ropes deteriorate with ultraviolet exposure: store out of direct sunlight.
- Natural fiber ropes can rot: do not store in wet or damp conditions.
- Whip, tie, or heat-seal rope ends to prevent fraying.

	Strength	Stretch	UV Resistance	Float	Handling/Tying
Coir	Poor–low	Considerable	Good	Yes / no	Good
Hemp	Low	Considerable	Good	No	Good
Sisal	Low	Considerable	Good	No	Medium–good
Manila	Low	Moderate	Very good	No	Difficult
Nylon	High	Considerable	Low	No	Good
Polyester laid	Medium–high	Moderate	Very good	No	Good
Polyester braid	High	Low–moderate	Very good	No	Very good
Polypropylene multifilament	Medium	Moderate	Poor	Yes	Very good
Polypropylene shattered film	Medium	Moderate	Good	Yes	Difficult–good
Polyethylene (Silver rope)	Medium	Moderate	Good	Yes	Medium–good
Dyneema®, Spectra® exotics	Very high	Almost nil	Good–low	No	Specialist use

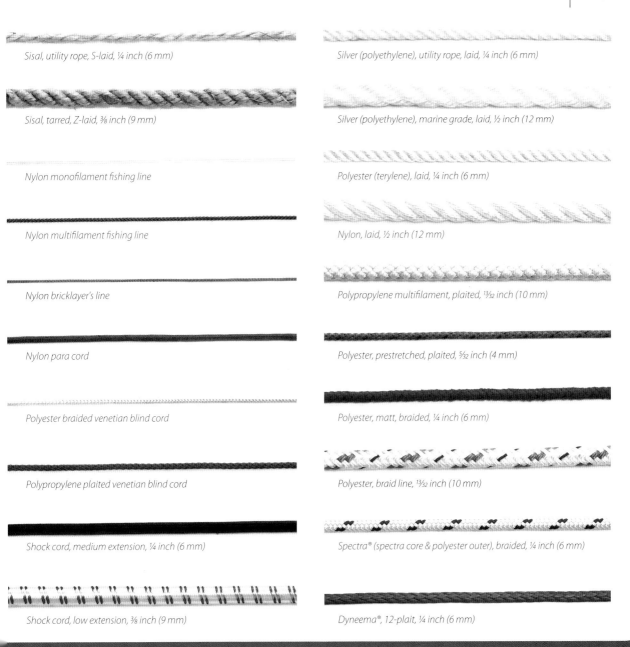

Sisal, utility rope, S-laid, ¼ inch (6 mm)

Sisal, tarred, Z-laid, ⅜ inch (9 mm)

Nylon monofilament fishing line

Nylon multifilament fishing line

Nylon bricklayer's line

Nylon para cord

Polyester braided venetian blind cord

Polypropylene plaited venetian blind cord

Shock cord, medium extension, ¼ inch (6 mm)

Shock cord, low extension, ⅜ inch (9 mm)

Silver (polyethylene), utility rope, laid, ¼ inch (6 mm)

Silver (polyethylene), marine grade, laid, ½ inch (12 mm)

Polyester (terylene), laid, ¼ inch (6 mm)

Nylon, laid, ½ inch (12 mm)

Polypropylene multifilament, plaited, ¹³⁄₃₂ inch (10 mm)

Polyester, prestretched, plaited, ⁵⁄₃₂ inch (4 mm)

Polyester, matt, braided, ¼ inch (6 mm)

Polyester, braid line, ¹³⁄₃₂ inch (10 mm)

Spectra® (spectra core & polyester outer), braided, ¼ inch (6 mm)

Dyneema®, 12-plait, ¼ inch (6 mm)

TOOLS

The most obvious tool for a person handling rope is a sharp knife. However, a knife is sometimes regarded as something to be used only in an emergency—a good quality side cutter is a more useful tool, as it should sever the rope or strand in one go. For very thick rope, there may be no substitute for a sharp knife, and exotic fiber ropes require a special knife (with a partly serrated blade), available from marine stores. Other useful tools include: a hollow or Swedish fid; a wooden fid; a marlinspike; a small engineer's, shoemaker's, or cabinetmaker's hammer; an awl or spike; waxed polyester whipping twine; electrician's PVC stretchy tape; and a cigarette lighter or a hot knife for sealing.

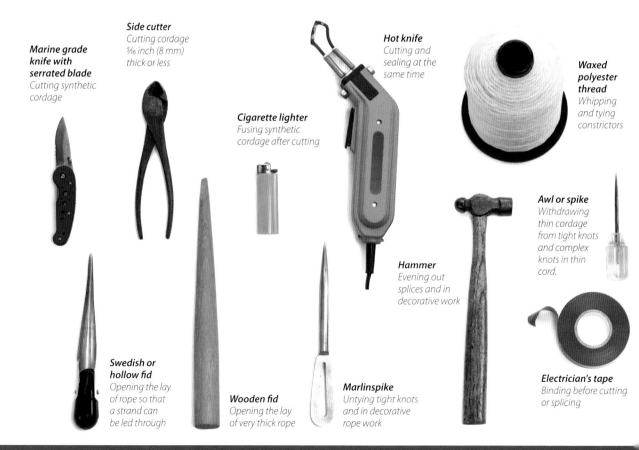

Marine grade knife with serrated blade
Cutting synthetic cordage

Side cutter
Cutting cordage 5/16 inch (8 mm) thick or less

Hot knife
Cutting and sealing at the same time

Waxed polyester thread
Whipping and tying constrictors

Cigarette lighter
Fusing synthetic cordage after cutting

Awl or spike
Withdrawing thin cordage from tight knots and complex knots in thin cord.

Hammer
Evening out splices and in decorative work

Swedish or hollow fid
Opening the lay of rope so that a strand can be led through

Wooden fid
Opening the lay of very thick rope

Marlinspike
Untying tight knots and in decorative rope work

Electrician's tape
Binding before cutting or splicing

CUTTING & SEALING

Before cutting rope with anything other than a hot knife, use knots or tape to stop the lay or braid from fraying. Tie a knot either side of where it is to be cut.

If using a knife, check that it is sharp. Alternatively, tape either side of the cut for thick rope, or tape once and cut through the center of the tape.

1 Tie a tight constrictor knot (pp. 28–9) on either side of where the rope is to be cut.

1 Make about three tight windings with electrician's tape at the site of the cut. For thick cordage, tape on either side of the cut.

1 Hold the rope above the cigarette lighter flame, not in it. Cautiously dab the end with moistened fingers or a wet sponge to tidy the edges.

2 Cut with a side cutter, or place the rope on a piece of wood and cut it with a very sharp knife.

2 Use a side cutter, or place the rope on wood and cut with a sharp knife. Press hard and cut through the center of the tape.

2 Alternatively, if you have access to a hot knife, cut the rope against a piece of wood. Cut thick rope in four- or five-second time segments.

WHIPPING

Whipping is the traditional method used to finish the end of a piece of rope, or its individual strands, so that it doesn't unlay, or come apart. Also, some knots can loosen when the load is removed or the rope is shaken. If the working end is whipped to the standing part, this will prevent the knot from coming undone. For whippings in the end of rope, it is usually best to begin near the end and work in the direction of the standing part. The recommended length for whipping is around one-and-a-half times the diameter of the rope, but this may be varied according to use or aesthetics.

COMMON WHIPPING

This is the quickest and most secure whipping. Both ends of the twine are tucked securely beneath the windings. It needs two lengths of twine: one about 3 feet (1 m) long for the whipping, and a shorter one, middled to form a bight, for the pull-through.

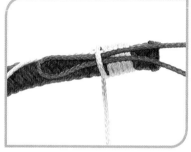

2 Wind about half way. Install the pull-through so that additional bindings will cover all but the end of the bight.

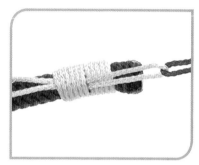

4 Maintain tension on the twine, and tug on the pull-through to draw the whipping under the bindings.

1 Make a turn around the end of the rope with the twine, and tightly bind along the rope and over the tail.

3 Continue binding tightly. When finished, pass the working end through the bight.

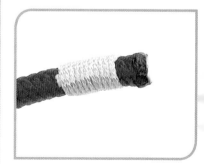

5 Trim the ends about ⅛ inch (3 mm) from the binding and fuse close to the binding with a cigarette lighter.

FRENCH WHIPPING

French whipping is a succession of tight half hitches. It produces an attractive spiral pattern. In thin cord, it can be used to cover a handle to improve its grip.

WEST COUNTRY WHIPPING

West country whipping secures each turn as you go. Should the whipping chafe at one point, it is less likely that the whole lot will come undone.

1 Tie an overhand knot (p. 17) around the rope with twine, so that the working end is proceeding in the direction that you are about to bind.

1 Start with 3 feet (1 m) of twine. At its center, tie an overhand knot (p. 17) around the rope. Tie all following overhand knots in the same way as the first—either left over, or right over.

2 Tie a half hitch (p. 6) to bind the tail to the rope. Push the hitch tightly against the overhand knot. Continue tying half hitches. The tail can be trimmed after five half hitches.

2 Turn the rope over and tie an overhand knot on the opposite side to the first. Continue alternating so that the knots progress along each side of the rope without overlapping.

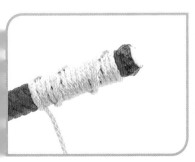

3 Make the last two half hitches with an extra tuck each, as in the multiple overhand knot (p. 17). Trim ⅛ inch (3 mm) from the binding and fuse with a cigarette lighter.

3 Finish each side with an extra turn around itself, as in the multiple overhand knot (p. 17). Trim the ends ⅛ inch (3 mm) from the knot and fuse with a cigarette lighter.

COILING ROPE

The easiest way to store or carry a length of rope is to coil it. However, simply gathering overhand turns can put a twist in the rope: a clockwise twist if you are right handed, a counterclockwise twist if left. The methods demonstrated here gather the coils with the right hand and collect them in the left.

1 Depending on the thickness and length of the rope, form a suitably sized overhand turn. Ensure that the short end hangs below the bottom of the turn so that it won't slip inside and tangle.

2 Pick up the hanging part with the thumb and index finger. As you raise it, turn the hanging part toward you with a clockwise turn of the wrist. Place this underhand turn next to the previous one in the left hand.

3 Make alternate overhand and underhand turns. If the rope is twisted and it is not convenient to shake it out, gather an over- or underhand turn or two out of order to accommodate the twist temporarily.

WRAPPED COIL

This coiling technique is particularly suitable for long-term storage or transport. It takes longer to tie than other methods but there is little chance of other ropes or coils tangling with it.

1 Tie a reef knot (p. 22–3) at the top, with each working end twice the length of the coil's circumference.

2 Wind the right working end over and around—and the left, under and around—to the bottom of the coil.

3 Where the working ends meet, tie another reef knot, so that the two knots are at opposite sides of the coil.

BUNDLED COIL

This is a quick method that can be easily undone, to secure a coil that can be tossed into a trailer, stored in a locker, or hung by the tail. It can also be used for stowing a jib sheet or other sailing rope, and for securing the unused portion of a rope when either the tail or the standing part is fixed.

1 Leave a working tail up to one-and-a-half times the circumference of the coil. Elongate the coil and at about one-third down from the top, wind the tail around the coil moving upward and over itself.

2 Make about four neat windings that do not overlap. Form a bight in the tail, pull it through the coil, and slip it over and around the top of the coil. Pull on the tail.

3 The coil can be hung on a peg, or tied by the tail to a rail using a clove hitch (p. 72) or a slipped overhand knot (p. 18). To undo the coil, slide the bight back over the top and through the coil.

DOUBLE SLIP COIL

The double slip method allows for very quick access to the coil. It works in a similar manner to the highwayman's hitch (pp. 80–1). If the coil does not need to be hung, or is to be placed over a peg, simply pull the slip overhand knot tight at the end of Step 2, and do not continue with Step 3.

1 Leaving a tail about one-and-a-half times the circumference of the coil, form a bight with its center about two hand spans from the top of the coil.

2 Pass the bight over and around the coil and tie a slipped overhand knot (p. 18). Hold both the coil and the overhand knot together in one hand.

3 Form a new bight in the tail, lead it into the coil, up, over, and to the right of the first bight, then under itself. Tighten. Hang the coil by the first bight. To release, unhang and pull on the tail.

STOPPERS

Stopper knots of the simple kind shown here are tied to prevent rope, line, or string slipping through a hole or other narrow opening. They also stop cord ends fraying. The overhand knot is the simplest, and is the starting point for many other knots. Try a multiple overhand knot when a bulkier stopper is required. The figure-of-eight knot, the easiest of the three to untie, is often used when sailing.

OVERHAND KNOT

- MULTIPLE OVERHAND
- SLIPPED OVERHAND

The simplest knot that can be tied, the overhand knot is the starting point for many other knots. On its own, the overhand knot works as a stopper, but when pulled tight, may be difficult to untie. The multiple overhand knot is more easily loosened. The slipped overhand knot can be released quickly, but be careful how you use it, as it may shake loose.

Pass the working end over and through the center of the turn, from back to front. Pull on both ends to tighten the knot.

With the standing part of the rope in the left hand and the working end in the right, make an overhand turn.

MULTIPLE OVERHAND

Feed the working end around the turn several times.

Begin as for Step 1 of the overhand knot, but before tightening, feed the working end around the turn another one, two, or three times.

If you need to untie a multiple overhand knot, try flexing it to loosen it.

The more times you take the working end around the turn, the more you will have to manipulate the knot when tightening to make it even and tidy.

Wind the bight, but not the end itself, over and through the center of the turn.

SLIPPED OVERHAND

Make an overhand turn as in Step 1 of the overhand knot (p. 17), but with sufficient length in your right hand to make a generous bight.

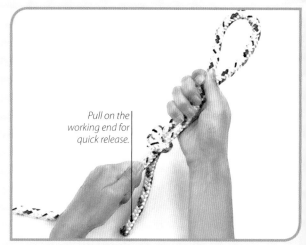

Pull on the working end for quick release.

Tighten by pulling on both the standing part and the bight. To undo, pull on the working end and the knot will slip apart easily.

FIGURE-OF-EIGHT KNOT

Deriving its name from the shape of the numeral 8, the figure-of-eight knot is almost as simple to tie as the overhand knot (p. 17). It can be tied quickly at the end of a rope. When pulled tight and put under strain, the figure-of-eight knot is much easier to untie than the overhand knot. For any application using pulleys or block and tackle, it is the best knot for preventing rope from running out through a block.

With the standing part in the left hand and the working end in the right, make an overhand turn. Tuck the working end behind the standing part and bring it forward.

Follow the shape of the numeral 8 and lead the working end through the overhand turn.

Direct the working end through the turn, from front to back, and pull on both ends. If it has been pulled very tight and is difficult to untie, bend the knot slightly to loosen.

BINDINGS

Binding knots are tied in a single piece of cordage around bundles of objects, such as coiled rope strands and bag necks, to hold them together or seal the opening. Bindings and lashings perform similar tasks, but bindings are temporary, can be used on pliable materials, and have just one or two confining turns rather than multiple windings. Bindings should not be used as bends to join two lengths of cordage, nor as hitches to attach load-bearing rope to an object.

SURGEON'S KNOT: BINDING

As the name suggests, this knot gained its name on the operating table. It is simple to tie and works particularly well in suture material and thin twine. The first half of the knot is capable of keeping tension on the object until the second half is secured. This binding version of a surgeon's knot is a variation on the surgeon's knot bend (p. 58) and has one extra winding in the second stage. When tied using fine line, it will be difficult to untie and may need to be cut.

2 What began as your left working end is now your right. Wind the new right working end over and around the left, and continue to make a second winding.

1 Pass the cord around the item or bundle and wind the left end over and around the right end—as for the first half of a reef knot (pp. 22–3)—twice, then tighten.

In some applications, a third winding is added to each half of the knot.

3 Tighten so that the two halves of the knot lie evenly side by side. Fine or slippery cord may slip slightly until the second stage of the knot is firmed.

BINDINGS

REEF KNOT
• GRANNY KNOT

The reef knot is easy to tie and untie, and is a very useful knot for tying bundles and securing parcels. The name probably comes from its use in reducing sail in bad weather—"reefing down"—by tying reef points around the excess sail. It must be tightened against a surface for stability. The granny knot is usually a reef knot gone wrong, and shown only so that you will recognize it. It is not reliable and when it does work, it is hard to untie. Of the two knots, the reef knot is far superior.

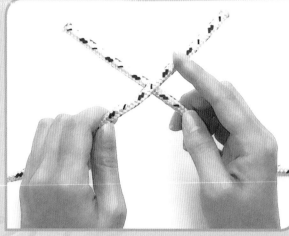

1 With an end of rope in each hand, lay the left working end over the right.

2 Wind the left end around the right end and bring it back to the front. What were once the left and right ends of rope are now reversed.

*Left over right,
then right over left*

3 Do the same as for Step 2, except wind the new right working end over the left. The rule is to wind the left end in the first half of the knot, and the right in the second.

GRANNY KNOT

5 For the granny knot, proceed as for the reef knot to the end of Step 2. Then instead of Step 3, wind the left over the right again.

4 Draw both sides of the rope tight to complete the knot.

6 Pull very tight. When the surface of the rope is slippery or smooth, the granny knot has a tendency to slip, especially when not pulled taut against a flat surface.

BINDINGS

POLE LASHING

Pole lashing, also known as the scaffold hitch and Oklahoma hitch, will bind long thin objects of assorted sizes and profiles. When used as quick lashing, the ends pulling through their respective bights work as a tackle, helping to draw the bundle up tightly before it is secured with a binding knot, such as a reef knot (pp. 22–3). If the shape of the bundle changes during tightening, the hitch can be adjusted. A pair of pole lashings can hold glued items firmly until dry. As a plank sling, it makes a quick and simple temporary shelf for the garage.

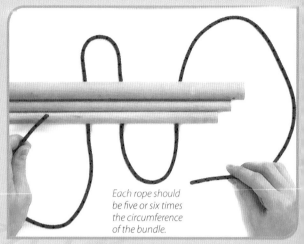

Each rope should be five or six times the circumference of the bundle.

1 To bind a bundle, you will need two lengths of rope—one for a pole lashing at each end. Arrange the rope on the ground in a Z pattern, and lay one end of the bundle on top.

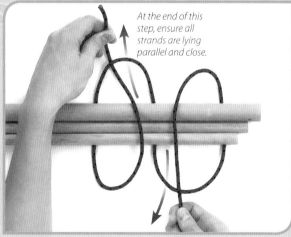

At the end of this step, ensure all strands are lying parallel and close.

2 There is now a bight on either side of the bundle. Pass each end of rope across the top of the bundle and through the opposite bight. Pull on the ends to tighten.

Reef knot reminder: left over right, then right over left.

3 Secure the lashing with a binding knot, such as the reef knot (pp. 22–3). With the lashing pulled tight, lead the left working end over the right.

PLANK SLING

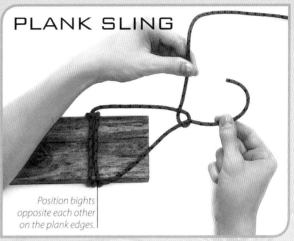

Position bights opposite each other on the plank edges.

5 When suspending a plank, arrange the bights at the edges of the plank, with all parts of the rope lying flat on the plank. A bowline (pp. 36–7) can be tied to join both ends.

4 Take the right working end over the left and pull tight. Repeat Steps 1–4 at the other end of the bundle. A bundle may splay apart unless secured in two places.

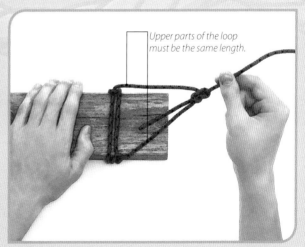

Upper parts of the loop must be the same length.

6 Make sure that the two upper parts of the loop are the same length, so that the bowline is centered and the plank will sit level when suspended.

BAG KNOT
• SLIPPED BAG KNOT

Well suited to securing the neck of a cloth bag, the bag knot is similar to the constrictor knot (pp. 28–9), so study both carefully—it is easy to confuse the two. A bag knot is held secure by the friction between the rope and the bag itself, therefore it may not work well using slippery rope. For small bags and fine cord, use a slipped bag knot to save time untying a tiny, tight knot or to prevent the bag from being nicked by a tool used to pick the knot apart.

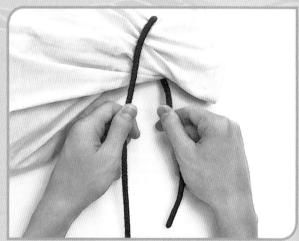

1 Make a turn over the gathered neck of the sack, placing the working end to the right of the standing part.

BINDINGS

2 Bring the working end to the top left, crossing it over the standing part.

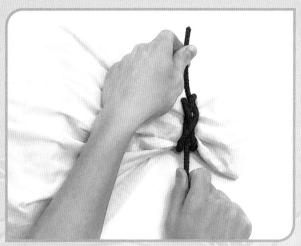

4 Lay the working end diagonally right across the knot and tuck it under the first turn made around the sack, feeding it from right to left. Pull tight.

3 Feed the working end around the back of the sack and place it to the left of the standing part.

SLIPPED BAG KNOT

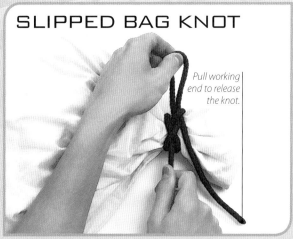

Pull working end to release the knot.

5 For a slipped version of the knot, make a bight in the working end before tucking it under the turn in Step 4. Pull tight. To release, simply pull on the working end.

CONSTRICTOR KNOT

• SLIPPED CONSTRICTOR KNOT

This is a useful knot for tying a bundle. It is similar to the bag knot (pp. 26–7), but relies on the friction between the parts of the rope itself, rather than between the rope and the surface. The constrictor can often be used instead of a clove hitch (p. 72): the constrictor is more secure but can be more difficult to untie. When tied in a colored thread, it can mark a particular point in a complicated knot.

1 Working from left to right, wind the working end over and around the bundle, forming a turn.

2 Cross the working end diagonally left over the standing part, and wind it around the bundle again.

To sever a constrictor knot, cut through this top turn with a knife. The lower turns protect the bundle from being nicked.

Ease the two halves of the knot together and pull tightly on both ends.

4 Take the working end over the top of the first turn that was formed and pass it underneath. The working end should now be in the center, between the two turns.

3 Proceeding from left to right, take the working end under the diagonal crossing. You have now formed a loose clove hitch.

SLIPPED CONSTRICTOR KNOT

Tug on the working end to quickly release the knot.

5 For the slipped version, begin with Steps 1–3 of the constrictor knot. Make a bight in the working end and complete Step 4 using this bight.

BINDINGS

BOTTLE SLING

The bottle sling, also called the jug sling, is a little more involved than some other binding knots. The knot provides a carry handle for a bottle, or any item, with a flange or shoulder large enough to prevent the knot from slipping off. The bottle sling provides an artistic way to display decorative bottles and lipped vases, and allows drinks to be hung over the side of a boat to cool in the water. The knot should be laid out spaciously on a surface, as the procedure is as much visual as it is mechanical. This example requires about 5 feet (1.5 m) of cord.

Center of original bight

2 Partially overlap the right ear over the left, so that the center of the original bight remains below the lower intersection of the ears.

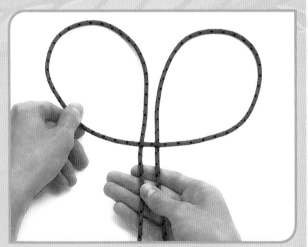

1 Middle the cord and place the resulting bight flat on the table. Draw the bight down over the standing parts to make two evenly sized "ears."

Keep the knot flat on the table.

3 Holding the pattern in place on the table with one hand, draw the center of the original bight under the knot at the point of the lower intersection of the ears.

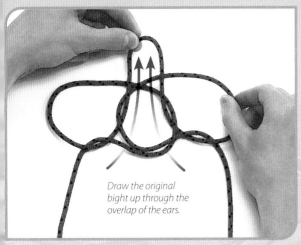

Draw the original bight up through the overlap of the ears.

4 Now bring the center of the original bight up through the space formed by the overlapping ears, to make a new bight at the top.

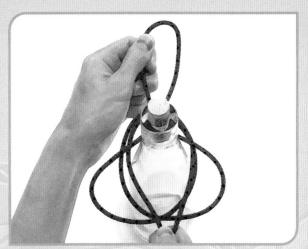

6 Lift the knot carefully and place the hole over the neck of the bottle. Tighten by pulling on the upper bight and evenly on the pair of ends.

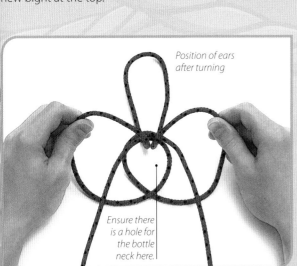

Position of ears after turning

Ensure there is a hole for the bottle neck here.

5 Using both hands, turn the ears and center part over simultaneously, with the top moving away from you. The top of the ears now finish at the bottom of the pattern.

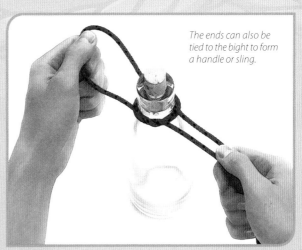

The ends can also be tied to the bight to form a handle or sling.

7 Work the knot to a snug fit around the neck of the bottle. The ends can be tied together to make a second handle, using a fisherman's knot (p. 56) or figure-of-eight bend (p. 55).

BINDINGS

TRANSOM KNOT

The transom knot is used to tie two poles together at right angles. It is similar to the constrictor knot (pp. 28–9). While not as strong or rigid as the square lashing (pp. 93–4) or diagonal lashing (pp. 95–6), it is quicker to tie and easier to remove. This makes it particularly suitable for light jobs with many knots to be tied. The knot can be reinforced with a second transom knot tied at 90 degrees to the first. Using less cord than a lashing, the transom knot is good for small, fiddly tasks. A drop of glue applied where the cord crosses will make the knot more secure.

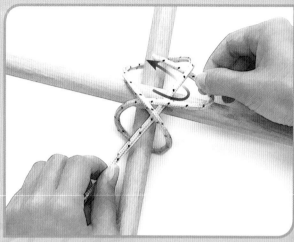

2 Firm the knot slightly. It should resemble two half hitches. Lead the working end over and under the right-hand portion of the first diagonal.

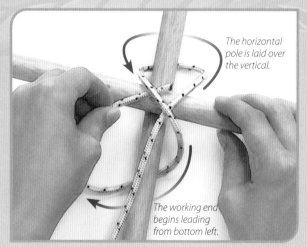

The horizontal pole is laid over the vertical.

The working end begins leading from bottom left.

1 Lead the working end diagonally across the intersection, left behind the vertical pole, diagonally across again, left behind the vertical pole, and under the last diagonal crossing.

To double the strength, tie a second transom knot behind the first.

3 Pull the standing and working ends in opposite directions If required, turn the structure over, rotate it 90 degrees, and with another piece of cord, tie the knot again.

LOOPS

Loop knots are closed bights tied either in the bight, which requires no access to the ends, or at the end of a rope. Single, double, or multiple loops can be formed. Fixed loops do not change size. Running loops are tied, then pulled tight around an object. When rope must be reused, select a knot that is easily untied. Some that are hard to untie after loading particularly suit disposable fine line and shock cord. Having an independent structure, fixed loops can be used for handholds, footholds, and reusable attachment points.

FIGURE-OF-EIGHT LOOP

LOOPS

This is a fixed single loop tied in the same way as the figure-of-eight knot (p. 19) but with a bight formed in the working end. It can also be tied along the length of rope—called a figure-of-eight on the bight—and can take a load on one end, both ends in parallel, or both ends pulling in different directions. Items to be attached to the loop can be threaded into the bight before tying, or cow hitched to the loop after tying.

Continue the figure-of-eight pattern and pass the loop, or the item that was threaded into it earlier, through the turn, from front to back.

Form a bight and make an overhand crossing. The bight will become the loop. Lead the loop around behind the standing part and the working end.

Pull the loop tight. A load may be applied to both ends or to the long standing part only. The loop is very secure but can be harder to untie than the figure-of-eight knot.

SURGEON'S LOOP

The surgeon's loop is a fixed loop that holds well in thin, smooth cord, fishing line, and shock cord. It is, in fact, a triple overhand knot tied with a bight. Single and double overhand versions are tied in exactly the same way but might not be as secure. It is a difficult knot to untie once loaded, so is best used for permanent loops or where the line will be cut once the loop is no longer needed. Wetting fine line will make it easier to work the knot tight.

Make a second and a third winding.

Wind the bight through the turn twice more to tie a triple overhand knot. For shock cord, the two extra windings should suffice. Three is best for fishing line.

LOOPS

Form a bight and make a loose overhand knot.

Begin with a bight twice the length of the loop that you wish to make. Form an overhand turn in the bight and tie an overhand knot (p. 17).

Work spiral section tight and even.

Hold the bight in one hand and the standing parts in the other: pull to firm the knot. It is important to the integrity of the knot to achieve an even, spiral appearance.

LOOPS

BOWLINE

- DOUBLE BOWLINE
- WATER BOWLINE
- BOWLINE: ALTERNATE

The bowline, a fixed loop, is a practical knot that is especially useful on a boat or dockside. The double bowline is used for very slippery rope, and the water bowline in cordage that may tend to jam when wet. Two ropes of different type and diameter may be joined by tying a bowline in each with the loops interlocked.

Begin with a working part twice the length of the circumference of the loop you wish to make.

Make a small overhand turn and lead the working end through it from underneath. The size of the finished loop depends on how much of the working end is pulled through

LOOPS

Make sure the working end is led correctly through the turn.

Having decided on the size of the loop, pass the working end behind the standing part, up and to the front, then lead it back through the turn, parallel with itself.

DOUBLE BOWLINE

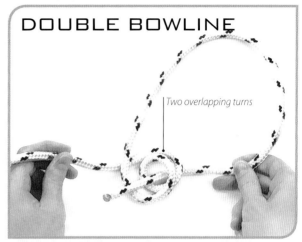

Two overlapping turns

For a double bowline, make two overlapping overhand turns instead of the single turn in Step 1, and pass the working end up and through both turns.

Grasp the working end and its parallel part in one hand, the standing part in the other, and pull. If the knot falls apart, the working end was led incorrectly in Step 1.

Continue the working end behind the standing part as in Step 2, then back and parallel with itself through both turns.

LOOPS

Tighten as in Step 3, and take the slack out of the knot. If the loop is now too large, ease it out on the parallel part and remove the slack by pulling on the working end.

Continue leading the working end behind the standing part, up and to the front, then back through each turn, following the same pattern as in Step 2.

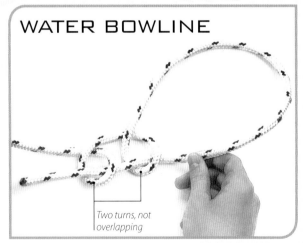

WATER BOWLINE

Two turns, not overlapping

For a water bowline, begin with Step 1, but make two distinct overhand turns and do not overlap them. Lead the working end up through each turn separately.

When using the knot, ensure that the inner half hitch holds the working end captive.

Inner half hitch

Tighten as in Step 3. Feed the slack out of the inner half hitch and transfer it to the loop. The loop can be adjusted if necessary as in Step 6.

BOWLINE: ALTERNATE

Use this method to tie a bowline directly around an object.

Tie an overhand knot, making sure the working end passes over the standing part and then under it. The working end must be long enough to allow a firm handhold.

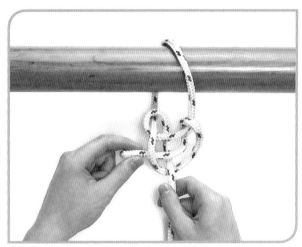

Take the working end behind the standing part from left to right, through the loop from front to back, then back over the standing part and under itself.

Capsize the overhand knot by pulling the working end downward until it is straight. The standing part forms a turn around it, as in Step 2.

Pull the working end upward and away so that it slides under the bottom of the turn and pops inside it. Pull it around the back and to the right to sit inside the loop.

LOOPS

BOWLINE ON THE BIGHT

This is a fixed double loop tied either in the bight or with a bight formed at the end of the rope. The parallel loops can function as two single loops or one thicker, stronger loop, and the load can be applied to one or both standing parts. Bar and brewery workers once used this bowline for hoisting and lowering barrels off trucks and into cellars. Like the Spanish bowline (pp. 50–1), it can be utilized to lift irregularly shaped objects.

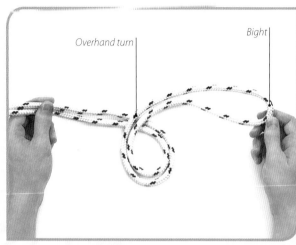

Overhand turn

Bight

Form a bight twice the circumference of the loop that you wish to create. The bight itself is the working end. Make a small overhand turn.

Make sure the working end is led correctly through the turn.

Lead the bight through the turn, from back to front. The portion that is not drawn through the turn will become the loop.

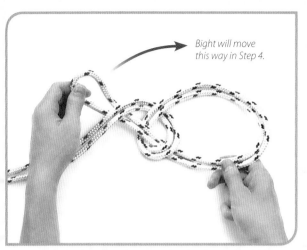

Bight will move this way in Step 4.

As with the bowline (pp. 36–7), take the end of the bight up and around behind the standing part.

Pull on the standing parts and the lower, or bight, side of the loop to tighten. You may have to feed some of the bight excess into the loop itself.

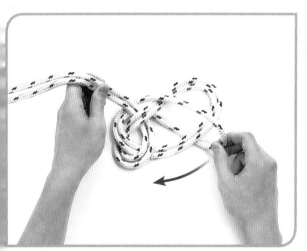

Open out the bight and slip it over and around the whole knot, so that it holds the two standing ends captive.

The two loops can be used separately or as one. If the knot is loosened and adjusted, one loop can be made proportionally larger or smaller than the other.

LOOPS

ANGLER'S LOOP

The angler's loop is a fixed single loop normally tied in an end. It makes a secure, permanent loop that holds well under load in fishing line and shock cord. It is important, however, to pull the knot up tight before use. In thin cord, fishing line, or shock cord, the angler's loop is difficult or impossible to untie and is best used where line can be cut once the loop is no longer needed. A clip, snap hook, or other item can be threaded into the bight at Step 1, or cow hitched to the loop later.

Begin with a working part twice the length of the loop you wish to make. Make an underhand turn and then form a bight in the working end.

Direction of rotation in Step 2

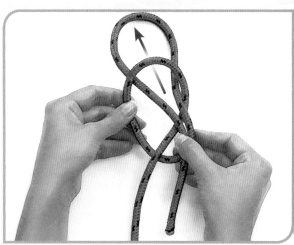

Rotate the bight right to left, then lead it through the turn from front to back. The bight, which is now the slipped portion, will become the loop.

Overhand knot

If the working end is excessively long, pull the extra cord into the loop. Work it out through the overhand knot and into the standing end.

Slide the working end under both strands of the loop, from right to left.

Thumb inserted to show channel the working end passes through in Step 5.

Lead the working end around behind the standing part, adjacent to the lower portion of the overhand knot.

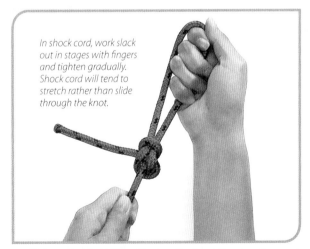

In shock cord, work slack out in stages with fingers and tighten gradually. Shock cord will tend to stretch rather than slide through the knot.

Tighten the knot by pulling on the loop, the standing part, and the working end. Pull hard on the loop and standing part to complete, particularly in shock cord, which stretches.

ALPINE BUTTERFLY KNOT

The alpine butterfly knot, or loop, also known as the lineman's loop, is an easily untied fixed single loop. It suits fishing line, cord, and thin rope, but is awkward to tie in thick rope. It can be loaded on either end or on the loop, so in a hoisting line, it provides both a load attachment loop and a ground control line. The knot can extend a damaged rope's life when tied with the weakened section in an unloaded loop.

Lay the left standing part diagonally over the turn.

Winding away from you, left to right, make a round turn and one extra turn around the left hand. Place the left standing part over the first turn and secure it with the thumb.

Extend this turn to create a long bight.

Pick up the bottom of the left round turn and, allowing the left standing part to run around the hand, extend a bight to at least triple the size of the turn.

Secure the two standing parts together with the left thumb, grasp the loop with the right hand, and pull to tighten.

Tuck the bight underneath all the turns on the hand.

Lead the newly extended bight to the right and tuck it, right to left, under all the turns that are wound around the hand to form a loop.

Work the knot into a tidy shape at the base of the loop.

The two standing parts can now be spread to restore the function of a continuous rope. You may need to work the outer turns of the knot inward and pull on the loop to tidy it.

LOOPS

BLOOD LOOP DROPPER KNOT

The blood loop dropper knot is a fixed loop that holds well in slippery materials, such as shock cord and fishing line. Its tight wrapping turns identify it as a member of the blood knot family, which includes the blood knot (p. 57). The loop is perfect for attaching droppers—separate lines with a hook or sinker, which give the knot its name—to a single line. Wetting fine line will make it easier to tighten the knot. When making a series of dropper loops, tie the loop furthest from the working end first.

Form an overhand turn at the required place along a line; secure it with your thumb and index finger. The size of the turn depends on the number of windings you make in Step 2.

Tie a multiple overhand knot with four, six, or eight windings. The thinner and more slippery the line, the greater the number required to make the knot secure.

Note that in doing this, half a turn is lost from the left part of the windings and another is added to the right.

Pick up the bottom center point of the original turn and lead it up through the hole to form a loop. Check that the hole is actually at the center of the windings.

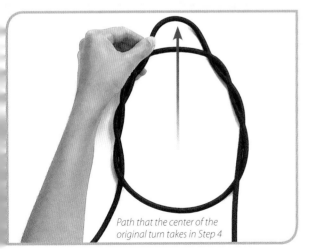

Path that the center of the original turn takes in Step 4

Find the center point of the windings and draw it slightly away from the turn to make a hole. Keep the hole open.

Secure the loop by pulling three ways: on the loop and the two portions of line. If necessary, slide the windings neatly up to the loop.

ARBOR KNOT

This knot makes a running loop that can be put around a post, spar, or drum, and tightened by pulling on the standing part. It is one of several arbor knots that can be used to attach fishing line to a reel, or arbor. This particular running loop can be collapsed without having to be untied: once the item in the loop is removed, simply pull on the standing part and the loop slips back through the knot, which collapses. Never use a running loop in any situation where it could get caught around a person's fingers or limbs.

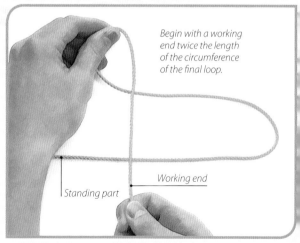

Begin with a working end twice the length of the circumference of the final loop.

Standing part

Working end

Form a bight, with the standing part as the lower strand and the working end above it. Make an overhand turn in the working end and lead it down over the standing part.

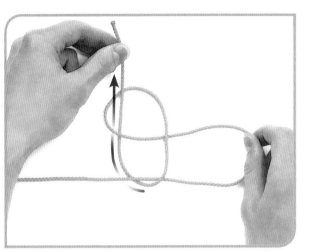

Tuck the working end under the standing part, lead it upward under the lower part of the turn, and up through the center of the turn. This forms one wind.

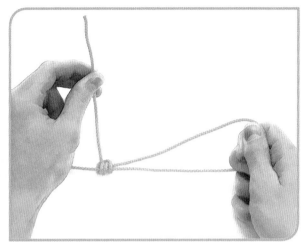

Pull on the bight and the working end to firm the windings about the standing part. Mold the turns into shape by rolling them between thumb and index finger.

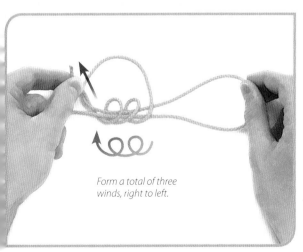

Form a total of three winds, right to left.

Wind the working end around the inside of the turn and the standing part, twice more. Work from right to left, and downward at the front and upward behind.

A reel can now be placed in the loop. Pull on the standing part and slide the knot hard against the reel. To remove the reel, slide the knot back along the standing part.

LOOPS

SPANISH BOWLINE

The Spanish bowline, like the bowline on the bight (pp. 40–1), is a fixed double loop tied in the bight, but with splayed loops rather than parallel ones. The size of each loop can be independently adjusted. Irregularly shaped objects can be hoisted using this knot as long as the loops are adjusted to fit snugly, so that slack isn't pulled from one loop into the other if the loops are unequally loaded. This bowline has been used in emergency rescue.

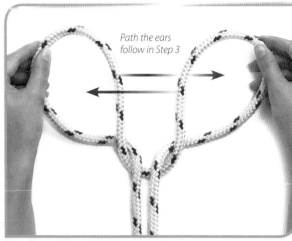

Path the ears follow in Step 3

Turn each ear over symmetrically away from you, to give the overhand intersections an extra winding.

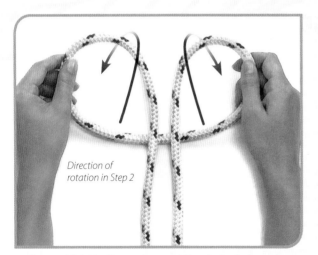

Direction of rotation in Step 2

Form a bight in the center, or at the desired place along a length of rope, open out the bight and turn it over and away from you to create two overhand turns, or "ears."

Crossing turn

Cross the two ears, sliding the left ear under and up through the right ear. Note that a crossing turn has been formed around the two standing parts.

Grasp the rope here.

Keep the pattern flat on the table, and pass the fingers of each hand into their respective ears from the rear. With the left fingers, pick up the left edge of the crossing turn.

Continue drawing your hands apart to create a new bight in each hand. Tighten by pulling on the loops together in one hand and the standing parts in the other.

Grasp the rope here.

Draw it slightly into the left ear. Repeat with the right hand, picking up the right edge of the crossing turn and drawing it into the right ear.

The inside part of each loop is fixed.

Adjust relative loop sizes by pulling on the outer edges.

The inside part of each loop is locked by the knot, but the outer edges can be slid to make one loop larger or smaller than the other.

LOOPS

JURY MAST KNOT

This knot allows an extra spar to be "jury rigged" as an emergency mast. The center eye sits over the end and the ropes holding the makeshift mast upright attach to the three adjustable loops. It can also be used for erecting a tent or flagpole, as long as there is a shoulder, through bolt, or other device to prevent the knot sliding down the pole. Laid flat, it is an interesting and attractive knot that can be stitched to a bag or jacket sleeve as decorative trim.

Lead the left hand into the first turn from underneath, over the left edge of the second turn, under the right edge of the first turn, and pick up the left edge of the third.

Working from left to right, make three underhand turns. The left edges of the second and third turns should overlap the right edges of the first and second turns.

With the right hand, lead over the right edge of the third turn, under the right edge of the second turn, over the left edge of the third turn, and pick up the right edge of the first

Center of second turn

Draw your hands apart far enough so that two loose bights begin to form. The remainder of the knot should be circular in shape with an obvious hole in the middle.

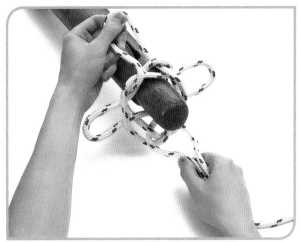

Place the knot over the end of a spar, and adjust to fit snugly. Tie both standing ends together about the spar. The three bights become attachment points for stays.

The second turn is still in the circular portion of the knot. Draw it out carefully at the top to form a third bight. Adjust the knot so that the three bights are of a similar size.

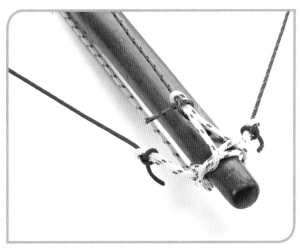

The stays—rope or wire supporting the mast—can be attached to the jury mast knot with sheet bends or double sheet bends (pp. 62–3).

BENDS

Bends join two lengths of cordage. Some bends are secure only in lines of the same size, or under constant load. Others can join lines of different sizes, or hold secure even when unloaded and shaken. A few are particularly suited to specific materials, such as shock cord. Some hitches, such as the anchor bend (pp. 76–7), are also called bends: in old sailing terminology "to bend" meant to attach a rope to an object, usually an anchor, or to join two ropes together. Such hitches should not be confused with actual bends.

FIGURE-OF-EIGHT BEND

The figure-of-eight bend is also known as a Flemish bend. It is a suitable knot for joining two lengths of cordage of the same diameter, but the bend can be rather bulky in some cordage. It is not suited to monofilament fishing line and shock cord. The tying process is simple and easy to remember, especially once you know how to tie the figure-of-eight knot, and produces a strong, reliable result.

2 Lead the second rope into the knot parallel to the first working end. Continue through the knot until the second working end emerges beside the standing part of the first.

1 Tie a loose figure-of-eight knot (p. 19) near, but not too close to, the end of the first length of rope. Then begin doubling the knot with the second rope.

3 Make sure the knot is neat and even. Pull alternately on the standing parts and the working ends to tighten.

BENDS

BENDS

FISHERMAN'S KNOT

- DOUBLE FISHERMAN'S KNOT
- BLOOD KNOT

These knots are suitable for joining two lengths of fishing line, shock cord, and thin rope of similar size and type. The fisherman's knot is also known as the angler's, English, halibut, and waterman's knot. The double fisherman's knot, which is less inclined to slip, is used by climbers, while the blood knot is mainly an angling knot.

2 Make an overhand knot with the second working end to capture the standing part of the first rope. Tie this second overhand knot in the opposite direction to the first.

1 Lead the working ends together from opposite directions and overlap them. Make an overhand knot (p.17) in one of the working ends so that the other rope is captured.

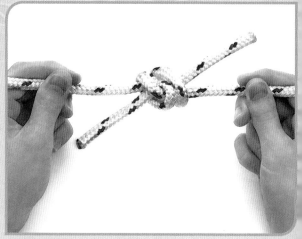

3 Pull each overhand knot tight, then draw the two together by pulling on the standing parts.

DOUBLE FISHERMAN'S KNOT

4 For a more secure version of the fisherman's knot, tie a multiple overhand knot (pp. 17–18) with two windings in each working end around the other rope's standing part.

The ends should be pointing in opposite directions

6 Repeat with the second rope around its partner, winding in the opposite direction for the same number of turns, and taking the working end back between the two ropes.

BLOOD KNOT

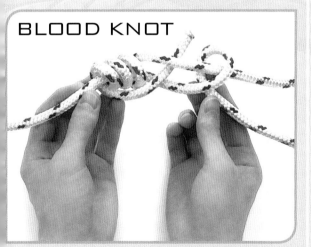

5 Begin with a slightly longer overlap than in Step 1. Wind one rope around the other four or five times. Return the working end over the windings and between the two ropes.

7 Pull on the standing parts to bring the two halves together, then firm up and neaten the knot by pulling on the working ends. Pull on the standing parts again.

BENDS

SURGEON'S KNOT: BEND

The surgeon's knot bend, also called the ligature knot, is a variation of a reef knot (pp. 22–3). The surgeon's knot works well in sewing cotton and twine, but it should not be made with shock cord or ropes of significantly different size and texture. For greater security when using fishing line, tie the knot with three windings in Step 1 and two windings in Step 2. Although it may initially slip with fishing line, the knot becomes secure when tightened properly.

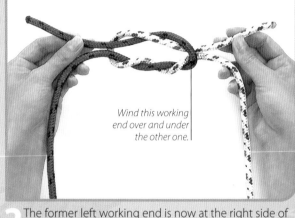

Wind this working end over and under the other one.

2 The former left working end is now at the right side of the knot. Pass this end over and under the left, winding it around just once, so it comes out the left side of the knot.

Start by winding the left working end over the right.

1 Pass the left working end over the right and wind it around as in Step 2 of a reef knot (p. 22). Continue and make a second winding in the same direction.

3 Pull tightly on both standing ends. The knot will assume a spiral appearance. The final result is a reef knot with an extra winding in the first half.

CARRICK BEND

The carrick bend can be used to join ropes of the same or slightly different sizes. Since there is not much manipulation in its tying, the knot is suited to joining large ropes. It capsizes under load but does not jam; even in large rope, a few knocks with a hammer will loosen the knot. Left flat, it can be stitched or glued onto an item as trim. Tied as for a binding knot in opposite ends of the same cord, the carrick bend forms the basis of several decorative knots, including the knife lanyard knot (pp. 118–20) and the double Chinese button (pp. 121–3).

BENDS

2 Continue feeding the working end of the second rope under the upper edge of the turn, over its own standing part, then under the lower edge of the turn to exit.

Overhand crossing

1 Form an overhand crossing with one rope. Lead another rope from the opposite direction, over the turn of the first rope, under the standing part, then over the working part.

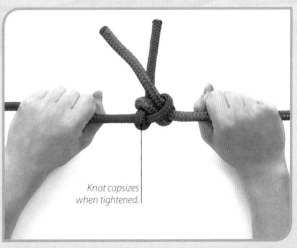

Knot capsizes when tightened.

3 Tighten the knot by alternately pulling on the working ends and the standing parts. It is normal for the knot to capsize as it is pulled tight.

BENDS

ASHLEY'S BEND

This bend can be loaded on the working ends as well as the standing ends. It can join two lengths of rope, or, with two long working ends, provide four usable standing parts. It can therefore make a four-way tie-down with the crossing point fixed in place, so that the ropes cannot chafe or shift as they might if simply looped around each other and led away to form two right angles. The knot works well in rope, shock cord, fishing line, and twine. It holds in dissimilar materials, such as rope and shock cord, as long as they are of similar diameter.

Working end under

1 To finish the knot with four standing parts, first decide at which point along the rope you will place the knot. Take the first length of rope and form an underhand crossing.

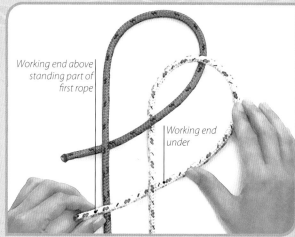

Working end above standing part of first rope

Working end under

2 Take the second rope and feed it into the loop of the crossing from underneath. Form an underhand crossing with the working end on top of the first rope's standing part

Ends together through center of both turns

3 Slide the two crossings closer together. Pick up both working ends in one hand and lead them down through both loops, as though completing an overhand knot.

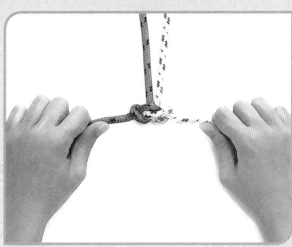

5 Pick up one standing part in each hand and pull them in opposite directions to finish tightening the knot.

4 Grasp the working ends in one hand and standing parts in the other. Pull on both pairs of ends to begin tightening the knot.

6 If four usable ends are required, the knot will need further alternate tightening to achieve uniform shape and stability. This is particularly important for shock cord.

BENDS

SHEET BEND
• DOUBLE SHEET BEND

Quick and easy to tie and untie, this is a very useful knot aboard boats, but be careful as a finger can easily be caught. Both bends can join ropes of differing sizes. The double sheet bend is less likely to shake loose when unloaded, and is the better knot if the sizes of the two ropes are markedly different. These bends are related to the bowline (pp. 36–7) and the double bowline (pp. 37–8). The knot is used to join in new threads for weaving and knitting, and for making and repairing nets.

This must be the thicker rope if diameters differ.

1 If the ropes are of different thicknesses, take the thicker one and form a bight with the working end on top. Pass the working end of the second rope up through the bight.

2 Lead the working end of the second rope up, then down underneath the bight, and to the front.

DOUBLE SHEET BEND

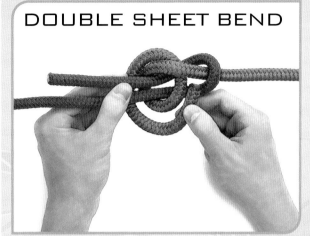

3 Now pass the working end under itself so that it lies across both strands of the bight.

5 To tie a double sheet bend, complete the sheet bend to the end of Step 3, but do not tighten. Continue the working end around the bight again and to the front.

Both working ends finish on the same side of the knot.

4 Firm the knot by pulling on the bight with one hand, and the standing part of the second rope with the other. The working ends must not finish on opposite sides of the knot.

6 Tuck the end under its own standing part and over both strands of the bight to exit. Again, the working ends must finish on the same side of the knot.

BENDS

ONE-WAY SHEET BEND

Also known as a tucked sheet bend, this is a method of joining two ropes to be pulled across a surface. The one-way sheet bend is a more secure version of the sheet bend (pp. 62–3) when the rope is to be pulled across a rough surface, through water or vegetation, or over obstructions or edges, such as a house roof gutter. However, the rope must be pulled in the correct direction, not the other way, or back and forth.

2 Lead the right working end down across the front of the knot. Tuck it right to left, under the lower edge of its previous turn.

1 Complete Steps 1–3 of the sheet bend (pp. 62–3). Leave the knot loose.

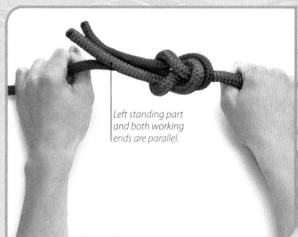

Left standing part and both working ends are parallel.

3 Tighten by pulling on both standing parts. The knot can be pulled, from left to right only, across rough surfaces and over obstructions without the ends catching.

RIGGER'S BEND

The rigger's bend, also known as the Hunter's bend, is ideal for tying both rope and shock cord, and for joining rope to shock cord. It works well in slippery rope and will also hold in fishing line once the knot is pulled very tight. As with most bends, it is best not to leave the working ends too short. Like Ashley's bend (pp. 60–1), the knot can provide four stable, usable ends. Some will find the rigger's bend quicker and easier to tie in the hand than Ashley's bend, or at least easier to get started.

BENDS

1 Lead the ropes from opposite directions, overlap them about 18 inches (46 cm), and create a turn, with the ropes exiting to the right lying under the ropes going left.

The rope pair should be flat and parallel, the lower rope on the outside of the turn, and the upper rope inside.

2 Take the left working end—the one belonging to the right-hand rope—and lead it through the turn from back to front. Hold it on the inner left-hand edge of the turn.

4 Pull the working ends completely through, then pull firmly on the standing parts to tighten. Make sure the working ends protrude from the knot at least a hand's width.

3 Take the right working end and lead it through the turn from front to back.

5 The knot will capsize and the two working ends will exit in opposite directions. If four usable ends are required, tie the knot near the center of the two ropes.

HITCHES

Hitches attach load-bearing cordage to spars, piles, anchors, bollards, fish hooks, trailer tie-down points, and many other objects. The choice of hitch is important if it needs to remain secure when subjected to shaking or flogging, or if the load is not constant. The angle at which the load can be applied to some hitches is also important, as is the end or ends that can be loaded. Despite their names, the anchor bend (pp. 76–7) and the topsail halyard bend (p. 85) are both hitches.

HITCHES

COW HITCH
- **PEDIGREE COW HITCH**
- **COW HITCH AND TOGGLE**

The cow hitch, also called a lark's head, provides a very simple method of attaching a ring or small object to a rope. It is especially useful for connecting rope items that have closed loops to keys, zipper tags, and other closed-eye fittings. The strain should be applied evenly to both ends of the rope. If you wish to finish with just one standing part, tie the pedigree cow hitch. The pedigree cow hitch will hold in fishing line and shock cord.

2 Widen the bight and fold it back over and around the ring so that the bight lies on its own standing part. Pull on the ring and standing parts to tighten.

1 Form a bight and pass it through the ring, from front to back. The ring must be able to pass through the bight.

If the ring is fixed or too large to fit through the bight, use a working end and follow Step 3 to tie the hitch.

3 Pass the end through the ring, front to back, left and to the front, cross over the standing part, make another turn around the ring, back to front, and under the crossing.

PEDIGREE COW HITCH

Feed working end into the hitch from its own side

Repeat Steps 1 and 2, but before tightening, lead the working end away from the hitch then back under its own turn and that of the standing part. Pull through firmly.

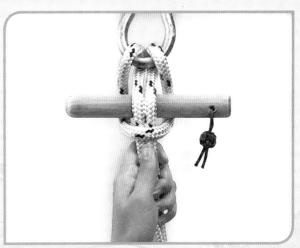

After inserting the toggle, pull on the standing parts to tighten. The load must be taken by both standing parts.

COW HITCH & TOGGLE

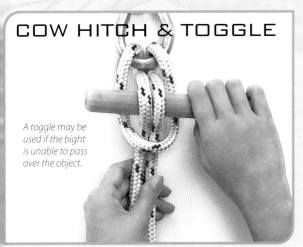

A toggle may be used if the bight is unable to pass over the object.

Lead the bight through the ring and bring it down over its standing part. Draw the standing ends partly into the bight, and insert the toggle.

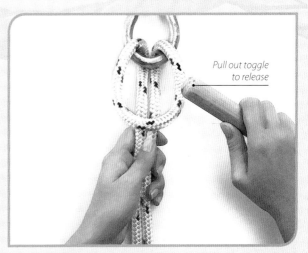

Pull out toggle to release

To release, pull out the toggle. A toggle is simply an item of convenient length that is strong enough to take the strain. The greater the load, the tighter the toggle will be held.

HITCHES

HITCHES

PILE HITCH
• DOUBLE PILE HITCH

Pile hitches can be used for attaching a dinghy to a post, or pile, or an anchor line to a bollard. They can be tied in the bight—requiring no access to the ends of the rope—or at the end of a rope. The length of the working end required to tie the hitch will depend on the diameter of the post. To untie, ease some of the working end back into the hitch until there is enough slack to lift the bight off the top of the post. The double pile hitch is very secure but a little more complicated to untie.

1 Form a bight long enough to pass several times around the post. Hold the standing parts in one hand. With the other, lead the bight around the post, under both standing parts.

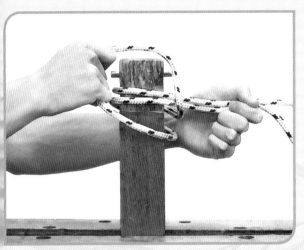

Widen the bight and place it over the top of the post.

DOUBLE PILE HITCH

Complete Step 1, then wind the bight around the post a second time before placing it over the post. The second winding is made lower down the post than the first.

Pull evenly on both ends to firm the hitch. If the rope is sticking and not tightening evenly around the post, you may have to help it, but be careful not to catch your fingers.

Adjust the hitch as for Step 3. With both hitches, make sure that you hold the ends together until the bight is placed over the post, so that both ends are captured.

HITCHES

CLOVE HITCH
• CLOVE HITCH: ALTERNATE

The clove hitch is a quick and easily remembered knot for attaching a rope to a pole, but it can slip on a smooth surface. The load can be applied to either end of the rope. Steps 1 and 2 show the clove hitch tied with a working end. The alternate "in-the-hand" method shown in Steps 3–6 allows the hitch to be readily tied in the bight—anywhere along the rope. This method can be used where you can slip the hitch over the end of a pole.

1 Lead the working end over and down behind the pole, then up in front and over itself to the left.

2 Lead the working end diagonally across the turn, around the back of the rail again, then upward under itself. You have formed two half hitches. Pull the ends to tighten.

CLOVE HITCH: ALTERNATE

Two similarly sized overhand turns

Direction the loops will move in Step 4

If you don't have easy access to the ends of the rope, tie the clove hitch using this alternate method. Begin by making two consecutive overhand turns.

When viewed from the side, the two half hitches can be identified. It is the same knot as shown in Step 2.

Left turn sitting over right

Slide the left-hand turn over the right, then slide the fingers of the left hand through the center of both loops.

Simply slide the half hitches over the end of the pole and tighten.

HITCHES

HITCHES

MARLINSPIKE HITCH

The marlinspike hitch can be used to temporarily secure a tool or to make a handle in thin cord to provide better grip. It was often tied around a marlinspike, which gave the knot its name, but may be tied around tool handles for hoisting up a tree or onto a roof. If there is no spike available, a pencil makes a good substitute. Before starting this method, tie off the standing part so that you can apply tension to the cord.

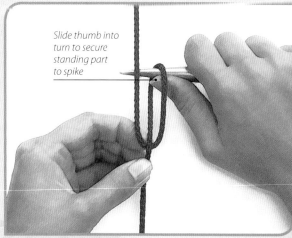

Slide thumb into turn to secure standing part to spike

Leaving the spike inside the turn, raise it, taking the loose portion of the turn with it, and slide the spike behind the standing part. The right thumb passes into the turn.

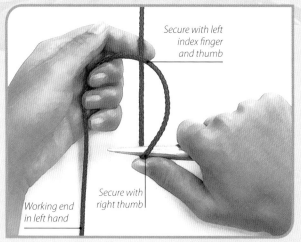

Secure with left index finger and thumb

Working end in left hand

Secure with right thumb

With the spike in your right hand, hold it against the cord with your thumb. Raise the working part above the spike, make an overhand turn, and secure the intersection.

Edge of turn behind tip of spike

Load the hitch in this direction only. When the spike is removed, the hitch will untie.

With the left fingers, pick up the forward edge of the turn take it left, over the standing part and slip it behind the tip of the spike. Pull down with the spike to apply tension.

BARREL HITCH

The barrel hitch is a quick and simple method of securing a barrel for hoisting upright. The same hitch can be tied around a box. Be careful that the rope is positioned under the center of the barrel, and that the upper hitches are located opposite each other, and well above the barrel's center of gravity. You will need a length of rope about three times the maximum circumference of the barrel.

Separate overhand knot into two hitches

Separate the overhand knot at its midpoint so that you have two opposing hitches. Maneuver the halves around opposite sides of the barrel.

HITCHES

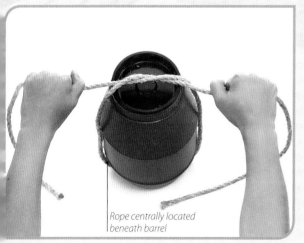

Rope centrally located beneath barrel

Slip the midpoint of the rope beneath the center of the barrel. Lead the ends up opposite sides of the barrel and tie a loose overhand knot (p. 17) at the top.

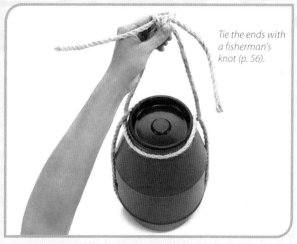

Tie the ends with a fisherman's knot (p. 56).

Ensure the rope is located correctly beneath the barrel and that the hitches are central and opposing. Maintain upward tension and tie the ends together to form a sling.

ANCHOR BEND

• ROUND TURN AND TWO HALF HITCHES

The anchor bend, also known as the fisherman's bend, is a quite secure knot but, perhaps because it looks so simple, is most often completed by the addition of a half hitch. It will hold in shock cord, however the extra half hitch is of no benefit. The round turn and two half hitches is particularly simple to tie, but it will not hold at all in shock cord.

HITCHES

1 Make a round turn through a ring, winding from back to front and left to right. Do not pull the turn tight yet, as the working end needs to pass through it first.

2 Lead the working end left behind the standing part, then to the front, and tuck it to the right beneath both windings of the round turn.

Pull tight

Pull on both the standing part and working end to tighten the knot around the ring. This is a completed anchor bend, but a half hitch is usually added.

ROUND TURN AND TWO HALF HITCHES

Round turn

First half hitch

Make a round turn through the ring as in Step 1. Pass the working end around behind the standing part, to the front, and under itself, to make the first half hitch. Pull tight.

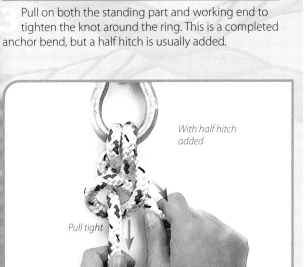

With half hitch added

Pull tight

Pass the working end around behind the standing part again, to the front, and under itself. Pull the working end as tight as possible.

Pull each half hitch very tight

Second half hitch added

Continue the working end in the same direction, around behind the standing part and to the front again, and make the second half hitch. Pull very tight.

HITCHES

PRUSIK KNOT

The Prusik knot, also known as the Prusik hitch, is excellent for attaching a loop of light line to a taut length of rope. Without load, the Prusik knot will release its grip and can be repositioned easily on the rope. Tighten the windings and apply load at right angles—that is, in the same direction as the rope—and it will grip once more. The strain must be applied evenly to both ends of the line, so tying them into a loop is ideal. To grip well, the line should be no more than half the diameter of the rope.

HITCHES

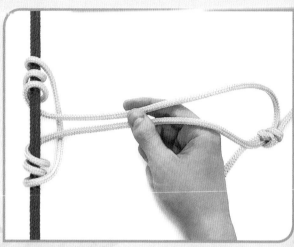

Open out the bight of the cow hitch. Wind the knotted end neatly around the rope and under the bight three or four times, so that each turn is inside the other.

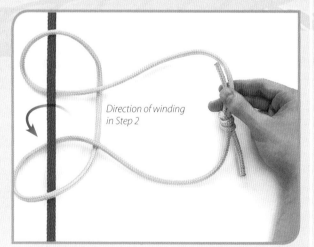

Direction of winding in Step 2

Take a length of line about 3 feet (1 m) long and tie the ends together with a fisherman's knot (p. 56). Form a loose cow hitch (p. 68) around the fixed, taut rope.

Windings must not overlap. Friction will prevent the knot from sliding.

Ease the two sets of windings together. Rotate the windings around the rope with your fingers to work the slack out of the bight and into the knotted loop end.

BUNTLINE HITCH

This hitch's name is from its use on square-rigged vessels, where it secures buntlines to the foot of a square sail. Although used as a hitch, the knot is actually a sliding loop. It is considered secure, no matter how much a sail flogs, or flaps, in the wind. When pulled very tight, it may need a marlinspike to help untie it. One solution is to tie a slipped buntline hitch by making the final diagonal tuck in Step 3 with a bight, so that a tug on the working end will release the knot, but this will not suit all applications.

Wind around behind the standing part and to the front, then cross diagonally left over the turn.

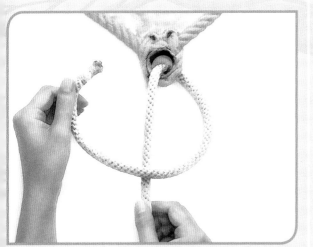

1. Lead the working end of the rope through the ring, from front to back and left to right, then back across to the left to make an overhand turn.

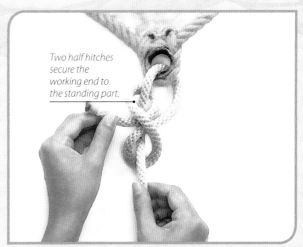

Two half hitches secure the working end to the standing part.

3. Continue around behind the standing part of the turn, then tuck left beneath itself. Tighten and slide the knot to the ring.

HITCHES

HIGHWAYMAN'S HITCH

While the name may conjure up visions of robbers in the Wild West tying their horses to a hitching rail, ready for a fast get-away, there is no evidence of this hitch's use in such criminal activity. It is a good knot to know because of the way it instantly releases with a tug on the working end. However, it is not the most secure of hitches: constant movement of the standing part, or the application and release of tension, can easily loosen it.

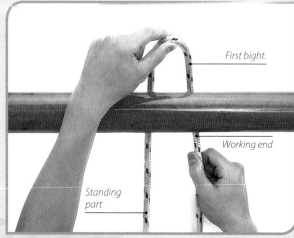

First bight.

Working end

Standing part

1 Form a long bight in the left hand, with the working end to the right of the standing part, and lead it up behind the rail. Leave a longish working end.

Second bight

2 With the right hand, form a second bight in the standing part, with the remainder of the standing part on the right side of this new bight.

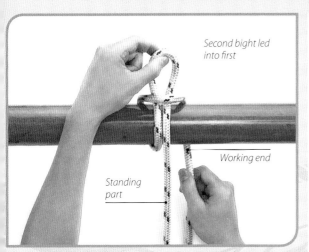

Second bight led into first

Working end

Standing part

Tuck this second bight up through the first, hold it in place with your left hand, and tighten the first bight around the second by pulling on the working end.

Third bight led into second

Lead this third bight fully up into the second, so that there is no slack around the rail.

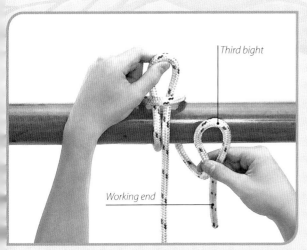

Third bight

Working end

With the right hand, form a third bight in the working part, with the working end to the right.

Pull on standing part to tighten.

Pull on working end to release.

Pull on the standing part to firm the second bight around the third. To release, pull on the working end and the hitch will slide apart.

HITCHES

HITCHES

TIMBER HITCH
• KILLICK HITCH

The timber hitch is an easy method of securing a rope to a pole, and it requires only a single passing around it, which is an advantage if the pole is heavy. With the timber hitch tied at the center of gravity, the pole can be hoisted. The addition of a half hitch forms the killick hitch, which allows the pole to be towed, on land or through water, with directional stability. The timber hitch is also used to attach nylon strings to a guitar bridge.

Use more windings for bigger, heavier poles.

2 Wind the working end around the turn again once, twice, or three times. Pull tight on the standing part and ease the slack out of the windings through the working end.

Alternatively, go over the turn first, then under it from left to right

1 Make a loose turn around the pole from the back to the front. Pass the working end behind the standing part, to the front, and under the turn.

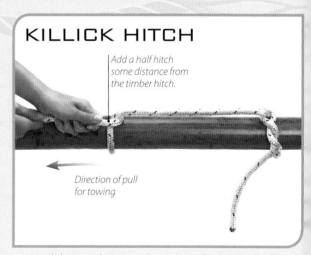

KILLICK HITCH

Add a half hitch some distance from the timber hitch.

Direction of pull for towing

3 Lead the standing part along the pole and tie a half hitch (p. 6). Tying it nearer the end provides better stability when towing, but too near the end and it will slip off.

ROLLING HITCH
•TAUTLINE HITCH

The rolling hitch is used to tie a rope to a pole or to larger rope, when the load is to be applied, at an angle between 45 and 90 degrees to the pole. The direction of the load, or strain, will dictate the way in which the knot must be tied. The hitches shown here take the strain from the right. To take a load from the left, the hitch can be tied as a mirror image, or tied the same way but from the other side of the pole. The tautline hitch works similarly, and is suitable for attaching a line to a taut rope.

Pass the working end diagonally left across both windings, then down around the back of the pole.

HITCHES

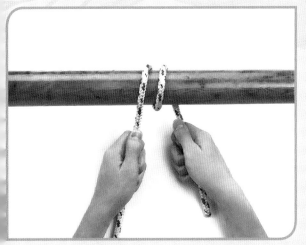

Begin the hitch with a round turn, proceeding up and over, and from left to right.

Tuck the working end up under the diagonal. Note that the rolling hitch is actually a clove hitch (p. 72) with an extra turn around the pole on the right.

Load the hitch from the right.

4 Pull both ends to tighten. The load can be applied from the right of the hitch. For loading from the left, begin tying the hitch as in Step 1, but winding from right to left.

6 Lead the working end up behind the rope, to the front, and tuck it under itself, parallel to the standing part. The knot looks like a cow hitch (p. 68) with an extra turn.

TAUTLINE HITCH

5 Tie this hitch in line that is half the diameter of the taut rope, or thinner. Complete Step 1 of the rolling hitch, then lead the working end left in front of the standing part.

Load the hitch from the right.

To apply strain at an angle less than 45 degrees to the rope, consider using a Prusik knot (p. 78), but note that both ends of the line must be equally loaded.

7 Pull both ends to firm the hitch tight around the rope. As with the rolling hitch, the strain can be applied from the direction in which the initial overhand turn was made.

TOPSAIL HALYARD BEND

The topsail halyard bend is ideal for tying a halyard to a spar, or a rope to a pole, so that it can be hoisted. Unlike a clove hitch (p. 72) or a rolling hitch (p. 83), where the strain tends to rotate the pole, the topsail halyard bend naturally accepts the load at the pole's center. It is a very strong and ingenious knot that has the added advantage of spreading the load evenly across the width of three windings, lessening the compression that would occur with a clove hitch.

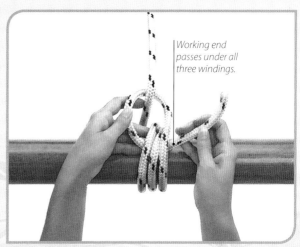

Working end passes under all three windings.

Bring the working end to the front and tuck it under all three windings. The turns must be loose—too tight and it will be difficult to lead the working end under.

HITCHES

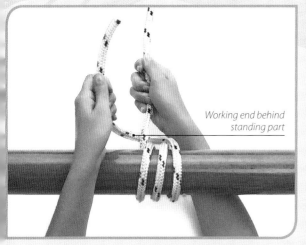

Working end behind standing part

Leading from above, make a round turn around the pole, from back to front and left to right. Add a single turn to form three windings. Lead the rope diagonally left and behind.

Working end passes over two windings, then under one.

Reverse direction and lead the working end right to left, over the top of the first two windings, then under the third. Tighten from the standing part to the working end.

HITCHES

PALOMAR KNOT

The palomar knot is a simple method for attaching fishing line to a hook, ring, or swivel. It is quick to tie and very strong, but not as resistant to abrasion as snelling (pp. 88–9). When attaching line to a hook, it is best to pass the bight through the eye from the tip to the back of the shank, especially where the eye is angled toward the back. This adds to the directional stability of the hook. Some argue that it makes the hook less likely to catch a fish; others counter that the hooked fish is less likely to get away.

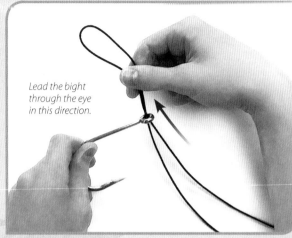

Lead the bight through the eye in this direction.

1 Form a bight slightly longer than the length of the hook. Pass the bight through the eye, from the tip of the hook to the back of the shank.

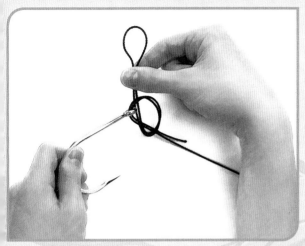

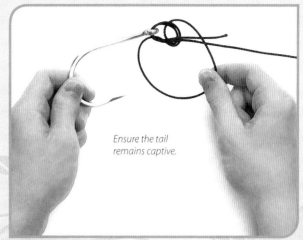

Ensure the tail remains captive.

2 Using the bight as the working end, tie an overhand knot (p. 17) around the eye, making sure that the end of the line, the "tail," remains captive.

4 With the hook passed completely through the bight, pull on the standing part and the working end to make the bight firm against the overhand knot.

Open up the bight and pass it around the hook.

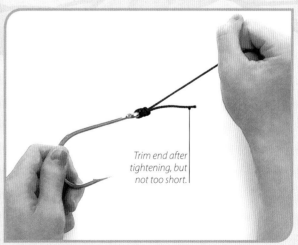

Trim end after tightening, but not too short.

3 Pull enough slack out of the overhand knot so that the bight can be passed over the end of the hook.

5 In stiffer, heavy breaking strain line, it can be difficult to firm up the knot. Wetting the line helps, but tends to make it more slippery in your fingers.

SNELLING A HOOK

Snelling was the only method of binding a line to a hook in the days when hooks had a flattened spade, rather than an eye, at the end of the shank. This snelling method is a little more awkward than the palomar knot (pp. 86–7), but is less affected by abrasion and less likely to be bitten through by a fish. Other methods of snelling a hook tend to be more complicated. When fishing line is either very fine or very stiff, keeping bights and windings under control while tying can be difficult.

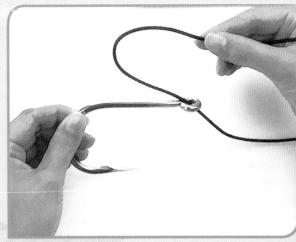

1 Pass the line through the eye in a direction from the tip of the hook to the back of the shank. Leave a working end about four times the length of the hook.

HITCHES

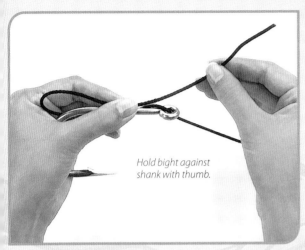

Hold bight against shank with thumb.

Lead the working end down the length of the shank, then back toward the eye, making a bight almost the length of the shank.

Lead the working end upward through the remaining portion of the bight. Pull hard to make sure that the windings are tight.

Wind tightly down the shank.

Hold the bight firmly against the shank. Beginning just below the eye, wind the working end around the shank and bight four or five times, or up to six times for a large hook.

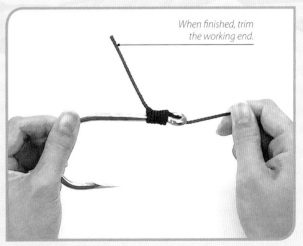

When finished, trim the working end.

Tug hard on the standing part to pull the bight tight around the working end and slide the knot up to the eye.

TRUCKER'S HITCH

The trucker's hitch is also known as the waggoner's hitch and dolly knot. As it can be tensioned further after tightening, it is suitable for tying tent stays, or securing a load on a trailer. The hitch provides leverage, allowing the rope to be pulled tight, and uses up any excess cordage. It requires a length of rope four to five times the distance from the hitch's starting point to the securing point. The trucker's hitch is only stable under tension, so make sure that there is no chance of the load shifting.

HITCHES

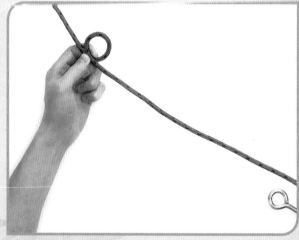

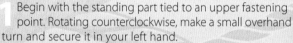

1 Begin with the standing part tied to an upper fastening point. Rotating counterclockwise, make a small overhand turn and secure it in your left hand.

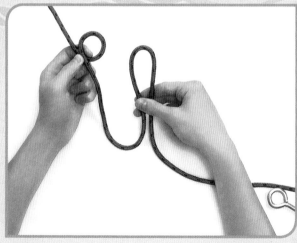

2 With your right hand, form a bight in the working part. It will need to have a length approximately half the distance from the turn to the securing point.

HITCHES

Lead the end of the bight into the overhand turn from below—not too far in, about a fifth of its length will do. Secure the bight and overhand turn in your left hand.

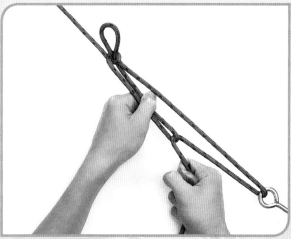

Lead the working end up through the shank from back to front. Apply downward tension to the working end. The turn will grip the bight and you can let go with the left hand.

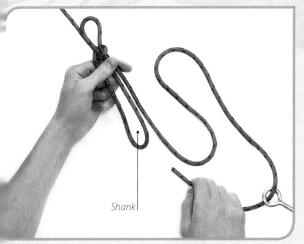

This forms a new, lower bight, called a shank. Lead the working end down and through the lower fastening point.

Shank

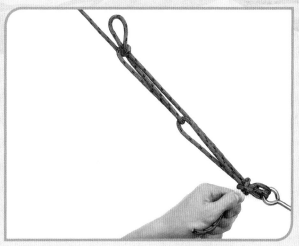

Pull the end as tight as necessary and tie it off above the fastening point—a couple of half hitches (p. 6) should do. The trucker's hitch requires some practice to master.

LASHINGS

Lashing is a method of fastening structural items together with cordage. When building a tree house, for example, use lashings to secure the beams, cross bracing, and supports. While bindings are temporary fastenings, and use just one or two turns of cordage, lashings are more permanent and use multiple windings. The cordage acts as a clamping mechanism, but also provides friction to help prevent the lashed items slipping against one another. Some lashings work best in cordage with some stretch.

SQUARE LASHING

Square lashing is a relatively easy way to secure two poles at right angles. It is stronger and more permanent than the transom knot (p. 32) but takes more time and cordage. Be careful with the tension and the number of windings: the lashing must be strong enough for the job, but not so tight that the poles are bent. The lashing can also begin with a timber hitch (p. 82), constrictor knot (pp. 28–9), or multiple overhand knot (pp. 17–18). Experiment to find out which works best.

Later additional windings will lock the tail securely.

Tie a clove hitch (p. 72) to the vertical pole. Wind the tail and standing part together. Place the horizontal pole on top of the vertical. Lead the ends over both poles to the right.

LASHINGS

LASHINGS

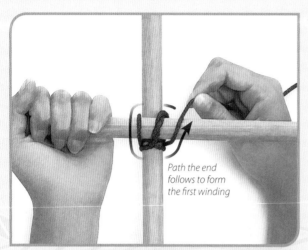

Path the end follows to form the first winding

Maintaining the tension, lead the cord behind the upper vertical pole, over and down in front of the left horizontal pole, around behind the lower vertical and to the front.

Frapping turns do not bind pole to pole but compress the existing windings.

Commence the frapping turns. Make a turn over the right horizontal, then wind clockwise between the two poles three or four times.

Repeat the winding process about four times. The number of windings will depend on the diameter of the poles and the thickness of the cord.

Clove hitch to finish

Stop at the top left and tie a tight clove hitch (p. 72) around the upper vertical, so the lashing can't slide or rotate under tension.

DIAGONAL LASHING

Diagonal lashing is used to pull cross-bracing poles together. The two poles don't have to be at right angles. The timber hitch (p. 82) at the start pulls both poles together without changing their relative position. However, if the poles are not already fixed by some other means, the angle can be difficult to maintain during lashing. The tension applied in the diagonal lashing process isn't as great as in square lashing (pp. 93–4), but there is less chance of the poles sliding.

Lead the cord away from you and around the back

Tie a timber hitch (p. 82) around both poles, at the intersection with the widest angle. Tighten the hitch and lead the cord away from you, around the back of both poles.

LASHINGS

Commence lashing through the wider angle first.

Wind tightly over the top of the hitch and around the intersection four or five times. Unless the poles are fixed, the tighter you wind, the wider the angle becomes.

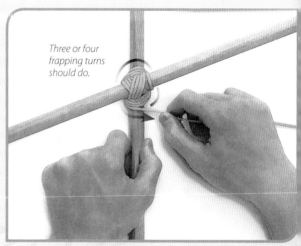

Three or four frapping turns should do.

Wind the cord counterclockwise by passing in front of the upper vertical pole, behind the left cross pole, in front of the lower vertical and behind the right cross pole.

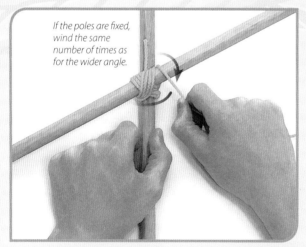

If the poles are fixed, wind the same number of times as for the wider angle.

Now wind across the narrower intersecting angle. If the poles are not fixed, apply pressure and continue winding until you achieve the angle you want.

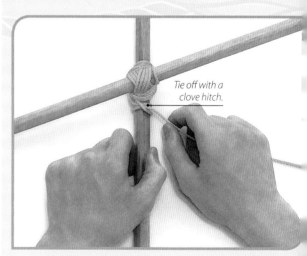

Tie off with a clove hitch.

Finish with a clove hitch (p. 72) around one of the poles Align it with the end of the frapping turns so that there is little chance of the hitch sliding or rotating under tension

SHEER LASHING

The sheer lashing can secure two poles longitudinally to reinforce or extend a pole, with one lashing at either end of the pair or at the overlap between them. Tied a little more loosely, it makes an A-frame lashing where the two poles are separated slightly and intersect at a narrow angle to form a support. The A-frame is also known as sheer legs. For an angle of more than 25 degrees, the diagonal lashing (pp. 95–6) may be a better choice.

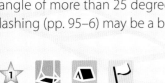

To make an A-frame, begin the lashing far enough away from the pole ends, so that the top of the frame is deep enough for the object it will support.

Lay two poles side by side and tie together with a clove hitch (p. 72). Leave the shorter end long enough to be secured underneath the windings.

Cover the short end of the clove hitch with the lashing.

Begin winding, but not as tightly for an A-frame as for securing two poles. As a rule of thumb, make the binding length no less than the width of the two poles.

LASHINGS

Make at least two frapping turns; there is unlikely to be room for more than three.

For the frapping turns, lead the cord behind the top pole and to the front between the poles. Wind across the existing windings, between the poles.

If tying poles together to reinforce or extend them, make a tighter binding, omit the frapping turns, and finish with a clove hitch around both poles.

Finish at the opposite end to the original clove hitch and tie another clove hitch (p. 72) around one pole, not both. The hitch must be tight, and snug against the lashing.

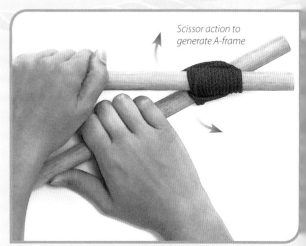

Scissor action to generate A-frame

To use as an A-frame, separate the poles by using a scissor action, stretching the cord equally at both ends of the lashing. Practice will help you apply the right lashing tension.

TRIPOD LASHING

There are different methods of tying tripod lashings but this one can be tied into a frame, transported to a site, and erected. After use it can be folded flat and taken elsewhere, with a temporary binding such as the pole lashing (pp. 24–5) securing the other end. However, it doesn't form the perfect shape of an equilateral triangle at its base. Like the sheer lashing (pp. 97–8), the angle at which the legs can be separated is determined by the length and tension of the lashing and the stretch in the cord.

Wind the short clove hitch end around the working end and lead both ends toward you across the three poles. This will help lock the clove hitch and its tail.

When beginning, allow for the width of the lashing and space to hang an item.

Lay three poles side by side, making sure the ends that will stand on the ground are even. Tie a clove hitch (p. 72) around the top pole at a suitable distance from the ends.

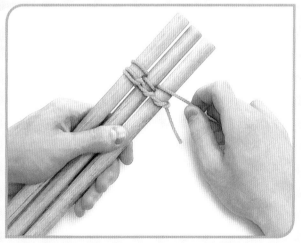

Start winding between the poles: under the bottom pole, over the center, under the top, then around and over, this time under the center pole, and over the bottom.

LASHINGS

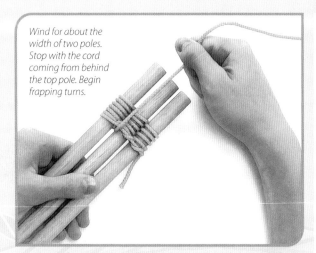

Wind for about the width of two poles. Stop with the cord coming from behind the top pole. Begin frapping turns.

Begin frapping turns by leading the cord down in front of the top pole, then to the back between the top and center poles. Form two or three turns around the windings.

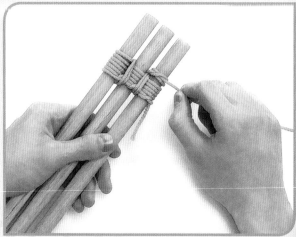

To finish, tie off with a clove hitch (p. 72) around the bottom pole. The frapping turn must lead straight into the hitch so that there is no chance of it rotating.

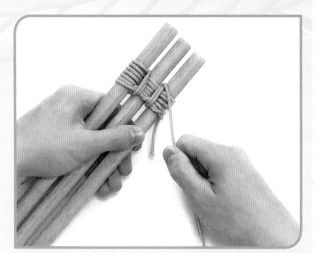

Lead the cord behind the center pole, and to the front between the center and bottom poles. Make a second set of frapping turns in the opposite direction to the first.

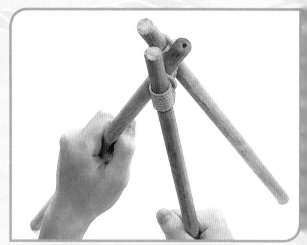

To erect the tripod, separate the outer poles and use a scissor action to swing the center pole in the opposite direction. This may be difficult if the lashing is too tight.

SPLICES

Splicing is a traditional method used to permanently join two laid ropes, add a branch rope to create a Y-join, or form an eye in the end of a rope. The splicing methods described in this book will enable you to complete all of these tasks. The eye splice (pp. 102–3) and short splice (pp. 104–5) are not difficult, however, they require a methodical approach and practice.

EYE SPLICE

An eye splice isn't actually a knot, but a means of forming an eye in the end of a length of laid rope. The method can also join a secondary piece of rope to the first to create a Y-piece, as long as the strain on each arm of the Y will be in a similar direction. A splice is used where a rope is fixed permanently to an item or slipped over a hook, pile, or bollard. Most laid ropes are Z-laid, meaning that the strands are wound clockwise, and these instructions are for Z-laid rope.

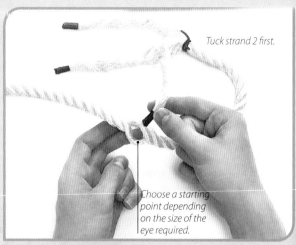

Tuck strand 2 first.

Choose a starting point depending on the size of the eye required.

2 Open the lay of the rope to raise one strand. Feed the central strand 2 diagonally left under the raised strand in the standing part. Do not pull it through completely yet.

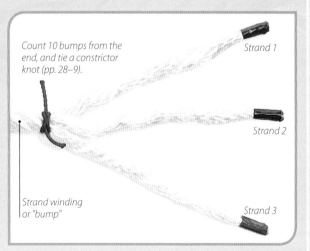

Count 10 bumps from the end, and tie a constrictor knot (pp. 28–9).

Strand 1

Strand 2

Strand winding or "bump"

Strand 3

1 Begin to unlay the rope. As you separate the strands, bind them with tape. Continue to unlay the strands up to the knot. Allocate each strand a number.

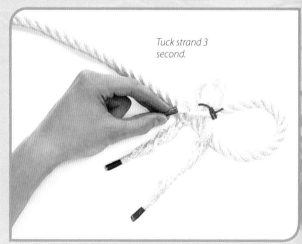

Tuck strand 3 second.

3 Feed strand 3, which is to the right of strand 2, under its corresponding right strand in the standing part, that is, the strand to the right of the one that strand 2 is tucked under.

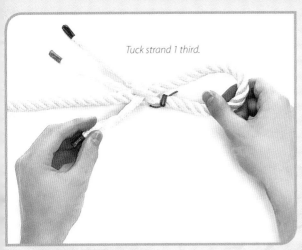

Tuck strand 1 third.

Rotate the rope slightly, and tuck the remaining strand 1 under its corresponding left strand of the standing part. Pull the three unlaid strands snugly up to the standing part.

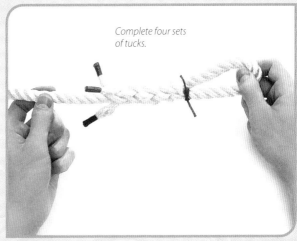

Complete four sets of tucks.

Maintain the even twist in the unlaid strands as you tuck. If you don't open the lay in the standing part sufficiently, the twist in the strands will increase as you go.

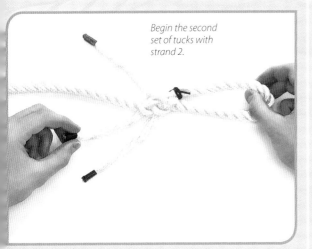

Begin the second set of tucks with strand 2.

Continue weaving the unlaid strands in this diagonal pattern until you have completed four sets of tucks. Three may be enough, but not if the lay of the rope is loose.

Trim and seal ends.

Thick rope may need the assistance of a fid for opening the lay. After the fourth tuck, the ends can be trimmed and either whipped (pp. 12–13) or heat sealed (p. 11).

SPLICES

SPLICES

SHORT SPLICE

This is a method of permanently joining two lengths of laid rope. It is not essential that the ropes be of exactly the same diameter, but they must be similar. When two ropes are joined with a bend, the knot will not pass over a pulley or through a block, but with the splice, as long as it is tapered and the rope size is comfortable in the sheave, it should fit through. There are other ways of joining two ropes that give a more slender result, but they are not as strong.

Begin tucking the left rope into the right.

2 Following the same procedure as for Steps 2–4 of the eye splice (pp. 102–3), begin to weave the left rope into the right. Make two sets of tucks.

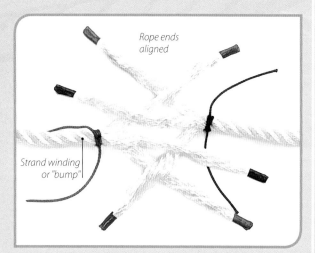

Rope ends aligned

Strand winding or "bump"

1 Tie a constrictor knot (pp. 28–9) around each piece of rope about 12 bumps from the end. Tape and number the strands and unwind them. Align the strands of the rope ends.

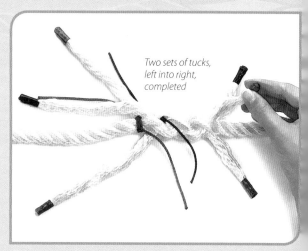

Two sets of tucks, left into right, completed

3 Make a set of tucks of the right rope into the left. Tighten the strands and adjust the alignment of one rope to the other. Loosen the constrictor knots as required.

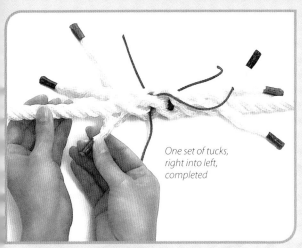

One set of tucks, right into left, completed

4 Make another set of tucks with the right rope into the left, so that there are two sets in each direction. Then make alternate sets until you have four in each direction.

Taper completed

6 An easy way to taper is to not tuck one strand of each set after three tucks, leave out a second strand after the fourth tuck, and make a fifth tuck with the one remaining strand.

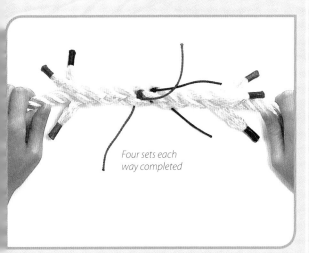

Four sets each way completed

5 The splice is completed and the ends can be trimmed and sealed. However, if you wish to taper the splice, proceed to Step 6.

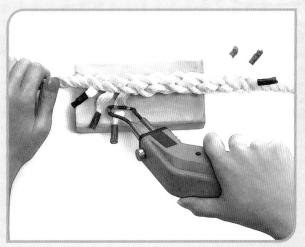

7 When the tucking of each strand is completed in the correct order, the splice will have an even and attractive taper. Trim and seal the ends neatly.

SPLICES

TRICKS

Rope tricks encompass seemingly impossible means of tying or untying a knot. They include manipulating a rope to enable a knot to be released, transferring a knot from one portion of a rope to another, and quickly turning one knot into a different one. Tricks in which apparently complicated knots are instantly untied either involve one or more slip knots, or incorporate an untying process that has the appearance of further complicating an already recognizable knot.

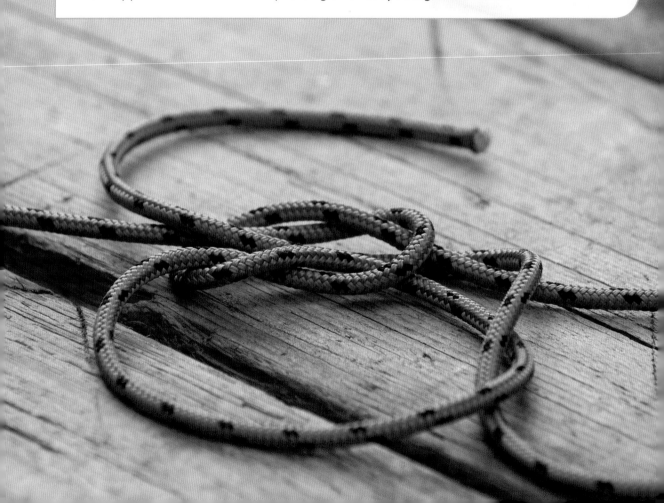

IMPOSSIBLE KNOT

Put a length of rope in front of your friends and challenge them to pick it up and tie a knot without letting go with either hand. The result must be a proper knot that does not collapse when the rope is pulled tight. Any kind of cordage will do, but a piece of rope will be easier to handle than thin cord. The rope or cord should be about 3 feet (1 m) long so you can comfortably demonstrate how the trick is done after everyone else has given up.

Keeping a firm hold on the rope, uncross your arms and move your hands apart, letting the rope slip over your wrists and hands as you do so.

Lay the rope on a table. Before picking it up, cross your arms over each other. Now lean over and pick up one end of the rope in each hand.

With this trick, you tie an overhand knot in the rope without letting go of either end.

TRICKS

HANDCUFFS PUZZLE

You and your friend put on rope "handcuffs" with a loop knot in each end for the wrists, and the two ropes linked. The kind of knot used to make the loops is not important, but the bowline (pp. 36–7) works well. The two of you must try to separate yourselves without removing the handcuffs, untying the wrist loops, or cutting the rope. This trick uses two ropes, each at least 5 feet (1.5 m) long. Thick, soft rope is best as it will not cause any chafing.

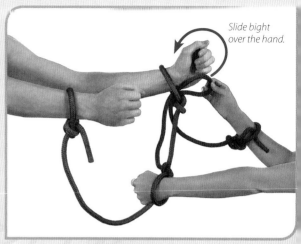

Slide bight over the hand.

2 Make a small bight in your rope and pull it toward you through your friend's wrist loop. Keep pulling until it is large enough to pass over your friend's hand.

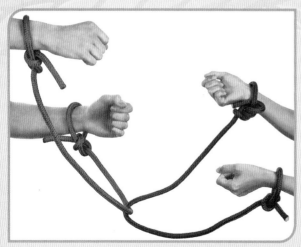

1 Interlock the two ropes and place the handcuff loops over your own and your friend's wrists. The loops must be big enough to slide easily over the hands and onto the wrists.

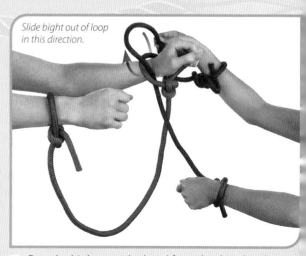

Slide bight out of loop in this direction.

3 Pass the bight over the hand from the thumb side to the little finger side. A gentle tug will pull it out of your friend's wrist loop, leaving you both free.

TRICKS

RING DROP

This trick allows you to remove an object threaded onto a loop, without letting go of the loop or breaking the object. The loop should be made from a length of thin cord about 3 feet (1 m) long and threaded through the center of a ring or bead. You can either hand the loop and threaded object to your friends and ask them to work out how to free the object without dropping the loop, or, once you have had a bit of practice, demonstrate the trick very quickly and let others try to work out how you did it.

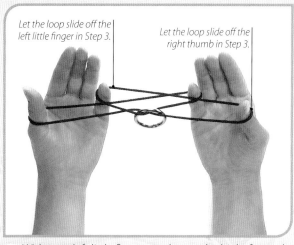

Let the loop slide off the left little finger in Step 3.

Let the loop slide off the right thumb in Step 3.

With your left little finger, reach over the bight formed by the right little finger, and hook it around the upper strand to the right of the ring, again from behind.

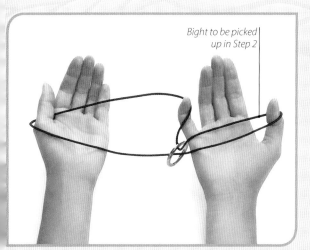

Bight to be picked up in Step 2

With the loop hanging over both your thumbs, hook the right little finger around the upper strand, to the left of the ring and from behind.

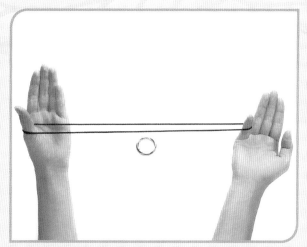

To free the ring, move your hands apart while letting the loop slip off the left little finger and the right thumb.

TRICKS

NOT A KNOT

This trick, which begins with a reef knot, looks very complicated but the seemingly secure knot falls apart completely when pulled tight. The final step is easiest to carry out if thin cord or flexible rope is used rather than thick or stiff rope. A piece of cord about 3 feet (1 m) long is ideal. You can either demonstrate the puzzle yourself, or give a reef knot to your friends and challenge them to make it collapse without untying it.

2 Lead the same working end through the center of the reef knot, again from back to front.

1 Form a loop and tie a reef knot (pp. 22–3). Pick up the working end that emerges toward the back of the knot and lead it through the loop from back to front.

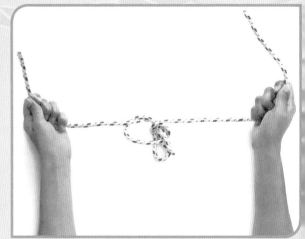

3 Pull firmly on both ends of the cord. The original reef knot will collapse and disappear completely.

DECORATIVE

Decorative knots are usually practical knots that are also attractive. The Turk's head has many applications, including improving grip on handrails and boat hook handles. Mats protect decks in high-wear areas or around deck fittings. Lanyards prevent small tools being dropped and lost. Sometimes a change of cordage can turn one design into a different object altogether—in thin cord, Solomon bar (pp. 133–5) can make a zipper pull, and in thick rope or old mooring line it can make a boat fender.

MONKEY'S FIST

Monkey's fists are a family of spherical knots, usually fitted with a core. The simplest is the best known. It weights one end of a heaving line for throwing between boats, and makes a good zipper, blind, or light switch pull. The monkey's fist can be used as a stopper where the knot is left permanently tied. With a hand grip made from a loop knot or an eye splice (pp. 102–3) in the short tail, it makes a dog's tug-of-war or throw toy. With a buoyant core, it keeps a key dropped overboard afloat, and hung up to swing on a boat, discourages seagulls.

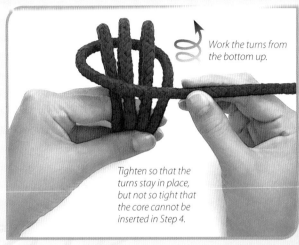

Work the turns from the bottom up.

Tighten so that the turns stay in place, but not so tight that the core cannot be inserted in Step 4.

Secure the turns between your fingers and thumb. Next, make three horizontal turns by leading the working end around the outside of the original turns, coiling upward.

The number of turns determines the size of the knot. Make more turns in Steps 1–3 to achieve a larger result.

Anchor the standing end with the thumb and take three vertical turns around the hand, pulling them up snugly so they are easy to secure in the following step.

The working end should leave the knot at the top left.

Work the third set of turns away from you as well as counterclockwise.

Lead the working end inside the first set of turns, above the second. Make a third set of three turns around the outside of the second, but inside the first, working counterclockwise.

DECORATIVE

Never use heavy cores in heaving lines, as serious injury can result.

Plastic ball core

Open a gap where any two sets of turns cross each other and insert the core. Close the gap to conceal the core.

KEY FOB / ZIPPER PULL

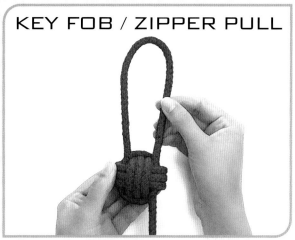

For a key fob or zipper pull needing a loop, pick up the working end behind where the first set of turns cross it and pull the amount of slack for the loop back into the knot.

Tuck one end inside the knot. Be careful not to pull it out again when tightening the knot.

Tuck the working end inside the knot. Gradually tighten the knot with an awl, working the slack from the standing end toward the working end. Fair up the knot with a hammer.

Cow hitch the loop to a zipper or single key. Attach a split ring for a multi-key fob.

Work the slack for the loop around the knot until it is in the center of the second set of turns. Cut off the working end and tuck it inside the knot.

DECORATIVE

KRINGLE MAT

This is known as the kringle mat because the basic knot resembles the pretzel-shaped kringle symbol on traditional Danish bakery signs. It is straightforward to tie, but make sure to keep the cord free of twist and the knots evenly sized. Five interlocking knots make a piece suitable to use as a small floor mat, decorative or heat-proof table mat, or drink coaster. Mats with six or more knots have a larger center hole and can be placed or formed around a central object, such as a lamp base, or around a deck fitting as a thump mat.

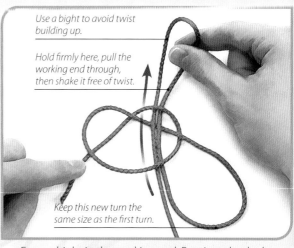

Use a bight to avoid twist building up.

Hold firmly here, pull the working end through, then shake it free of twist.

Keep this new turn the same size as the first turn.

Form a bight in the working end. Pass it under the lower strand of the first turn, over the working end that was laid across the top of it, and under the top of the turn.

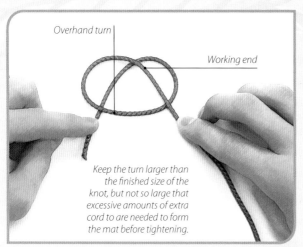

Overhand turn

Working end

Keep the turn larger than the finished size of the knot, but not so large that excessive amounts of extra cord to are needed to form the mat before tightening.

Make an overhand turn and lay the working end across the turn. If using light cord, the kringle mat can be tricky to keep in place. Try pinning the work to a cork tile.

There are now two identical and interlocked knot forms. There will be six knots in this completed mat.

Lay the working end over the new overhand turn. Repeat Step 2 to tie a third knot linked with the second. Continue until the work has five knots, one short of the final number.

DECORATIVE

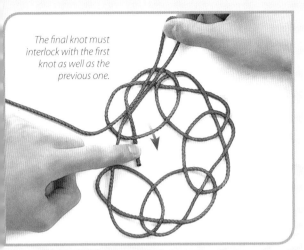

The final knot must interlock with the first knot as well as the previous one.

Lead a working-end bight over the first knot's upper strand, under the standing end, and—following the arrow—over the first knot's lower strand.

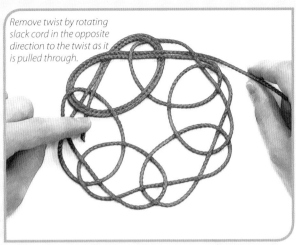

Remove twist by rotating slack cord in the opposite direction to the twist as it is pulled through.

Double the knot by following the standing part with the working end. Follow the knot around as many times as necessary, gently working the slack out of the knot.

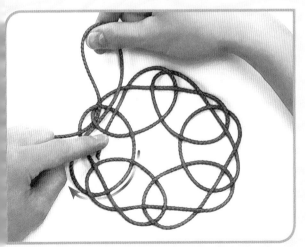

Lead a working-end bight under, over, and under, through the previous knot. Lead it over and under once more to tie next to the standing end on the outside, and pull through.

For greater stability, stitch adjacent strands together on the underside in 2–3 places.

Cut and heat-seal the ends and stitch them to the adjacent strand on the underside of the mat.

OCEAN MAT

Also known as an ocean plait mat, this oval mat is an excellent way to recycle old rope. Thicker cord is the best practice material, and finer cord may be pinned as for the kringle mat (p. 114–15). Begin with an overhand knot (p.17). Rotate it 180 degrees so that the ends are at the bottom. One end may be kept short, so that all slack is pulled out of the mat in one direction, or the cord may be middled first so that the mat is worked in both directions.

Keep the spaces open.

Lead the left-hand loop to the right and lay the right-hand loop over the top of it. Keep the spaces open as the ends will be woven through them in following steps.

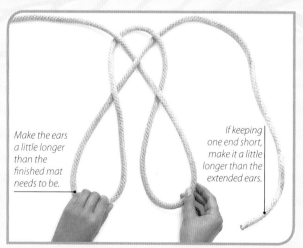

Make the ears a little longer than the finished mat needs to be.

If keeping one end short, make it a little longer than the extended ears.

Move the left-hand end upward clockwise and the right-hand end upward counterclockwise, opening two "ears" in the knot. Extend the ears and twist both clockwise.

Pick up the top right end. Lead it over the bight at the top of the long loop that now slants to the left, under both strands of the other long loop, and over once more.

DECORATIVE

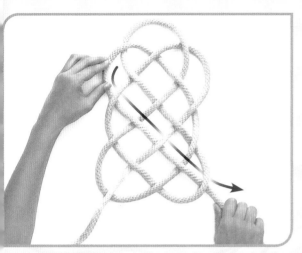

Lead the other end under, over, under, over, and under to lock the knot. Make sure that the mat shape is even, symmetrical, and slightly larger than the finished mat is to be.

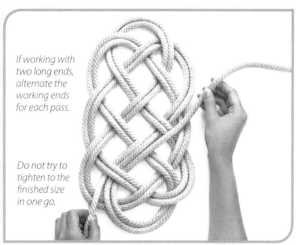

If working with two long ends, alternate the working ends for each pass.

Do not try to tighten to the finished size in one go.

Continue to follow the knot as many times as necessary to fill out the spaces. When finished, work the slack out from the standing end in two or more complete passes.

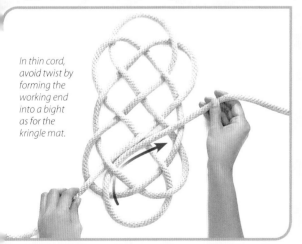

In thin cord, avoid twist by forming the working end into a bight as for the kringle mat.

The short left end becomes the standing end. Lead the working end over and under the next two bights so it is parallel to the standing end. Continue doubling the knot.

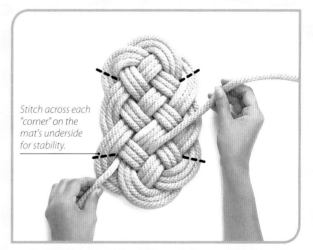

Stitch across each "corner" on the mat's underside for stability.

Cut and heat-seal the ends, and stitch or whip them on the underside. Unless the mat is small and the cord very stiff, stitch adjacent strands together on the underside.

DECORATIVE

KNIFE LANYARD KNOT

◆ CHINESE BUTTON

The single knife lanyard knot makes a simple zipper pull or key fob. When tightened up as the Chinese button, it makes an attractive small stopper that is traditionally used as a soft button or frog-style toggle fastening on bags and jacket fronts. The double Chinese button (pp. 121–3), double knife lanyard knot (pp. 124–5), and 4-lead, 3-bight Turk's head (pp. 127–9) are all based on this same method of tying the knife lanyard knot in the hand.

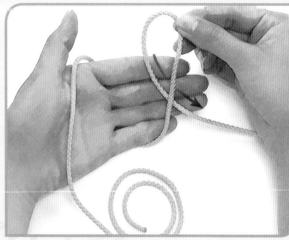

Middle a length of cord and hang it over the hand. Make an underhand turn in the end that lies across the back of the hand.

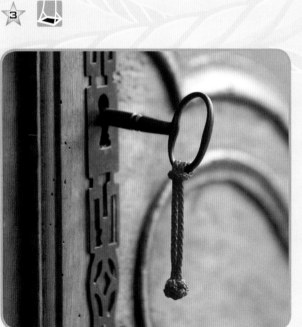

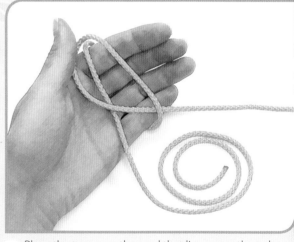

Place the turn over the cord that lies across the palm of the hand. Hold the turn in place with the thumb.

DECORATIVE

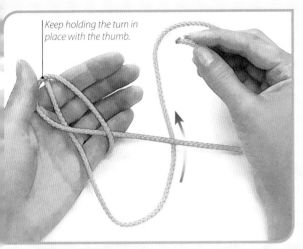

Keep holding the turn in place with the thumb.

Lead the other end behind the end leading out of the turn.

Tuck one end up through the opening in the center of the knot from underneath. This creates the Chinese button. For the knife lanyard knot, follow the arrow instead.

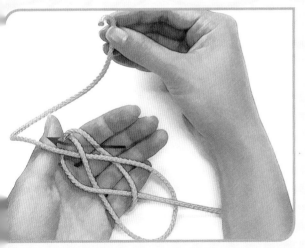

Tuck this end over the turn, under itself, and over the other side of the turn to create a carrick bend (p. 59) tied in opposite ends of the same cord.

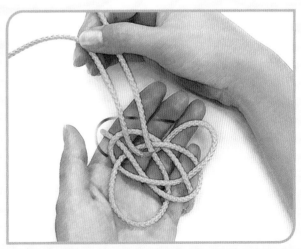

For the Chinese button, tuck the other end up through the center in the same way. For the knife lanyard knot, follow the arrow instead. Work excess slack out of the knot.

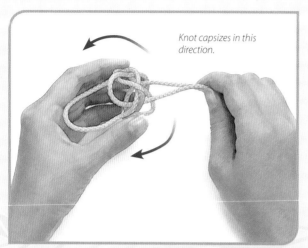

Knot capsizes in this direction.

Slide the knot off the hand, hold it loosely, and pull to the left while pulling the ends to the right. Work slack out of the knot, from the base of each side of the loop to each end.

The loop may be cow hitched onto a zipper or key.

When the knot is tight and evenly shaped, the ends can be cut off flush and fused together, left longer as a pair of tails, or unpicked with an awl to make a tassel.

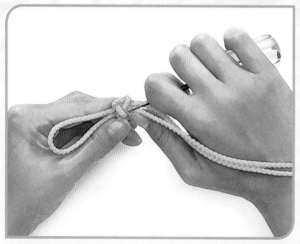

Tighten the knot with an awl, again working from the base of each side of the loop. Fair the knot into an even shape with a hammer, then tighten once more if necessary.

CHINESE BUTTON

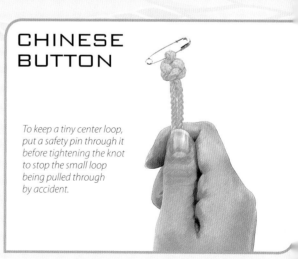

To keep a tiny center loop, put a safety pin through it before tightening the knot to stop the small loop being pulled through by accident.

Working the loop almost out of the knife lanyard knot when tightening it produces a Chinese button. The button may also be tightened so that the loop disappears.

DECORATIVE

DOUBLE CHINESE BUTTON

The double Chinese button is used in the same way as the single—or "undoubled"—Chinese button (p. 120): as a soft button or frog-style toggle fastening on bags and jacket fronts. The double button is larger and bulkier than the single and is tied without the single button's optional small center loop.

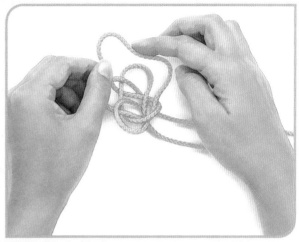

Push the center of the top loop down flat across the middle of the center opening.

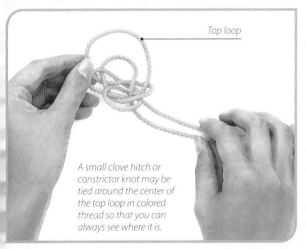

Top loop

A small clove hitch or constrictor knot may be tied around the center of the top loop in colored thread so that you can always see where it is.

Follow Steps 1–6 of the knife lanyard knot (pp. 118–19), keeping the center opening fairly large. Palm downward, slide the knot off your hand onto a work surface, top loop up.

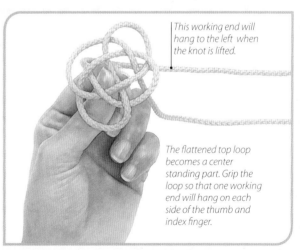

This working end will hang to the left when the knot is lifted.

The flattened top loop becomes a center standing part. Grip the loop so that one working end will hang on each side of the thumb and index finger.

Pick up the knot and hold the center of the flattened top loop firmly from underneath, taking care not to disturb the shape. Work the slack out of the knot.

DECORATIVE

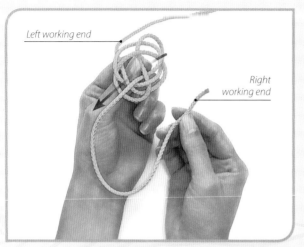

Left working end

Right working end

Pick up the right working end. Lead it upward to the left of the center standing part, keeping it below the thumb. Pull the slack through and let it hang over the top.

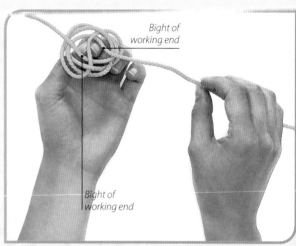

Bight of working end

Bight of working end

Pull the slack through once more. The bights of the working ends will be pushed together in the next step.

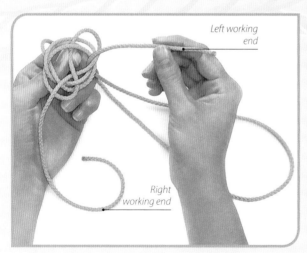

Left working end

Right working end

Pick up the working end that is hanging down on the left hand side. Lead it upward to the right of the center standing part, keeping it above the index finger.

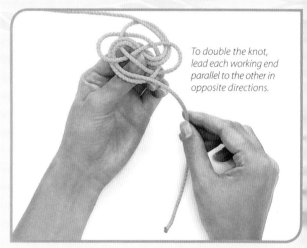

To double the knot, lead each working end parallel to the other in opposite directions.

Push the bights of the two working ends together and transfer your grip to these bights. Begin doubling the knot by leading each working end parallel to the other.

DECORATIVE

Continue doubling the knot until the working ends lie on either side of the center standing part.

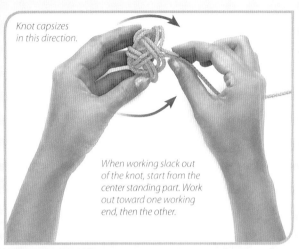

Knot capsizes in this direction.

When working slack out of the knot, start from the center standing part. Work out toward one working end, then the other.

Holding both ends in the right hand, capsize the knot toward the working ends in a mushroom shape. Work the slack out of the knot with an awl.

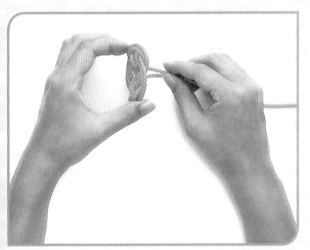

Pick up both working ends in the right hand and hold them close to the knot. Lightly hold the rim of the knot with the left hand, ready to capsize it into its final shape.

Fair the knot up into an even shape with a small hammer, then tighten once more if necessary.

DECORATIVE

DOUBLE KNIFE LANYARD KNOT

•TOOL LANYARD

The double knife lanyard knot, like the single knife lanyard knot (pp. 118–20), makes a zipper pull or key fob but with a bulkier knot that is easier to grip. The larger knot also allows one working end to be fed back into the knot to create a second loop for cow hitching to a tool or ornament, such as a knife. The item can then be hung from the neck or wrist. Be careful, as this knot has no safety release catch.

Continue following the knot with this end until it emerges from the knot parallel with the other end.

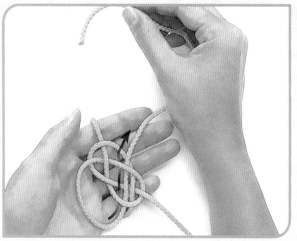

Begin with Steps 1–4 of the knife lanyard knot (pp. 118–19). Lead the left working end under the adjacent bight, over the other end, and under the next bight to form a loop.

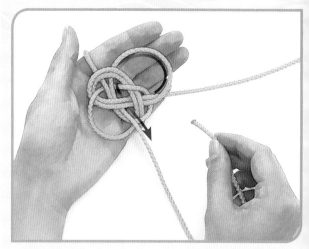

Now lead the second end over the first and under the adjacent bight to form a second side loop. Weave it through the knot parallel to the existing strands.

DECORATIVE

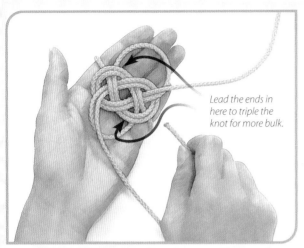

Lead the ends in here to triple the knot for more bulk.

The knot is now doubled. To triple the knot, lead each end parallel with the side loop and into the knot. Follow the knot again until each end emerges in the side loop center.

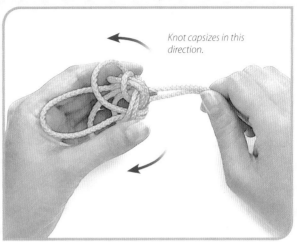

Knot capsizes in this direction.

As in Step 7 of the knife lanyard knot (p. 120), slide the knot off the hand. Capsize it into a 3-dimensional form by holding it in the left hand and pulling the ends to the right.

After doubling, or tripling, lead each end through the center opening from underneath. Gently pull the slack of the ends out through the knot.

The ends can be left as short tails, unpicked to make a tassel, or cut off flush and pushed back inside the knot with an awl to hide them. Cow hitch the loop onto a zipper or key.

Work slack out of the knot, then tighten with an awl, working from the base of each side of the loop. Fair up into an even shape with a hammer, then re-tighten if necessary.

DECORATIVE

TOOL LANYARD

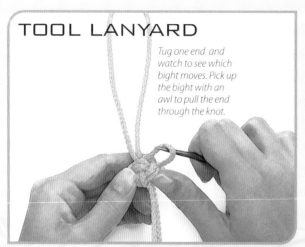

Tug one end and watch to see which bight moves. Pick up the bight with an awl to pull the end through the knot.

Tie the double knife lanyard knot (pp. 124–5), adjusting the loop to fit the neck or wrist. Find the last bight formed by either working end and pull it back through the knot.

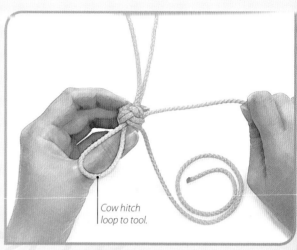

Cow hitch loop to tool.

Repeat Steps 8 and 9 three or four times, pulling out the first end and pulling the second end through the channel. This ensures that the loop will hold securely.

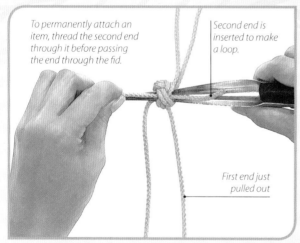

To permanently attach an item, thread the second end through it before passing the end through the fid.

Second end is inserted to make a loop.

First end just pulled out

Push a fid through the channel left by the working end just pulled out. Thread the second working end through the hollow of the fid. Pull it through the knot to create a loop.

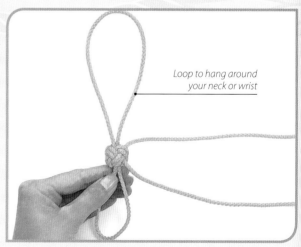

Loop to hang around your neck or wrist

For the final tuck, do not remove the first end but instead lead the second end alongside it. Make sure the knot is once again tight, then cut the ends off flush.

TURK'S HEAD (4-LEAD, 3-BIGHT)

• TURK'S HEAD (4-LEAD, 3-BIGHT): ALTERNATE

Turk's heads are a family of knots with one famous member, the Scout "woggle." They have long been associated with nautical ropework, both decorative and practical. Even today, the practice of tying one to mark the king spoke of a ship's wheel continues. Turk's heads are described by the number of leads, or interwoven strands forming the knot, and the number of bights, or curved edges along each rim.

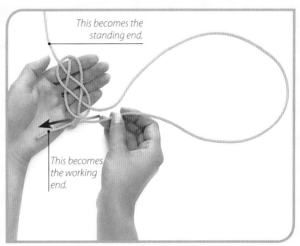

This becomes the standing end.

This becomes the working end.

Begin with Steps 1–4 of the knife lanyard knot (pp. 118–19). Lead the right, or lower, working end through the loop at the back of the hand, pull it through and let it hang.

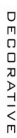

DECORATIVE

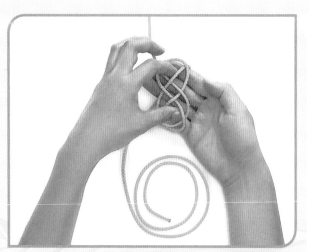

Slide the knot onto the fingers of the right hand. Poke the left index finger and thumb into the spaces above and below the center opening and pinch together.

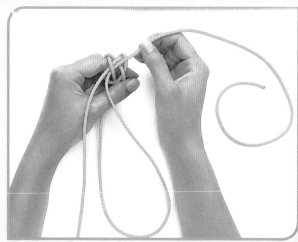

Slide the knot onto the index finger. Lead the working end into the knot parallel to, and below, the standing end. The knot is now locked and ready for doubling.

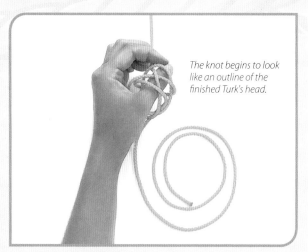

The knot begins to look like an outline of the finished Turk's head.

Slide the knot from the right hand, leaving it around the left thumb. Keep the knot very loose, but adjust the slack so that the knot is even and symmetrical.

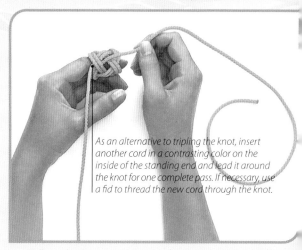

As an alternative to tripling the knot, insert another cord in a contrasting color on the inside of the standing end and lead it around the knot for one complete pass. If necessary, use a fid to thread the new cord through the knot.

Follow the knot until the working end reaches the beginning once more. The knot is now doubled.

DECORATIVE

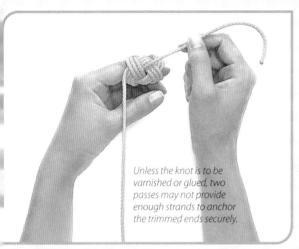

Unless the knot is to be varnished or glued, two passes may not provide enough strands to anchor the trimmed ends securely.

Follow the knot again once or twice and slide it onto the item to be decorated. Work out the slack with an awl. Cut he ends off close and push them under the standing parts.

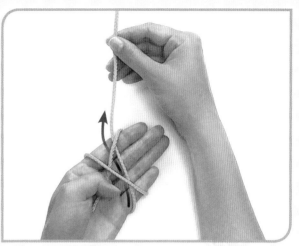

Lead the working end under both standing parts at the front of the hand to the right of where they cross.

TURK'S HEAD (4-LEAD, 3-BIGHT): ALTERNATE

While shown on a hand, this alternate method can be used to tie the knot around a fixed spoke, when you can't slide it over an end.

Anchor the standing end with the thumb. Lead the working end to create two crossed standing parts at he front and two parallel standing parts at the back.

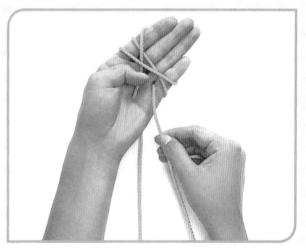

Now lead it behind the hand, across the left-hand standing part at the back, and to the front, left of all standing parts.

DECORATIVE

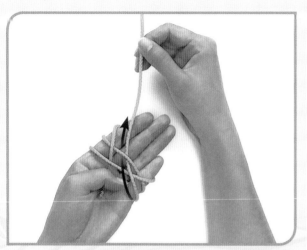

Bring it up over the first standing part and under the second, then turn the hand over.

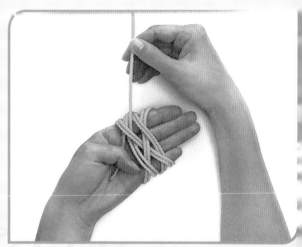

Lead the working end parallel to the standing end to lock the knot, then double it.

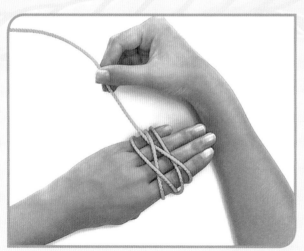

Take the working end over the first standing part, under the upper right of the crossed standing parts and then over the upper left. Turn the hand over.

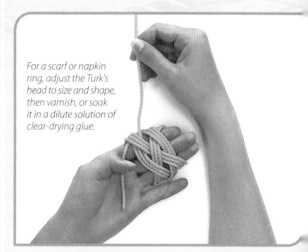

For a scarf or napkin ring, adjust the Turk's head to size and shape, then varnish, or soak it in a dilute solution of clear-drying glue.

As for Steps 5 and 6, follow the knot around as man[y] times as required. Trim and conceal the ends.

DECORATIVE

TURK'S HEAD (3-LEAD, 5-BIGHT)

The three-lead, five-bight Turk's head produces a narrower band than its four-lead, three-bight cousin when tied in the same cord for the same number of passes. It is a circular version of the three-stranded plait used for long hair and for decorating horses' manes and tails. Turk's heads tied around the fingers can be slid over the end of an object before tightening but the same method is used to tie the knot directly around an object such as a fixed railing.

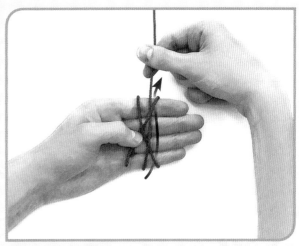

Lead the working end over the bottom right standing part and under the top right standing part.

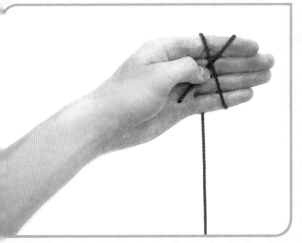

Anchor the standing end with the thumb. Lead the working end to create two crossed standing parts at the front and two parallel standing parts at the back.

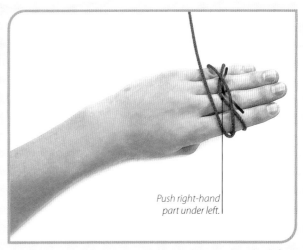

Push right-hand part under left.

Turn your hand over. Lead the working end to the left. Push the center of the right-hand standing part under the left to create two crossing points with a center opening.

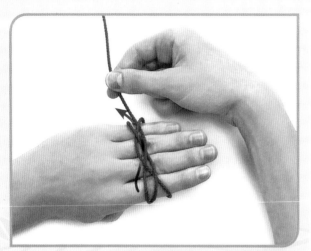

Lead the working end up through the center opening from underneath. Now lead the working end under the standing part at the top right.

For a scarf or napkin ring, adjust the Turk's head to size and shape, then varnish, or soak it in a dilute solution of clear-drying glue.

Ease all the crossing points around the knot with an index finger until they are equally spaced. Follow the knot for as many passes as needed to make it the required width.

Turn the palm of the hand to face you once more. Lead the working end parallel to the standing part to lock the knot.

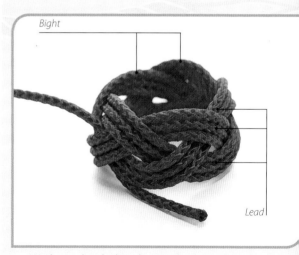

Bight

Lead

Work out the slack with an awl in several passes, cut the ends off close to where they emerge from the knot and push them underneath the standing parts.

DECORATIVE

SOLOMON BAR

Also called Portuguese sennit, Solomon bar is best known as a macramé knot used to make pot-plant hangers. Solomon bar zipper pulls and key fobs have a flat rather than spherical profile, and the same pattern can be used to make sturdy boat fenders in very thick rope. Combined with other knots, it makes an attractive, washable, and waterproof bracelet, or a hat band that can be pulled apart if necessary to provide extra cordage when camping. Solomon bar is wide enough to make a comfortable carry handle that won't cut into your hands.

Take the top end in front of, then behind, the right end, behind the bight, and up through the center of the loop formed in Step 1.

Middle a length of cord and, with the bight facing toward you, form a loop with the left-hand end by leading it in front of the bight and to the right.

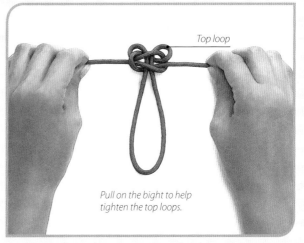

Top loop

Pull on the bight to help tighten the top loops.

Now reverse the tying process: lead the end now at right across the front, and the end at left in front of, then behind it, behind the bight, and up through the loop.

DECORATIVE

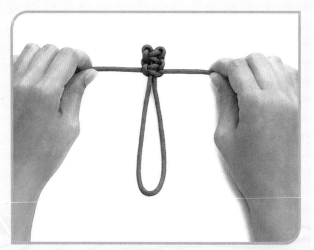

Continue knotting by taking the end that goes across the front of the work from the opposite side each time. If you take the end from the same side, the bar forms a spiral shape.

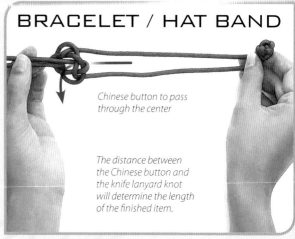

BRACELET / HAT BAND

Chinese button to pass through the center

The distance between the Chinese button and the knife lanyard knot will determine the length of the finished item.

Middle some cord and tie a Chinese button (p. 120). Tie a knife lanyard knot (pp. 118–20), with the Chinese button section forming the loop around the back of the hand.

Heat-sealed or glued end

When the piece is long enough, cut off each working end close to the knot and heat-seal or glue it in place. Cow hitch the loop onto a zipper or key, or attach a split ring.

The double loop will fasten over the button.

Push the Chinese button through the center of the knife lanyard knot. Tighten the knife lanyard knot around all four strands, after adjusting the length of the double loop.

DECORATIVE

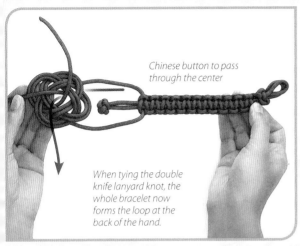

Chinese button to pass through the center

When tying the double knife lanyard knot, the whole bracelet now forms the loop at the back of the hand.

Begin the Solomon bar with the two long working ends. Continue to within 1 inch (2.5 cm) of the button. Tie a double knife lanyard knot (pp. 124–5).

HANDLE

Make sure this cord is the length needed for the finished handle.

To fit a carry handle, middle some cord, cow hitch it to one side of the item, and loop it through the other side. Make sure it is long enough to grasp comfortably.

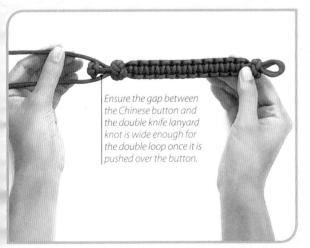

Ensure the gap between the Chinese button and the double knife lanyard knot is wide enough for the double loop once it is pushed over the button.

Push the Chinese button through the center of the double knife lanyard knot, and tighten the knot close to the end of the Solomon bar pattern. Cut working ends off flush.

Begin the Solomon bar pattern with the working ends and when the strap is finished, cut off and heat-seal or glue the ends as in Step 5.

DECORATIVE

ROPE LADDER

This portable, collapsible rope ladder is quick and simple to make, cannot rust, and is gentle on boat topsides and bare, wet feet. The ladder can be pulled apart easily and stowed as a rope coil when not in use or when the rope is needed for other purposes. It is light enough for children to carry, and to raise and lower. Because the rungs are not rigid, the ladder should be made only a little wider than a human foot. Space the rungs so that the distance from one to the next is comfortable for the smallest person who will use the ladder.

Tie a figure-of-eight loop (p. 34) in the middle of the rope. Make two bights in the right leg, forming a flat S-shape. The width of the S determines the width of the finished rung.

DECORATIVE

Pass the left leg from front to back through the eye of the upper bight and under both parts of the lower bight.

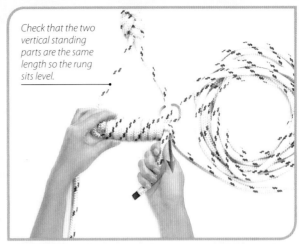

Check that the two vertical standing parts are the same length so the rung sits level.

Wind to the right until only the eye in the lower bight is exposed. Lead the leg over the rung to the back, around the right standing part, then feed it down through the eye.

Pass this leg away from you over the top of the bights, then bring it behind the bights to the front. Continue winding it tightly around the bights to form the first rung.

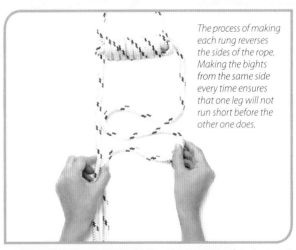

The process of making each rung reverses the sides of the rope. Making the bights from the same side every time ensures that one leg will not run short before the other one does.

The second rung is made the same way: by forming an S in the right leg, passing the left leg through the top bight and under the second, then winding from left to right.

GLOSSARY

ARBOR *The central part of a spool or reel about which line or cordage is wound.*

AWL *Thin metal spike with a handle, used to make holes in leather and canvas for sewing, for prising cordage out of knots where fingers can't reach and for pulling knots up snug.*

BEND *(noun) A knot joining the end of one rope to the end of another; (verb) To attach a rope to a spar or object, to attach a sail to a spar by means of a rope, to tie two ropes together at their ends.*

BIGHT *Any part of the cordage in between the two ends. Also, a section of rope bent back on itself in a flattened loop, ready for working into a knot.*

BINDING *Knot in a single piece of cordage that closes a bag opening, or confines, constricts, or lightly secures objects or coiled rope strands together.*

BLOCK *Enclosed device containing a sheave through which a rope passes in order to change its direction; a more nautical term for a pulley.*

BRAID LINE *Marine term for braided rope.*

BRAIDED ROPE *Cordage with interwoven strands proceeding both left and right, usually composed of one or more layers around an inner core.*

CAPSIZE *Distort a knot's layout, either accidentally by mishandling or overloading, or intentionally when tightening or working up a knot.*

CARABINER *Device similar to a snap hook but having features that make it particularly suited to climbing: it has a gate to prevent accidental release, and provision for rope to be belayed around it so as to be used as a brake.*

CLEW RING *The eyelet or cringle for attaching a sheet (controlling rope) to a sail.*

COIL *(noun) Rope neatly arranged so that it can be conveniently stored and transported; (verb) To arrange rope in a uniform shape so that it is manageable and doesn't tangle.*

CORDAGE *General term for any rope, line, or thin cord.*

CORE *The inner portion of a braided rope, usually the strongest part of the rope.*

CRINGLE *Metal sleeve, circular in shape, which can be sewn into a sail, or around which rope can be spliced. Its use is similar to that of a thimble.*

DOUBLE *To lead cordage, whether a new piece or a knot's own working end, exactly parallel to another to double the knot's bulk or width.*

EYE *Smallish circular formation in a hook, object, or rope, usually just large enough to allow the cordage, or bight of the cordage, to pass through.*

FAIR UP *Work or adjust a knot, usually decorative work, before and after the final tightening pass, so that it is evenly tensioned with a symmetrical or balanced appearance; may be done by lightly tapping all around with a hammer.*

FIBER *The basic material that the rope is made of—polyester, hemp, etc—or an individual strand of that material.*

FID *Spike or longish conical channel that is used to prize apart and open the lay of rope, wire, or knotting, so that another strand or piece of cordage can be fed through.*

FOLLOW *The process of leading a piece of cordage parallel to another.*

FRAPPING TURN *Non-structural lashing, applied more or less at right angles to an existing lashing, to compress or deflect it and increase its tension.*

GAFF *Spar, usually affixed to the upper, or upper forward, edge of a sail.*

HALF HITCH *The knot formed by making an underhand turn around an object, then leading the working end over the standing part.*

HALYARD *The cordage used to hoist a spar, sail, or flag.*

HEAVING LINE *Piece of light cordage with a bulky knot or small object attached to one end for throwing to another person or vessel.*

HITCH *(noun) A knot connecting a load-bearing rope to an object; (verb) To tie a half hitch or a succession of half hitches.*

JURY MAST *An emergency replacement mast, rigged around either a broken mast or another spar.*

LASHING *(noun) A knot, or succession of windings, that secures two or more structural items; (verb) The process of completing the knot or windings.*

LAID ROPE *Rope, traditional in appearance, that usually has three diagonally wound elements.*

LANYARD *Cordage, often decorative, that restrains an object, keeps it at the ready, or prevents it from being lost.*

LAY *The strands of the rope and the way that they twist. Hard and soft lay describes whether the strands are tightly or loosely wound.*

LOCKED *The state of a knot once the locking tuck is made.*

LOCKING TUCK *The final tuck with the working end that completes the knot structure.*

LOOP *Fixed or adjustable eye in a rope that can be attached to, or placed over, something; a knot that creates single or multiple, fixed or adjustable, loops.*

MARLINSPIKE *Metal or hardwood spike used to untie difficult knots, open the lay of rope or wire, and assist knotting procedures.*

MESSENGER/MOUSE *Line used to guide or pull a heavier rope into place.*

MIDDLE *To locate the center point of a length of rope.*

MONOFILAMENT *Single strand extruded filament.*

MULTIFILAMENT *Cordage made from fine strands of spun, wound, or plaited material.*

ON THE BIGHT *Term for a knot tied along a length of rope at a point other than its end.*

OVERHAND CROSSING *Similar to an overhand turn but the loop formed is not a perfect circle.*

OVERHAND TURN *Circle made by passing the working end over the standing part.*

PASS *The process of working once through a knot's complete structure, either leading the working end through to double the knot, or working a small amount of slack right through the knot and into the standing end.*

PASSING TURN *Pear or circular shape, formed almost accidentally by an independent process during the tying procedure.*

PENNANT STAFF *The rod or stick to which a small flag is attached when it is to be hoisted clear of the top of a mast and its rigging.*

PLAITED ROPE *Cordage with interwoven strands proceeding either diagonally left and right, or in the longitudinal direction of the rope.*

REEF POINT *A length of line attached to a sail for the purpose of gathering it in to reduce the sail area in a strong wind, or an eyelet to accept such a line.*

ROPE *Cordage of a thickness that can be comfortably worked or used in the hand.*

ROUND TURN *The formation made when a rope passes around an object one-and-a-half times.*

S-LAID *Less common form of laid rope, where the diagonal direction of the lay is left-handed.*

SENNIT *An item or length of cordage made by plaiting, braiding, or knotting.*

SHACKLE *U- or bow-shaped metal fastening device with a screw pin for closing and locking it.*

SHACKLE KEY *Slotted metal tool used to tighten and undo the screw pins of shackles; a shackle key and marlinspike are often combined in one tool.*

SHATTERED FILM ROPE *Rope made from flat, sheet-like strands rather than round fibers; relatively inexpensive and often made from residual material.*

SHEAVE *Wheel-like device over which rope runs in a block or pulley.*

SHEET *The cordage that performs the task of trimming a sail at its aft edge.*

SHOCK CORD *Elastic cordage, usually with a thin braided outer, with strands of rubber as an inner core.*

SIDE CUTTER *Tool for cutting light, single-stranded wire and nails, but also excellent for severing small cordage.*

SLING *An arrangement of a length of cordage that lifts and supports an object at the same time.*

SLIPPED KNOT *Knot tied with a bight made in the working end and used to make the final tuck. The knot can be released quickly by pulling the working end.*

SNAP HOOK *Hook with gate-type device that is quick to attach and has a spring loaded catch or pin for either quick release or to prevent it coming undone.*

SNUG *Pulled or worked until firmly up against something, or until all slack is removed.*

SPAR *This can refer to practically any pole on a vessel used for setting sail or supported by rigging; does not normally refer to the mast.*

SPLICING *The process of weaving or otherwise locking some, or all, of the strands of one rope to another.*

STANDING PART *The portion of rope leading up to, and into, the commencement of a knot; usually the part that is loaded.*

STOPPER *Knot preventing cordage from running through a hole or confined space.*

TACKLE *Blocks or pulleys, arranged to make a load easier to handle.*

TAIL *The leftover working end, once a knot is completed.*

THIMBLE *Metal or plastic sleeve, usually pear shaped, around which rope is spliced; its purpose is to prevent chafe and stop rope from closing tight around its fastening point.*

THIN CORD *Small-diameter cordage— also known as "small stuff"—too thin for practical handling under load but useful for decorative work, lanyards, and light-duty tasks.*

TOGGLE *Simple metal or wooden object, sometimes tailored for the purpose, that separates or secures portions of a knot, or joins the bights in separate lengths of rope.*

TUCK *(noun) The result after one strand has been fed under another; (verb) the process whereby one strand is fed under another.*

TURN *(noun) Cordage led over a spar, object, or another piece of rope, either simply draped over in u-shape, or fully passed around through 360 degrees; (verb) Leading cordage around a spar, object, or another piece of rope.*

UNDERHAND CROSSING *Similar to an underhand turn but the loop formed is not a perfect circle.*

UNDERHAND TURN *Circle made by passing the working end under the standing part.*

WHIPPING *The process in which rope, or its individual strands, is bound to prevent fraying, or when rope is bound to itself to form an eye.*

WHIPPING TWINE *Fine cordage used for whipping or heavy duty sewing.*

WORKING PART *The portion of the rope that is actively tying the knot; may be a bight.*

WORKING END *The end of the rope that is actively tying the knot but is not yet part of the knot; when the knot is completed, the tail or portion left over.*

Z-LAID *The common form of laid rope, where the diagonal direction of the lay is right-handed.*

		★							WHAT'S IT FOR?
44	Alpine butterfly knot	2	✓	✓	✓	✓	✓	✓	Attach flag clips, carabiners, and sinkers; simple ladder
76	Anchor bend	1	✓	✓			✓	✓	Attach anchor; secure tent stays; lift manhole cover
42	Angler's loop	2	✓			✓	✓	✓	Attach swivel to line; tether dinghy; loop in shock cord
48	Arbor knot	2	✓			✓			Attach rope to a drum, or fishing line to a reel; sliding loop
60	Ashley's bend	2	✓	✓			✓		Join different ropes; join fine lines; four-way tie-down
26	Bag knot	1	✓	✓				✓	Secure the top of a bag or sack or a rolled mat or bundle
75	Barrel hitch	1	✓					✓	Hoist a barrel, statue, or square-based box
46	Blood loop dropper knot	2				✓			Attach branch line to main fishing line
30	Bottle sling	3	✓	✓	✓			✓	Lift or carry a bottle, flask, or canister
36	Bowline	2	✓	✓	✓	✓	✓	✓	Practical knot; attach rope to a pole; join dissimilar rope
40	Bowline on the bight	2	✓			✓	✓	✓	Form twin loops in fishing line; irregularly shaped objects
79	Buntline hitch	2	✓				✓	✓	Attach sheets to a sail, clew ring, or snap shackle
59	Carrick bend	1	✓				✓	✓	Join heavy ropes
72	Clove hitch	1	✓	✓		✓	✓	✓	Attach rope to a pole; make a temporary barrier fence
28	Constrictor knot	1	✓	✓		✓	✓	✓	Tie bundles of pliable material; secure strands of a laid rope
68	Cow hitch	1	✓	✓		✓	✓	✓	Attach a ring to a closed loop, or a lanyard to a camera
95	Diagonal lashing	2	✓	✓				✓	Scouting activities; secure poles at odd angles
121	Double Chinese button	3	✓						Bulkier soft button or frog-style fastener
124	Double knife lanyard knot	3	✓				✓		Bulkier zipper pull or key fob; lanyard for small objects
102	Eye splice	2	✓				✓	✓	Make an eye in the end or join two pieces of laid rope
55	Figure-of-eight bend	1	✓	✓	✓		✓	✓	Join ropes of the same diameter; add length to stays
19	Figure-of-eight knot	1	✓	✓	✓	✓	✓	✓	Stop rope from running through a hole; a decorative knot
34	Figure-of-eight loop	1	✓	✓	✓	✓	✓	✓	Attach item to a rope; make a fixed loop; hang an object
56	Fisherman's knot	2	✓	✓	✓	✓	✓	✓	Join line, rope or cord; adjustable fastenings for necklaces
108	Handcuffs puzzle	1	✓						Escape from interlocked rope handcuffs
80	Highwayman's hitch	2	✓				✓	✓	Secure a dinghy temporarily
107	Impossible knot	1	✓						Tie a knot without letting go of either end of the rope
52	Jury mast knot	3		✓			✓	✓	Rig a jury mast, tent post, or flagpole; decorative trim
118	Knife lanyard knot	3	✓						Simple zipper pull or key fob; soft button or fastener
114	Kringle mat	2	✓			✓			Functional or decorative floor or table mat; drink coaster
74	Marlinspike hitch	2	✓			✓	✓	✓	Provide good grip on thin cord; hoist a tool by the handle

			☆							WHAT'S IT FOR?
112	Monkey's fist	3	✓	✓				✓	✓	Heaving line; key float and fob; zipper pull; dog toy
110	Not a knot	1	✓							Make a reef knot disappear without untying it
116	Ocean mat	2	✓					✓		Easy-to-tie functional or decorative oval mat; doormat
64	One-way sheet bend	2	✓	✓	✓	✓	✓			Pull a large rope along a dock; hoist a rope up a cliff
17	Overhand knot	1	✓	✓	✓	✓	✓	✓	✓	Prevent rope from slipping through a hole
86	Palomar knot	1	✓				✓			Attach hooks or other items to fishing line
70	Pile hitch	1	✓					✓	✓	Tether a dinghy to a pile or bollard; tie between posts
24	Pole lashing	1	✓	✓					✓	Tie a bundle of poles; suspend a plank
78	Prusik knot	1	✓	✓	✓			✓	✓	Climbing rope handhold or equipment attachment
22	Reef knot	1	✓	✓				✓	✓	Tie reef points in sails; tie parcels; flat knot in cloth
65	Rigger's bend	2	✓	✓	✓			✓		Join ropes of similar size and texture; join slippery ropes
109	Ring drop	1	✓							Remove a ring threaded on a loop without letting go
83	Rolling hitch	2	✓	✓				✓	✓	Fasten rope to take load at an angle
136	Rope ladder	2	✓	✓				✓		A soft, collapsible, light-weight, transportable ladder
97	Sheer lashing	1	✓	✓					✓	Reinforce or extend a pole; create an A-frame
62	Sheet bend	1	✓	✓				✓	✓	Join ropes of equal or different size
104	Short splice	3	✓					✓	✓	Permanently join two lengths of laid rope
38	Snelling a hook	2				✓				Attach fishing line to a hook
133	Solomon bar	2	✓	✓				✓		Flat zipper pull or key fob; bracelet or hat band; carry handle
50	Spanish bowline	2	✓						✓	Hoist and suspend irregularly shaped objects
93	Square lashing	1	✓	✓					✓	Scouting activities; build light framework or garden trellis
58	Surgeon's knot: bend	1	✓	✓		✓			✓	Join cotton and thread; join fishing line
21	Surgeon's knot: binding	1	✓	✓		✓				Leatherwork; any tying-off using fine line, twine, or thin cord
35	Surgeon's loop	1	✓			✓			✓	Permanent loops in the end of shock cord or fishing line
32	Timber hitch	1	✓	✓					✓	Lift and haul a log; attach nylon guitar strings to the bridge
135	Topsail halyard bend	2	✓					✓		Hoist a pennant staff or topsail spar; lift a pole
32	Transom knot	1	✓	✓					✓	Temporary lashing; craft; gardening trellises; kite frames
99	Tripod lashing	2	✓	✓					✓	Support for suspending bell or pot; frame for teepee
90	Trucker's hitch	2	✓	✓					✓	Tie a load to a trailer; tension tent stays
131	Turk's head (3-lead, 5-bight)	3	✓					✓		Tubular knot; grip or trim on handle; napkin or scarf ring
127	Turk's head (4-lead, 3-bight)	3	✓					✓	✓	Tubular knot; grip or trim on handle; napkin or scarf ring

HOW DO I?

Keep rope from tangling in the car boot or a rope locker	Wrapped coil, bundled coil
Hang hanks of rope for storage	Bundled coil, double slip coil
Tie tent ropes so they can be tensioned	Trucker's hitch
Tie down a load on a trailer, secure a cover over it	Trucker's hitch
Tie a tool to a rope for hoisting aloft	Marlinspike hitch, bowline on the bight/Spanish bowline
Tie a rope to the handle of a bucket or paint tin for hoisting	Round turn and two half hitches on the handle
Hoist a paint tin with no handle	Barrel hitch
Make a zipper easier to grab hold of	Solomon bar, knife lanyard knot, or a monkey's fist
Stop the end of a rope from fraying	Common, French, or West country whipping
Hang items with a knot that can be untied from the ground	Highwayman's hitch
Join pieces of shock cord; tie a loop in shock cord	Ashley's and rigger's bends; angler's loop
Tie planks or branches together for carrying or lifting	Pole lashing
Put a new carry handle on a case	Solomon bar
Join two ropes with a knot that won't catch when hauled	One-way sheet bend
Make a transportable lightweight ladder	Rope ladder knot
Tie a load onto roof racks	Rolling hitch, anchor bend, round turn and two half hitches
Weight the end of a line for throwing	Monkey's fist
Stop the end of a rope passing through a block	Figure-of-eight knot
Tie a fish hook in fishing line	Palomar knot, snelling a hook
Get a good grip on small or slippery line to pull hard	Marlinspike hitch
Put a loop in a rope when the ends are not accessible	Alpine butterfly knot, figure-of-eight loop; bowline on the bight or Spanish bowline
Suspend a plank as a temporary shelf	Pole lashings finished with bowlines; alternate bowline for attaching to support points
Suspend a pot over a campfire	Tripod lashing
Decorate a walking stick, a ship's wheel or tiller handle	Turk's head
Improve grip on varnished or slippery wheels or tool handles	Turk's head, French whipping in cord rather than twine
Attach a closed loop to a ring or other closed eye fitting	Cow hitch
Rig up a temporary clothesline in a tent or between tents	Tautline hitch
Make a temporary swing with an old tire	Bowline with standing part threaded through loop around the support; alternate bowline around tire
Fit a cable tie to an electrical lead for securing the coiled lead	Constrictor knot midway on lead with ends long enough to tie a reef knot round the coiled lead
Stop a dressing gown cord from fraying	Overhand knot, figure-of-eight knot
Secure a bead to cord to make a lamp switch pull	Overhand knot, figure-of-eight knot; monkey's fist
Make a doormat from old rope; make drink coasters	Ocean mat; kringle mat
Hang items from vertical tent poles or rope	Prusik knot
Make frames and trellis for the garden	Transom knot; square and diagonal lashing
Stop small tools being dropped or lost	Tool lanyard made from double knife lanyard knot
Stop keys dropped in the water from sinking	Monkey's fist key fob with buoyant core

INDEX

ACKNOWLEDGMENTS

The publishers wish to thank Bob Doel, David Glasson, Colin Grundy, Geoff Magee, Gordon Perry, the Rushcutter Shipchandlers, Geoff Smithson, Angie Turnbull, and Jonny Wells for their assistance in the production of this volume.

About the authors

Neville Olliffe and **Madeleine Rowles-Olliffe**, both members of the International Guild of Knot Tyers (IGKT), have run a small business making and selling handmade items of knotting and rope work for almost 20 years.

Neville began sailing as a teenager and, in 1968, took on a job in the marine trade and began a part-time writing career. He and Madeleine own one of Sydney's oldest yachts, which keeps them up to date with whipping and splices. Neville's focus is on basic knots and their usage, and various splicing techniques.

Madeleine, a systems engineer from an electronics and telecommunications background, is interested in applied and decorative knotting, and participated in IGKT public demonstrations at Hobart's biennial Australian Wooden Boat Festival in 2007 and 2009.

Disclaimer

While the material in this book has been prepared with your safety and the security of your property in mind, the authors and publishers accept no responsibility for the manner in which rope and knots are used. Be aware that a rope or knot that is suitable in one situation might be inappropriate in another, and caution must always be taken. Any suggested or implied usage is based on historical or common application, and ultimate responsibility lies with the common sense of the reader. Always proceed in a careful and cautious manner and seek qualified specialist advice from a professional before undertaking anything risky.

Neville Olliffe

Madeleine Rowles-Olliffe (left) seen here with Jasmine Parker, giving instructions on how to tie a knot.